# GHOST CATS

———∘∘∘⟩⟨∘∘∘———

Jaycee Clark
Elaine Corvidae
Shelley Munro
Michelle M. Pillow
Mandy M. Roth

Paranormal Romance

New Concepts                    Georgia

Be sure to check out our website for the very best in fiction at fantastic prices!

When you visit our webpage, you can:

* Read excerpts of currently available books
* View cover art of upcoming books and current releases
* Find out more about the talented artists who capture the magic of the writer's imagination on the covers
* Order books from our backlist
* Find out the latest NCP and author news--including any upcoming book signings by your favorite NCP author
* Read author bios and reviews of our books
* Get NCP submission guidelines
* And so much more!

We offer a 20% discount on all new ebook releases!
(Sorry, but short stories are not included in this offer.)

We also have contests and sales regularly, so be sure to visit our webpage to find the best deals in ebooks and paperbacks! To find out about our new releases as soon as they are available, please be sure to sign up for our newsletter (http://www.newconceptspublishing.com/newsletter.htm) or join our reader group (http://groups.yahoo.com/group/new_concepts_pub/join) !

The newsletter is available by double opt in only and our customer information is *never* shared!

Visit our webpage at:
www.newconceptspublishing.com

Ghost Cats is an original publication of NCP. This work has never before appeared in book form. This work is a novel. Any similarity to actual persons or events is purely coincidental.

New Concepts Publishing
5202 Humphreys Rd.
Lake Park, GA 31636

ISBN 1-58608-707-X
The Revenge © copyright October 2004, Jaycee Clark
Rain on the Mountain © copyright October 2004, Elaine Corvidae
Lynx to the Pharaoh © copyright October 2004, Shelley Munro
Animal Instinct © copyright October 2004, Michelle M. Pillow
Best Intentions © copyright October 2004, Mandy M. Roth

Cover art (c) copyright 2004 Amber Moon

All rights reserved, which includes the right to reproduce this book or portions thereof in any form whatsoever except as provided by the U.S. Copyright Law.

If you purchased this book without a cover you should be aware this book is stolen property.

NCP books are available at special quantity discounts for bulk purchases for sales promotions, premiums, fund raising, or educational use. For details, write, email, or phone New Concepts Publishing, 5202Humphreys Rd., Lake Park, GA 31636, ncp@newconceptspublishing.com, Ph. 229-257-0367, Fax 229-219-1097.

First NCP Paperback Printing: 2005

Printed in the United States of America

# THE REVENGE

By

# Jaycee Clark

### Prologue

The Chosen watched as they circled, circled and snarled at the one in the center. The girl was sentenced to death. No need to worry about her. She'd turned on them, she'd tried to leave.

And the betrayed never tolerated traitors. It was the code. And the code was never broken.

The Chosen looked up into the night sky. The full moon was dark this night. Silvery light should have shone down, bright as daylight, but the tall pines hid what they did. The moon itself seemed to turn a blind eye, the light was different, probably from the forest fires. The pregnant orb appeared almost a dull red, its light muted and dark.

A snarl pulled the Chosen back to the present and what went on in the clearing.

Water falling over the rocks didn't deter any of them.

A whimper from the center didn't change what was to come.

They toyed and played, snarling and snapping, stalking until she sat huddled, all but giving up.

Really, she could at least *try* to fight them. There were plenty of sticks and logs around, broken branches from the pines. Ineffective, but there all the same.

The Chosen sighed and shook its head.

A large boulder at the edge of the clearing was the perfect

overlooking point. The Chosen smiled as they closed in.

A pity really. She had been a nice girl, one of the followers, but now her life was forfeit.

With a small signal to the leader below, they all leapt onto her.

She didn't even scream. And if she had, it wouldn't really have mattered either way. She would still have died.

A hoot owl whispered through the night.

Tonight's work was finished.

The Chosen called its followers. This was not the only traitor. There were still others to take care of. The Chosen needed victims and treason seemed as good a reason as any to ordain their deaths. But it was not for them. The punishment was for a higher cause--to draw the enemy out.

And what better place to do it, than here. Here where the enemy thought they were safe?

The Chosen had waited a long time and now it was all within reach.

Nothing was sweeter, yet as bitter as revenge.


## Chapter One

The girl was dead.

Detective Lorenzo Craigen looked down at what remained of her and hoped to hell he was wrong. But in his gut he knew he wasn't.

Sael was back.

And there was no damn reason the son of a bitch should be.

"What do you see?" one of the locals asked him.

Craigen didn't answer. He tuned the young man out and looked around at the blood soaked ground.

His gut tightened. This should have been a sacred place and was, once upon a time, long ago, forgotten by most. Too damn peaceful of a place to have killed her, or should have been. Where the water ran off the mountains. He took a deep breath. The strong scent of pine and clear air was muffled and wrapped in the smell of death.

Cool New Mexico winds blew down off the Sangre de Cristos and he zipped his jacket against the autumn air.

"Chief Neilson said we should call you in," the young officer continued.

Craigen looked over his shoulder at the earnest and worried face. The name tag read White.

They seemed to get younger, smarter in some ways and completely naïve in others. It was in the still soft features of the officer's face, in the still-bright 'I'll change the world' eyes.

"This your first?" he asked White, turning back to study the ground around what remained of the victim.

"Y--yeah."

Craigen studied the break in the branches and weeds along the ground, all around the victim as if she'd been circled. The grasses flat, the twigs of bushes broken until about thigh high on him.

He stood. "You tell the ME where you tossed your breakfast so we don't waste time or money running tests on your puke?"

"Yeah." An edge of belligerence to hide shame.

Craigen walked around the clearing, heard the stream gurgling. Not too far from Sipapu, or any of the many little tourist rest stops along the way. But then, that was probably the point. Took a chance didn't he? Or rather they. God, they'd all but shredded her. Hair, once blond, was streaked dark with blood. Her body was broken and ripped, brutally so. Hell of a thing to see first thing in the morning. No wonder the kid lost his breakfast.

He nodded to White.

"Good. My captain reamed my ass for not doing that on my first. It was in a meeting that I remembered that what they were listing was what I'd had for breakfast. Smarter than I was starting out." He stopped and looked over at White. "How the hell did you find her?"

White's blond brows beetled. He looked like he should be on a poster ad for some designer underwear or some such shit. Kid looked out of place in the black uniform of Taos Police Department.

"Got a call into the station, said there was a body out here near this mile marker by the stream."

"Man or woman?"

"Hell if I know, Janice, the Chief's secretary answered it." He shrugged. "I live out here and Chief called me to ask me to check it out. I called him, apparently, he called you."

"No, he called my boss and my boss called me."

Craigen was sure the local Chief would be here shortly. Neilson would want this wrapped up quickly, and he had no qualms turning a murder investigation over to the state boys. Fine with Craigen. Neilson had enough to keep him busy by keeping the mayor of a tourist economized town happy.

"You did good securing the scene, White."

"Thanks."

Craigen walked towards the gurgling brook, watched as the sunlight shot white streams of light off the ripples. Should have peaceful here.

He took a deep breath, and caught the faint whiff he thought to never smell again.

Nothing would be peaceful until Sael was caught. And the bastard was supposed to be dead.

\* \* \* \*

Reya hurried into *Horizons*. "What? What is going on?" She flipped a strand of her long, straight black hair behind her shoulder and dropped her bag by the register area.

Mica sat crying on the stool behind the counter. Charlie leaned over from a display case and whispered, "Her friend was killed."

She started to say, "Oh is that all?" But thankfully thought better of it. The way Mica had blubbered all over the phone, she'd thought someone had been found dead here in the gallery, or maybe everything had gotten stolen, or perhaps something had happened to Mica herself.

Not to seem insensitive, but live as long as Reya lived and deaths came and went. She'd lost too many in her life to be truly affected by the inevitable.

However, she could say none of those things. Once, in a time forgotten, Reya would have felt Mica's pain. Instead, she walked to the girl and pulled her close. "I'm sorry, Mica. Is there anything I can do?"

Mica shook her head, the short mess spiked and tousled from Mica's hands running through it. It was the ever popular bed head look that Reya would never understand nor like, not that hair styles mattered at present.

"It was her roommate at the Institute," Charlie whispered.

"Oh, honey." She awkwardly patted the young girl's back. She wasn't the best person in these sorts of situations. "Why don't you take the day off? Tomorrow too, and the next day. As much time as you need."

Charlie nodded. "Yeah, you don't need to be here."

"But I--I just can't go back to the dorms. Everyone is so upset and they all want to ask me questions, like I know anything. And the policeman said they'd stop by and talk. I'd probably have to answer some more questions." She shuddered.

Reya studied the girl, stepped back and went to get her a cup of coffee. When she returned, Charlie, bedecked in his normal Docker pants and pullover, was cleaning the display cases.

He looked up and rubbed the back of his hand over his short goatee.

Reya handed a cup of coffee to Mica. "I thought you didn't like your roommate. Is this the same one? Or was it another?"

September was just around the corner and school had been on for a few weeks. Mica had complained about the new roommate at the Art Institute, but Reya didn't know if that one had been replaced or not. Last year, Mica went through three.

She shook her head. "No, this one was new. Just moved in last week after Holly moved out."

"Oh."

"Her name was Tanna." Mica wiped her eyes again, her face crumpling. "She was really great and we'd already gotten really close, ya know? Same interests and classes. Her mom called here a bit ago and was crying."

Reya took a deep breath. "Tell ya what. If you don't want to go back to the dorms, then why not go through the boxes of inventory in the back? See what all we need and check the emails for any interesting queries or photos that *Horizons* might be interested in, or if you don't feel like doing that, just go rest in the office."

Mica nodded and slid off the stool. Her sandals slapped against the hardwood floors, echoing in the shop.

Charlie huffed out a breath. "She's been like that since the phone rang earlier. I guess it was the mother's call that set her off."

"Understandable." Reya bent and picked up her purse, briefcase and bag. "Anything interesting as of yet?"

Charlie shook his head and went to the next display case. "Nope. But then, technically, we're not open yet, so who knows what else the day may bring."

"If we're lucky, hopefully, nothing."

"Funny thing about expectations and days and what fate deals out. They rarely work together as we'd like them to."

Charlie had the annoying habit of spouting off sage advice as if he memorized little Confucius quotes.

And Reya hardly needed Charlie to let her in on that little

secret. She'd been around plenty, long enough to know that life, or in her case, lives were never what was expected. Filled with twists and turns and unexpected surprises.

Her motto--expect the unexpected.

She worked through another half hour, rearranging things, setting things as she wanted them, then rearranging them again. She needed to change the bedding in the window display case to something lighter. The sun had already faded the black material to gray in places ... then again....

Something shimmered along her nerves. She glanced out the window, scanning the street, but nothing alerted her.

"What is up with you? Is it this thing with Mica?"

Reya pulled herself back and rolled her eyes. "You're such a sympathetic soul, Charles."

He hated his proper name. Which was why she wasn't surprised to see his frown. "I am sympathetic. I just meant...."

"I know, and no, that's not ... at least...." She shrugged. She couldn't explain it to Charlie. He was ... she tilted her head. Normal, as far as the locals went.

The man had worked for her for three years since she bought the property from him. He'd leased the spot as an art gallery, but she'd wanted more, a shop, a jewelry boutique. But she had liked that he was settled and somewhat established even if he was tired of the day to day and wanted something else.

Strange. He'd just sort of stayed on.

He was the same height as she, had that distinguished, gray-templed dark hair and character-lined male face that could fall anywhere between forty and sixty. His eyes were sharp hazel.

If she were guessing, she'd have to say almost fifty. Maybe a couple years older.

"What?" His salt and peppered brows beetled.

"Oh, um...." Reya shook her head. "You look nice today."

He flashed her a smile full of charm and the hint of the devil. "Black and beige are my colors, I've always said."

"How old are you?"

"Is that a come on?"

"Charles."

"Fifty-two." He straightened one of the black velvet busts that held a strand of citrine and topaz, wrapped and linked in bronze. He licked his lips. "Care to go out to dinner with a fifty-two-year-old?"

If she were what she appeared, the man was old enough to be

her father. But then things were never what they appeared to be.

She grinned and ran a hand down her tunic jacket. "I'll think about it."

The bell above the door chimed and energy tingled along her skin. She knew without turning around who stood there. Like a bolt of lightning, electricity arced through her, shooting from her head, swimming along her nerves, twisting her gut to pool at the base of her spine.

Reya swayed and closed her eyes, taking a deep breath. And she smelled him.

Slowly, she turned. He stood there in his starched Wrangler jeans, boots and button down, a gun clipped to his belt along with a badge. His black hair a bit longer than most, just grazing the top of his collar. His face was still the same, not too narrow, nor wide or blunted. It was a strong face, chiseled with sharp angles and lines. The dark of his eyes shimmered beneath harsh slashes of brows as his gaze met hers, and she couldn't help running a look down the long, lean lines of him. His corded neck, tanned and swarthy as always peeked out at her from his collar. His chest was as wide as she remembered and those hands, those hands. She wiped her damp palms on her thighs. Long fingered and deceptively elegant, she remembered how his fingers had grazed over her body. Her eyes rose back to his, noticed everything about him was the same, even the way one brow seemed to arch more than the other.

She sighed again.

"Hello, Reya."


## Chapter Two

Craigen stood in the doorway, tucked his shades in the vee of his shirt and watched as she schooled her features.

So controlled was Ms. Reya Lynx, owner of *Horizons Gallery*.

She licked her full lips and he ran his gaze over her. No one had changed more, and yet, changed less than Reya. She still favored long flowing lines of clothes, and they worked well on her willowy frame. Today she wore a dark blue tunic and pants suit, sleeveless he could easily see the muscles of her arms. A long pendant hung down and glinted in the sunlight. The stone was dark and familiar.

He grinned as he stared it, watched her fist it in her hand before he let his gaze run back up to meet her eyes and let her know he remembered.

Her eyes narrowed.

Apparently, she remembered as well.

He chuckled. "Been awhile."

"I've been here three years."

So she had. And they'd steered the hell away from the other.

He frowned when he realized he was actually, on some level, happy to see the woman. The energy that always followed her, followed them, flowed around the room and over his skin. He took a deep breath and smelled the shampoo he knew she still made herself with rosemary, flowers and a hint of citrus. Some light as air perfume that was new. And yet under both was the smell that would always and forever be Reya to him. No other woman, or being, was like her. It was a smell as sultry as the night and just as elusive as moonlight.

Her stubborn jaw jutted out and he knew the frown between her brows would be next. That one there that caused a slight crinkle in the bridge of her nose.

God, he'd missed her.

"Charles Carpenter, please meet an old ... friend, Lorenzo Craigen." Her voice could still melt the ice off the Sangre de Cristos or charm a single flake from the fallen snow. It was sultry, smooth, yet just a bit throaty.

His gut tightened and he took another deep breath.

She grinned, glanced down, then back up to meet his eyes. He didn't miss the challenge in the pale depths of hers--a color somewhere between smoke and sky.

An image of what they had looked like clouded with passion jolted through his brain, and he slammed the door shut on that one.

He turned to the man she'd introduced him to. Charles Carpenter. He knew of Carpenter. The man had owned the shop when it was *Deep Cave Galleries.* Hell, all Taos needed was another gallery. The streets were lined with the damn things. Art--or in his opinion, in some cases, what was supposed to pass as art--sculpture, paintings, clothing, crafts. Junk, in his opinion. Whatever. Once the *art* was stuck in a place and the locals slapped a gallery sign in the front window ... ta-da. And it worked. More tourists stopped in and would pay some god-awful, hocked up price for merchandise in a gallery.

His gaze roamed around this shop, and he admitted it had an artistic feel to it. *Horizons* was known for its handcrafted, one of a kind jewelry pieces that the people with too much money and time didn't bat at eye at buying.

Chunks of crystals and rocks glittered in display cases along with bracelets, necklaces, pendants, rings ... the shimmering went on, contrasting against the dark velvet back drops. Or in one case, sand. Black sand created a bed for the hammered bronze jewelry. Bracelets? No arm bands and maybe a torc, pendant, and rings.

Craigen cleared his throat and looked back at the former owner of the shop and gave the man a bare nod.

He caught the slight rueful look Charles tossed to Reya before the man said, "I'll be in the back with Mica." He patted her shoulder as he walked by.

The movement didn't really bother Craigen. Not really. They weren't together. He'd know if they were.

When they were alone again, Craigen shoved his hands in his pockets. "Nice place you have here."

Reya shrugged one elegant shoulder and turned her back to him, reaching into the solitary display case with black sand and rearranging the ornaments inside.

"It's good to see you."

Her eyes rose to his, her gaze tumulus beneath her lashes. He could all but see the anger swirling tighter and tighter around her. But then, like elusive smoke, it streamed away.

He grinned. "You've gotten even better."

Her incredible eyes narrowed at the edges. "Some of us always had control of our urges."

Definitely still angry.

To defend or deflect? Neither. Ignorance. His boots clicked across the hardwood floor and he laid a picture of a bracelet before her. "Seen this?"

She dropped her gaze from his to pull the photo across the glass surface towards her. She frowned.

"*Wolf Moon.*" She looked back up at him. "We sold the first several so quickly, and the demand was in, that it is one of the few things we keep in stock. Thankfully, the artist is agreeable to that venue versus a one time creation like most of the pieces we feature here."

Craigen leaned over the display case and trapped her gaze with his. "Would the artist have a name?"

"That's confidential, unless the artist deems otherwise and this one hasn't," she said softly.

His gaze dropped to her lips. "Maybe not, but I know you could persuade them to help us out. Especially since we're dealing with murder."

One brow arched. "Isn't it always?" She tilted her head and studied him. "What's this all about?"

"Murder."

"No, there've been others before this. Why are you here?"

Was she fishing for a compliment? "The girl was wearing a bracelet, as you notice, that you carry. Her roommate works for you. Seems here would be a good place to start."

"True. So what is the poor girl's name?"

"Tanna Barvendez. Heard of her?"

She looked at the picture, reached out, traced the bracelet with her nail. "No. Not until this morning. Mica called hysterical and I rushed over and learned her roommate had been killed."

He grabbed the photo up and tucked it into his breast pocket. "She here?"

"Mica? Yeah." Reya nodded and tucked a strand of hair behind her ear, motioning to the doorway behind the counter. "She's in back. She mentioned the police might want to talk to her again."

He shifted his gaze to the doorway. "We didn't get a lot out of her this morning."

Her hand skimmed across his. Just the barest of touches, a glance of her skin on his skin, but it felt like a sucker punch to his system. She quickly drew her hand away.

To hell with this. "Reya, we need to talk. It's important."

"Isn't it always with you?"

Looking straight into her eyes, he said. "This was Sael's work."

She paled and swayed slightly, slamming a hand down on the display case that still separated them.

Craigen reached out and grabbed her hand. "I won't let him get near you."

She shook her head, her breathing shallow. Dark shadows danced in her eyes, widening the pupil.

"Reya," he snapped.

She swallowed, licked her lips, and then cleared her throat. "Y-you're wrong. You have to be. You--"

"I hope I am."

Her eyes rose back to his, and at any other time he might have been amused at the fact she was trying to hide her fear from him.

"He won't hurt you. I swear it."

A slight tremor ran through her.

"Sael?" She shook her head. "It can't be. He's dead. What…?" She ran a hand through her hair. "Where … why?"

"Reya, look at me." He tightened his hold on her hand until she complied. "Did I let you down before?"

She blinked. "With Sael?"

He bit down. "Yes, with Sael."

"No, no, you didn't let me down about that."

Craigen took a deep breath. "We've both made mistakes."

And they had, both proud, both hurt, both refusing to budge.

She swallowed and waved her other hand. "I know. I know, I can be petty."

"And selfish, but you're still the prettiest damn woman I've ever laid eyes on."

A small smile tugged at the corner of her mouth and he wanted it to reach her eyes.

"At least I'm not arrogant, rude and a dozen other things." She linked her fingers with his.

"Reya, we have to talk."

This time instead of arguing with him, she nodded.

Relief loosened the muscles in his neck. "Good. First, I need to talk to Mica for a bit. I've several calls to make, leads to track down and then maybe this evening we can get together. How about tonight?"

Again she only nodded.

He turned, heading to the doorway she'd pointed to earlier. "I'll be in the back talking to Mica if you need me. Be careful."

Craigen was almost at the doorway when he heard her.

"He swore … do you remember, Lo? Sael swore we'd both pay. I can still see his eyes, all golden, hating me…." She trailed off.

Lorenzo Craigen took a deep breath. It had been a long time since she'd called him Lo. That more than anything told him how rattled she really was, even if he could see she was still too pale, her eyes too shadowed. He regretted that this--murder, Sael--is what bought him into her gallery today.

He turned back, knowing that if he saw Sael now, he'd just kill him and be done with it, and this time he'd make damn certain the bastard was dead.

"Lo?"

"Yeah?"

"He's mine this time." She turned and faced him and he inwardly swore at the determination fueled by rage in her eyes. "This time I take back my own."

Without answering her, he turned and walked away. He'd almost lost her before and no matter what lay, or didn't, between them, he'd be damned if he came even close to losing her like that again.

No matter what she wanted.

## Chapter Three

The late summer evening was slow to give up the light. It was almost nine and still enough daylight that the lighted lanterns on the tables didn't do much to cast more glow than the fading sun. The little black iron tables made for cozy eating, the setting sun, a nice romantic backdrop.

She sincerely hoped that had not been his plan this eve.

Reya studied the man across from her and wished her pulse didn't still kick up when he looked at her like that, straight on as though he could see all the way to her soul. But with Lorenzo, that was normally how he was. Straight on, no lies.

Which was why she was still so pissed at him.

He'd lied to her.

The waitress brought them a bowl of thin crispy tortilla chips, a small mortar of salsa and took their drink orders.

Reya wanted the house margarita. If she was dining with Lo, she knew she'd need all the help she could get to calm her nerves. He, as usual, just ordered water.

"What?" he asked as the waitress walked away.

"I'm here, so talk."

He merely picked up a chip, dunked it and said, "Still so blunt." The chip crunched in his mouth. "You look great, by the way."

She ran a hand over her thigh, the silky material of her sundress reminding her how she'd stressed over what the hell to wear. "Thank you, but you already told me that."

One side of his mouth lifted on a grin and her stomach tightened. This man was the only one in history that kept her tied in knots every time she was around him. Even before when they'd been together, so long ago it seemed, yet like yesterday.

A wicked gleam danced in his eyes. "I did, yes, but it was either tell you, you looked great again, or...." He leaned closer to her, his dark eyes dropping to her mouth.

She pulled her bottom lip in. "Or?"

His gaze ran from her mouth, to her chest, down to her thighs, and with him this close, she could feel the heat of his breath.

"Or tell you that I'd really rather take you back to my place, the moonlight shining through the windows, that silky dress on the floor and you on my bed," he said, his voice low and gruff. "I figured you'd rather hear that you looked great."

His eyes rose back up to clash with hers.

"Why does it have to be your place?" *Where the hell did that come from?*

He grinned, his eyes crinkling at the edges. "Because I want to claim you."

Her breath whooshed out. Lorenzo Craigen would only break her heart again if she let him. He was the only man who had that power, and she'd be damned if she gave it to him again.

"I won't hurt you," he whispered.

She leaned back in her chair. "I remember now what I found so aggravating about you. You always tried to read my mind."

"Was that it? And all this time I've been worried it was something else."

The waitress arrived with their drinks. After they'd placed their orders, she the spinach and mushroom quesadillas and he some combo plate, they waited to resume the conversation until the waitress left them in peace

"So tell me, Merria, what have you been up to?"

"My name is Reya."

"You just shortened it and changed the spelling. You'll always be Merria to many, though I do wonder where you came up with the nickname." His eyes danced in the fading light.

He knew damn well where she'd come up with it, he'd given it to her. And why *had* she picked that name?

His smile slowly faded. "I've missed you."

Instead of agreeing the truth of that statement, she looked down and took a drink of her lime and tequila. Their time had come and passed long ago. It would be nice to get some of it back. Not that she'd let him know that. She looked back up and again her stomach tightened at that intense look.

"Why'd you come back here?" he asked, eating another chip.

"I thought it time to come home." And it had been. Little did she know that he had come home as well, only days before her own arrival. They'd met at the local grocer and shocked the hell out of each other. After that, they'd kept their distance.

"Do you like your job?" she ventured.

"Do you like yours?" he countered.

"Yes, I love the gallery. It's one of the few things I've done that I've felt I'm where I'm supposed to be." She twirled her straw between her fingers. "I haven't felt that way in a long, long time."

His hand reached across and lay atop the hand she had on the table. "You've always been talented and I could always see you doing something artistic like this. You do belong here."

Sensing the dark currents that threatened the evening, rising from the past, she tried to lighten the mood. "You're just trying to butter me up so later when you beg me to go back to your place, I won't put up a fight."

For a moment, she thought he would say something else, as a chill seemed to emanate from him, a muscle ticked in his jaw. Lo took a deep breath and then grinned, but this time it didn't reach his eyes. "It won't be me begging, Reya, it'll be you."

"That sounds almost like a threat."

His hand squeezed hers. "I'd never threaten you. That was a promise." He gave her hand another squeeze and leaned back. "So tell me more about yourself."

"I want to hear about you."

"You know me and what I do. I'm a cop."

And always short on words about himself. Some things would never change. This evening he had on another pair of jeans, starched like the first, a beige cotton button down and a brown leather jacket. All the man needed was jeans and boots and somehow he could dress them up and down and it aggravated her that she'd probably taken a lot longer to get ready than he did. She took a deep breath and smelled his expensive cologne, woodsy with a hint of spice and under that heady, tempting fragrance, was Lorenzo. Reya shook her head.

"Why jewelry?"

She grinned and leaned up on her elbows. "Because I've always liked pretty sparkling things and I'm vain enough to admit that I love the thought of being surrounded by them."

His gaze raked over her. "Yet you don't wear more than the basics and yours never sparkle. And you're not vain."

He would be one of the only ones that ever saw through that front. She shrugged. "I wanted to come home and I wanted to do something. I had some experience in Italy with jewelry and decided I wanted to do that. I helped run a shop out in San Francisco and knew that's what I wanted to do here. But I didn't want the average or lots of new age. I wanted something that blended them, but definitely had the feel of the American Southwest. I only take artists from New Mexico, Texas, Utah, Arizona, Colorado and Nevada. Though there are two from California and one from Montana, but normally, it's just the surrounding states."

They talked until their food came, during dinner, through the desert of fried plantains. She told him of artists of dreams, how they were working on updating their online catalogue and acquire new clients online.

Lo watched her talk, the way her hands moved, the way the low light caught with a dull sheen on the wide silver bracelet she wore, the way it winked from the dark black stone of her pendant.

The pendant he'd given her still hung around her neck, between her breasts. Her eyes might glare at him, and he knew she might never fully trust him again, not like she had once upon a time, but she still felt something for him. She still wore the damn pendant. He remembered the little jeweler from the shop in Spain.

Shaking off the memories of the past, he focused on what she was saying. "I want another drink."

He motioned to the waitress. Other tables had already seen their share of diners come and go, but they'd stayed, talking more than eating and she'd already had three margaritas. Not that he really cared. But she'd never been one to drink and when she did, it didn't take much for her to get wasted. He wondered what she was trying to get away from.

Her cheeks were flushed, her eyes bright with the tequila and whatever other poison, probably triple sec, they mixed in their margaritas. "So glum. Why so serious? You were always so serious, Lorenzo Craigen."

"And you were always laughing."

She waved a hand. "That was before." Plopping her chin on her fist, she asked. "So why a cop?"

"Can you honestly see me as a banker?"

She chuckled and the sound pulled a smile from him.

Definitely enough drinks.

"Nope. Though you're driven enough you could have your own business again, just like before." She leaned over as if to whisper something and he couldn't help but glance to the vee of her dress and admire the view of her cleavage. He slowly ran his gaze up, noting the pound of her pulse in her neck, the way her collarbone dipped and curved, the way the candle light made her appear even more beautiful.

Without thinking, he reached over, his hand curving around the back of her neck, to tangle in the silkiness of her upswept hair. He leaned towards her. Stopping just shy of laying his lips on hers, he looked in her eyes, saw the excitement and the want there. Smiling, he kissed her. Her lips were as soft beneath his as he remembered. And she still tasted of cool desert evenings and warm sun drenched mornings.

Her lips parted beneath his and he tilted his head, deepening the kiss. Reya swayed, her hand gripping his thigh to stay upright.

It was she who pulled back, and the fact they were in public was the only reason he let her. She licked her lips, her eyes staring at his mouth as she whispered, "I wish you would have stayed away."

Lorenzo tightened the hand at her nape. "We don't always get what we wish for."

He jerked her to him and kissed her like he wanted to, felt his inner soul claw to get out. The damn woman would make him forget his own head. Abruptly, he jerked back. He ran his hand from her neck, over her shoulder, down the bare inside of her arm and felt her shiver as she watched him. "We're leaving."

He tossed enough bills on the table to cover the meal and drinks, nodded to the waitress as they made their way off the little patio and to his Dodge pickup truck.

"Boys and toys," she muttered.

"And how the hell practical is a damn Beemer when the roads are covered in ice and the ground in snow?"

She walked with him to the driver's side and climbed in, sliding over to the middle seat and straddling the stick shift.

He started to tell her to move over and buckle up, but to hell with it. He climbed in after her, his truck rumbling to life. He shifted the truck into reverse and couldn't help but notice how his hand grazed the inside of her thigh, and with that damn flirty little skirt, it didn't do much to help him out.

Lo cursed as he turned the truck out of the parking lot and

pulled onto the highway.

"I don't want to go home yet," her voice was lower than normal. "I want to see where you live."

Yeah, he'd make it through this night. He had *no* intention of sleeping with her tonight. None. They had things to talk about. Important things to plan. Not ... not.... Well, damn. He hadn't planned on getting her in his bed, not that he would have argued.... Damn it, if Reya didn't still twist him up into freaking knots.

The memory of what it was like to be inside her, to have her lithe limbs tangled around him as she came apart in his arms shattered through his well meant plans. He reached over and flipped the stereo on, punching the scan button on the radio. It landed on a cultural station.

"I should take you home," he said through his teeth as he shifted again, his hand once again grazing a thigh. Again and the gear shift, and his hand was all too close to the heat of her, tangling memories with reality.

Her hand on his thigh tightened as she leaned over and nipped his ear. "I said I don't want to go home, Lo."

When they were on open highway, he rested his hand on her thigh, the skirt bunched up so that bare skin met his.

He stared at the highway and tried not to think about what lay a few inches from his fingers.

The ride to his home outside of town flew by in a blur. His sprawling one story adobe house sat a couple miles off the highway at the base of the Sangre de Cristos on a hundred acre ranch. Not that he had time to ranch, though he did keep a couple horses in the barn for when he felt like riding.

Like now.

But it wasn't his horses he wanted to ride all damn night long.

He had to lift his hand from her leg to downshift as he turned into his drive. His lights cut across the deep porch with the rockers and a swing.

"Nice place you have here. I'm impressed, if not surprised."

Spanish guitar music played low and slow on the radio, a seduction of sound. Lorenzo could no more stop himself from kissing her again than he could the rise of the moon.

She shifted in the seat, facing him more. His hands cupped her face as he kissed her slow and deep before retreating to tease her lips with his tongue.

His hand ran down her neck, over her chest, to slip between the vee of her dress. His other hand found the hem of her little skirt. Warm, hot skin met his as he felt the curve of her breast with his other hand. Her soft inner thigh tightened at his touch and he grinned at the bunch of muscle beneath his hand.

Her mouth opened and she tilted her head, her hand grazing his thigh in long strokes.

He could feel the heat of her on his hand and he wasn't even at her center yet. She moaned in her throat and he jerked back, his heart slamming in his chest, his skin prickling with desire. His other half wanting her other being.

They were connected in more ways than one. She was his mate. He'd known it. All along he'd known it and there wasn't a damn thing he could do about it until now. He'd known the minute she made plans to move back and had come home himself.

Looking into her eyes, well aware of where her hand rested, the fact that he could take her here and now, he said, "Let's go inside."

She smiled, slow and catlike. "I was hoping you'd say that."

Lo helped her out of the truck and hurried into his house, unlocking the back door. They stood in the dark of the kitchen, the full bright moon shining down through the window to bathe them in white light.

For so long he'd kept control of his inner self, his emotions, but now all threatened to rip him to shreds. He'd conquered shifting so that he only changed when he needed to, and not when the beast itself wanted to, or when the moon wanted him to.

He was a werecat. His pride of lions lived here in Northern New Mexico and southern Colorado. Mountain lions when they could no longer be humans.

Reya's eyes glowed.

"Not yet," he whispered.

She smiled and pulled him to her, backing up to the counter, even as she kissed him. He felt the need in her, heard it in her breaths, saw it in the furious beat of her pulse in her throat.

He leaned in and nipped her neck as she tilted her head to the side. At the counter, she stopped. Lo picked her up and set her on it, nudging her knees apart to step between them. He felt her wiggle her feet against his legs, her sandals clattering to the floor.

"I want you, Lo," she gasped as he unbuttoned one button and then another.

He stopped. "Do you?"

"Yes."

"Why?" He hooked his finger beneath the lace edge of her bra and flicked it over the center of her breast.

Her breath shuddered out.

Lo ravaged her mouth, his hand kneading her breasts even as she scooted closer to the edge of the counter. He pushed the cups of her bra down so that he bared her, her breasts pushed up high for his touch, for his mouth. He kissed her neck, down over her collar bone. Her hands fisted in his hair. He kissed one breast, laved it and pulled the center in his mouth. She moaned low and deep, jerked his head up so that she could kiss him.

Her kiss met his, hot and wet, demanding and taking.

His hand slowly traced patterns on her inner thigh. He grazed his fingers over her center, bands tightening around his chest as he noted she was already as wet as he'd known she would be. She shuddered in his arms, her mouth ravaging his.

"Easy," he whispered.

"It's been too long." Her hands fisted in his hair. "I don't want easy."

He slipped one finger under the edge of her panties and watched her eyes widen, watched the change begin as her pupils grew, the irises glowing a dark blue through black. God she was beautiful, and hot and still so damn responsive.

He ripped the flimsy lace away from her. She gasped, her eyes starting to change. Lo grinned as he traced her center in long sure strokes with his thumbs, staying away from the one point he knew would shatter her.

"Please, Lo. Please." She muttered in their forgotten language.

He smiled. It wasn't simple need in her voice, or her face ... it was more.

Still watching her, he slid his fingers deep inside, closing his eyes at the hot, wet feel of her. Even better than he remembered.

She moaned, and he opened his eyes to see her close her eyes and throw her head back, exposing the long length of her neck. There was something very arousing about the fact that she was half undressed and vulnerable while he was fully clothed. He leaned forwards and kissed the column even as he worked his fingers, deeper and faster, shallow and slow until she was begging. She smelled of dark promises and still tasted of heady pleasures.

"Please, please, Lo. Oh, yes ... right...."

He barely pressed the hidden buddle of nerves and watched,

felt as she shattered in his arms, her inner muscles vising around his fingers and he wished to hell he was buried as deeply inside her.

She purred as she fell against his shoulder, her tongue licking his neck. Lo picked her up, carried her to his bedroom and knew that unless she was sober, he wasn't about to give in to his own wants. There would be no excuse she could hurl at him tomorrow morning. When they came together again, it would be because they were both lucid and wanting it.

He laid her on his four poster, pine bed, watched as she cuddled into the pillows. "Join me," she whispered.

Carefully, he unbuttoned her dress all the way down the center. Leaning over, he kissed her deeply as he tossed the dress aside and pulled her bra off her arms, laying it on the nightstand. Her hands came up and started on the buttons of his shirt. Lo, gently circled her wrists, pulling back and ending his kiss.

"In a minute." He kissed her again and stood. He covered her with his quilt, watched as she snuggled deeper into his bed, the soft sound of a purr rumbling in the room.

"Hurry," she said, her voice heavy with sleep and desire.

She never could drink and not fall asleep. He grinned and walked back to the kitchen, checking all the doors and windows.

He stood in the living room looking out across the wide expanse of plain, watching the headlights of distant cars on the highway speed towards and away from Taos. The cluster of lights from the town slowly trickled out to his ranch and beyond. The dark shadow of Rio Grande Gorge snaked across the silvery landscape.

He watched as a shadow shifted, walking down his road, followed by another. He narrowed his gaze, listened carefully and knew.

Kade and Darrell. He wanted to know if they'd found out anything. Another shadow moved out by the barn. He stood there waiting until he knew ... Dena. Well, she was probably pissed, but it was hardly his fault if she wanted him. He'd told her no. She'd just have to live with the fact that Reya was here. And his.

While he waited for his cats to come to him, he opened the sliding door, heard the rustle of the wind as it wove across the vast basin. He'd always liked the fact he could hear the wind before it ever reached him. There were few places it did that. New Mexico was one of them. He could still remember the smell of it as it had been in his childhood long, long ago in Chaco Canyon, the way he could smell rain on the air hours before the storm would come rumbling down the prairie.

Even then there had been an enemy. And now?

Somewhere out there, the enemy waited again.

## Chapter Four

The Chosen looked around at the group gathered. Some were still in their human form, others in the form of their animals. There were wolves and coyotes alike. Hunters and scavengers.

The Chosen wished the blood was still pure, still untainted, still pure wolf, but things and time changed one's perspective. When the cause was large enough, alliances could be born in hell.

After all, needs want when the devil drives. Though, the devil was a very subjective thing. No doubt evil existed, but The Chosen had never met the Christian's devil, though evil could easily be touched.

The amusing thing was that so many often never realized they were in contact with that which they so abhorred. They liked their scary movies, their ghost stories, the idea that something might go bump in the night, but they never truly wanted to be faced with it.

The Chosen smiled while listening to the others talk, their whispers filling the air and twining with the pine smoke from the fire. The sound of the brook gurgled through the night. The Chosen rose, pulling the jacket tighter around its frame. A storm was rising, building to the west. The smell of rain and chill hung in the star studded night. Pine and aspens speared up, black against the midnight sky, their shadows long on the silvery moonlit ground.

"Why are we here?" one of the members asked. Avis was the newest of the group and the most outspoken, but without a doubt the most eager to prove himself.

The Chosen waved him down, noted the tattoo on Avis wrist in the sign of the wolf moon. Perhaps that had been a mistake, asking everyone who signed, who joined to receive the mark of their order. The mark of the wolf.

The werecoyotes rumbled amongst themselves. They were merely the expendable. The trace, if it were found, would lead mostly to them. The tattoos, the groundwork, even this meeting place.

Legend told how the coyote had closed the sipapus of the ancients, closing the doorways between the underworlds and this so that only the kachinas could pass through. The Chosen had no idea if that were true or not, nor did the Chosen care.

Right now the reason for the unorthodox alliance with the coyotes had nothing to do with the old legends and everything to do with a carefully laid plan. By the time The Chosen was finished here in the Four Corner's region, the Prides and their orders would no longer be an issue and neither would these mangy werecoyotes or their packs.

And it would again be The Chosen's rule, the time of the wolf.

## Chapter Five

*Merria of the Water walked out of their house and carefully climbed down the ladder to the ground. The pueblo was dark and the packed dirt hard under her feet. She could hear the gentle lap of the Sacred Blue Lake as it met the shore. She looked up at the night shrouded mountains. The smell of pine tingled in her nose, mixed with the smoke from the fires.*

*Chants floated heavy and elusive on the air. The men were in the kiva. This was a time of special meetings.*

*The baby, Little Moon, cried out and Merria bounced her on her hip, holding the water jar in her other hand. She'd learned to do things with Little Moon, she had to be resourceful. The water jar was tied to her waist. She had made a plug out of a pine branch to fit in the top so that she would be able to carry water and the baby both up the ladder.*

*At the edge of the lake, she leaned down and filled the jar up. The water was cool, the moon, full and bright, shimmered on the waves.*

*The drums beat from deep in the kiva, and she felt the vibrations through the ground, watched as the water trembled.*

*Little Moon cried again, but Merria set her daughter down and hurried to fill the water jug.*

*Then she heard it.*

*A low growl.*

*The hairs on the back of her neck stood, her arms prickling with dread as the sound graveled across the night.*

*She jerked to look to the right.*

*Another sound from the left.*

*She carefully stood, gathered Little Moon to her, trying to quiet the child's cries. Looking one way, then the other, she slowly backed up the path away from the sacred waters. She should not have come out this night, but she'd been so busy with the baby before, she hadn't had time to gather the water. She had thought there would be enough.*

*She should have waited until morning.*

*"Reya," her husband had told her, "do not go out after dark. The elders have been talking… there are things...." He'd shaken his head.*

*"Lorenzo," she whispered. Why hadn't she demanded he tell her? She knew of things in the night. She was one of them. He was one of them. Their child was a child that should not have been by all legends, but Little Moon was.*

*She held the child tight to her as she came to the edge of the trees.*

*The growls seemed to whisper along the ground at her feet, building and building.*

*The drums from the kiva beat faster, harder, louder.*

*Chants rose on the air. Fear slithered across her.*

*Please, please let her get her daughter to safety.*

*Merria turned and ran....*

*The animal leapt from the side of the brush, knocking her off her feet, and she felt Little Moon fly from her arms.*

*"No!" she screamed, her anger and rage summoning her beast with such a power, pain knifed through her. She had not changed form in many, many moons. While she carried their child, while she nursed their babe still.*

*Merria whirled, slashing at what attacked her. A yell, part human, part howl, rent the air.*

*Little Moon was crying, crying, crying.*

*She whirled, ready to fight whomever she must.*

*Another wolf, larger than most, picked her child up.*

*"No...." she pleaded. "Please. I'll do anything. Anything … not my child. Please."*

*The wolf slowly changed back into the man he was. And she gasped, fear twisting her gut.*

*Sael. The black shaman. He had left her for dead long before, when her people had lived in the Canyon. His face was pale in the moonlight, his eyes as black as his soul and the magic he practiced.*

*And now?*

*"Sael?"*

*He tsked. "You left."*

*She had. He had taken her then, given her to Chinu, the leader of the Lynx. And he had turned her. Why?*

*Little Moon was crying. The shrill noises building and echoing in the woods, bouncing off the water.*

*"Do you hate me still?" she asked, licking her lips. She tried to step forward, but others slinked nearer, growling low in their throats, their fur standing on end.*

*Lorenzo! She screamed in her mind.*

*"You were to be mine," he said, in that slow, smooth voice that was as dark and flat as the Coyote's eyes. "Not the other's."*

*And he'd punished her husband then too. Giving Lo to the Chief of the Lions of the Mountains. It had taken them so long to find each other again.*

*And now ... now here was the man who had wanted her, and who she had always loathed.*

*Little Moon cried again, even louder. Panicked the baby gasped for breath before letting loose another shrill cry.*

*Merria held her hands out, begging. "I will be. Now."*

*"Now is too late." With no warning, he tossed Little Moon aside. Her child fell onto the rocks with a sickening snap.*

*"Nooooooooo!" She ran forwards and they let her pass, one nipping her heel.*

*Merria fell to her knees, picked her baby up. A wound cut across the child's temple, matting the dark hair, blood trickling down the side.*

*The child was still, silent, not breathing.*

*"No. No. NO!!!!!" Tears fell from her eyes and she gently placed a kiss on her daughter's cheek before laying her down. Pain ripping out her heart. A stick lay to the side of her baby.*

*"No!" Rage like no other clawed through her as she turned and let loose all her fury, all her power. Lightning flashed, wind roared down the mountain.*

*"Reya!" someone called.*

*"I will hate you for as long as the moon hangs in the sky!" She pulled her arm back to sink deep into Sael's cold heart, but something slammed into her side and the world faded.*

*She heard Lorenzo's roar, but blackness closed over her as she felt herself being lifted and smelt, not her husband's scent, but that of Sael.*

\* \* \* \*

Reya opened her eyes and realized she was crying. The dream. She closed her eyes again and wished to be there, she wanted to smell Little Moon, the child she had not held in almost a thousand years. That child that could still wake her in the night with the ghost cry. The child of her womb and Lo's seed.

No. No. She was not going to allow that black cloud of depression to sweep over her.

Yawning, she shoved the dream and its remnants away. Stretching, she turned her head into the pillow and breathed deep, the sheets gliding against her skin ... her naked skin....

Lorenzo.

She rolled over, reaching across the bed....

It was cold.

She sat up, shoved her hair out of her eyes and looked around. She was naked. Memories from the night before, the ride, the truck, the kitchen ... she buried her face in her hands. Oh, God, the kitchen. Reya flopped back against the pillows and stared at the ceiling.

What was worse? The fact she'd begged a man she didn't know if she loved or hated? Or that he gave her passion, yet didn't take any in return?

She frowned and stared at the tall stucco ceiling, the large wooden beams cutting across it, offering no suggestions.

Smooth, real freaking smooth. She hadn't spoken with the man in more years than she cared to count ... what? A hundred? Two? She'd seen him off and on through the years, but they'd never again spoken. Not after the last tangle with Sael. Sael....

Nausea greased her stomach and she shoved it aside.

Think of Lorenzo and talking to him again.

Well, they were speaking now. And here she'd begged him to make love to her. Her blood warmed, hummed through her veins at the memory. His hands were still the same, firm, yet gentle, demanding and offering protection yet no quarter to allow her to keep something from him.

He had that power over her. Only Lorenzo had ever had that power over her. She'd had sex with other men since their parting, but none ... no one had ever made her heart skitter, her stomach flip at the simple look at him.

Tears pricked the backs of her eyes and she flung her arm over her face. Things should have been so damn different, but they weren't. And there wasn't a damn thing she could do about it. Not a damn thing.

Sael had ripped them apart and now he had bought them back together?

It seemed too clichéd, but there were clichés for a reason.

Sael....

Fear slithered through her at the mere thought of the evil man. What he'd done, all he'd stolen....

And yet, she and Lo kept meeting up and every time she believed that this time, this time would be different and Sael wouldn't win, everything changed and her world would be shattered.

Like the last time. She actually believed that Sael had died, she learned that Lorenzo--then known as Lucian--had tracked the werewolf to a mountain village in France. And he had killed him, slowly, taking his revenge for all the man had ever stolen from them. She had been allowed to watch some, but then Lorenzo had ordered her from the room and Darrell had carted her off. She'd been angry and run, too many emotions and no way to release them. She'd returned later, to Paris, to Lorenzo only to find him shacked up with a blonde countess.

Anger shimmered through her. It didn't matter. It was all in the past. Live and let live, as the old saying went. She'd almost shifted that day in that town house, but Lorenzo had stopped her and it was a good thing, she would have easily killed the poor countess. After that, she didn't speak to Lo again.

But he'd killed Sael. Lo had killed their enemy. She had heard the story later from Darrell.

She sat up. Sael had to be dead. Lorenzo would never have lied to her about that. Never about that. He had sworn if it took him all his lives, he would hunt the man and kill him.

So what if they were wrong? Who would commit heinous acts, so similar to Sael, in this town, now that both she and Lo were here?

Shaking off the thoughts, she crawled out of bed, and pulled her bra and dress on, looking around for her shoes.

The thick robust smell of coffee filled the air. The bedroom door was shut. She quickly used Lo's bathroom, admiring the terracotta tiled floors, the deep inset tub. Reya washed her face and used his mouthwash and toothbrush.

The man had always been so meticulously organized and some

things would never change.

She opened the solid pine door and walked down the hall, her feet cold on the tile floors, noting things she'd missed the night before. The beautiful southwest artwork on the walls. In the living room, above the fireplace hung a painting.

Reya halted, her pulse slowing, the oils drawing her closer.

She'd seen this in the window of one of the galleries when she'd first moved back here. She'd decided to do something else and then go back to purchase the painting. But when she'd gotten back, it was gone. She'd tried to find out who had bought it, who the artist was, but the gallery owner wouldn't give her a name.

It was what would be considered folk art of the native southwest. It was a picture of a village in the mountains here, pines around, the pueblos almost orange in the fading sun. The sky washed in colors blending from the lightest pinks to deep purple to blazing orange. A mother stood looking towards the water, the wind blowing a strand from her braid across her neck. And in her arms, she held a child.

Reya had wanted it for the simple reason that the child looked like Little Moon and perhaps the woman looked a bit like herself. It was a heartbreakingly familiar painting that had called to her then and called to her now.

Her heart ached. And on top of that damn nightmare, she couldn't help the despair that rose up at the poignant, lifelike painting.

"Well, it's about time you woke up."

Reya whirled at the voice from the kitchen. And there stood an old friend. Darrell Hawkins, still tall and sinewy, reminded her of the aspens. Dark hair, swarthy skin and brown eyes that held the devil's own mischief. He grinned that crooked cocky grin at her and Reya felt herself smiling back.

"What are you doing here?" she asked, walking to the kitchen.

"Following orders. I was about to wake you because the big man knew you'd want to go home and change first."

Relief warred with a large dose of disappointment at the fact Lorenzo wasn't here. Reaching for the coffee mug Darrell handed her, she asked, "Where's he at?"

She saw it, the shuttering of the gaze, the way he blanked his features and she felt the wall he threw up between them.

"He got called out late last night, early this morning."

She looked out of the large picture window that gave her the

Sangre de Cristos at dawn. "There was another murder wasn't there?"

Darrell shrugged. "I have no idea, I just followed orders."

She snorted. "You know every damn thing that ever goes on." She took a gulp of the coffee and glanced at the clock, she really had to get going.

"You ready?" he asked her.

"Yeah, I've got to go change clothes." And get to the shop and figure out what the hell she was doing.

"Cool, can I watch?"

Reya tossed the rest of her coffee on Darrell. "Shut up, Darrell."

He grinned and wiggled his brows. "Now we *both* have to change."

"My God, what have I gotten myself back into?" she asked as they walked out of Lo's house, Darrell locking up behind them.

He slung is arm over her shoulder and pulled her close. "Come on, babes, you *know* you missed me."

"Only in your dreams."


Chapter Six

Lorenzo was sitting in a conference room with someone from the state bureau of investigations and trying to pay attention.

The newest murder victim was a male, young, early twenties, Caucasian. Five foot ten, blond hair, green eyes and his parents from the Midwest were being notified. Same tattoo as the first and same bracelet. The *Wolf Moon*.

The fact that the jewelry came from *Horizons* was not lost on him. He knew, knew in his gut that it was not a mere coincidence.

And as if his thought pulled the question to light, the Chief of Police asked, "Craigen, what of the jewelry and tattoos? They seem to match."

Lo nodded. "They do. The owner of *Horizons Gallery* told me it was called *Wolf Moon*, and one of the few pieces they keep stocked and factory line made. Nothing really special about it. She said she'd talk to the artist and see if he would talk to us, she was also going to go through receipts and see if she could learn if the victim yesterday morning had purchased the bracelet or if someone else did. Hopefully I'll have a list later today."

Everyone nodded and started to file out. The Chief called him back.

"I don't like this and I want it wrapped up as soon as possible. Reporters get a hold of this crap and you'll be hearing rumors of cults and shit. With the festival the town has planned, the mayor will not be happy."

*And we're sorry two young kids died.*

"Autopsy and tox screens should be back on the first vic. Get them, I want a brief on my desk before you leave today."

"Yes, sir."

The day just kept improving.

He ran a hand over his face.

"Craigen?"

Lo looked at the Chief. "Yeah?"

"I often get itches that I'm being left out of something." The man's gray eyes zeroed in on him.

Lorenzo stared back. "And?"

The Chief's eyes narrowed. "I've got that itch now."

No one ever accused the man of being dumb. Smiling, Lo said, "They have medication for that."

With one last hard look, the Chief strode away to his office, hollering at Janice, "Where the hell's my coffee?"

Janice rolled her eyes and Lorenzo turned and left. Just a pleasant morning all the way around.

Outside, he could hear the traffic over on *Camino De La Placitas.* He hurried to his truck and breathed deep. Yes, the air foretold of the cold weather to come soon, and the rain with it.

He drove the streets over to *Horizons*. He didn't see Reya's SUV parked out front, but then she'd be the type to use the parking lots over several blocks and walk to work. Darrell better damn well be with her. He didn't want her alone. Not for one minute.

Bells chimed when he opened the door and stepped into the cool interior of her shop. He saw Darrell sitting behind the counter thumbing through a magazine.

He turned and relief trickled through him at the mere sight of the woman. She stood in the corner helping a customer bedecked in red pants, turquoise boots and screaming red and black shirt. The ensemble was topped off with a turquoise hat. This was what he hated about Taos, the rich or simply dumb tourist who thought they would dress like the 'locals' and only ended up looking like complete fools.

Reya on the other hand wore light skinned boots, dark denim jeans that encased her long, lean legs, and a tight fitted, fawn colored vest with crochet work holding the wide strips of leather together and decorating the buttons, hem and collar. Today, again, her arms were bare, the muscles defined even more by the silver armband she wore. And still the pendant hung from around her neck. Today her hair was long and free down her back in one silken black wave.

Her eyes locked with his and a soft smile played her mouth before being replaced by a frown.

Over a thousand years and he had yet to figure the damn woman out. Some might call him slow, but he knew that where females were concerned a man could live forever loving the same one and still find mysteries about her after that many years.

He grinned and walked over to Darrell. "Anymore problems?"

"None."

"Good, keep it that way."

He leaned against the display case at the front, looking through her selection of items and saw nothing that really interested him. Well, he did like the cat pin. But Reya wasn't a pin wearing kind of woman.

When the fashion bedecked customer paid an unholy amount of money for a pair of earrings and bracelet he sighed in relief and waited for her to leave. The door chimed shut.

" 'Bout time. How the hell do you sell to people like that?" he asked.

She shrugged. "I am not picky on what they want, or how much they spend as long as they spend in my store. The more the merrier."

A jewelry story owner, he thought.

"Gallery owner," she snapped, reading his thoughts.

He grinned, a rusted laugh chuckling out. "Semantics."

She tapped her fingers, the short nails clicking on the counter as she asked, "Did you need something?"

Lo sighed. "Darrell, go get something to eat and drink, bring something back for Reya."

"I can get my own food, if I wanted any, which I don't, thank you very much."

Darrell patted her shoulder and leaned close. "Don't worry, I'll bring you back another caramel mochachino." He kissed her cheek.

Lo couldn't stop the growl that purred deep in his throat. He knew about their damn weekend in the Caribbean a century ago and it still pissed the hell out of him.

Darrell grinned. "Oh, boss man, don't worry, she's yours. Always has been, always will be."

Lo kept his eyes on Reya, as Darrell walked by, Lo shot his hand out and grabbed his friend by his throat. "Don't ever kiss her again."

Darrell laughed and ripped free of Lo's hold. The door chimed behind him.

Arrogant prick.

Reya's eyes bore into him. "I don't need a baby sitter."

"No, you don't."

"Then why has that annoying testosterone jokester been with me since I got up this morning?" She leaned over with her elbows upon the counter. The vest bunched. Unfortunately it was buttoned clear up to her throat.

He reached out and ran a finger down the soft lambskin, watched as his finger grazed over the swell of her breast. "He's guarding you when I can't be around." His gaze rose back to her.

"Baby sitter, guard, semantics."

Lo leaned close and said quietly, "You can fight me on any number of things, and most I'd let you win on, but not on this."

Her pale eyes locked with his. He saw the argument building. "I can take care of myself."

"You won't win."

"You have no say in anything I do anymore, Lorenzo."

His hand snaked out, wrapped around her neck and jerked her half over the counter. Nose to nose he bit out. "Don't pull that with me. You're mine. You always have been and you always will be. Better get used to it."

He crushed his mouth to hers, not surprised to feel the heat of her anger, then the waning as she opened her mouth and kissed him back. He slowly released her.

"I'm still mad at you for Paris."

"Yeah, I know, and I'm still pissed at you for the men you've slept with since then. I could kill every one of them. Almost killed Darrell." He didn't think she wanted to hear how he actually *had* killed two, but they had deserved it after he found out that they were only using her. And one had been a truly sick and twisted bastard. How the hell she'd gotten mixed up with that guy, Lo would never figure out.

Reya sighed. "It's not going to work, you know."

"What won't work?"

"Us, together, happily ever after. We're not created to be that way."

"As I said, you won't win, you might as well give it up." He straightened and pulled another photo from his pocket. "I need to ask you more questions."

She looked at the enlarged photo of the tattoo, and luckily the there was no way to tell that the person it was attached to had been mauled and mutilated. Beside it he laid the picture of the bracelet.

"The *Wolf Moon*," she whispered. "This person is dead too, isn't he?" Her eyes rose to his.

"Yes, a young male."

She nodded, studying the pictures. "I dreamed of Sael last night," she shrugged and added, "this morning. It was that night at the lake."

Her pain rolled off her in a tidal wave and slammed into him. Lo reached over and took her hand. "I'm sorry I wasn't there to hold you."

She gave him half a grin and shook her head. "The past is the past and can't be changed."

God if only it could be changed. He'd prayed and begged his own gods when he and Reya had first been separated. He'd thanked similar gods years and years later when he found her again, cursed them still when they'd allowed his family to be taken from him. Centuries later when the Spaniards swept through and converted the area, he'd prayed to the Christian's God and had found her, had slain his enemy and yet, had still lost Reya again.

But now, here they were, and he'd be damned if he lose her again, in any way.

"I'll have Darrell bring you out to the house tonight," he said.

"What if I don't want to…?"

"That's not the way it works, and you know it. You'll be there. We need to figure out how to trap Sael." And he wanted to seduce her. The way she'd purred and screamed in his arms spiked through his brain in one hot rush of lust.

Reya looked at the man across from her, knew he'd only grown more powerful through the years. She was a modern independent woman, but part of her had always been his and they came from a different time. She was his to call, she belonged to him, even if they were different. They had bonded before they were turned into shifters, bonded long after they were created and then bore a child together in love, part human, part lynx, and part mountain lion.

"Why?"

"Why what?"

"Why do you want me there? You know it's been so long you could choose anyone."

Fire lit in the dark of his eyes, his features hardened. "I won't dignify that stupid question with an answer."

She shrugged. "Fine, I'll see you tonight."

The door chimed again, and he turned. Charles walked in smiling. "Morning, all. Did you two have a pleasant night?"

Reya glanced at him, then turned to Charles. "Well, the dinner was great, wasn't it, Lo? But the rest of the evening was rather quiet and unmemorable."

Anger still radiated out of him, but he smiled at Charles. "And when given a remark like that? What's a man to do other than promise that tonight will never be forgotten?"

With that, he zeroed in on her again, his hands fisted on the display case and said, "Darrell stays. Period. I ordered it."

"I--" She started to say didn't have to take orders from him. A muscle ticked in his jaw and his pupils were widening. Sighing, she said, "I'll be leaving here around six or so, probably seven. It's a Friday night and we're open later tonight."

"Fine. Did you get the receipts of all that purchased the bracelet?"

The switch in topics stalled her for a moment. "Um ... yeah. In the back, let me get them."

She hurried into the back of the gallery, past the supply room where Mica was opening a new shipment of boxes to the office. On her desk she grabbed the envelope and decided to check and see if the artist had answered her email request about releasing the artist's identity.

Nope.

She heard a growl and spun around. Across the hall Mica cursed at the styrofoam she was attempting to pull from a box.

Lord, she was hearing danger in the simplest of things. Hurrying over, she helped the undergrad.

"Sorry, why didn't you holler for help?" Reya asked as she held the box and let Mica pull the packaging free.

"I can do everything myself, didn't you know?" Mica, her hair still spiked, wearing jeans and a tight fitted grunge shirt, shrugged and straightened. The bracelets on her arms jingled. "Need anything?"

"Oh, no, I was just wondering if you're okay, if you're sure you don't want to take the day off."

Mica shook her head. "No, I'm fine. Really."

Reya walked back out to the front of the shop. "Here." She handed the envelope to Lo. Taking a deep breath she couldn't help but smell that damn spicy cologne. The man probably wore it simply because he knew it was an aphrodisiac. He stopped in mid sentence to Charles and turned to her, a wicked smile curving the edge of his mouth.

"Sorry," he said, turning back to Charles. "I've been up too long and need more coffee."

"Don't worry about it." Charles walked to the back.

"Tonight."

She licked her lips, grinned as she saw his eyes follow the movement. Shutting her mind off to him, she flipped her hair back off her shoulder and waved a hand in front of her. "Man, I shouldn't have worn this leather vest thing. It is hot." Watching his eyes narrow, she undid the top button, then the next, and then another.

"That's enough," he strangled out. His eyes met hers and her stomach tightened at the hot look in them. He stepped closer. "I meant what I said earlier."

"Which time?"

His breath was warm on her face. "Darrell. The fact you're mine." He closed the distance between them and kissed her, nothing spectacular, just his lips on hers. "And the fact that you sure as hell won't forget tonight."

## Chapter Seven

The Chosen knew that the time had come. The Chosen had planned to wait until tomorrow, but things were in place. Today would work. Tonight would be perfect. The storm would hit this eve and they would have no clue where the danger came from.

Reya and Lorenzo....

The two made The Chosen ill. What they had done ... they

must pay and pay they would.

The Chosen knew impatience hindered carefully laid plans. The original plan had been to ruin Lorenzo's reputation, strip him of his power, and make his peers question him. The Chosen wanted to pin the murders on him and then at the end have him watch as The Chosen's followers devoured Reya.

But.... Things and plans change.

The Chosen picked up the coffee cup and drank deep, knowing that tonight was the night.

\* \* \* \*

This time when Reya arrived at Lorenzo's she could admire some things she'd missed in the dark. To be honest, she really hadn't paid all that close attention. She'd become modern, lost in the modern world, often forgetting that she was different from everyone else. And what she was, like anything else, took discipline to master. She was like the runner who realized they hadn't jogged in months.

Last night she could have noted everything she was now, but she hadn't. The large sprawling adobe home was like most in the area, sun washed to a light tan, the large logs protruding from the sides, a barn set off the back of the house and she could see the black snake of the gorge in the distance. Two horses stood in the paddock. No Dodge truck, no Lo. Someone sat on the porch.

When she and Darrell got out, she didn't recognize the woman. Darrell spoke up. "Dena, this is Reya."

Dena stood, was on the short side, muscular and didn't look like she smiled much.

"Reya, as in *the* Reya?" A humorless smile flitted over her mouth. "Well, isn't it nice to finally meet you?"

Reya frowned.

"Ignore her, she's just jealous because Lo never paid attention to her other than to notice she was great at her job."

Oh. "And what job would that be?"

"Protecting your ungrateful ass," the woman shot back.

"Joy. Friends and enemies, they're always so damn tangled." Feeling her anger rise at the rude woman and really not wanting to waste the energy, she opened the front door and strolled into the house as if she owned the place.

Lo wanted her to be here. *You're mine. You always have been. You always will be.*

Fine. She was his. She'd just make damn certain that this time he understood that was a two-freaking- way street.

She tossed her purse onto the entry table and carried her bag into his room, Darrell following close behind. She heard Dena's mumbled, "Bitch."

"Is she always so friendly?" She opened the closet, opened the dresser to find it was half empty. She looked over her shoulder at Darrell.

"Hey, don't look at me. He's known where you were for years. Why the hell do you think we moved back here?"

Sadness and sweetness collided. The closet, likewise was half empty. As if he'd just been waiting.

"Don't let Dena get to you," Darrell said, dropping her other bag on the bed.

She chose not to answer. The other woman was cute and honestly looked more Lo's type. She looked like she could handle her own in any situation. Probably knew how to shoot a gun and took all sorts of martial arts or something.

Reya tossed her underwear into his drawer. And stopped. Why the hell was she doing this? Why hadn't she just bought enough along to stay the night?

*Because she was hoping for more?*

So why announce it to all and sundry that she was easy?

She wasn't easy, she just didn't want Dena to think she had any place here.

"She doesn't," his deep voice said from the doorway.

He stood there, leaning against the door frame, his hands in his pockets, his jeans starched as always, his button down shirt not even wrinkled after he wore it all day.

"Lo." She shoved the drawer shut. "I figured if you're going to be all macho, I'd just bring some clothes with me so I wouldn't have to keep going to my house." She looked back to him and noticed Darrell was gone. "Where's Darrell?"

He stepped into the room and shut the door. "I sent him to check things out, find out where some of the others are and to bring them all here later."

"Oh." She walked to the bed. "For what?"

"A meeting." He walked to her, wrapped his hands around her from behind and pulled her against him.

"For?"

He kissed the side of her neck. "Later."

"Now."

He whirled her around, "Okay, since you asked so nicely." His hands cupped her breasts, caressing them through the soft leather of her vest.

"That's not what I was talking about."

He grinned down at her, slid his hands up under the back of her vest and unhooked her bra. The release of the elastic made her sigh. Lo's hands glided up her bare arms, his fingers grazing on the tops of her shoulders until he pulled the straps of her bra off her arms. Grinning he jerked the lacy material out from under the front of her shirt.

She reached up to unbutton it.

"No, leave it for a minute." He cupped her breasts again.

"Why?"

He gently rubbed the soft leather against her, flicking his thumbs over her nipples. Desire twisted from her breasts to tighten her gut. She sighed.

"Don't you miss the feel of leather against bare skin?" he whispered hot in her ear.

"Sometimes," she whispered back.

He licked her ear, his tongue causing goose bumps to spring along her arms, dance down her spine to tickle the base of her back. "I hate when you do that," she softly said, closing her eyes.

"No you don't." His hands continued to play the leather against her skin until she was warm, her blood humming, her breasts and nipples so sensitive that the slightest shift of material had her gasping.

Lo pulled back and unbuttoned her jeans. "I want these off of you. Now."

He stepped away and walked to the dresser, picking up a remote and clicking a button, sultry Spanish guitar music heated on the air. He sat in the chair by the fireplace.

"Take your clothes off for me."

She stood there, panting. "What?"

"Take. Them. Off."

"But...."

"Now."

His rough voice aroused her. How had she forgotten this? That he could make her want by simply speaking. How he liked to be in control, and yet he'd hand the reins to her if she asked.

She wasn't in the mood to ask. On the next song, she began to peel her jeans down her legs. Part of her should feel stupid. It had been so long since she'd been with Lorenzo, but she didn't. One look at the smoldering look in his eyes, the tightened features of his face, the fact he was lounged back in the chair just waiting....

Reya had missed the quickening of her blood, the way her whole body tightened in wanting a single touch from him.

She kicked her jeans to the side and swayed to the music.

"The rest."

Her eyes locked with his as she slowly rolled her panties down her legs and tossed them to him. He picked them up from his lap and held them. "You're wet."

She smiled.

"The shirt."

Reya rubbed the material against her torso as she swayed and danced for him.

"God, I've missed you," he said, his voice harsh. "Come here."

Reya shook her head and slowly unbuttoned her shirt until it hung open.

"Come here."

She smiled and slowly pulled one arm free, then the other. "In a minute."

Naked she swayed and danced to the music that pulsed in the air as humid as the desire and passion.

She heard the rustle of his clothing and opened her eyes in time to see him standing in front of her. "I said, come here."

"You came to me." His mouth crashed down on hers, fighting for control. His fully clothed body rubbed against her naked one. His shirt grazed her sensitive nipples and she gasped.

He walked her back until they fell on the bed, her head barely missing her bag. He muttered something and shoved it aside. His hands were everywhere, branding her, claiming her, marking her.

Reya closed her eyes, the feelings too much to control. She had missed him unbearably through the years. How in the hell had she ever thought she was over him? How?

"You will never be over me. Never," he swore, rising up on his elbows, the features of his face pulled tight.

His eyes dared her to contradict him. She brushed her hand over his jaw, and felt the shimmer of his other self just beneath.

"Our souls needed to merge. We've starved them, Reya."

She closed her eyes as he kissed her again, the denim of his jeans rough against her inner thighs, his shirt almost coarse against her torso and breasts. His hands were everywhere, cradling her face, then skimming the tops of her breasts, only to pinch a nipple before kissing it gently.

Reya growled and arched. The air shimmered around them.

His fingers traced circles on her breasts even as he pulled them deep and suckled.

Reya reached between them, and tried to unbutton his shirt. He pulled up. "No."

"But I want."

"My way."

Next time, she would....

His smile was tender. "Next time you can do whatever you want. I've wanted this for too damn long."

His mouth met hers again, his tongue licking the seam until she opened beneath him. His groaned low in his throat and dove deep. His fingers trailed over her stomach, grazed lower until he finally touched her.

She felt the air shimmer harder with her inner beast, she opened her eyes and saw the air was turning green.

She remembered this from before. Before with Lorenzo when the spirits knew it was special … the air changed, charged, and became part of them.

His fingers played over her center in long slow strokes that had her shuddering. Finally, his fingers pierced her and she cried out.

His breath was hot on her neck as he worked his fingers deep, and deeper, faster and slower.

"Lorenzoooo," she moaned.

He chuckled against her belly, his tongue wet as he twirled around her navel. He blazed a trail to the juncture of her thighs and she stopped breathing all together until she felt his breath blow a stream of cool air against her heat.

She closed her eyes and gave herself up to him.

"Finally," he whispered. "You are mine, Reya. Always. Forever. No one can do this to you, but me."

His mouth kissed her, even as his fingers worked within her, she could feel herself building, building. His wicked tongue darted, licked, laved until she was twisting. Building up to....

"No." He stopped and quickly stood.

Her entire body pulsed, her breaths panting out. "What?"

He stood on one foot and pulled off a boot, then the other, tossed his socks aside, quickly shucked his jeans and boxers, and all but ripped his shirt off.

She couldn't help it, she laughed.

Lorenzo looked at the woman sprawled out on his bed, smiling, her eyes filled with the love that had always been between them.

He walked to the foot of the bed, crawled up the bed, crawled up her body until he was right back where he'd started. His length lay atop hers, her breasts soft and pliant beneath his chest, the heat from her core all but scorching his groin.

He kissed her softly, slowly, urging her to join him. Pulling back, he kneeled between her open thighs. Lo looked down at her pink female flesh and felt lust lightning through his veins. He ran one finger from her pubic bone down until he slipped into the wet center of her. He watched as he loved her with his fingers, watched her face as her eyes slid closed. When she was riding his hand, he slowed, moved closer and positioned himself at her entrance, groaning as her wet heat touched the tip of his erection.

"Reya."

She opened her eyes and looked at him.

He entered her in one hard thrust.

She screamed.

He grabbed the sides of her face. "If you ever again leave me, I will hunt you down and chain you to my side. You are mine. You rule beside me, from here on." He thrust deep and deeper still, felt the air shimmer with the last of his control. "Say it."

"I'm yours, Lorenzo. I always have been. Yes." She rocked against him and stopped, fisted her hands in his hair, "If I ever find you in bed with another woman I will do more than walk away and not speak to you for two hundred years."

He grinned, and lost himself in the feel of her. They moved in the dance that was older than they were, their breaths mingled and the air crackled. He could feel them, their other halves joining as well, their bodies loving and becoming one as their magic and their souls merged.

Their cats growled, Lorenzo thrust again, taking her up with him. She wrapped her legs around his waist and let him ride her as he wished, meeting him with her own passion. A roar ripped from deep within him as he felt them both going over the peak, shifting together as they were completely joined.

Reya shattered in his arms, her muscles squeezing him until he couldn't see, her own roar echoing in the room.

Lorenzo thrust deep and shared his soul with her and wished more than anything he could again give her a child. One day, one day he would it give all back to her.

## Chapter Eight

The phone jarred them awake.

Lorenzo fumbled up and realized it was his cell. Finding his pants, he pulled the small technological blessing/curse free and answered. "Craigen."

Reya shifted and pulled the quilt up to cover her breasts. Her black hair cascaded over the pillows. He wanted back in bed with her.

"What?" he asked the other person on the phone.

"There's been another murder over at that gallery you been going to. Chief wants you there, ASAP."

The pleasantness of what had finally happened slid away into the black meaning of Janice's words.

"Thanks, Janice. I'll be there in about ten minutes." He flipped the phone shut and quickly dressed. Three deaths in less than three days. Good God.

Reya sat up. "What? What is it?"

"Nothing," he automatically said. What if she'd been at the damn shop instead of in his bed?

"Don't lie to me. It's something. Is it another murder? What? Tell me." She grabbed his shoulder and pulled him around.

Truth or lie. "Yes, another murder, and I'm supposed to get there now."

He buttoned his pants and pulled on his boots and shirt.

She quickly stood. "Let me get you something to drink to take with you or--"

Lorenzo leaned down and kissed her. "Go back to sleep and whatever you do," he said, pulling back, grasping her shoulders, "do *not* leave the house. You understand?"

"You've had it blessed?"

"Hell, I've had it everything." He quickly buttoned his shirt, grabbed his badge and gun off the dresser and looked back at her again. Leaning in one last time he said, "Promise me, Reya, we both know this has to do with you. I need to know you're safe."

She sat back on the bed, wrapped in his quilt. "Yes, yes. I'll stay here. I won't leave."

"Good." He gave her one last kiss and walked to the door. Dena sat in the kitchen.

"Have fun, Tom Cat?"

He rarely used his rank as their leader to intimidate, but he let the power growl his voice. "Knock it off. You're ordered to guard her with your life and if you fail me, so help you, there is nothing that will save you from my wrath."

Her face paled and she nodded. "Yes sir."

He hurried out of the house, thunder rumbling off the mountain, wishing he didn't have to leave. As he sped to town, his hazards flashing, he wished this was all behind them, but knew it was a futile wish.

\* \* \* \*

The Chosen waited in the barn as the truck drove away. In such a hurry he didn't even notice the lack of sound near his home. The storm was picking up.

It was time for pay back. By the time he returned, all would be over and he would have no one to blame but himself.

The Chosen looked at the werewolves, the werecoyotes and said, "Watch them."

Their captives sat tied and bleeding, two of them dead, on the floor of the barn. Seems the pride's leader had been otherwise occupied when his followers needed him.

And it had been a merge. The Chosen had only seen one other and that had been at least eight hundred years ago and between two werewolves in Europe. The Were people could sleep with humans, being part human themselves, they could find mates like them, but few found the perfect mate ... their soul mate.

And those two had merged. All the more reason for them to die. They could actually build a dynasty.

And that would just never, never do.

"Let's play," The Chosen said and made its way out of the barn and towards the house.

Lightning jumped off the Taos peak and ripped the thunder down the valley. The Chosen smiled. The full scope of vengeance was so close the taste was like nectar from the gods.

\* \* \* \*

Reya dressed in her jeans and pulled on a sweatshirt and some tennis shoes she dug out of her bag. The tiles were cold beneath her feet and she'd always enjoyed warm weather herself. It wouldn't be long and the cold winds of winter would be arriving.

Dena sat quietly at the kitchen counter eating a sandwich.

Damn. Reya had forgotten all about the woman.

Animosity could be tiring and she was feeling too good to feel petty. "Hi."

Dena looked up and Reya could have sworn she read fear in

the other woman's eyes. "Hi. I'm ... uh ... sorry about earlier and all."

Reya laughed. "Did he do the voice thing to get you to say that? Really, don't take it personally. Lorenzo just has a problem with sharing." Reya jerked open the refrigerator door

"And one thing he'll never share is you."

Reya shrugged. "Oh he shared me before now, but I think I just promised that he never would again." She frowned.

The other woman asked, "What did he do the voice thing with you too?"

Reya laughed. "Honey, he did everything with me." Realizing she might be rubbing noses, she asked, "Were y'all involved?"

Dena shook her head. "Nope. He only had a thing for one woman and that was you."

Reya pulled a bottle of water out and kicked the door shut, twisting the lid off. "I am sorry. If anyone had asked me yesterday morning if I cared he was with you, I would have told them no."

She took a drink of water.

Dena narrowed her gaze. "Then you would have been lying."

Reya shrugged. "True. But I could have convinced myself of it."

"You look like the woman in his painting."

Thunder rumbled outside down the mountain, slamming into the side of the house.

She paused then took another drink of water. "Do I?"

Dena nodded. "Yeah and in most of his other paintings as well."

"What other paintings?" Reya asked.

The look on Dena's face clearly said she wished she hadn't said anything. "Ummm...."

"What other paintings?"

"Just forget I said anything...."

"Nope, nuh-huh. What other paintings?" Reya asked, snatching a chip from Dena's plate.

"I--"A knock at the door interrupted them.

Reya started for the door, but Dena shoved her aside. "I was told to guard you, and regardless of whether or not I like you, I will."

"Oh good grief."

Dena opened the door and Reya looked out onto the portico to see Mica standing there crying.

"Reya?" she burst into tears.

Dena turned with a raise of brow. "You know her?"

"Yeah, a college student that works for me."

"Great you can handle her then, because I don't do the tears and there-there thing."

"Isn't that a surprise," Reya muttered. "Mica? What's wrong? What happened?"

Dena turned back and motioned Mica inside. "Don't let the storm in."

Mica wiped her eyes with the back of her hand and reached into her coat pocket. "Did Charles call you yet?"

"No, why?"

Her face crumpled and she cried again. "It's so horrible. Someone was found at the shop. What if I'd gone back? I was terrified it would be you and … and … and...."

Reya reached through the doorway and jerked Mica in. "What? What are you talking about?"

Mica shook her head. "Someone found a body at our shop."

"Are you high?" Reya asked.

Mica's face was streaked with tears.

Dena suddenly asked. "How did you know she was here?"

Mica frowned. "She told Charles if he needed her, this was where we could get her if she wasn't at home."

Dena's brows furrowed. "So how do you know what happened at the shop and why didn't Charles call here?"

Mica shook her head. "I don't know. I have no clue. I just...."

"Put your hands where I can see them," Dena's voice lashed out.

"What?" Mica and Reya asked at the same time.

"Now, Mica, put them where I can see them."

Mica nodded. "Okay."

She jerked her hands out of her coat and fired a shot so quickly, Reya didn't realize what happened until the gun was pointed at her.

"Mica?"

Reya glanced quickly at Dena, saw only her legs from behind the huge arm chair, but blood seeped in a stream across the tiles.

"Mica?" the college girl asked in her flighty voice. Then before Reya's eyes, the spiked haired girl slowly began to change. Morphing.

Whoever or whatever she was, she was a morpher.

The face changed into that of herself, with her own voice. "Oh,

Lo, how lovely to see you again."

Reya stumbled back.

The face and body changed to Charles, "Reya, would you date a fifty-two-year-old?"

She bumped into the other armchair. The form changed into a dead body on the floor. A face she didn't know or recognize. Then the form shifted, melding into boots and jeans and a white button down. Blood pooled over his chest.

"Lorenzo!" Without thinking, she rushed forward, then stopped.

Think, she had to think.

His form still lay at her feet, her heart slamming in her chest. No. No. It couldn't be. She would know, she would.

A cold wind blew through the house.

*"Lorenzo!"* she screamed in her mind. This wasn't happening. Her breath panted out and she closed her eyes against the nausea. She was powerful. She was. So stupid not to have stayed in shape.

Reya sensed a blur of movement and shot her eyes open, and her hands out, throwing a shield up, but it was too late.

Something slammed into the side of her head, and her world tilted.

"Lorenzo," she whispered as she fell.

All she could see were the boots. His boots as she tried to pick herself up off the floor.

"We're going on a little trip," his voice whispered in her ear.

The cold seeped deep within her until blackness closed over.


Chapter Nine

Lorenzo pulled up in front of Reya's shop and knew he should have told her, but he didn't want her here.

An urgency pulled at him. Was the new vic someone she knew? And now in her damn shop? Rage roiled through his blood.

Just as he opened the door an image flashed white hot in his mind.

*Reya backing away. No. No. It can't be.*
*His house. His chairs. The tiles.*

*"Lorenzo!" she screamed.*
…her voice echoed within his soul.
"'Bout time you got here," one of the guys said.

Without a word, he started the truck and shoved it in gear. His tires squalled on the asphalt. "Please, please, please."

He never should have left her. Never. Just like before. Damn it.

He tried to bring the image back, even as his cell rang and the radio sputtered. He flicked the radio off and sped through town, narrowly missing one car.

He reached deep within him and shoved his power to her. He couldn't see her, all he could feel was the deep cold of death.

Lorenzo chanted words he'd forgotten he'd remembered. He called on all his cats.

\* \* \* \*

Reya opened her eyes and felt the rain on her face. She looked through her lashes at the woman on the rock. It was raining.

Pain pulsed through her head and she dared not move. She heard one of the growls. Not a cat's growl, but one from her nightmares.

The wolf.

And something else, she could sense them. They were not the wolves of her nightmares, they seemed … lesser somehow.

She waited, listening to the woman.

"My followers. This is a great day. A great day in deed. Do you see the woman before you?"

Murmurs filled the air.

The wind roared across the plains with a vengeance. Whistling just behind the figure. She narrowed her gaze to see in the darkness and hoped the others wouldn't know.

Whistling, the wind … darkness wasn't relieved behind the figure, the leader. Whoever or whatever the thing was. She stayed still.

"This, this woman is our great enemy. She is the Lioness of this Mountain Cat order. She always has been. It was her lover, who killed Sael, ripped his body apart piece by piece. It was because of her that Sael was killed. And now we shall avenge my brother."

Selinna....

Relief slid through her at the words. Sael *was* dead.

Darkness beyond. Where were they?

Lightning staked down not a hundred yards away and thunder shook the ground. But she saw, and Reya knew. The Gorge.

She tried to see along the ground and in the distance, she could see the cars, cars from the highway as they crossed the bridge over the chasm. But it was miles over to the highway....

She couldn't be too far from Lorenzo's ranch.

This time she closed her eyes, left the shield up, and channeled straight to Lorenzo ... The Gorge, the house, the bridge.

\* \* \* \*

Lorenzo jumped from his truck and didn't even both to cut the engine. He flew to the house. The door stood open. He decided now was not the time to be a human. He concentrated and shifted in one smooth motion.

He smelled blood and hurried into the house, the night's rain roaring closer. He saw Dena on the ground. Reya!

He turned and raced outside the cold wind rippling along his fur.

In the barn he found others. Darrell was hurt, barely alive. He went to him first. Lorenzo licked his friend's face, nudged him and then growled, batting at Darrell's hand until he called forth his friend's beast. When shifted they could heal much quicker than they could as humans.

A noise at the door had him crouching low.

"Lorenzo?" a voice asked.

He could hear other voices outside. Then a growl and purrs. His cats.

"Shift," he commanded them. "We're hunting."

And then an image pierced his mind. He could feel the rain on her face, see the lightning, the gorge, the bridge and cars in the distance.

They were still on his land.

He roared out of the barn and took off across the valley towards the point he knew them to be at. It was a place he'd always liked to go to think and it had a path that led to the bottom of the canyon. It was on the border between his ranch and his neighbors. They'd both used the trail.

"Sire?" one of his asked.

The rain sheeted down upon them, cooling against his skin, but doing nothing for his rage.

He looked to the side and saw Charles, sleek, if a bit older than most in both cat and human form. He owed the man much for keeping an eye on her. "We hunt to kill, they've taken Reya."

Charles turned and roared to the others. The message was passed. There would be no mercy.

## GHOST CATS

\* \* \* \*

Reya watched and listened. She heard the roars even over the rain.

Silently, she shifted. "You would do well to remember who comes for you. And last time I checked you were nothing here." She rose and stalked around the woman. Now she could see her clearly. Not Mica, but the woman who had always hated her.

Selinna was different now, her eyes still a dark green, almost black, her hair shorter, but her face was scarred.

Reya licked her lips. The shifting for her had not been as easy as she wished. "You always were jealous, Selinna of Sael. You were jealous of me. Come to think of it, you were jealous of just about everyone."

She looked out over the group and realized they were larger than she expected, but still rather small. Werewolves and coyotes. Ahh....

"You've been a naughty girl, Selinna," she chided. "The coyotes? You've really lowered yourself." She turned to one who snarled at her. "Tell me, did she share with you her absolute hatred of your kind?" She circled him. "I bet she lets you coyotes do all the dirty work, tells you something along the lines of you being the true soldiers."

The idiot nodded.

"You poor thing, she's going to kill you when you're done serving her."

"That's not true," one of them said.

Reya laughed. "I must commend you, Selinna, you've managed to do what no other wolf leader would ever lower themselves to doing. You went to bed with the enemy."

"Isn't that the pot pointing to the kettle?" Selinna jumped down and shifted into a black wolf, her green eyes showing. The woman shifted as easily as she'd morphed into the other humans, slick and smooth as liquid silver.

How had she not recognized the woman, recognized the beast even as she thought it friend?

"I never willingly slept with your brother," Reya snarled.

"You've become so complacent with the times, Reya, you never even knew it was me. I kept waiting you know, kept waiting for you to look at me and really, really see. To at least *sense*."

"Did you? I guess I had better things to do."

Lightning flashed, again all too close. Thunder shuddered

down the mountain.

They circled each other. The others backing up, making a larger circle around them.

"Did you ever know he slept with me?"

"Your brother? That's not something I would brag about, Selinna." Still they circled. *Come on, Lorenzo. I can take her, but not all of them!*

And then she heard his voice. Part of her had been terrified that Selinna had morphed into him because she'd killed him.

*Wait for me.*

*I'll try.*

"No, you little slut. Your precious Lorenzo. Did you know it was I in his bed in Paris? It had taken me that long to hunt the bastard down and I would have killed him if you hadn't shown up." The last growled across the air between them.

"Really? Well, lucky for me and him then. You're not the only bitch he's slept with you know." She stopped, crouched low. "And for that plan alone I could kill you."

They sprang at each other, claws and teeth ripping fur and flesh. She used her tail to bat at Selinna, ripped her claws down the wolf's back pleased when she heard her scream. Reya roared as Selinna's jaws clamped on her neck, stinging where they locked. She twisted onto her back, planted her feet against Selinna's belly and threw the wolf off.

"Did your brother die painfully?" she asked. "I hope so, I've prayed so. I rejoiced when I heard he'd died. Sael was evil and never deserved to live." Reya realized they were closer to the edge than she'd thought. She danced closer, taunting. "Come at me, puppy, and let's dance again."

She was waiting. Selinna sprang through the rain at her. Reya waited, waited until the last possible moment and then used her own momentum to catch the wolf that landed on her. Again she twisted, rolled and sank her own teeth into Selinna.

The wolf howled and clawed back. Reya felt her own skin rip open, the sting of the rain strangely exhilarating.

They fought and bit, clawed and danced. At last....

This time Reya was on her back, prayed it would work and waited until Selinna sprang onto her again. She was ready.

Reya caught Selinna in the soft underbelly with her back paws. Still she rolled up and shoved her legs out.

The wolf howled as she flew over the edge and down into the dark depth of the canyon. Her relief was short lived.

The growls and barking calls tightened around her as they all drew closer.

Then he was there, leaping over all them to stand in front of her.

Roars filled the air as the werecats met the werewolves and werecoyotes.

He broke two of the wolves' necks. She tossed another off the side of the cliff.

"I told you to wait for me," he growled.

"I'll have to work on listening to you."

The battle didn't last long. Lightning flashed and strobed, thunder ripped though the valley just as the claws did. Blood filled the air as the dead wolves and coyotes lay on the ground. One of them growled out, "The elders will not be pleased with you, Lorenzo."

Lorenzo leaned down low. "The elders will understand when I explain that you were killing innocents and leaving them for the humans to become involved in."

The old wolf laughed. "I told her not to bring them in. They were new, not known of our ways, they turned and wanted out. She had the werecoyotes kill them."

The old wolf took another breath and died.

"It's time to go home, Reya."

She stood there, panting. "Selinna? Of all the damn women you had to pick to sleep with. Why in the *hell* did it have to be her?"

The other cats circled them as they walked home, guarding them.

Apparently it was time to come back to the pride, but she wasn't certain she was ready.

"You're mine. Don't forget it."

"Yeah, well considering I just killed one of your girlfriends, I'd say you better not forget it."

The rain washed the blood away and by the time they returned back to the house, most of all their wounds were healed. Both she and Lo batted Dena's beast to come out so that she could heal herself. Darrell was carried into the house by two other werecats who had shifted back into human form. Apparently there were more than she realized here.

"There is much for us to talk about," Lorenzo told her.

Apparently.

## Epilogue

Reya stood in the shop looking at Charles and wanting to ask him if she'd really seen him there that night. She thought she had, but then hadn't been sure. She decided she was better off not knowing.

Autumn hung heavy on the air, the mountainsides a quiltwork of gold, red, and orange, aspens broken by the dark green of pines. Snow had already fallen on the higher elevations.

She and Lorenzo were seeing each other, but she moved back to her place wanting things to go slowly and get to know him again. He thought it was a load of shit and maybe he was right. Maybe it was just an excuse.

But they were together regardless and time would tell if she wanted that to be permanent.

There were no more murders and the newspaper and locals had wondered what had happened to all the coyotes and wolves out on the lip of the canyon several miles from town. A rancher, Lo's neighbor, discovered the rotting bodies when the buzzards started circling.

Detective Lorenzo Craigen had no idea what had gone on out there and had rushed home because someone had called claiming to be the murderer and had kidnapped his girlfriend. Of course, that turned out to be a humorless prank and he was left explaining to both Taos Chief of Police and his own boss for leaving the scene of a murder investigation.

The murders were listed as unsolved though he still asked around and the state police would call her once a week to see if there was anything new.

She went into the police station several weeks ago to let someone know that her assistant, Mica, hadn't shown for work in a week and couldn't be reached on the phone. Apparently she hadn't been to classes either and no one had seen her since.

And Reya, she just tried to figure out what she wanted out of life. Right now she was studying with a local bruja to work on building and honing her powers. No sense in being caught off guard again.

Lorenzo was still pissed at her about that.

All things considered, life was pretty good. She took a deep breath and smiled at the customer that walked through her door.

\* \* \* \*

Lorenzo sat in the barn loft, the tang of turpentine and oil paints thick on the air. He was so mad he couldn't see straight, but damn it, he'd make her come around. She should be living with him, not in that other empty apartment.

He gathered paint on the tip of his brush and finished the scene of the Reya naked in the moonlight.

He grinned. She'd kill him if she saw this. Come to think of it, maybe he'd just offer to set this in the gallery that showed his work if she didn't move back out here with him. She was his wife, no matter how damn many centuries had passed.

No, no one would see this painting but him. Though he might show her.

He whistled to the wooden flute music soothing from his speakers.

Time.

He would never understand the woman.

He was also currently trying to explain to the elders what the hell had happened that night. Not wanting a huge were war to begin, they were having meetings with a liaison who, though werecat, worked within the packs. He'd see how it went.

Lorenzo studied the painting. God she was beautiful. Grinning he kept painting.

\* \* \* \*

The cave was damp, but then it always was. Winter was coming on and food would be harder to find. She had no idea why she couldn't shift, but for now, her powers held her captive in wolf form.

That was all right, her time would come … if the winter didn't kill her off first.... One day she would gain her vengeance on those she hated....

One day....

# RAIN ON THE MOUNTAIN

By

Elaine Corvidae

*Hun*
(One)

Thunder rumbled in the distance, breaking up the monotony of the hot, humid air. *Another summer day in the south,* I thought as I picked my way across the cornfield where my missing persons case had just turned into a homicide.

The crime lab technicians were casting nervous glances towards the west, where the afternoon thunderstorms were building great, black anvils of cloud in the sky. I hoped that the rain held off at least long enough for them to get finished-- although the storms seldom lasted long, they were usually ferocious, and precious evidence could disappear forever into the red clay.

My partner, Charles Gardener, was already there, standing off to one side amidst the broken stalks of corn. He cast me a glum look as I came up, then went back to watching the body as it was zipped into its black bag. The smell of decay still hung in the air; the flies would have been at work from the moment the corpse was left here, in this remote corner of Pickerel County. I was just as glad that I had arrived late.

"Took your time, Starnes" Charlie said morosely. Sweat plastered his blond hair to his head; it was thinning on top, and his scalp was already starting to turn red from the sun. He wore a suit and tie, and I remembered that he had been in court that morning.

"Are we sure this is our girl?" I asked, resisting the temptation to remind him that today had theoretically been a day off for me.

"Physical description matches, at least superficially. She's going straight to the forensics people up at Chapel Hill, so if it is her, we should know soon." He bit his lip, then shrugged. "She was decapitated."

"Christ." I swallowed hard against unexpected nausea. Charlie and I had worked murder cases before, but most of them were the straightforward kind. Quarrels among relatives that ended up settled with shotguns, drunken brawls that evolved into stabbings, the occasional robbery gone bad ... but nothing like this. "That'll make identification harder."

"Not really. We found her head a few feet away from the rest of her."

I tried to put aside the mental image. "That doesn't make sense. Usually perps cut up a body to make it harder to ID."

"Not always." Charlie patted his pockets, looking for a package of cigarettes that wasn't there. When he remembered that he was supposed to be quitting, he swore softly. "Let's take a walk, and I'll fill you in."

Charlie's briefing didn't take long--at this point, there wasn't much to tell. Two boys out on their ATVs had stopped near the field when they smelled something dead. Curious, they'd gone into the corn to investigate, which was when they had discovered the body.

The victim had been a fully clothed white female who seemed to match the description of Debra Simpson, an NC State student gone missing over the weekend. Decomposition was rapid in 98-degree heat and high humidity, however, and it would take the regional forensic team to make a positive ID. There had been no sign of a purse or wallet.

We emerged from the green fortress of the cornfield, but stopped well behind police lines. As usual, a crowd of onlookers had gathered despite the remoteness of the spot.

"Reporters," Charlie said with a nod, as if I could have missed the six big news trucks, assorted cameramen, and talking heads, not to mention the helicopters circling overhead.

I gestured at my sweaty shirt and muddy jeans--I'd been working the garden when I'd gotten his call. A proper picture of the Pickerel County Police Department, I was not. "You're the one in the suit."

He grumbled under his breath, squared his shoulders as if preparing for battle, and marched resolutely in the direction of the reporters who were already converging on him like wolves on a sheep. Quietly blessing my good luck, I took a moment to survey the rest of the onlookers who lined the narrow road.

Besides the swarm of reporters, there was a large contingent of old men, farmers mostly, who'd stopped to gawk and discuss the sad state of the world. A few housewife-types who had been out running errands stood in a nervous gaggle, and a car full of teenagers had pulled off the curb to watch as well. But as I swept my eyes over the crowd, there was one figure who stood out enough to make me take a second look.

His hair was so black it shone in the sun, and hung to just below his shoulders. A red bandanna held it out of his dark eyes, contrasting nicely with his coppery-brown skin. I pegged him as one of the Hispanic immigrants who worked the nearby farms. He wore a battered jacket over a t-shirt, jeans, and heavy boots, none of which were at all out of the ordinary.

So maybe it was his features that caught my attention. They were fierce and proud, as if one of the figures on a Mayan stele had come to life. Or maybe it was the way he stared back at me-- not challengingly, but steadily, intently, as if he was memorizing every detail.

The wind came up, and I smelled rain and lightning. Thunder crashed, startlingly near, and I jumped and glanced automatically towards the darkening sky. When I looked back, the man was gone.


## *Caa*
### (Two)

"Shit." I put down the stack of photos and sat back in my chair.

Charlie picked up one of the pictures, then dropped it again. He looked faintly haggard, like he hadn't slept well. Having seen the images of what I'd missed at the scene yesterday, I understood why his dreams might have been bad.

When he didn't respond, I reluctantly returned my gaze to the photos. Many of them showed what was left of Debra Simpson's body--dental x-rays had confirmed her identity overnight. Other photos showed the blood-spattered corn stalks, while a few documented the field as it had looked before a horde of police had tramped around in it. "Looks like she was killed on site," I said. "There's too much blood on the corn, otherwise."

"Yeah." He nodded vaguely at the pictures. "Take a look at the close-ups of the wounds."

"Christ. What kind of weapon would rip the skin like that?" It looked as if someone had literally torn Debra Simpson apart.

Charlie only shook his head. "That's what the forensic report is for."

"So what next?"

"We already had an APB out on the boyfriend," Charlie said. "Who, by the way, her parents insist couldn't possibly have been her boyfriend."

Debra's boyfriend was one of the reasons we'd been investigating her disappearance in the first place. When she had failed to return to school on schedule, her roommate had grown worried enough to call the police. According to the roommate, Debra had been on her way here to meet one of the many immigrant workers who had flocked to the agricultural jobs in Pickerel County. A quick visit to the farm where Miguel Santiago had worked had shown that he had disappeared at the same time, which had made him suspect number one in the case.

"I'm afraid to ask," I said. I had the feeling I wasn't going to like what Charlie had to say.

"I managed to get them on the phone--the mother anyway; the father is under heavy sedation. Mrs. Simpson wasn't too happy to talk to me. Seemed to think I ought to be out scouring the county for clues instead of calling her. I asked her about Santiago, but she explained to me in no uncertain terms that Debra already had a boyfriend on campus, a very respectable young fellow name of Mike Woodward. Then she added that even if Debra hadn't been seeing the frat boy, she certainly wouldn't have gone out with one of 'those people,' and suggested that maybe Santiago was a stalker instead. Or that Debra had met him while doing some kind of mission work, which would explain why she was on her way out here in the first place. I tried to explain that Santiago is Catholic, but she wasn't too interested in listening." Charlie shrugged.

"Hell. What about the on-campus boyfriend?"

"He's got an alibi--was seen by fifty other people at a frat party. Not that it clears him without a firm time of death yet. Or means he wasn't involved."

"True," I said. I looked back down at the photos of a young woman's mangled body, feeling seriously out of my depth. Violent murders like this didn't happen in Pickerel County. This case belonged down in Charlotte, not out here in the boonies.

But as I stared at the photos, I realized that something other than the gruesome nature of the crime was bothering me.

I stood up abruptly. "Come on, Gardener."

"Where are we going?"

"To the donut shop, where else?"

He muttered something about smart-ass cops, but grabbed his suit coat and followed me out.

\* \* \* \*

"Why are we back here again?" Charlie groused.

The ride out to the crime scene had failed to improve his disposition, but I decided to cut him some slack--after all, he'd had a rough time of it yesterday, between court and the murder and the press--so I ignored his surly tone. Charlie and I had worked together for almost three years now, and for the most part we got along. But our partnership was no different than most relationships--if you wanted it to last, you had to know when to keep your mouth shut and let something slide.

Not that I was an expert on relationships. My record long-term boyfriend hadn't lasted six months.

"Because I wanted to see the scene again, without a thousand other people mucking around," I replied.

"Then why did we have to take this death trap? I would have been happy to drive."

I ignored his snide comment as I maneuvered my full-sized truck off the road and onto the muddy shoulder. Pickerel County was mostly farmland, which is another way of saying it was dirt poor. The county could barely afford to pay its detectives, let alone spring for a car, so we were stuck driving our personal vehicles.

For some reason, Charlie had never liked riding in my truck. The fact that it's got more rust than paint showing might have been part of it. Or that the thermostat was stuck on "heat," which meant any air coming through the vents was even more ovenlike than the air outside. But I liked to think that those little flaws were part of the truck's charm.

We climbed out, Charlie slamming his door shut with a loud thump. The now-deserted cornfield lay before us, like the scene of a battle once all the soldiers have gone home. A piece of yellow police tape had snagged in the corn, and hung limp and unmoving in the still air.

"Notice anything about the corn?" I asked.

Charlie rolled his eyes. "It's got ears."

"I see why you were top of your class at the academy. It's all bent and broken, right?"

Charlie searched for a non-existent cigarette, then sighed. "You win the gold star for the day, Starnes. Of course it got busted up, with all of us tramping around in it. Tell me we didn't drive all the way out here for that."

"But it wasn't broken to start with." I held up one of the crime scene photos that I'd brought with me for him to see. This one had been taken from a slight elevation--probably the little forested hump that ran just to the north of the field. "Are you going to tell me that our perp forced a woman to walk in there, killed her, and then walked out himself without damaging a single plant except for the ones she was laying on?"

"Maybe he walked down between the rows."

"Then where are his footprints, Gardener? You were here for the initial investigation--I don't see anything in the report that tells me how either Debra Simpson or her killer got in the field. The only footprints noted belonged to the boys who found the body."

"There aren't always footprints or tire tracks. You know that."

"What I know is that it's rained every afternoon for the last five days--since before Debra Simpson disappeared. That field is pure mud--I know I scraped enough of it off my shoes yesterday evening."

Charlie frowned, obviously not sure if he bought my theory or not. "So?"

"So? Doesn't that seem odd to you?"

"Even if you're right, I don't see what it could mean."

I didn't, either--that was the problem. But before I had to admit it, Charlie's cell phone rang. He took the call, rolled his eyes, and gestured to indicate that he would be a while. From his side of the conversation, it sounded like the case he'd put in a court appearance for yesterday wasn't going too well.

Leaving Charlie to his call, I circled around the muddy field to the low rise and its thin strip of forest. Maybe standing at an elevation, even if only of a few feet, would help me get a new perspective on things.

Pines and sweetgums waved green arms against the intensely blue sky. A battalion of blackberry brambles encircled the trees, and I swore as their thorns stabbed me through my clothes. By the time I extricated myself, I was hot, sweaty, and scratched, and less sure all the time whether my ideas were worth anything. Yanking a final bramble free, I took a step into the shade of the trees ... and looked up into a pair of amber eyes.

It took a minute for my brain to interpret what I was seeing, because it was just so damned unexpected. There, not fifteen feet from me, a big cat crouched in a fork in one of the larger trees. The thing was huge and built like a linebacker. Its yellow-red fur was spotted, so it had to have been a leopard--or a jaguar.

Even as all these thoughts went through my head, I felt a cold hand run down my spine. Some atavistic fear awoke in the pit of my gut, left over from the time when humans had been the prey of creatures like this one. I'd faced down violent men armed with shotguns, raving drunks, and crazed addicts, but at that moment I couldn't have forced myself to move for any amount of money.

My gun felt heavy at my hip, and I told myself to just grab it. I wasn't going to shoot the animal unless I was positive it was going to attack, but if nothing else I would feel better with a weapon in my hand. But still I couldn't move.

And then the eerie stare was simply gone. A shadow flashed through the trees, vanishing with a swiftness I could scarcely credit. My heart hammering, I yelled for Gardener and yanked my gun out of its holster. Trying to get the animal back in sight, I stepped deeper into the wood, out of the sunlight.

A figure seemed to materialize beside me. With a startled yelp, I spun, bringing my weapon up--only to find myself looking into the dark eyes of the stranger from the day before.

*Ox*
(Three)

I swore silently, both for letting someone sneak up on me and for displaying surprise when he did. Neither, as Gardener would no doubt remind me, was good for police image.

"Did you see that cat?" I barked, trying to cover the fact that I was flustered.

He gave me the same look he had from the day before--calm, but utterly steady. It reminded me uncomfortably of the stare of the jaguar. The stranger was even cuter up close than he had been across a field, and I noticed that he had a small jade plug through his lower lip.

"Except for the two of us, I have seen no creature here," he said. His light accent was odd, and didn't remind me at all of the other Hispanic immigrants I'd met.

At that moment, Charlie ran up. "I saw some kind of big cat," I told him. "A jaguar, maybe, or a leopard. It was in the tree right there."

Charlie gave the stranger a quick once-over, and I knew he was wondering what the guy was doing here. So was I.

A hasty search turned up no sign of the big cat, however--it was as if the creature had simply vanished into thin air. There was nothing to see at all, except for a set of muddy footprints that belonged to the man who had surprised me. Although he wasn't going to say it aloud in front of a civilian, I knew that Charlie was starting to think I'd imagined the entire incident.

Frustrated and a little spooked, I turned to the stranger, who had been watching us with a sort of bemused interest. "You mind if I ask you some questions?"

He shrugged, somehow making the gesture more graceful than I would have thought possible. Taking that as a yes, I said, "I saw you here yesterday, and now you're back today. Do you live near here?"

"No." He smiled slightly. "And before you have to ask, my name is Pacal Bahlum, and yes, I am in this country legally. I will be happy to show you my green card, if you wish."

I got the impression that Pacal was used to being harassed about his card, and I felt a vague sense of guilt. Charlie, however, didn't seem to share the feeling and took Pacal's wallet when it was handed over, carefully checking the identification against the man standing in front of us. When he grunted and handed it back, I wondered if he was disappointed to find everything on the up-and-up.

"So what are you doing hanging around here?" Charlie asked, glowering a little to make up for not finding anything wrong with the card. "There are laws against trespassing. You got permission to be here?"

"No," Pacal admitted, which surprised me. Most people caught doing something wrong would at least try to cover. "I suspect I am here for much the same reason you are. Because of this terrible crime that has occurred."

"And what's your interest?" I asked, even if I wondered if he might be a friend of Santiago's. Or--if we were really lucky--might even know where Santiago was hiding.

Pacal sighed, and for a moment I thought he wouldn't answer. Even people in the country legally were often wary of talking with the police, expecting that they would have to pay bribes just to avoid being harassed. "I am here because of the murders of some of the workers in the surrounding area," he said at last. "Because I fear that they were killed by the same man who has done this thing."

I exchanged a look with Charlie. "There haven't been any unsolved murders," Charlie growled.

Pacal favored him with the same eerily-steady gaze that he had given me earlier. After a moment, Charlie was the one to look away.

"Not of wealthy young white women, no," Pacal said. His tone was oddly gentle, as if he spoke the obvious to a pair of children. "If you have no more questions, I will be on my way. As you pointed out, I am not a guest on this land."

He turned and walked back towards the road. Caught off our guards by his strangeness, and without any real pretext to hold him, Charlie and I could only stand and watch him go.

* * * *

"I'm telling you, there's something funny about that guy," Charlie insisted.

I leaned back in my chair and rubbed tiredly at my eyes. Ever since we'd gotten back from the crime scene, he'd been repeating the same vague accusation. "So your background check pulled up something?"

"Nada." Charlie looked disgusted. "Zip. Nothing. Not so much as a speeding ticket--not that there's any record of our Mr. Bahlum owning a car anyway. But I know there's something up with him. Call it cop's instinct."

I stood up and turned off the window-unit air conditioner. The building that housed Pickerel County's finest dated from the early 1900s and looked every minute of it. The ceilings and windows were tall--a must from a time without central A/C--and a fan hung down from high above, turning listlessly but not doing much to stir the tepid air. Without the window unit, we would have been roasting.

"I'd rather call it a day," I replied, getting a roll of the eyes from my partner. "See you tomorrow, Gardener."

"It's only four-thirty, Starnes. Wouldn't want to rip off the fine taxpayers of this county by leaving early, would you?"

"It's only four-thirty, but the library closes at six."

"What do you want at the library?"

I shrugged. "Call it a hunch, all right? You keep running down our mysterious Mr. Bahlum, and I'll start checking into what he said about the murders."

Clearly, Charlie though I was out of my gourd. "You mean the murders that somehow haven't been reported to the police, because this is the first either of us have heard of them?"

"Come on, Gardener--you know that a lot of times these workers don't report things to the police. They can't speak English, or they come from some place where the authorities want a bribe to do anything, or both."

Charlie's scowl eased a little. "If there have been any odd disappearances that haven't been reported, I'll bet you five dollars it's because our Mr. Bahlum is behind them. Probably burying them in his backyard. Except there's no local address on him, so maybe he's burying them in somebody else's backyard."

"Just keep thinking those happy thoughts, and maybe we'll get somewhere with this case."

My truck started on the third try, rumbling to life like a dinosaur woken from sleep. Make that an elderly, cranky dinosaur with a bad back. As I steered out of the dusty gravel parking lot and into the street (smaller cars fleeing in terror before me), I thought about what Charlie had said about Pacal Bahlum.

Hanging around a crime scene was suspicious, no doubt about it. Killers frequently enjoyed watching the show their actions had caused. It wasn't unheard of for murderers to join volunteer groups scouring the landscape for the very person they had caused to go missing. They assumed they were superior to the police and everyone else, and visiting the scene of their atrocities was a sort of joke to them, a smug laugh at the expense of all those trying to solve the case.

That wasn't the vibe I had gotten from Pacal Bahlum, though. There *was* something odd about him, no doubt about that, but was it because he was a murderer or because of something else?

*Or is he really weird at all? Maybe all this is just a cultural misunderstanding. Maybe my "vibe" is perfectly normal where he comes from. Just because he speaks pretty good English doesn't mean he's just like me.*

My speculation hadn't gotten me anywhere by the time I pulled into the library parking lot. The library was a tiny brick building from the same era as the police department, the courthouse, and the rest of downtown. Something it did have going for it, however, was three computers and all the local newspapers on microfilm.

"Hey, Tricia!" called the woman behind the counter when I came in. As my sun-dazzled eyes adjusted, I saw that Emily was as immaculately-coiffed and dressed as always. Emily Bumgartner was the kind of woman you just knew would never do anything so unfeminine as actually perspire, no matter how hot it was. Her hairspray never seemed to give up halfway through the day, and her makeup stayed firmly in place no matter how long it had been since she'd put it on. We'd gone to high school together, and back then her perfect poise had made me feel large, sweaty, and awkward. Nothing much had really changed since then.

Fortunately, Emily was so nice it was impossible to resent her. "Hi, Em. I need to get some research done."

She gestured to the empty library. "Help yourself."

I pulled everything I could find on immigrant worker deaths. Six o'clock rolled around before I was halfway done; Emily just told me to turn off the lights and lock the door before I left. Grateful for her help, I lingered long after closing. When I finally emerged from my reading, it was past eight and starting to get dark outside.

I leaned back, conscious that my neck hurt and my stomach was empty. *And what do I have to show for missing dinner?* I asked myself, eyeing the stack of printouts in front of me.

*Not a hell of a lot,* I replied. *Not even enough to show Gardener without him laughing his ass off at me.*

Finding reports about worker deaths hadn't been hard. In fact, it hadn't been near hard enough--according to what I'd just read, most occupational deaths in the US involved immigrants. Even little old Pickerel County had its share, not to mention the surrounding counties, all of which were heavily agricultural as well.

Most of the deaths were fairly cut-and-dried accidents with plenty of witnesses. I dismissed those for now, deciding that it wasn't likely our murderer was plying his trade right out in front of everyone yet somehow getting away with it.

But that still left several deaths on my list. One poor bastard had been found run through an industrial-sized wood chipper that had mangled his body pretty good. No one else had seen the accident--they hadn't even found his body until coming in for work the next morning. The obvious conclusion had been made, and the death investigation hadn't gone very far. But it occurred to me that dropping a body through a wood chipper was a good way to get rid of evidence of murder.

Another man had complained of feeling ill while working in a field in ninety-degree heat. His employer didn't provide water for the workers--but the foreman was selling beer on the side. No one seemed to know if the victim had hastened his demise by buying any, but he promptly disappeared after that and wasn't seen again until what was left of him was found a week later. The medical examiner had judged the body too decomposed to determine exactly what had killed him, but noted that the most likely cause was dehydration. Case closed.

I wondered how hard the ME had tried, how cursory his exam had been. Obviously the death investigation had stopped with him; there had been no remains hurried to Chapel Hill for the forensic experts to look over. Why bother? The deceased was just a worker, and an illegal alien to boot.

I didn't know if either of these deaths or any of the others on my list had anything to do with Pacal Bahlum's accusations. I didn't know if any of them had been outright murders, although I privately thought that anyone who worked men in the fields in the summer without providing water was at least guilty of manslaughter.

*And if they are murders ... if a killer is covering his tracks by choosing his victims from people no one will work too hard to defend ... then what does Bahlum have to do with it? How does he know? Is it because he's the killer? Or does he know the killer?*

*And either way, why did the murderer suddenly decide to kill Debra Simpson instead? She doesn't fit the profile.*

*Unless Miguel killed those men, and Debra somehow found out about it. He might have murdered her to cover his tracks.*

I resolved that first thing next morning I would put in a call to the medical examiners in the various cases, see if they could at least fax me the paperwork, maybe give me their off-the-record impressions. But for now, I was starving and tired, and I wanted nothing more than to go home, take a bath, and rot my brain in front of the TV before falling into bed.


*Can*
(Four)

The heat of the day still radiated up off the blacktop, but with the sun down the air was finally starting to cool. I steered my truck along the winding road leading home, blithely ignoring potholes, the windows cranked down and the radio cranked up. The wind blew my hair wildly around my eyes, and I let go of the wheel long enough to wrap a hair band around it.

Pines lined the road to either side, their monotonous gray-brown trunks broken up now and then by an orange "no trespassing" sign. Fireflies flashed like yellow Christmas lights amidst the trees. I slowed a little as I navigated a curve, just in case a deer decided to dart out in front of the truck.

Something passed overhead, but my view of it was almost entirely blocked by the roof of the truck. I jumped, startled, and tried to think what it might have been. The shadow had been far too big for an owl--more like a small plane. But there hadn't been any engine noise.

*Stop being so damned paranoid, Tricia,* I told myself. I was tired and hot--no wonder I was imagining things.

Something slammed into the roof of the truck, so hard that I thought for a moment that a tree had fallen on me. I shouted and slammed on the brakes instinctively. There came the shriek of something hard and sharp scraping across the metal roof ... then nothing.

My heart pounding, I jumped out of the truck, expecting to see a dead deer, or some hapless raccoon that had fallen out of a tree at just the wrong moment. But road was empty except for me and the truck.

*Shit, the truck....*

The roof bowed downwards in the center, as if something heavy had struck it. Long sets of scratches scored the rusty paint, revealing the gleaming metal underneath.

*What the--?* I had hit something--or, rather, something had hit me--the dent proved it. But what? I turned around again to look back up the road, and that was when it grabbed me.

It was huge and dark, a thing as large as a man but with a squashed, misshapen head that belonged to nothing human. Something soft and clinging enmeshed me, even as it sank claws into my arms, and a tiny part of my mind wondered if my attacker was wearing a cloak. Then its stench enveloped me: the smell of graveyards, of offal, of a butcher's dumpster on a hot summer day.

Even though I was choking, training and instinct took over. I kicked hard, and my foot connected with something. The thing holding me grunted, and its grip loosened just a bit. Taking every advantage of the situation, I twisted loose and jumped back, trying to put enough distance between us to draw my gun.

My foot caught some irregularity of the road, and I fell heavily. The pavement ripped my palms, and I swore, rolling onto my side and pulling my gun at the same time.

"Freeze! Officer of the law!" I shouted.

I could just see the thing that had attacked me, standing at the very edge of the glow cast by the truck's headlights. The rational part of my brain had just decided that it was a man in a cloak with some kind of odd Halloween mask, when it took two steps forward and dropped to all fours. Only its forelimbs weren't human, but rather the wings of a giant bat.

It dipped its head a little, and I saw the ridged, furrowed ears, the small eyes, the triangular nose like a knife sticking up out of its snout. Its mouth opened, strings of drool splashing the road, and revealed a pair of blade-like incisors.

This was no costume. This was real.

But again, while the rest of my mind froze, the training took over. I squeezed off a series of shots, but the creature skittered first to one side, then the other, moving faster than I would have imagined possible. In the movies, the good guys always hit what they aim for, but so far as I could tell all of my shots missed. Then there was nothing but clicking--the gun was empty.

The thing seemed to realize that I had run out of ammo, because it stopped skittering. Instead, it reared up on its hind legs, its mouth splitting in a grin made more hideous because there was something still recognizably human in it. Its wings spread out to either side, dark and ragged as something that had been rotting in the sun. I lay paralyzed on the pavement and knew that it was going to kill me.

A yellow streak moved through the headlights, too fast for me to track. An instant later, the creature that had attacked me fell back, its great wings sweeping wildly for balance. Something big had come between it and me, and I had to blink my eyes several times before realizing what I was looking at.

A jaguar.

The jaguar's fur bristled, but it moved in a slow, sleek prowl. Its huge paws made no sound on the pavement, and its black lips drew back in a silent snarl, exposing prodigious canines. Its amber eyes remained fixed on the bat-thing, and its ears were flat against its head.

The bat-thing stared back, seeming to have forgotten all about me in favor of this new threat. It hissed--and then, horribly, it spoke. I didn't recognize the language, but its tone sounded faintly outraged, as if it felt itself wronged in some incomprehensible way.

By that time, I half-expected the jaguar to start talking back. But my protector seemed more inclined to action than talk; it sprang towards the bat-thing, its powerful hindquarters launching it a startling distance. For an instant, the two grappled, and I saw the jaguar sink its claws deep into the bat-thing's back, releasing a spray of blood.

The bat-thing shrieked and twisted sharply, flinging the jaguar to the ground. The big cat was back on its feet almost instantly, but the delay was just enough. The monster brought both wings down in a powerful beat, flinging a cloud of road grit and stench over me. Its body shot into the air, as if propelled by a cannon, and a moment later the shape was gone.

The jaguar watched it go, tail lashing. It let out a single, coughing roar that echoed and reechoed amidst the pines. Then it turned and looked at me.

I found myself captured by that amber stare. Steady and frightening, it seemed to probe my innermost thoughts. I wondered blankly if all prey felt that way, felt the predator looking for the weakness that would spell its death.

Then the jaguar seemed to shiver, like a bit of mist blown apart by the wind. The amber eyes darkened to brown, fringed by long lashes. In one final insult to my sanity, I found myself staring not at a jaguar, but at my suspect, Pacal Bahlum.

## *Hoo*
(Five)

"Are you all right?" he asked.

"Hold it right there," I said, pointing my now-empty gun at him. My hand, I noted, wasn't any steadier than my voice.

He did as I asked, crouching in the light of my truck's headlamps and looking at me with an expression of concern. His long, black hair half-hid his face, but I could see a shallow cut along one high cheek.

"All right," I said, with what I thought was admirable restraint, "what the hell is going on here?"

"You're bleeding." He gestured to my arms, and for the first time I felt the sting of the lacerations. "If you will allow it, I'll tend your wounds."

"Just stay where you are and tell me what's going on! What was that--that thing? And you! How did you...?" I trailed off, unable to make myself say the words.

Pacal sat back on his haunches and look at me, amusement in his dark eyes. "As you wish. I'm a jaguar shaman--my forefathers have been taking the shape of the forest king since before whites ever dreamed there was even a continent here. As for the evil thing which attacked you ... that, I fear, was a follower of Camazotz, vampire god and one of the lords of Xibalba."

After a moment of silence, I lowered my empty gun. "Maybe you ought to get in the truck," I said.

\* \* \* \*

I gripped the steering wheel so tightly that my knuckles were white, expecting to see a dark shape swooping down at any moment. Pacal sat quietly belted into the passenger side, one arm out the window. He looked the very picture of relaxation, but when I risked a look at his proud-featured face and wind-tossed hair, there was a watchfulness in his eyes that reminded me of a cat that is only pretending to sleep. A backpack sat on the floorboard between his feet, and I wondered if he was staying anywhere or was simply a transient.

*I can't believe this is happening.* My brain floundered, trying to come up with some rational explanation for what I had witnessed. But there was none. I was just going to have to accept the fact that I was driving around with a shape-shifting jaguar shaman in my truck.

*Unless I'm going crazy.* Nah. I had too much self-respect to buy that.

"Tell me again what's going on," I said. "The extended version that actually gives information, if you please."

"The extended version? That will be difficult. It started long ago, at the beginning of this age of the world, when the Hero Twins went to Xibalba, the underworld. When Camazotz tore the head from Hunahpu in the House of Bats." From his faint smile, I had the odd feeling that he was teasing me. "We will be a very long time if I tell you that."

"Shorter version, then."

"Very well. As I have told you, I am a shaman among my people."

"Who are--?"

"The Maya. I am from Guatemala, originally, although I have lived much of my life in this country." A shadow passed across his face, and he turned towards the window, so I couldn't see his eyes anymore. "But that, too, is a tale for another time. I came here hunting a killer, Detective Starnes, but no ordinary killer. Rather a creature of darkness, a man who has dedicated his soul to the gods of the underworld. They despise all life, and so in turn does he. They have filled him with a hunger for blood and have given him a shape in which to slake that thirst."

I thought of the monstrous bat-thing in the road. I've always liked bats, to tell the truth--some of them are downright cute seen up close. It hadn't been the bat-ness of the thing that had so terrified me, I realized, but rather the pervasive sense of *wrongness* that it exuded from every pore. "So ... are you saying he's a shape changer as well? Like you?"

"Not like me," Pacal said, sounding offended. I had to admit that he had a point--no such feeling of wrongness had come from him.

"But how ... I don't understand how that's possible. I mean ... if things like this happen ... are capable of happening ... wouldn't someone know?" I asked helplessly. I had the sudden urge to call up all my old teachers, from Mrs. Caudell in kindergarten to my instructors at the police academy, and demand to know why they hadn't told me about all this.

Pacal smiled, a flash of white teeth in his brown face. "But people do know, Detective. Many people, both in my homeland and elsewhere. Is it their fault that you whites dismiss it all as quaint folktales?" He held up a hand, as if to forestall any further questions. "That is not the reason I've come here, though. As I said, I came to track a killer. And now that you know--now that you believe, having no choice to do otherwise--perhaps we can combine forces."

There was a faint note of sadness in his voice, and I wondered if he was lonely. I supposed that chasing down a monster no one else believed existed would make you lonely pretty quick. I was already trying to figure out what to say to Charlie and coming up with nothing that didn't sound like I needed some leave-time in a padded room.

We pulled up into the driveway in front of my house, and I killed the motor. The white paint of the old farmhouse looked ghostly in the night, and I felt a shiver work its way up my spine. Towering oaks clustered around it, providing shade for a house built when things like central heating were for rich city folks in New York or someplace like that. The trees cast too many shadows, and my paranoid brain turned every one of them into a bat-shape.

Normally, I wouldn't have even considered bringing a strange man to my house. But the guy had already been beat up defending me from a creature from the netherworld; after that, none of the ordinary precautions seemed to apply. I climbed out of the truck and beckoned him after me.

The wooden porch creaked under our feet; he wore a pair of sturdy boots, still caked with clay. I led him into the living room, then hesitated, uncertain of the niceties. "Can I get you something? Tea? Beer? Catnip?"

"A beer would be fine. And perhaps some bactine. As for the catnip, I'm trying to cut back--they have a twelve-step program for that, I believe."

I laughed despite myself, then left to get two cold beers and one extensive first aid kit. When I came back, it was to discover that Watson, my overweight calico, had wandered into the room. Pacal crouched on the carpet in front of the ancient woodstove, petting her.

"If you're looking for a date, she's spayed," I said. He gave me a sharp look, and I sighed. "I'm joking, okay? Not very well, maybe, but give me points for trying to deal."

Pacal insisted on treating the wounds on my arms first. At least they were all below the sleeve of my t-shirt, so I didn't have to take off any clothes. The scratches stung like crazy, and the edges had turned an angry red color, but they didn't seem too serious.

Pacal hadn't been quite so lucky. He took off his jacket and shirt to reveal a series of deeper lacerations across his shoulders. When he held his long hair out of the way so I could clean the wounds, I noticed that he had a gold plug in each earlobe, as well as the one is his lip. I've always had a thing for guys with piercings.

Like the jaguar, he was powerfully built. Not artificially bulked-up like some weightlifter, but lean and compact. Whatever he did--and what the hell did a shaman do, anyway?--it had kept him in good shape.

"Why don't you tell me what you know about this bat-creature," I said as I swabbed iodine over the cuts. I figured getting my mind back on a series of grisly murders would keep me from thinking how long it had been since I'd gotten laid.

The window unit hummed and buzzed loudly in its heroic effort to cool the humid air. His voice was almost lost beneath it, and I had to strain to hear him. "Its killing spree began in Guatemala," he said. His dark eyes seemed to be watching something I couldn't see. "I first became aware of it after it had killed a number of men on the local police force."

I felt a chill. "It's got something against cops, then?"

His expression was unreadable. "No. I believe that their deaths were ... personal. But even if that is the case, once it had begun to feed its bloodlust, it could not stop, and its murders became less targeted.

"I do not know if it sensed that I had begun to track it, or if some other urge motivated it to leave Guatemala and come to America. The signs I saw were unmistakable, however, and so I followed it here."

"Seems like the border guards might have noticed a giant man-bat trying to get in," I muttered.

"Ah, but he--I believe it was once a man, at any rate--does not always appear as such. During the day, he could stand before you, and you would never know it."

That was a scary thought. "There's no way to tell? None?"

"Not for you." He winced slightly as I pressed a bandage down too hard. "I believe that I could perceive the difference, see the monster behind the mask of flesh."

Well, that was something, anyway. "Go on with your story."

"I suspect that, in his human guise, he took work on one of the farms near here. At first he was cautious, but with the slaying of the young lady it seems that he has become bolder. Perhaps he feels he cannot be caught. Perhaps he simply can no longer control himself at all. I am uncertain why he attacked you, but if I had to guess, I would say that he saw you at the scene of the young woman's death, either in person or on the television."

The heart-stopping fear I'd been trying to put behind me returned full force. I could still see the thing's face every time I blinked, as if the hideous muzzle and malformed wings were etched on the inside of my eyelids. "So ... do you think it might try again?"

"I don't know." Pacal pulled his t-shirt back on, moving carefully so as not to pull too hard on the bandages. "Certainly it is possible."

Not the most reassuring thought. "How did you know? I mean, you showed up at just the right moment to save my life. How did you know I was going to be attacked?"

His smile returned for a moment. It was a nice smile; I liked it. "I wouldn't be much of a shaman if I couldn't predict anything, would I?" he asked.

"Hmm. I don't suppose that you can predict where we might find our perp?"

Pacal shook his head, his long hair whispering over his shoulders. "No. Dark magic protects him, hides him from my eyes. I am strong enough to know that he is in this general area, but beyond that, I cannot be more precise."

I thought back to the last moments before the creature had fled. "It spoke, didn't it? Before it flew off? Did you understand it?"

"I did. The words were in a Mayan language, one that was spoken in the mountains where I grew up." Pacal's mouth thinned in displeasure. "I have long suspected that he is Mayan as well; this simply confirms it. As to what he said ... the gist was that he accused me of betraying my blood by defending you. He seems to believe that because he and I share the same heritage, I should therefore condone his murders. He has forgotten that his lords are the enemies of all life, whether that life comes from America or the Guatemalan highlands."

I sat back against the couch, absently chewing on a thumbnail. Watson climbed in my lap, and I began to pet her. Her purr thrummed against my fingers. I wondered if Pacal ever purred.

Hadn't I read something about big cats not being able to purr? Or was that just an urban legend? I couldn't remember.

"I looked into the other murders you mentioned," I said at last. "That's why I was out so late tonight. I found a few unexplained deaths that might fit the pattern. You want to tell me which you think are the work of the creature, so I can bug the medical examiners tomorrow?"

I retrieved the stack of printouts I'd made, and let Pacal ruffle through them. "These three," he said at last, and laid them down on the coffee table between us.

The first was the man whose corpse had gone through the wood chipper. The second was a man whose body had been found hung up in some branches in the river. He'd been in the water for a while, and was highly decomposed. And the third had been discovered on a construction site, crushed beneath a collapsed wall, which hadn't been shored up according to OSHA regulations.

Disappointingly, the worker who had died from heat stroke wasn't among the ones Pacal had chosen--just pure human stupidity and malice, there.

"This was the first to die here in America," Pacal said, touching the brief report of the supposed drowning victim. "Or at least I think he marks the beginning of the killer's activities in this country."

"Why?"

"Because of the date. He was last seen on June eighth."

"So?"

Pacal sighed. "I forget that you aren't as sensitive to these things as someone from my village would have been. Something very important happened on that day. By our calendar, it was 5 Zotz 1 Ik. That is, the fifth day of the month of the bat.

"The planet you call Venus, which we call Lahun Chan, is a malevolent force in our beliefs. Some fear him so greatly that they will put up shutters so as not to be touched by his light. On the fifth day of the month of the bat, he crossed over the face of the sun, Kinich Ahau. A very bad omen indeed, just the sort of day that would call to a dark creature such as we hunt." He fell silent for a moment. "At night Kinich Ahau, the Sun-faced Lord, descends into Xibalba, the underworld, where he takes on the form of a jaguar to battle the monsters that would keep him from rising the next day."

I shook my head, too tired to understand what it might all

mean. Hard to believe that just that morning I would have thought anybody going on about Mayan astrology and ancient gods was a nutter to be locked away for his own good. I felt as if I'd aged twenty years since lunch alone.

"I don't know if it helps," I said, "but Debra Simpson was supposed to have an illicit boyfriend out here. One of the workers. According to her roommate at college, she was dating one guy on campus to keep her parents happy and seeing this guy on the side. She was supposed to be coming out here to visit him when she disappeared. Could he be our killer?"

"Perhaps. I would have to meet him to be certain." Pacal's dark eyes met mine, and I again felt his unnerving, steady stare. "Have you questioned him?"

"We haven't been able to find him."

"If you do, you should take me to see him."

I frowned, wondering what excuse I could possibly give Charlie for bringing Pacal with me. "Maybe." The grandfather clock in the hall chimed. Midnight. I roused myself with effort. "Do you need to me to run you home? Or wherever you're staying?"

He shook his head. "No. We don't know if our quarry will seek to attack you again. I will stay and guard you. Everything I need is in my backpack, so do not worry for my comfort."

I didn't know what I thought about having an uninvited houseguest, let alone one who had ideas about guarding me. But remembering the horror of the supernatural attack, I had to admit that I felt better having him there.

"All right," I said, "you can stay. Just don't eat the houseplants or claw up the furniture, okay?"

*Uac*
(Six)

A shrill ringing woke me the next morning.

I slapped groggily at the alarm three times before I finally realized that the ringing was coming from the phone. Half picking it up and half knocking it off the cradle, I somehow managed to get it to my ear and grunt into the right end.

"It's me." Charlie's voice wasn't the most melodious thing to hear at oh-my-God in the morning.

"Christ, Gardener, the sun's not even up," I said, struggling into a sitting position. The faint gray light that precedes dawn leaked through the white curtains, and an ambitious rooster was crowing out in the yard.

"Tell me about it, Starnes. I just got a call from the highway patrol. Seems some early bird decided to get some fishing done in a pond out on Glowenhour Road. His first cast caught on something--they think it might be a car."

I said goodbye to any delusions I'd harbored about getting back to sleep. "All right. Give me directions. I'll meet you there as soon as I get some coffee."

My problematic houseguest was sleeping on the sofa in the living room. His shirt was neatly hung up over the back of a chair, his socks and shoes stowed beneath it. His brown skin shone in the dim light coming through the front windows, and I had the crazy urge to touch it.

*Pathetic, Starnes. Face it--the only way you can get a cute guy to spend the night is to be attacked by a giant bat. And even then he stays on the couch.*

I reminded myself that I ought to be glad Pacal had turned out to be a nice guy--not that I hadn't locked my bedroom door last night, just in case. Still, the whole situation struck me as a sad commentary on my complete lack of any kind of social life.

Pacal came awake all at once, just like a cat disturbed from its sleep. I envied him the ability to go from totally zonked to bright-eyed and watchful in two-point-ten seconds.

I told him about Charlie's phone call. When I was done, he nodded. "I will go with you."

"How am I going to explain you to my partner?" A sudden thought struck me. "Maybe you could show him, too? Charlie might be hard-headed, but even he would believe it if you turned into a jaguar right in front of him."

Pacal's mouth tightened slightly. "It is not a trick, not something to be done without thought, without good reason."

"Assuring my partner doesn't think I'm crazy seems like a good reason to me."

"I'm sorry, Detective, but I don't wish to put myself in further danger. It was a calculated risk to reveal myself to you last night, but I had no choice. I'm sure you can come up with a good story to explain my presence."

"Fine," I said, turning back to the stairs and feeling vaguely annoyed. "In that case, I need a shower. And coffee. Lots of coffee."

\* \* \* \*

By the time we pulled off the road beside the pond, my brain was beginning to function. "Stay here," I told Pacal, before climbing out and heading towards the solemn group standing around the red clay shore.

The pond was the kind you usually find on farms, dug out of the clay to provide water and a cool place for livestock. Runoff had turned it a murky shade of orange, making it impossible to see more than a few inches beneath the surface. An elderly man with a fishing pole and tackle box stood talking to a reporter-- already, the local newshounds had come sniffing, and I was willing to bet that there would be crews all the way up from Charlotte within a few hours. Charlie stood by himself, watching as divers worked to attach chains to something in the water. A tow truck with a heavy winch stood ready to pull it out as soon as they were done.

"What's the word?" I asked as I came up beside him.

He didn't spare me a glance. "The word is 'bad.' They think there's a body inside."

If there was a body, then the car wasn't Debra Simpson's missing vehicle. I swore under my breath and hoped like hell that the divers were wrong. We needed evidence in the case we had, not a whole new death investigation.

"You can still see some faint impressions in the dirt where the car ran off the road. Probably some drunk missed the curve and wound up in the pond instead." Charlie shook his head in disgust. "Find anything at the library?"

I told him about the questionable deaths I'd found but kept silent about Pacal. I still didn't know how to explain him tagging along with me. But Charlie only seemed to be listening with half an ear, and I realized that he thought I was barking up the wrong tree.

If only he knew how wrong he was.

"We ought to look into these deaths more closely," I said at last.

"Some of them weren't even in our county, Starnes."

"I know. I guess I don't mean us, specifically. But all of us. The justice system."

"Yeah, cause we don't have enough to keep us busy already."

I ground my teeth in frustration, even though I understood his point. "I just think we might be missing something, that's all.

What if the rush to sign a death certificate meant that something was overlooked? Did anybody even bother to check beyond the obvious? There might be something going on here, Gardener, and we--everybody--might be missing it. And if there is, and it comes to light--you don't want another Henry Wallace case, do you?"

Henry Louis Wallace had been a rarity--an African American serial killer--who lived down in Charlotte. His victims had been African American women, and he'd had to kill nine of them before somebody finally realized that there was a connection between their deaths. A lot of angry citizens had thought their deaths hadn't been investigated with the same energy that would have been expended had a string of whites been violently murdered. I didn't personally know the truth about that--it had been well before my time on the force--but I didn't have any trouble imagining the same charges being brought against us over the murdered workers.

Apparently, Charlie had no trouble imagining it, either. He glumly took out a cigarette--it looked like he was off the wagon again--and stuck it between his lips. "All right. We'll look at the medical examiners' reports, ask some questions. What the hell. My wife left me and you can't even get a date--what else are we going to do with our copious free time?"

I ignored his sarcasm with dignity. "Thanks, Charlie."

The divers had finally hooked up the chains to the tow truck. The huge winch began to turn, and slowly pulled an expensive white convertible from the pond. Water cascaded out of it, and silt covered most of its surfaces, but I could make out the license plate. I didn't have to check my case notes to know it matched that of Debra Simpson's car. Finally, a break.

But my relief was short-lived, because I could also make out a dark shape slumped in the passenger side, held in place by a seatbelt. The divers had been right. It was a body.

"Shit." Charlie flung his cigarette onto the ground and stomped it a few times before walking towards the car. As I followed him, I heard a door slam. Turning, I saw Pacal walking towards us.

Charlie had seen him too. "What the hell is he doing here? And why the hell did he get out of *your* truck?"

My tongue froze; I couldn't think of anything to say. But Pacal had overheard Charlie's outraged exclamation. As he approached, he smiled confidently and extended his hand. "A pleasure to see you again, Detective Gardener. Let me explain, please. I am with the Guatemala City police department."

He took something out of his jacket and flashed it at Charlie. It caught the rays of the rising sun, and for a moment I couldn't decide if it was some kind of small mirror, surrounded by a frame of glyphs and figures, or a police badge. Charlie got the full effect of the reflected sunlight, however, and seemed to have no doubts. Apparently, turning into a jaguar was only one of Pacal's tricks.

"Why didn't you tell us before?" Charlie asked as Pacal tucked the mirror back into his jacket.

"I wasn't certain what your reaction would be. I must confess, I have found some of your counterparts in other counties to be less than pleased by my presence. After all, I have no jurisdiction here. But when Detective Starnes came to question me last night at my hotel, I realized that you two were serious about investigating these murders--*all* of them."

Charlie glared at me. "You didn't mention any of this to me."

I gave him a lame smile. I felt bad that Pacal had put some kind of mojo on Charlie, but at the same time I wasn't sure what to do about it. "Sorry, Gardener. I was getting to that."

"She was kind enough to stop by and pick me up on the way here this morning," Pacal continued. "You see, I had been investigating a series of murders at home in Guatemala. I received a tip that the murderer had fled the country and come here, but the source was not the most reliable. Because I already had legal residency in America, I decided to come on my own and see if it was true."

Charlie still didn't look happy, but he shrugged. "All right. You can tag along. Just stay out of the way."

"Of course. Thank you, Detective."

As Charlie turned away, Pacal gave me a small smile. I resisted the temptation to give him a good kick in the shins in return. The bastard could at least have told me about his little trick with the mirror beforehand.

Ignoring Pacal for the moment, I followed Charlie to the car, where the crime lab techs were already starting to go over it. The flashing bulbs as they photographed every inch of it made me realize that I had a headache.

We opened the car from the driver's side, to keep the body from falling out. The smell was everything you might expect, and I saw Pacal actually take a step back. And had he gone a shade paler? I felt a little twist of vindictive pleasure as I turned my attention back to the car.

There was a purse on the seat, stuck in the middle, as if it had been sandwiched between the driver and her passenger. The driver's license and credit cards inside confirmed that it had indeed belonged to Debra Simpson.

It took longer to get to the ID of the other victim. Sliding the wallet out of the water-logged back pocket of a dead guy was not one of the more pleasant things I've done. By the time I opened it, I already guessed what I would see.

"Miguel Santiago," I said, holding the drivers license so that Charlie and Pacal could see.

Charlie fished a pack of cigarettes out of his pocket and lit up. "Guess that rules him out as a suspect after all," he said.

\* \* \* \*

"None of this makes any sense," Charlie complained. We were back in our office, trying to catch up on paperwork while discussing the events of the morning. Pacal had come back with us, but had been so quiet the entire time that I almost forgot he was there.

But wasn't that how cats hunted? Quiet, so quiet that the prey never saw them coming until it was too late?

Now he stirred a little; he had been leaning against my desk, his long, jeans-clad legs stretched out before him. "Perhaps you could explain, Detective."

Charlie gave Pacal a dark look--I had the feeling that nothing was going to make my partner take to the shaman. "Sure. No problem. We've got a girl killed in a cornfield. Except the car she was presumably driving wound up in a pond by a road. No skid marks. Her boyfriend's still in the passenger seat along with her purse, but the seatbelt on the driver's side--where she should have been sitting--looks like it was forcibly broken. Can you come up with an explanation for all that?"

"Maybe her killer abducted her first," I said. "Maybe once he had her subdued, he did something to Santiago--knocked him out--then pushed the car into the pond to hide the evidence." Santiago's body had been too far gone to be able to easily tell what had happened to him; it would take a careful autopsy. His last remains were on the way to Chapel Hill, to join those of his girlfriend. Reunited one last time, or something like that.

"Maybe." Charlie didn't look convinced.

I put in my requests to the medical examiners' offices for the paperwork on the worker deaths. When lunch rolled around, I volunteered to take Pacal to the nearest diner. Charlie seemed just as happy to let me.

Ciro's was a little restaurant that specialized in southern cooking, ironically run by a Greek transplant and his equally-Greek wife. After this morning, I wasn't feeling too hungry, so I just got a salad and a peach milkshake. Pacal ordered a hamburger and fries; he seemed bemused when the burger came topped with coleslaw instead of lettuce.

"Your partner doesn't like me," he said, before taking a tentative bite out of the burger.

I shrugged. "Charlie doesn't like anybody. Why do you think his wife left him?" I took a sip out of my milkshake, then glanced up. Pacal's dark eyes were watching me with that eerie-intent stare he had. I noticed that he had the longest lashes I'd ever seen.

"So what do you think happened?" I asked, to give me something to think about that didn't involve Pacal's gorgeous eyes. Or any other part of him.

He sighed and looked back down at his food. "I think ... I think that Debra Simpson's death may have been random. I think she and her friend were driving along the road with the top down, enjoying the evening air, when the monster simply swooped down and snatched her from the car."

"Explaining the broken seatbelt."

"Yes. Without its driver, the car simply swerved off the road and crashed into the pond. No doubt everything happened far too quickly for Miguel to do anything. Or, if he did see the monster, he was too terrified to move even to save himself."

I nodded and drank some more peach shake. "Sounds reasonable. We haven't gotten back the autopsy report on Debra yet, but I bet they find bruises and lacerations where the seatbelt was."

"Not to mention where the monster gripped her as he carried her off." Apparently Pacal had decided that coleslaw on a burger was a good thing; he took a bigger bite, chewed, and swallowed. "He took her to the cornfield next. Am I right in thinking that the two sites are close together?"

I shook my head. "Ten or fifteen minute drive, easy."

"In a car, yes. But as the bat flies?"

"Hell. Yeah. There aren't any direct short cuts by road, but it wouldn't take long at all in the air. And that's why there weren't any tracks going in or out of the field--he didn't take Debra in on foot. He dropped her from above."

"After first tearing away her head, as Camazotz tore away the head of Hunahpu in the House of Bats, and drinking her blood."

"You mentioned that before," I said. "Last night, when I asked what was going on. What does it mean?"

Pacal put down the rest of his sandwich, as if I'd asked him something too important to be interrupted by mere eating. His dark eyes were very solemn. It occurred to me yet again just how long it had been since my last boyfriend.

"It is an old story," he said finally. "The first story, the story of how the world came into being. It is recorded in the *Popol Vuh*, which you might think of as a holy book of my people. The entire tale is very long, but I will do my best to summarize the relevant part for you now.

"Long ago, a pair of twins, Hun Hunahpu and Vucub Hunahpu, were playing the ball game. The noise they made angered the lords of the Xibalba--the underworld--who commanded the twins to appear before them. The twins were given a series of tests, which they failed. For their failure, they were sacrificed, and the head of Hun Hunahpu put on a tree. When a maiden of the underworld came to pick the fruit of the tree, the head spit into her hand, and she became pregnant. After fleeing to the upperworld, she gave birth to a second set of twins--Hunahpu and Xbalanque."

"How many Hunahpus does that make in this story so far?" I asked. "Didn't the gods have more imagination than that?"

Pacal gave me an exasperated look. "Please, Detective Starnes, this is important."

"Sorry. And I let guys who save my life call me by my first name, you know. Tricia."

"Very well, Tricia." A faint smile ghosted over his face and was gone. "When they were grown, Hunahpu and Xbalanque also became ball-players. Again, the noise disturbed the lords of Xibalba, who demanded they appear before them as their father and uncle had. The twins were very clever, however, and passed all of the tests, until they reached the final one. They were placed in the House of Bats for a night, where a host of bats waited to kill them. The twins climbed into their blowguns and hid from the bats there, but as dawn approached Hunahpu put his head out to see if it was safe, and at that moment Camazotz tore it off.

"There is a great deal more to the story, but suffice it to say that eventually Hunahpu's head was miraculously restored, and the lords of the underworld were defeated. Defeated, but not killed. They lurk still in the dark places, and not only must the sun face them every night after he sets, but the souls of the dead must pass through as well if they are to find paradise beyond."

Pacal fell silent, watching me. Waiting for my reaction, perhaps.

"I don't know that I understood everything," I said finally. "But I get the gist. You're saying that the murderer has thrown his lot in with Camazotz and the rest--the bad guys. And he's basing his MO on something from an old story."

"In this one case." Pacal went back to his burger. "He has not killed the same way every time. The earliest murders that I became aware of were more ... ritualistic, I suppose is the word. Their hearts were cut out, their jaws torn off."

"Ugh. Some ritual." I made a face. "This case just keeps getting better."

## *Uuc*
## (Seven)

I'd really hoped that Miguel Santiago had been our killer, because with his death my list of suspects had officially gone down to zero.

Pacal and I were alone in the office that afternoon; poor Charlie had been called back to testify in court again. I took out the list of the three immigrant workers Pacal said had been killed by our monster and plotted the locations of their murders on the map. Then I added a marker for Debra Simpson, and another for her car. If there was a pattern, I couldn't see it, except that the locations were all within twenty miles of each other.

"It might be that our killer worked the same farms that these men did," Pacal suggested.

"Maybe." I stared at the pins in the map, as if I thought they would suddenly spell out the killer's name for me. "But I don't see how that helps us. People move around from job to job, and half the time they're being paid under the table. Even if they aren't, no one is going to keep a reliable record of who worked their fields on what day."

"We could try questioning the workers on nearby farms. I think if I was to come before our killer, I would recognize him even if he was in human form."

I imagined trying to convince some foreman that I needed his men to do a lineup for me. Then I tried imagining that half of them wouldn't slip out the back at the first sight of the police to begin with. "If we don't have any other choice." I turned my back on the map and stared at the clutter on my desk, feeling suddenly depressed. "I'm done for today, either way."

Pacal followed me out to the parking lot, obviously intending to climb into my truck and ride home with me. "Don't you have anywhere else you need to be?" I asked. Not that I particularly wanted to get rid of him--it wasn't as if men followed me around like puppy dogs all the time or something. But I didn't know what he expected of me, or what he thought his role was.

"I returned to America to find this killer," he said. My truck was unlocked--nobody was going to steal the thing, after all, when they could nab plenty of cars made in this century--and he opened my door for me before going around to the passenger side. "Not only are you my sole ally in this task, but you have already been attacked once. Where else should I go?"

I began the long process of cranking the truck, having it stall, and cranking it again until the engine finally revved to life. "I don't think there's much left to do tonight, unless you have any ideas you haven't shared with me. I was planning on going home, crashing on the couch, and killing a few brain cells in front of the TV."

"Perhaps we should stop for a pizza on the way."

I laughed incredulously. "Do jaguar shamans like pizza?"

"This one does."

I shook my head, shoved the sticky gearshift into "drive," and headed out the parking lot.

\* \* \* \*

We stopped at Pizza Hovel on the way out of town, then headed down the road towards home. The pavement uncoiled in front of the truck like a lazy blacksnake, striped with the shadows of trees cast by the setting sun. I cranked up some tunes on my CD player--Charlie calls it my "devil music"--and sang along with Ill Ni"o for a few miles. Pacal hung his arm out the window, his eyes slitted like a cat who isn't quite asleep yet but is giving the prospect serious consideration.

There came a loud crack, and the windshield suddenly spider-webbed. For an instant, I thought a rock had come of the road and hit us; then, I realized that the neat hole in the center had been made by a bullet.

"Shit!" I jerked the wheel to one side and stood on the brakes. The tires squealed in protest as they left rubber on the pavement, then bounced wildly onto the shoulder. The pizza box went flying off the seat and slapped wetly into the dash before falling on the floor. "Pacal! Are you all right?"

I turned to check on him and saw that he was staring at the seat beside me in horror. There was a hole in the upholstery barely an inch away from my shoulder.

There was no crack this time, but I heard the gunshot, and a puff of dirt exploded in front of the truck. Swearing furiously, I threw open the door and rolled out, putting the truck between myself and what I hoped was the direction of the shooter. I didn't remember pulling my own gun, but it was already in my hand. "Get to cover, Pacal!"

A moment later, he rolled out of my open door and joined me. "Stay down," I said, and chanced a look over the bed. "There's a rise and some trees--the shooter must be in them."

Pacal nodded. "I'll find him," he said grimly.

My heart lurched. "Are you crazy! Stay put, damn it!"

He touched my arm lightly, a comforting gesture. And then he was moving away from me, running in a strange, loping crouch. I shouted after him, but he disappeared into the tall grass of the field that lay between the truck and the trees.

The idiot was sure to get himself shot. I risked another look over the bed, firing off a round in the general direction the shots had come from, hoping to distract the sniper from Pacal. Then I scrambled back to the cab and radioed for help.

It seemed to take forever for Pacal to come back. I crouched with my back against the truck, listening for any further shots-- or, worse, for a shot followed by a cry. But all was silent.

Pacal returned just before the police cruiser responding to my call arrived. One moment I was alone; the next, he was just there, as if he'd beamed in. I jumped and yelped, almost pointing the gun at him before I realized who it was.

"Damn it, Pacal, don't do that again!" I shouted. I was angry-- angry that someone had shot at me, angry that Pacal had taken such a risk despite my telling him to stay put.

"I found nothing," he said. His eyes seemed to have lightened from dark brown to blazing amber, and I realized that he was angry, too. "I would have hunted him longer, but I feared that he might circle around and come for you if I was gone too long."

"We don't even know it was the killer, and not just someone with a grudge. Or even a random loony," I pointed out.

"It doesn't matter." His eyes continued to burn, and his lips pulled back for a moment, revealing fangs. Dark spots appeared on his skin like exotic tattoos--the jaguar was close to the surface. "You might have been killed! You almost were killed!"

Like I was supposed to be happy about it? If one of us should have been losing his cool, I felt pretty sure it should have been me, as the almost-victim. "Calm down," I said harshly as the wail of the cruiser's siren got louder. "Or run--they can't see you like this."

He took a deep, shuddering breath and looked away from me. By the time the cruiser pulled up, tires spraying gravel everywhere, he seemed to be back to normal.

Since no further shots had come, and Pacal hadn't been able to find the sniper, I felt it was probably safe to stand up. I did so and went around to meet the officer getting out of his vehicle. It turned out to be Joel, the newest recruit on the force. I swear he looked like he was about twelve.

As I hailed Joel, the crazy zigzag of the broken windshield caught my eye, and I stopped. The full enormity of what had happened finally sank in, and I felt a flush of fresh anger.

"That--that bastard! He shot my truck!"

Now it was personal.

\* \* \* \*

It was strange to be the victim in a case. I answered questions, watched the crime lab extract the bullet from my truck's frayed upholstery, and generally felt useless. Even as I tried to answer Joel's questions, I struggled for answers to my own. *Could* the sniper attack be unrelated to my murder case? Was it possible that some perp I'd helped bust was out on parole and looking to get even? Charlie was testifying in a case involving large quantities of bathtub gin (Pickerel County was dry, which meant the moonshiners had a field day)--could some cousin or friend of the bootlegger have shot at me to send Charlie a warning? Had the shots come from a poacher with really bad aim who didn't realize he was shooting towards a road? Or was it the work of a random crazy person?

It was almost dark by the time Joel and the crime lab left. I climbed morosely back in my truck, wondering how much it was going to cost to get the windshield replaced. "So," I asked Pacal, who had been quiet ever since his earlier outburst, "do followers of the bat god believe in using firearms to settle their scores?"

"He cannot take his bat form while the sun journeys across the sky," Pacal said. "Perhaps he knows that we are onto him--that you and I have joined forces--and does not dare confront us more directly." He sighed and stared unhappily out the window. "I do not know. I have failed you, Tricia."

"Listen up," I said as I guided the truck back onto the road. I was jumpy as fat on a griddle, certain that I'd hear the deadly crack of a bullet at any second. "Just because you don't know who decided to take potshots at us doesn't make you a failure."

He looked down at his hands, and his nostrils flared slightly. "No. That isn't what I mean. I have failed, Tricia. I failed in my sacred trust, and I am ashamed to tell you just how badly."

I didn't like the sound of that. "Tell me anyway."

"I have not spoken much of my life before this, but for you to understand everything, it is important that you know at least some of my history. Let me tell you without interruption, and then you may ask what you will, agreed?"

"Sure."

He lifted his head, and the setting sun blazed through the window, limning his proud features in fire. "I was born in the highlands of Guatemala. Even for that area, the village I lived in was remote. So far were we from others that even our closest neighbors thought us strange. The Spanish never reached us, and our religion remained untouched by western beliefs. Not to say that it is just as the ancients practiced it--as I said before, even other Maya thought us aberrant.

"When I was a child, however, a man came to our isolated little village. He was the first white man any of us had ever seen. His name was Joseph, and he was an ethnologist. He had heard of us from the other villages and wished to learn our tales and beliefs, so that he might compare them to the rest he had gathered in the region.

"Joseph lived with us for some time, and he became special friends with my family. When the time came for him to leave, he made a generous offer to my parents: he would take me back to the states with him as an adopted child, so that I might be educated here in the US.

"My grandfather was vehemently opposed to this, but my parents were not so certain it was a bad thing. Not only would I get an education, but even in our remote locale we had heard of the violence that plagued our country.

"Perhaps you have heard of it as well. Guatemala's troubles began in the fifties. The government of the time wished to support labor reform and redistribution of land to the poor. The corporations who depended on the plantations did not like this, of course, and so Guatemala's democratically-elected president was overthrown with the help of the CIA, and a regime sympathetic to the plantation-owners and corporations put in place.

"Over the next forty years, hundreds of thousands of my people were killed, and tens of thousands 'disappeared'--taken away for torture, their bodies disposed of far away from their families. Entire villages were wiped from the face of the earth. Greed and racism ruled the country, and the lives of the Maya were as nothing to anyone."

Pacal fell silent. I could hear my heart beating, the unsteadiness of my breathing. I could feel his grief like a live thing, and a sense of shame came over me, as if my ignorance of the events he related somehow made me complicit in them.

"So I came to America," he said at last. "I could go on for hours about my first impressions, about how overwhelming everything seemed. How alien it all was to a child from a farming village where nothing had changed in centuries. My first few weeks were filled with terror, but eventually I adapted, and with the resilience of a child I ultimately took to my new life as if it had been the only one I had ever known. I went to high school, and then to college. My adoptive parents were very proud of me.

"But when I graduated from university, I realized that I wanted to return home again. I wanted to see my own parents, my grandparents, my friends, my brother and sisters, none of whom I had seen in a very long time. By then the civil war had largely ended, and I felt it was safe to go back.

"And so I returned to my village. I took a bus as far as I could, then accepted rides from other travelers, first in trucks, later in carts. At long last, I came to the land where I had been born.

"There was rain on the mountain that day, and I remember it made me happy, because it would make the crops grow strong. The smell of lightning in the air, of wet earth and growing things, was so evocative of my childhood that I felt I had never left at all. I ran the last mile up the steep path, feeling light as a bird.

"The village ... was gone. The houses had been burned, and I found bones lying among them that had been left to the elements for years. If there had been any survivors, they were gone as well. Disappeared."

"I'm so sorry," I said, forgetting my promise not to interrupt. Tears pricked at my eyes, making the road blurry, and I blinked hard.

"Thank you," he said. "I will not try to convey my feelings. Some of it perhaps you can imagine, and the rest ... it would do no good to tell you, for no one who has not had such overwhelming loss can truly understand what it is like. I think for a while I went a little insane.

"I moved to the nearest city and simply ... existed. Drank myself into oblivion whenever my loneliness and grief became too much to bear. I thought about returning to America, but that would have required action, and in the state I was then in it seemed too difficult even to make the decision.

"Eventually, however, something penetrated the haze I existed in. There were signs that even I could not ignore, telling me that something terrible was happening. If nothing else, it broke me out of my self-pity long enough to take up my duties as a shaman. My grandfather had been our shaman, before his death, and had trained me since I was very young, hoping that I would take over for him once he was gone. My departure for America had disrupted that plan, however, and at first I remembered little of his teachings. It shamed me to think that I had dishonored his death by ignoring his wishes, so I did my best to return my feet to the proper path. I went back to the highlands, both to the ruin of my home and to any neighboring villages that had survived, both to remember and to learn.

"I believe that the one we hunt must have taken his path at much the same time, and that the signs I had seen resulted from the disturbance he had made. Even as I was finishing my own initiation, he was beginning to make the first sacrifices to his dark gods.

"And now we come to the place where I must confess my own sins to you, Tricia. For his first victims were evil men who had either commanded the massacres or participated in them. These men had never faced justice, you see. How could they, when they themselves had never been removed from power? When they still filled the military, the police?"

"That sucks!" I exclaimed, appalled. "I mean, why didn't anyone do anything? They ought to be locked up in jail, not running the place!"

"I cannot argue with you," he said wryly. "I felt ... I felt as though perhaps some retribution had finally been exacted with their deaths, even if they accounted for only a few among hundreds. So I did nothing. I let the killer do as he would and turned a blind eye. And so it is that we have come to today, with innocents dead and your life in danger. My own inaction has brought us to this pass."

We pulled into my dusty driveway, and I killed the motor. For a long moment, we sat in silence, as I tried to think of something to say that could possibly make up for even one iota of what he had suffered. There wasn't anything.

"I'm sorry," I finally settled on. "But it isn't as simple as you make it sound, Pacal. I mean ... these guys he killed to start off with ... should they have just gone unpunished? How could you be expected to protect assholes like that?" I realized that I was gripping the steering wheel so hard that my knuckles were white, and I forced myself to relax. "Look, you lived here long enough to know our justice system doesn't always work. Bad guys get away. Innocent men get locked up. Rapists and child molesters are released on parole every few years so they can do it all over again. I'm sworn to uphold the law, but I'm not blind to the flaws in the system. But no matter how screwed up it is sometimes, it's better than what your people got. When you have mass-murderers running the police department, where do you go for justice?"

I realized that I was babbling and stopped. "What I mean is that you're human, most of the time anyway, and if some higher powers or whatever wanted you to protect the bastards that maybe killed your own family, they should have taken that into account. Any gods that made humans ought to know better than to ask such a thing of anybody."

"Tell that to Debra Simpson's parents."

"Damn it, Pacal! You aren't responsible for everything. You sure aren't responsible for some crazy guy who decided to turn into a bat and go on a killing spree."

Pacal was silent. In the growing dark, I couldn't see his expression. "I think ... I think that perhaps he did this thing because he wished for justice against those men," he said at last. "Or at least revenge. And I ask myself what is really the difference between us?"

I understood where he was coming from. At the same time, I wanted to beat his head against the dashboard a few times and knock some sense into his thick skull. "The difference would be that you aren't a blood-crazed murderer. A technicality, I know. That was sarcasm, in case you missed it there."

He laughed softly, despite everything. It was a nice laugh; I thought I could hear the jaguar's cough in it. "I did not. It is good to smile, Tricia. You have lightened my heart."

"Yeah, well, servant to the public and all that," I said, suddenly embarrassed. I wasn't used to people saying things like that to me. Especially not in that serious tone, like he was referring to something a lot more important than one of my lame jokes.

"Come on. Let's go in. You can have a shower and I'll dig a couple of beers out of the fridge, okay? I'll find something to nuke for dinner."

\* \* \* \*

The pipes in the wall rattled while Pacal showered in the old, claw-footed tub upstairs. I was still cursing the bastard who had shot at us--not only had he hurt my poor truck, but he'd ruined our pizza so that I had to cook. I wondered if I could sue him for the $12.99 it had cost me at Pizza Hovel. Or at least hide it somewhere in my next expense report.

Nah--it'd probably bankrupt the county.

The water shut off, which was just as well, because I'd been pretty tempted to creep upstairs and sneak a peek at my houseguest in the buff while he was busy lathering up. After a few minutes, I heard the stairs creak under his tread; then the door to the front porch screeched open and closed again.

A few minutes later, I carried the food and beer out onto the screened-in porch. Pacal was sitting in the swing at one end, absently petting Watson, who--being strictly a house kitty--was as close to the great outdoors as she ever got. Pacal had put on a pair of jeans but left off his shirt and shoes. His black hair was still wet; trails of water dripped across broad, brown-skinned shoulders. In the faint light coming from the lamp in the living room, I saw the gleam of metal in both nipples.

My mouth went dry, and I was suddenly conscious of how bad I must look. In the summer, the temperature in the kitchen was a preview of the fires of hell, and standing over a hot stove meant that my face was bright red and soaked in sweat. I spared a thought for librarian Emily--she probably would have come out fresh as a rose.

"Red beans and rice," I said, passing one bowl to him as I took a seat beside him on the swing. "It was the fastest thing I knew how to make. Sorry--it isn't much of a dinner, I guess."

"It smells wonderful. Thank you." He took the bowl from me, then held it up out of Watson's reach when she tried to stick her head in it to investigate. I threw a bean across the porch, and she took off after it, certain that anything we were eating must have been a thousand times better than that expensive premium-brand cat food I gave her.

"So what next?" I asked after we'd finished eating. I thought about taking the dishes into the kitchen, decided that they could wait, and stacked them on the floor. The swing rocked gently under our weight, and I realized that it was oddly comfortable to sit there in the dark with Pacal. I don't know why I trusted a guy I'd only met the day before so completely, but there was something about him that relaxed all those defenses a woman has to have just to stay halfway safe. I would have said we "clicked," but that didn't really describe it.

"I am not certain," he said after a while. I realized that he always waited a moment before answering a question, as if he were giving it serious thought in order to give me the most complete answer possible. As if every question I asked really mattered. "I may try to consult the divination stones again, if we have no other options, but as I said before I cannot determine his precise location that way."

I nodded. I wanted to come up with some brilliant plan, but at the moment my brain was too fuzzed. It had been a long, stressful day, and I wasn't at the top of my game to say the least.

Pacal shifted towards me. He smelled like my shampoo, but beneath that was a faintly musky scent, wild and clean and dark as a rainforest. I thought I could feel the heat off his skin even though inches of air separated us.

"I'm sorry that this thing has put you in danger," he said. "I would not have chosen for it to be so. But now that it is ... I find that a selfish part of me is glad to have your help in this."

His fingers brushed my face very lightly, peeling back some of the stray hairs that sweat had stuck to the skin. I closed my eyes, then opened them again, my heart rabbiting in my chest. "And I do not say that just because you are a beautiful woman," he added seriously.

I wanted to laugh--did I mention that I was sweaty, dirty, and dressed in jeans and an old t-shirt? But before I could, he leaned over and kissed me. His mouth was hot and tasted like the beer we had drunk. It wasn't one of those slobbery kisses, either.

A part of my brain wondered if it was smart to get mixed up with someone who was part of a case I was working, no matter how weird a case it was. I told it to shut the hell up and kissed him back. His skin felt good under my hands, smooth and tight over lean muscle. When my fingers encountered the nipple rings, I leaned back and grinned at him.

"Are these all the piercings you've got?" I asked, and gave one ring a playful tug.

His eyes slitted in pleasure. Amber burned in their depths. "No. One other."

"Where?"

He leaned forward and kissed my neck, his breath warm against my ear. "Why don't you find it?" he asked.

So I did.

*Uaxac*
(Eight)

That night I had a dream.

Most of my dreams were pretty ordinary. I would dream that I was late to work, or that I was back in high school and had a test I didn't study for, or that I was driving somewhere but didn't have any directions to get there. Then there was that one about Johnny Depp--but never mind about that.

This dream was most definitely not one my run-of-the-mill dreams. It seemed to start gradually, although maybe I just can't remember the beginning. All I know is that I finally became aware that I was walking down a long, dark tunnel. Four owls flew in front of me; they were carrying an object between them that sometimes looked like a lump of resin and sometimes like a bloody heart. It seemed that I'd been walking a long time, that I was walking to the center of the earth or the other side of eternity.

Then the tunnel opened up into a great cavern. The owls disappeared into the shadows, but that was okay--I didn't need them to guide me anymore. The cavern floor sloped down, and I followed it, until I came to the river.

From a distance, I didn't know what the river was made of, but it seemed to flow more sluggishly than mere water. But as I drew closer, I realized that I could smell it. Blood. Lots of blood.

By the time I reached the bank, the stench of blood was almost overwhelming. It flowed and lapped restlessly in its channel; bright arterial blood mixed in with streams of darker. It had started to separate in places, the clear serum riding on top. Great clots clogged the river like ice flows. The whole thing made me want to gag.

It was dark on the other side of the river, but I could sense something moving in the shadows. Make that many things. A wind blew from that side, and it smelled of decay and disease, of gangrene and filth. The bat-creature had smelled that way, and I suddenly realized where I was. Xibalba. The underworld. And the things on the other side of the river, the things I couldn't see, were the lords of this place, and they hated me with a malevolence that went beyond mere human emotion. They longed for my death, for the slow, agonizing death of every living thing. They wanted the world itself to wind down, until there was nothing left but ash and darkness. And in the infinite silence of oblivion, they would finally be content.

I was paralyzed with fear. I wondered where my gun was, but even as I did so I knew that no bullets would stop these creatures. They were gods, after all, weren't they?

Then, gradually, I became aware that there was a light moving through the darkness. I couldn't make it out at first, because of all the shadowy figures that stood between it and me. But as it got closer, the figures fell back, crying out in anger and fear. A roar shook the very foundations of the cavern, and a moment later I saw the jaguar.

It was huge, bigger than any living animal could possibly have been. It wore a headdress of bright feathers, and its red tongue lolled out as it snarled at the lords of the underworld. Its eyes burned like suns, so bright I could barely stand to look at it. I thought that there might have been a figure walking beside it, a girl with brown hair who looked a lot like the photos of Debra Simpson when she had been alive, but the glare from the jaguar made it hard to be sure.

"The sun makes his nightly journey through the underworld," Pacal said.

I jumped, because I hadn't heard him come up. Instead of his usual clothes, he wore an elaborate headdress, cloak, and loincloth. Jaguar spots made dark rosettes on his brown skin, and his eyes were amber. He wrinkled his nose a little, making his long cat-whiskers stand out.

"The sun doesn't go anywhere," I pointed out reasonably. "The rotation of the earth just makes it look that way."

Pacal laughed, but it came out as a jaguar cough. "Yes. That is also true."

"It can't be both."

Amusement sparkled in his amber eyes, and he smiled, revealing fangs. "That is a very western way of thinking. But it will not serve you in this battle."

The sun jaguar roared, scattering the misshapen lords of death from its path. I wondered if they were stupid or just very determined. After a few thousand years of nightly battle, you'd think they would have given up by now.

"This is the source of our enemy's power, but he is not here." Pacal said. "And you should not be here, either."

He reached out claw-tipped fingers and gently, gently shut my eyes. I heard the sun roar, and the sound echoed and echoed in my ears, until it turned into the howl of my alarm clock.

\* \* \* \*

I groaned and slapped at the snooze button. Pacal mumbled something incoherent--it didn't sound English--and flung an arm around my waist. His body was snuggled up tight against mine, which felt nice. Really nice.

I was relieved to find that I didn't regret the previous night at all. Maybe later I would, but right now the whole experience got the Tricia Starnes Stamp of Approval. I didn't know if what we had would turn into a relationship, or even if I wanted it to. Was I in love with him? I didn't know that, either, but maybe it didn't matter right now. We were friends and enjoyed each other's company, and for the moment that was enough.

The alarm went off again. Pacal yawned and stretched; I watched admiringly. He opened his eyes halfway and gave me a smile that did all kinds of things to my hormones. "Turn it off?" he suggested.

"Love to. But I'm afraid the good people of Pickerel County expect me to show up for work today."

"Mmm. I suppose that isn't entirely unreasonable." But he sounded like he regretted it. Hell, I certainly did.

Despite my obligation to the taxpayers who kept me living in the lap of luxury, we did find time to take a shower together. Watson lay on the bathmat, staring at the shower curtain, and probably thinking I'd turned into a total slut. But she was spayed, so what did she know about it, anyway?

\* \* \* \*

A couple of faxes from the medical examiners waited for me on my desk when I got in. None of them were particularly informative, and in most cases the remains had been sent back to Mexico or wherever the deceased came from, so there was no chance of an autopsy that might reveal signs of foul play. Charlie was already behind his desk, his feet up and a scowl on his face. It deepened when he noticed Pacal trailing in after me.

"What the hell are you doing getting shot at?" he asked bluntly.

"Glad to see you too, Gardener. I'm fine, thanks for asking."

"I'm serious, Starnes. You should have called me."

I sighed. Charlie had never been the over-protective type, and I didn't want him to start now. Of course, maybe it wasn't being over-protective to be upset when people started taking potshots at your partner. "Joel said he was going to swing by my place on his patrol last night, just to keep an eye on things," I told him. I hesitated a moment, wondering if I should get into my relationship with Pacal, then forged ahead. "And Pacal was there, so that's another pair of eyes looking out for me."

Predictably, Charlie didn't look thrilled by this news. He gave Pacal a scowl and said, "I need to talk to my partner in private. Got it, amigo?"

Pacal raised an eyebrow at me. I shrugged. "I will find the water fountain," he said diplomatically, and left.

Charlie didn't waste a minute. "Look, Starnes, maybe this guy was a big shot back in Guadalajara--"

"Guatemala."

"--or whatever banana republic he's from, but he's not a cop. Not here."

"I know that. I don't see what it's got to do with anything. I can only date cops now or something?"

"It isn't that. But the guy doesn't count as protection. There are gun laws in this state, and I'd rather you had somebody with you who has a license to carry one."

I wanted to tell Charlie that Pacal was probably better protection against the thing we were hunting than a carload of AK-47s. But I'd promised Pacal, so I just bit my tongue instead. "I'm not stupid, Gardener. I take precautions. You know as well as I do that anybody in law enforcement can become a target. How many cops have gotten shot over traffic stops?"

"I'm just saying be careful. You don't know this guy all that well."

"Is this stay-alive advice or relationship advice?"

Charlie threw up his hands. "Does it matter? You aren't going to listen to me."

"It matters. I just want to know if I'm taking advice from my partner who's a damn good cop, or from my partner who gave me a front-row seat at his messy divorce."

After a minute, he let himself smile a little. "All right. Fair enough. I won't say anything more. For now."

I privately wondered how long that vow would last, but I nodded. "Good. So what's on the agenda today?"

"We finally heard from Debra Simpson's legitimate boyfriend. Or rather, his lawyer," Charlie said. "He's willing to let one of us in to question his client, if we drive all the way to Raleigh ourselves. Oh, and, he wanted to make sure we understood that he would be present at all times, in case we decided to start beating the kid with rubber hoses or something."

"Damn, and I packed mine special and everything." I perched on the edge of the desk. "Actually, I think you ought to be the one to talk to the kid."

"And why do I get the honor of driving all the way to Raleigh?"

I felt bad about deliberately sending Charlie on a wild goose chase. After all, the chances that our killer was Mike Woodward were pretty much zero, unless he had a secret interest in ancient Mayan gods that I didn't know about. But what was I supposed to tell him? That I was chasing the bogeyman?

"For one thing," I said, "you can pull off the whole good old boy act if you need to. If the lawyer or the kid are anything like the parents were, you can play the prejudice card--how you're sure that a fine upstanding white boy like little Mikey couldn't have anything to do with the murder, although you could see how he might be upset if he found out his girl was out slumming with some taco trash."

"Jesus, Starnes, you've been watching too many old movies." By the resigned way he said it, I could tell that Charlie had given in. "What are you going to be doing while I'm off reinforcing bad stereotypes about white southern males?"

"Asking questions around the farm where Santiago worked. And before you ask, yes, Pacal is going with me. Most of these guys don't speak a lot of English, and I need somebody to translate." Damn, I really was lying like a dog to poor Charlie. I made a mental note to try and make it up to him, while at the same time hoping that he never found out.

"Good luck. I'm sure they'll be really happy to see you."

I shrugged. "We've got to do it, Charlie. See you later."


*Bolon*
(Nine)

Needless to say, the day turned into an exercise in frustration. We visited three farms that day, two where workers had been killed and the one where Miguel Santiago had worked, on the off-hand chance that he and Debra hadn't really been completely random victims. We pulled up beside vast fields of tobacco or some other cash crop, where dozens of sweating men toiled in the hot sun. I started to get the odd feeling that if I had jumped back in time two hundred years, the scene would have been almost identical.

A foreman would come up, and I'd explain to him why I was there and what I needed. He would argue that it was impossible to stop work even for ten minutes to answer my questions. I would point out to him that I could stop work a lot longer if I needed to in order to get answers, and that I would rather we all stay friends and keep it short and sweet. He would finally give in, and I'd end up looking at a whole lot of tired, sweaty, closed faces of men who didn't want to talk to me out of fear that I'd end up having them deported. The language barrier was another problem. The foremen generally helped with that, since Pacal, as it turned out, didn't speak a word of Spanish. I worried that my questions or their answers weren't being translated right, or fully, no matter how simple I tried to keep things.

"Did you know the deceased? Did anyone seem unusually interested in him? Did anyone else disappear around the time he did? Was anyone acting suspicious? Did he have any enemies? Get in any arguments?"

And when we finally got back in the truck, one last question: "Did you sense anything?"

Pacal's answer was inevitably "no."

By the time we drove around to the fourth farm, I was hot, sweaty, and depressed. The sun was going down, and I worried the workers would have already quit for the day by the time we got there. Pacal seemed pensive; he hadn't spoken much for the last few hours, and I guessed that he shared my frustration. To make things worse, the evening thunderstorms were chasing us east, a stack of monumental black clouds that seemed to have erased everything on the horizon. Gusts of wind buffeted the truck, and I belatedly realized that the bullet hole and cracks in the windshield were going to have a major effect on the truck's ability to stay waterproof.

As we bounced along the muddy track running through a peach orchard, I saw that the workers were all grouped around an open-bed truck. Some of them were already sitting in the back, while the rest finished putting away their equipment. All of them were casting anxious glances towards the sky, no doubt eager to get the hell out of there before the rain came. Well, if I had to get wet, so did they.

The men looked up curiously as I guided the truck to a stop. Pacal had his window down, and had been dangling his arm leisurely out of it. Suddenly, he sat up straight, his eyes going wide. I followed the direction of his stare, and had only enough time to glimpse a confused impression of brown skin and dark hair before the other man turned and ran.

Pacal shouted something in a language I didn't understand--an imprecation, maybe, or an order to stop. If it was the latter, the other man didn't listen. With a curse of my own, I bailed out of the truck, pausing only long enough to grab a flashlight out of the glove compartment.

I flashed my badge at the startled foreman who had started to approach. "Police!" I shouted, even as I broke into a run. Even though Pacal had only a small head start on me, I could barely see him in the rising gloom. A cold flash went through me, and I realized that on the other side of the massive clouds the sun was going down. If we didn't overtake the fugitive soon, he'd be able to revert to his other form.

I came up on Pacal crouching beside a tree. He signaled me over, and I joined him. He was staring intently out into the growing dark, his pupils so dilated I could barely see the brown ring of iris around them. His nostrils flared, scenting, and the dark rosettes of the jaguar's spots rippled over his skin.

The wind came up, and I smelled rain the instant before a deafening crash of thunder rent the air. Right on its heels came the rain; I felt the first cold drops only an instant before I was engulfed in a deluge.

"Damn," I hissed. This was going to make it harder than ever to track our killer. The hair tried to stand up on the back of my neck at the thought of him circling around and tracking *us* instead.

Pacal glanced at the sky as thunder rumbled again. "The rain god Chac is coming, striking his axe against stones," he said. I had no idea if that was meant to be a good thing or not. "Stay here. I will find our quarry."

Before I could object, he ... well, it's hard to describe, really. He sort of leaned over, sort of *flowed* ... and a moment later the jaguar was racing away from me, its powerful legs carrying it into the storm so fast it was like he just disappeared.

*Damn.* First the storm, and then my partner in this decided to go off on his own. Then again, he had ways of finding the killer that I didn't, even discounting the sensitivity of a jaguar's nose. Cursing him silently, I checked to make certain my gun was fully loaded, then settled in to wait.

The sky got steadily darker, except for the moments when lightning lit up the world like a bulb popping as it finally burned out. The wind picked up, driving the rain almost horizontal. The trees trashed madly, and unripe peaches pelted me as they were ripped from their branches. *Tornado weather.*

And then, between one boom of thunder and the next, I heard the jaguar's cry. It was a cry of anger--but also of pain.

My heart leapt into my throat, and it was an effort not to shout out his name. Instead, I bolted from my hiding place. The darkness was absolute, so I switched on my flashlight, even though I worried its light would give me away. Wet leaves clung to my face, and branches clawed at my hair. I stumbled over the uneven ground, cursed, and forced myself to keep going.

I was on them almost before I knew it. The beam of my flashlight flickered over a form; then, the sky exploded from a near-by lightning strike. The brilliant flash threw the orchard into stark relief, and I saw two figures. The jaguar was pressed against a tree, his lips drawn back in a snarl, one foreleg held up against its body. Something darker than water dripped from his fur.

And in front of him ... stood a man. An ordinary man, or at least I would have thought so if I'd met him under any other circumstances. His black hair hung in his face, plastered there by the rain, and his handsome features were twisted into an expression that defied my ability to read.

Even as my brain tried to assimilate everything, I brought up my gun and trained it on the stranger. "Police! Get your hands in the air!" I shouted.

The man looked at me, squinting at the glare of the flashlight that I kept trained on his face. Slowly his expression eased into a horrible, rictus grin. He lifted his arms, as if he was going to comply after all.

Except that by the time he finished the gesture, he was spreading wings, not arms.

Somehow, I had forgotten how awful and terrifying the creature was. The horror of it hit me like a physical blow, and I almost dropped my flashlight. Its eyes glittered, and its muzzle opened, revealing the blade-like incisors. It might have been laughing at me.

I squeezed off a shot, and it flinched. Good God, had I managed to hit it?

If so, the bullet didn't seem to do much damage. The bat-thing brought its wings down, lifting itself into the air. Even with the rain and the wind, its stench reached me, the smell of rot and sickness and death, as if it carried plagues on its wings. I swung the flashlight around, trying to track it, but it moved too fast.

"Shit," I whispered. "Where did it go?"

Something heavy slammed into my back, knocking me to the ground. I tried to bring the gun around blindly, but agony slashed down my arm. Hot blood--my own--hit my face, and I felt the gun fall out of nerveless fingers. Darkness blotted out the sky above me, and the shaking beam of my flashlight revealed the monstrous face getting closer and closer as it bent down over my prone body. Its lips pulled back, and I saw that its two incisors were covered with my blood. It had gotten a taste, and now it was going to take it all.

I hit it with the only weapon I still had. The flashlight smashed into its face with all the strength I possessed. The creature jerked back, squealing in shock.

Two things happened. One was that I heaved as hard as I could, trying to throw it off me. The second was that Pacal hit it with all the weight of his compact body. It went over backwards, the jaguar roaring in rage. There was a flurry of claws and blood, and Pacal leapt back, stumbling as his weight came down on his injured leg.

I dropped the flashlight and scrambled wildly for my gun. My right arm had gone completely numb, and I was afraid to look at the extent of the injury. My left found the gun by touch, and I wrapped my fingers around it awkwardly.

The beam of the dropped flashlight intersected with the monster. I got a glimpse of it as it twisted, saw that it was bleeding as well. One of its great wings was in tatters from Pacal's claws. Letting out a hiss of hatred, it drew back from us--then headed skyward once again.

"No!" I shouted wildly. Pacal yelled something--it sounded more jaguar than human. I fired a shot in the direction of the fleeing monster, and at the same instant the sky opened up.

The lightning bolt seemed to rip open the belly of creation. I'd never been that close to a lightning strike; the sound was more like tearing cloth than the rumble of distant thunder, and so loud I could still hear it ringing in my ears even after it had ceased. The bolt turned the world into a stark place without color, and in its heart I glimpsed the twisted figure of the bat, wings stretched to their fullest and back arched in agony. Then the light went out, and all I could see was a negative of the image, imprinted on my retinas.

The smell of burning hair and flesh came to me, and I blinked wildly to clear my vision. The beam of the flashlight showed a human hand, its fingers twisted in pain. Pacal brushed past me, and I swore. Shoving my gun into the holster, I grabbed the flashlight again and pointed it where the thing had fallen.

A man lay there now. Our killer. Smoke leaked from beneath his clothes, and his eyes stared blindly. Even so, I saw the faint movement of his chest. He wasn't dead. Not yet, anyway.

Pacal had taken back his human form, and went to kneel by the man. He looked ... puzzled, mostly, as if someone had given him a riddle he couldn't answer.

"I ... I know him," he said slowly, although he didn't sound sure.

The man stirred at the sound of his voice. Cracked lips parted, and a faint thread of sound came out. "P ... Pacal?"

I came over, uncertain whether I was going to have to pull my gun or administer emergency aid. "Who is he?"

Pacal didn't say anything. The killer swallowed convulsively. "Don't ... you know me? It's Yaxun."

Pacal hissed, his eyes going wide in horror. "No. You're dead. You...."

Yaxun laughed weakly. "Yes. I am ... dead, brother." He coughed, and blood bubbled out between his lips. "I died ... the day they came ... they killed everyone."

Pacal closed his eyes. "I know. I know. But why did you do this thing?"

His brother didn't answer, and for a moment I thought he'd died. Then he stirred. "They came ... you don't know what they did ... they put a gun to my head. The things they forced me to do." A sob broke his voice and then he really was silent.

I swore and dropped to my knees by him, intending to administer CPR as best I could with one hand. But Pacal reached out and grabbed my wrist. His eyes were closed, but I thought not all the water on his face came from the rain. "No. It is better this way."

"But--"

"What would you do--save him and then put him in jail?" he asked. There was so much bitterness in his words that it hurt just to hear him speak. "You know that can't be done. Leave it."

I didn't understand everything that had happened, but I knew he was wounded, both inside and out. "He was ... your brother?"

He nodded, then looked away. "I haven't seen him since we were both children," he said, so quiet I could barely hear him. "I thought he died with the rest of our family in the massacres. I just ... please. Don't ask me anything else. Not now."

I didn't. Instead, I stood up shakily and held my hand out to him. After a long moment, he got up and took it. Battered and bloody, we limped out of the orchard together.

*Lahun*
(Ten)

Yaxun's funeral was a very small affair. Other than Pacal and myself, there wasn't anyone but the guys hired to put the coffin in the ground. I thought that Pacal might have said some words or done some kind of shaman-thing, but he did nothing. He still seemed stunned, as if the lightning bolt had hit him instead of his brother, and I wondered how long it would take him to fully wake up.

My right arm was still swathed in bandages. It had taken too many stitches to close the wound, and I'd lost a lot of blood thanks to some kind of anti-coagulant in the bat-thing's saliva. Of course, my report said that the wound had come from the same knife that had stabbed Pacal. A search of Yaxun's bunk in the cement building where some of the workers lived had turned up a rifle that matched the one that had fired the bullet at my truck. And a forensic exam of the bunk's blankets had found a hair that matched Debra Simpson's, so it seemed that my case was as closed as it could officially be.

Charlie had been furious at me. As soon as I got out of the hospital, he'd ranted and raved about how I had to be insane to go chasing a dangerous suspect through a thunderstorm without backup. I tried to convince him that he would have done the same in my place, but he staunchly denied it, even though I suspected that I was right.

When the backhoe began dumping earth on the coffin, Pacal and I turned away and started back to the truck. I had taken his hand, and although he didn't say anything, the way he held it tight made me think he was grateful.

"I'm sorry," I said, when we were out of earshot of the gravediggers.

"So am I." Pacal sighed and shook his head. "I always wondered why the signs that came to me were so clear. It was because of our shared blood, I think. He was my brother, and I was responsible for him. That was what he meant, that night I met you on the road. When he said I had betrayed my blood in defending you."

"You didn't know, Pacal. There was nothing you could have done. He ... it sounded like he'd been through hell. If anyone's to blame for this, it was the men who tortured him and killed your family. Not you."

"So I tell myself. But I still wonder what might have happened if I had looked harder for him when I returned to Guatemala. I assumed that he had died along with the rest, but I should have made sure. I should have tried harder."

"No." I stopped and turned to face him. His dark eyes looked so sad and troubled that it broke my heart. "You didn't know. You aren't omniscient." I shook him gently. "He was an adult, and in the end he's the one who made his decisions. You couldn't have done that for him. You have to forgive yourself."

His mouth twitched wryly. "I know. But it's hard."

We started walking again. I took a deep breath, telling myself to be brave, to ask the question I'd been scared to ask for days. "So ... what will you do now?"

"I had thought about going to see my adoptive parents again," he said. His fingers tightened gently on mine. "But I do not think they would believe me if I told them what had happened."

"Probably not. It is pretty fantastic."

"Indeed." We had reached the truck; he stopped and turned me towards him. He was still stiff from the stab-wound in his side, and he winced a little when he raised one hand to touch my cheek. "And if I left, then who would look after you and make certain that your truck does not acquire any more bullet holes?"

I smiled shakily. "Yeah. And it would break Watson's heart. She's really attached to you."

"And we would not want to disappoint Watson."

"No. We wouldn't."

He slid his hand around the back of my neck and leaned in to kiss me. "Then I suppose it's settled." He let go and opened the truck door for me. "I do have two working arms, you know. I could drive instead."

"Like hell! Nobody drives my truck but me, purr-boy." I shoved him lightly out of the way and climbed in. "Now get in and hang on."

His lazy smile made me think of a sleepy, well-fed cat. "Perhaps when we get home."

Meow.

# LYNX TO THE PHARAOH

By

## Shelley Munro

Chapter One

*Patria Oasis, Egypt, 1835*
A blood red moon shone down over the desert. An omen, the locals whispered as they bolted for their camel-skin tents, dropped the flaps and hid from the fearsome sight.

Sethmet stared into the darkness, sensing the upheaval in the air with every particle of his tense body. Muscles twitched beneath his skin, itching for the freedom of a nocturnal run across the dunes at the edge of the oasis. It was his normal routine, but tonight, he resisted, testing the air. Listening.

Evil whispered from the shadows. Menace thrummed in the air, making the night birds jabber uneasily in their roosts. Sethmet sensed danger too but had no intention of running to hide like the villagers. His was a secret duty, sworn in blood many centuries ago and passed down through the generations from father to son. A sacred promise to the pharaoh to protect the tombs of the cat.

The wind picked up, sending the scent of exotic spices and perfumes from the caravanserai swirling through the air. The reeds on the edge of the lake rattled, warning of the approaching storm.

Sethmet walked briskly from the oasis, past the caravanserai--the inn where travelers resided--and past the pens where restless camels were hobbled and bedded down for the night. When the faint glow of lamps and candle light faded, he rapidly stripped off his boots, coat, silk cravat, shirt and finally his trousers. He stuffed them under a rock he'd used in the past then stood for an instant and let the chill of the rising wind caress his body. Finally, his broad chest rose and fell and he let the cat take him, reveling in the pleasure-pain of the transformation from man to beast. Bones lengthened, stretched. Hands converted to clawed paws and a fine brownish red fur formed on his skin. Sethmet dropped to all fours, his large fur-tufted ears twitching with pleasure and the buzz of intensified senses.

The caracal tested the air. Along with the storm and the myriad of scents from the oasis, he smelled the campfires of the English tourists. Sethmet had visited them already, but not as the cat. Their canvas tents rattled in the gusts of wind. A sand storm was fast approaching, screening the moon from sight. His eyes scanned the vicinity for anything suspicious. All clear.

Sethmet's slow trot hastened into a full out run, just for the pleasure of feeling his muscles work, for the speed and the heady rush. He rounded the end of a rolling sand hill, his sharp eyes picking up the camp at the base of the next sand hill. Then, a flicker of a lamp caught his attention. Apart from the main site and moving slowly in the opposite direction. Sethmet checked the air, smelling for danger then paused in surprise. Subtle perfume--flowers of the lilac. Woman.

He sat on his haunches, blinking while the human thought about this new development. It was unusual for English women to come to his family's oasis since it was so far from the big towns. Perhaps she came with one of the men. A wife or a lover. The steady retreat of the light piqued his curiosity.

On the unprotected side of the dunes, the wind tugged at his fur, blew particles of sand in his eyes, but something inside the cat urged him to keep following. A flash of white petticoat told him he'd almost caught the woman. His heart beat harder, faster. Shifting wasn't an option, not with an English woman, but would she take fright at seeing the cat? His ears flicked rapidly back and forth while he tried to decide. Even if she were linked to treasure hunters intent on finding the lost tombs, she was in danger out here alone in the approaching storm. What was her protector thinking?

A powerful gust of wind, the dull roar of the rising, swirling sands and the startled squeak from the English woman made up his mind. Sethmet padded up to the swaying form of the woman, intent on herding her to safety.

Long ebony hair streamed out behind her while black skirts blew up and outward, baring her legs and white frilly undergarments. His heart jumped, astonishing both beast and man. The urge to shift and claim her sprang into his mind, shivered the length of his body. Suddenly, he wanted to sink into the warm softness of this woman. The need to touch her soft skin beat like an urgent drum inside his head. A soft snarl erupted in protest from the cat.

The woman heard, despite the wail of the wind. She whirled, her big blue eyes widening in astonishment.

But not fear, Sethmet thought with a sense of pride. He knew then this woman would be a worthy consort for the man who claimed her. In that moment, Sethmet desperately wanted that man to be him.

Charlotte froze, staring at the big cat that stood a foot from her. Its golden eyes were fixed on her, unblinking and solemn.

"I hope you're not hungry," she whispered, not taking her eyes from the caracal. What had her stepbrother called them? That's right. Desert lynx. The cat prowled closer. In the flickering light of her lamp, the cat seemed big--huge--and heavily muscled. Its pointed ears looked long because of the black tufts at the tips. Golden eyes gleamed with intelligence. Was it hungry? Or curious? Either way, uneasiness skittered through her veins, and she inwardly cursed her stupidity in thinking it was safe to walk alone at night. Her husband would have scolded her soundly and no doubt shut her in her room with only bread and water to eat for punishment.

Charlotte squared her shoulders. Since her husband's death, she'd made decisions on her own, be they good or bad. The consequences too. She clutched her easel and paint box a fraction tighter. Perhaps painting by moonlight hadn't been such a good idea. Charlotte scanned the sky, seeing nothing but black before she glanced back at the still cat. Imagine capturing the beauty of the beast on canvas. Her gaze traced the muscular lines of the animal before the scant light faded. Clouds obscured the red moon, defeating her urgent need to capture the scene in a painting.

"I ... ah ... think I'll go back to camp now," she said. "But I've no idea why I'm telling you." Charlotte sidled toward the cat then at the last moment, when she was almost past, it moved blocking her retreat. Her heart thudded. Was it her imagination or had it opened its mouth a bit wider? Charlotte tried to keep each breath even and attempted to step around, despite her knocking knees. "Good, kitty. I don't have time to play now. Off you go, kitty. Back to your friends."

The cat's lips curled and a hiss, scarcely louder than the wind, trembled in the air between them. Charlotte stilled then rapidly backed up without taking her gaze from the cat's golden eyes. So, she'd go back to camp the long way. She had her lamp. And she had all night.

The wind rose, a strong gust sending her stumbling and her skirts flying up around her waist. Embarrassed, she fought to push them down and dropped the lamp. It rolled end over end down a slope with a loud clang. The flame flickered then blew out leaving nothing but deep, pulsing darkness.

A soft cry escaped Charlotte. Her teeth bit into her bottom lip. Run or not run? Before she could decide, something brushed against her hip.

*The cat.*

Her mouth dried, and she fought to draw a shaky breath into her starved lungs. A sharp nudge against her hip pushed her away from camp in the opposite direction. Off balance, her arms flailed. Her painting materials fell from her grasp and dropped to the ground. Charlotte scrambled to retrieve them, but another sharp nudge moved her three unladylike steps before she could dig her heels into the shifting sands.

"My paints," she protested. "I don't have any more."

A growl stopped further complaints cold. Her life was more important than a box of paints and her drawing book. Another impatient nudge made her move, but it was in the slow, uneasy gait of a blind person.

"How can I see where I'm walking?" Charlotte muttered crossly, coming to an abrupt halt. The cat seemed to understand her difficulty and stepped so close to her, she could have run her hand down the animal's back without stretching. Her hand slid across the soft fur and curled into the cat's scruff for better balance. It surprised her that she wanted to stroke the beast, to feel the sensual slide of fur beneath her fingers. Her heart jumped erratically while her breasts peaked beneath the stiff stays she wore. Astonished by the unusual reaction, she missed her step and tripped over a partially embedded rock. She hit the sand with a thump before sitting to rub her leg briskly. How could she see where she was going when she couldn't see her hand in front of her face?

The cat paused and prodded her with its head. Seconds later, she felt a damp sweep over her cheek. A little rough, but not unpleasant. The wind howled, and the cat gave a low growl followed by a sharp, insistent push on her upper arm.

Charlotte pushed to her feet. The sand stirred, blowing in pounding waves like the ocean. It roared like a ferocious beast in a foul temper. A shiver crawled across her body at the fanciful thought.

The cat kept moving steadily through the night without hesitation. Charlotte wondered if she were wise to place her trust in a beast that could eat her for dinner as quick as look at her. She hesitated, her steps faltering and almost decided to turn back, to go with the survival instinct that shouted she was a fool. Then, the ground under her stout boots changed from sand to rock. Footing became easier. Unerringly, the cat moved through the darkness before stopping. The cat's low growl sounded as if it wanted her to do something.

"Kitty, I wish I could understand you," Charlotte murmured.

The cat rubbed its head against her hip, giving a soft purr before shunting her toward what felt like a wall of rock. Charlotte held out her hand to stop herself from pitching forward and thumping her head. Her palm caught the edge of an overhanging rock then nothing.

"A cave," she said, not trying to hide her amazement. "Good, kitty." Charlotte stumbled into the dark cave, fully trusting the cat now that it had brought her to a refuge from the growing storm.

Outside, the wind wailed. Sand whipped through the air and inside the mouth of the cave. Charlotte moved cautiously, making her way deeper into the dark hole in the rock. Once she was out of the range of the wind and sand, she sank to the ground, settling in a sandy patch with her back against the rock wall. The cat sat beside her, a welcome warmth in the damp cave. Bone deep weariness seeped through Charlotte. Her eyelids drooped after her adventure. She fought the tiredness, but the soft breathing of the cat at her side lulled her senses, and she fell asleep.

\* \* \* \*

Sethmet guarded the woman throughout the night, content to doze at her side. When the storm passed, he stood. He studied the sleeping beauty, intrigued by her presence with the English. His top lip curled at the thought. Tomb robbers disguised as tourists. His gut instinct had never failed him before. His eyes drifted across her peaceful face. It was difficult to believe that a woman with the innocence of an angel could endanger his family with her greed. A part of the deception? Or the innocent she looked?

Time would tell.

Sethmet *would* protect the tombs from robbers. He would not fail in his duty to his family and that of the pharaoh. Shape shifting was part of their heritage. A gift they treasured and did not intend to give up lightly. If the woman was involved, he'd find out and deal with the matter. Meanwhile, it wouldn't hurt to get to know her better.

Decision made, the cat prowled to the mouth of the cave. Sethmet tested the air. With nothing to alarm him, he moved swiftly out into the night. He paused by the spot where the woman had dropped her paints, but they had disappeared with the wind. No matter. His sisters had paints and books they could spare. He moved on, a silent sentry in the early dawn as he stopped to survey the tourist's camp.

The English camp had escaped serious damage--a supply tent slanted drunkenly and some of the items left out overnight were strewn across the surrounding desert.

Sethmet loped along at an easy pace back to his clothes. Acute anticipation pulsed through his mind, the like of which he'd never felt before. Though eager as he was to return to the woman, he didn't forget the caution that had become second nature. He paused by the rock where he'd left his clothes. Nothing disturbed the still of the storm-washed dawn, so he seamlessly shifted from caracal to man. He pulled on his clothes with a sense of purpose and haste. Suddenly, the chore of protecting the pharaoh's treasures and ensuring his comfort in the afterlife had taken an interesting turn. Sethmet's mouth curled up in a slow, feral grin. If the woman wasn't under the protection of another man, he could use that. *Use her.* Gain inside information and find out what the English were up to. She'd felt the simmering attraction between them even if she hadn't fully understood. The smile eased up into intense and carnal. He prayed she was unclaimed by another male. A surge of heat shot straight to his groin. He'd teach her to call him kitty.

Sethmet ghosted through the oasis, his silent, rapid footfalls eating the distance between the English camp and his family villa on the hills at the opposite side of the oasis. The mournful bray of a donkey broke the silence, reminding Sethmet that it wouldn't be long before the people stirred. As he hurried through the village, past the market place, the bathhouse and the gracious columns that decorated the square, he felt a trace of satisfaction and pride. The oasis of Patria was prosperous, the inhabitants happy yet hardworking. The Gods and the pharaoh had been generous indeed.

A sleepy servant let him into the villa. Half way across the marble floor, he paused and turned.

"I would like food and drink to take with me."

The servant nodded, more alert now, and hurried off to carry out his instructions.

Restless, Sethmet wandered the villa before finally seeking out his mother to ease the sudden tension and restlessness he felt inside.

"Son, you are up early."

"Mama." Sethmet smiled and bent to kiss both wrinkled cheeks before leaning against a pedestal, almost toppling the bust of the pharaoh that stood proudly on top.

"Take care, Sethmet." The wooden rocking chair his father had purchased in Cairo squeaked when she set it in motion.

Sethmet's eyes widened fractionally then narrowed. He'd tried hard to hide his impatience to go to the woman. Obviously, his mother knew him too well, and despite her partial blindness, she'd sensed his turbulent emotions. The push and pull as he grappled to balance desire for the flesh and execution of his duties.

"Do not forswear love in the pursuit of justice, my son."

A powerful shudder wracked his body as he studied his mother's face.

The red moon.

The storm.

And now his mother speaking of love and justice.

Mayhap, the arrival of the English woman was a personal omen, sent to try his devotion to protecting the pharaoh's tomb. A test to see if he'd succumb to temptation.

## Chapter Two

Once the first rays of the sun peeped over the horizon, Sethmet gathered his basket of food from the kitchen and strode from the villa. The meeting would appear casual, yet it would be anything but since he'd planned everything carefully while she'd slept. Sethmet had chosen to remain in the English style of clothing rather than his traditional garb of galabiyya. The English seemed to accept him more readily if he dressed and spoke like them, something he'd learned well from his father and subsequent experience. Veiled ridicule for wearing a full-length robe that looked like a dress wasn't the greeting he hoped to achieve. His thoughts drifted back to the woman. They turned carnal before he had time to blink. Questions of how she'd feel as their bodies joined and slid together, how she'd taste....

But he was getting ahead of himself. He wouldn't--refused--to act if the woman was taken.

Sethmet entered the small cave cautiously, not wanting to scare her and start off on the wrong terms. He scuffed out the paw prints he'd made last night and this morning with his foot, leaving only the woman's tracks and the new ones he'd made in human form. Early morning light spilled through the mouth of the cave eliminating most of the shadows.

"Hello!" he called. "Is someone in here?"

A soft gasp sounded, caught by his acute hearing. When he rounded the bend in the cave, the woman was sitting, her long, ebony hair tangled and tumbling loose around her shoulders. His heart gave an uneven pump as he looked his fill, tracing her full, pink lips, her apprehensive blue eyes and pale skin with his gaze. His eyes swept over her breasts, her trim waist and came to a halt on her hands. Disappointment thumped his gut, searing in its intensity. The English woman was beautiful, and he wanted her more than ever, but she wore a wedding band on her left hand.

\* \* \* \*

Charlotte blinked up at the man who'd woken her. Nervous at the way he towered over her, Charlotte scrambled to her feet. Sudden shooting pins and needles in legs cramped from staying in one place made her wobble precariously. The man moved so quickly she didn't register until her hand tightened around his forearm. Warm skin greeted her touch along with a shudder of awareness at his stark masculinity. He was tall and lean with a build that hinted at muscles beneath the fabric of his clothing. Dark, curly hair framed his head, unruly enough that she had the urge to smooth it with her hands. In fact, she acknowledged that her hands itched to stroke more than his hair. Charlotte jerked up her chin, wary yet enthralled by the stranger. It took her an instant longer to let go of the man's arm.

"I must have fallen asleep," she said, uneasy with the intimacy of the cave and the glow she could see in his tawny eyes even though the light in the cave was dim. "I need to return to camp before my stepbrother starts to worry." Or loses his temper with me. Charlotte wrinkled her nose at that thought. William's temperament seemed uncertain these days, and his wrath was a sight to make a grown man or woman tremble. All the more reason to hurry back to camp.

"Let me escort you back." The stranger paused to smile and offer his arm. The flash of even white teeth pushed her awareness of his raw sexuality even higher, and she felt unaccountably nervous. But not frightened, she realized in puzzlement. How peculiar.

"Your brother has hired me as a guide. I am Sethmet."

"Our guide?" Charlotte snapped her mouth shut as she heard herself parrot the man.

"That's right." He glanced down at his arm then back at her. One dark brow rose in silent mockery, and Charlotte realized she'd been staring. Her gaze shot to her half boots before she extended her hand and placed it on the hard sinews of his arm.

They strolled across the sand and rock floor of the cave as though they paraded in one of London's finest ballrooms.

The silence between them intensified. Charlotte swallowed as she fought to think of suitable chitchat to fill the void. Aware of the social chasm between them yet desperately wanting to breach it, she blurted, "I saw a cat last night."

He paused, just inside the mouth of the cave, and looked down at her with an impassive expression. The seconds dragged out.

"It was beautiful," Charlotte said.

"There are no footprints out here."

His voice was low, husky and it strummed along her nerve endings. Charlotte shivered as a picture formed in her mind. Two people together--man and woman--naked, rubbing their bodies against each other. A small gasp of shock emerged when she saw their faces. His--Sethmet's--and hers. Heat pooled in her cheeks while nerves danced in her stomach. She wanted him sexually. The realization stunned her since intimacy with her late husband, George, had been anything but inspiring. Certainly nothing more than duty. Charlotte swallowed and struggled to regroup.

"Perhaps the storm covered the prints, Mr. Sethmet."

He grinned without warning, as if something amused him. "It's just Sethmet."

"I am Charlotte." It seemed pointless to keep to formalities when she was so far from home. "Charlotte Webster."

"Charlotte." Sethmet rolled her name, making it sound unusual. Exotic. "Come. It is early still. No one stirs in your camp. Would you like to watch the birds on the oasis and break your fast with me?" He indicated the basket he held in his other hand.

Ribbons of color streaked the morning sky, a faint splash of orange and a deep pink. Charlotte sighed, feeling more at home in this foreign place than she'd ever felt amongst society in London.

Charlotte strolled at his side, very aware of the flex of muscles in his arm and the brush of his trousers against her skirt. "Can we go past the camp first?"

"If it would put your mind at rest."

They slid down a short rocky slope and rounded the base of a dune. In the distance, the canvas tents of the camp were visible. A faint plume of smoke rose, indicating that the cooks were awake. If she returned now she'd have to go to her tent. It seemed a shame to waste such a beautiful morning.

"I'd love to visit the oasis," Charlotte said, ignoring the feminine pride inside that warned her she would not look her best after sleeping in her clothes. She risked a glance at him, and the silent gleam of approval in his eyes warmed her all over. This early in the morning, she couldn't blame the heat of the sun.

"What made you decide to travel to Egypt?"

Charlotte paused then found herself wanting to tell the truth. "My husband died eight months ago. I wanted to have a break." A break from the sympathetic tabbies and the puckered brows when she so much as spoke to an unmarried man.

"Ah," he said.

Charlotte wondered what he meant by that since his face didn't yield a clue.

They arrived at the edge of the oasis more quickly than

Charlotte would have liked. Countless questions trembled at the tip of her tongue. Curious as a cat. That's what George used to say, always in a chiding manner.

Sethmet stopped by the edge of the lake, in a small private spot, screened from the main path.

A gentle breeze played a musical tune as it blew through the reeds. Not far from them, a heron stabbed the water with its beak and came up with a wriggling silver fish.

He placed his basket on a flat rock and helped Charlotte sit on another rock that made the perfect seat. Her lack of primping and fussing gained his approval. Not that she needed to preen. Sethmet opened his woven basket. He had to stop the urgent need to touch, to run his hands across her silky cheek. A bark of laughter escaped at the thought. No doubt, Charlotte would slap his face at the presumption.

"Is something funny?"

"Not a thing," Sethmet said. "Would you care for flat bread and cheese?" He spread out a blue woven cloth on the ground beside them and set out the food. The instinct to serve and nurture Charlotte came as a surprise. Most women ran after him, but being with Charlotte felt right. He wanted to protect her, even if she came from the English camp.

Charlotte was no longer committed to a man.

Satisfaction swelled within Sethmet along with an urge to kiss her. Hell, he wanted to do more than that. He wanted to claim her as mate.

He glanced up from laying out the food and saw Charlotte studied him avidly. For an instant, open desire shimmered in her blue eyes before her lashes lowered to screen the emotion.

Sethmet acted on instinct. He leaned toward her and took possession of her lips in a slow, easy kiss of exploration. When she didn't object, he deepened the contact, sliding his tongue across her soft, pink lips and urging her to open her mouth so he could taste. Charlotte sighed, and he took advantage, delving into her mouth with raw need. God, he needed to touch Charlotte and with more than his mouth. He needed it as bad as breathing. Without further thought, Sethmet gave in to the desire, entwining his fingers in her hair and cradling her head, drawing her closer. Still, it wasn't enough. He trailed one hand down her back, pressing her against his chest so her breasts brushed his thin cotton shirt. Charlotte moaned softly. The low, throaty sound drew a shudder from Sethmet. So much. So fast. He shuddered again, his cock tight and heavy with need. His fingers trailed down her neck, tracing over smooth skin and coming to rest on a rapidly beating pulse at the base of her neck.

Pure physical desire, the like of which she'd never known, kicked Charlotte in the belly. It was a primitive throb in her veins, and she didn't want to stop. Charlotte sucked in a hasty breath as his mouth slid from hers and laid a trail of kisses down her neck. Sethmet was a stranger yet she felt as though she'd known him forever.

Sethmet pulled away from her without warning leaving Charlotte bereft in an ocean of turbulent emotions. She didn't want to stop the magic. She wanted more of the same. Charlotte opened her mouth to protest, but Sethmet raised his finger to his mouth in a gesture of silence. Approaching footsteps halted the unladylike begging that trembled on her lips.

A woman bearing a stoneware urn came into sight. She froze upon seeing them then addressed Sethmet in a foreign tongue. He replied, and the woman giggled then stooped to fill her urn with water from the lake. She hurried off, but Charlotte noticed the intent curiosity in the woman's eyes when she glanced back over her shoulder.

"Would you care for some juice?" Sethmet's husky voice vibrated along her nerve endings leaving moist dampness between her legs. Wonder made her gape at him since no man had touched her emotions in this way. It was as if they were already intimate, as if they'd known each other in another life. Yet how was that possible?

"You are frowning. Perhaps you do not care for juice of the orange fruit?"

A soft blush suffused her cheeks. The burst of heat intensified under his dark gaze.

Sethmet reached out to stroke one finger down her cheek. "We must eat, or I will give in to temptation and make love to you."

His blunt words thrilled her when they should have shocked. God forgive her, but she wanted to make love to Sethmet. Somehow, she sensed it would be powerful and moving and would change her life forever.

Charlotte swallowed and moistened her lips. Finally, she lifted her eyes to meet his gaze. "What if that's what I'd like too?" she blurted.

Sethmet's tawny eyes glowed. He didn't answer her question, but instead reached for her. His arms wrapped around her shoulders then he lifted her so she sat in his lap. Charlotte was enveloped by warmth and his exotic scent--a whiff of sandalwood and something else that reminded her of a cool English forest.

"Are you sure?" he whispered against her lips.

Charlotte closed the remaining distance between them, eager to taste him again. Their lips touched, their tongues sliding together in a slow, sensuous dance. Moist heat exploded on her senses, and she stirred restlessly needing more.

"Sethmet," she breathed against his lips. Charlotte tugged Sethmet's cravat free from his collar and slipped one hand in the opening she'd created. Warm skin greeted her touch. Charlotte undid another two buttons revealing more skin, golden and hot to the touch. She leaned forward and pressed an open mouthed kiss to his collarbone. His erection nudged her buttocks, and Charlotte squirmed. Anticipation bubbled through her, the sensation of rigid masculine flesh beneath her legs readying Charlotte for his possession. Her breath caught as she wondered what would happen next.

"I want to touch you, Charlotte."

The husky voice made her melt inside. Then Sethmet smoothed his hand under her skirt, tracing the tender skin behind her knee. Charlotte shuddered. "Yes," she whispered.

Sethmet pushed the food aside and laid Charlotte on the cloth he'd spread out earlier. He leaned over her and stared down into her eyes, serious and intent. "I wish I could take the time to undress you. But this is not the time or place to linger."

Anyone could interrupt them. Charlotte knew she risked scandal and censure but didn't care. The taste of freedom was heady stuff. And she wanted to explore whatever this thing was between them. "But we have some time?"

He smiled then, a slow grin that spread across his lips and up to his eyes. "We have time enough."

The hand under her skirt traveled higher over bare skin. One slender finger slipped through the slit in her drawers. He stroked the length of her cleft, dancing his fingers across her clit. Charlotte released her breath on a gasp. A shivered worked the length of her body. She lifted her hips, silently pleading for more. Her eyelids closed leaving Charlotte adrift in a world of pure sensation.

"Do you like the way I touch you, Charlotte?"

"Yes," she whispered. His finger circled her clit then shifted lower, and he inserted a finger into damp, feminine flesh. A squelch sounded, loud and undignified. Charlotte flinched, her eyes flying open in consternation. George had liked to couple in complete silence with the lights off and removal of minimal clothing.

Sethmet laughed. He splayed her legs and bent over her. Charlotte wasn't sure what he intended. Her heart pounded, and she tried to wriggle away.

"Stay," he whispered in his husky voice. "Let me taste you. Let me pleasure you."

Charlotte thought her heart might thump out of her chest as she glanced down at Sethmet. His dark head was bent between her spread legs, hiding his expression. His finger thrust inside her again. Charlotte swallowed, aware, now more than ever, of possible discovery.

Then he licked across her clit.

A blaze of sensation arced through her body. Charlotte bit her bottom lip, trying to hold back the unladylike moan that trembled at the back of her throat. Sethmet raked his tongue across her sensitive bud again.

"Let go, Charlotte. Come for me." He cupped her bottom, lifting her to his mouth and sucking gently.

"Sethmet," Charlotte cried. Hot pleasure spilled over. She convulsed, a violent spasm streaking down her legs right to the tips of her toes.

Sethmet lifted his head and smiled up at her, a grin of supreme masculine satisfaction. "Tonight, Charlotte, will be even better."

## Chapter Three

Charlotte walked at Sethmet's side, intensely aware of their physical and mental closeness. The terracotta glow of the rocks near the dunes, the green of the plants surrounding the lake seemed brighter, the rich, loamy scent of the soil, the dryness of the sand and Sethmet's sandalwood musk richer and more intoxicating than before.

The plaintive grunts of camels filled the air while their masters bade them sit. A number of workers scurried around the campsite while members of William's group finished breaking their fast and sauntered off to their tents.

"Charlotte, where have you been?" William glared from his post outside the equipment tent.

"I was awake early and decided to take a walk. Mr. Sethmet met me by the lake and escorted me back to camp."

Charlotte hoped he didn't notice anything amiss with her appearance. She'd tidied and fastened her hair with a strip of cloth. Sethmet had assured her she looked beautiful, but even so, she hoped evidence of what they'd been doing wasn't emblazoned over her face.

"I wish to leave in half an hour," William said, directing his displeasure at Sethmet.

Sethmet bent from the waist in a subservient manner that drew a frown from Charlotte. An act. If ever a man was born to lead it was Sethmet, yet he was acting the role of servant. Uneasily, she wondered why.

"I am prepared to leave. I will check to make sure all else is in readiness." Sethmet dipped his head with a courteous nod at Charlotte then retreated leaving Charlotte and her stepbrother alone.

"You mustn't wander off on your own. It's not safe with the savages that roam the desert."

Charlotte disagreed but knew better than to verbalize her opinion. "Where are we going today?" Anticipation stirred inside at the thought of exploring more of this mysterious land. And Sethmet, she thought wickedly.

"We ride to explore the ancient ruins to the west of the oasis."

"That sounds wonderful," Charlotte said. "I must get my sketchbook."

Half an hour later, Sethmet helped Charlotte and the men of the party clamber aboard their camels. The train moved off with much protest from the camels. A laugh escaped Charlotte as she rolled from side to side and backward and forward almost as if she sat in a rocking chair. The beasts were not unpleasant to ride but they never ceased their noisy protests.

At the head of the column, Sethmet halted his camel and allowed the others to move ahead after indicating the direction they needed to travel. When Charlotte rode past him he nudged his camel into a walk beside her.

"Was your brother angry?" he asked in a low undertone.

"He was worried," Charlotte said.

Sethmet looked across, his eyes glowing with an inner light. "You are safe here. No harm will come to you."

Charlotte blinked, the intense golden light mesmerizing. Her breasts seemed suddenly tender while her womb ached and wept for the pleasure she knew he could give. Charlotte wished they were alone. With William in this difficult mood, it would be hard to escape for private moments with Sethmet. A slow grin swept across her lips. Hard but not impossible.

After riding the camels for half an hour, the ruins appeared as a dot on the horizon. The sun beat down strongly despite the fact it was still early morning.

"We should reach the ruins before the heat of the midday sun," Sethmet said as if he read her mind.

Charlotte wiped her brow, wondering why she'd taken the time to wash and change gowns before they'd left when she felt grubby already. At least her straw hat kept the worst of the sun off her face but she feared freckles would appear soon. She glanced over at Sethmet and tried in vain not to blush. After the intimacies they'd shared, she should have hidden in shame. Instead, Charlotte couldn't wait for tonight to arrive.

"William said we'd spend the day exploring and not start back until late in the afternoon."

"You'll have plenty of time to sketch the ruins."

"I just hope I'm able to walk after riding a camel again. The ride to the oasis was bad enough." She patted the jewel bright rug she sat on. "I think I need more layers."

Sethmet laughed out loud attracting a frown from her stepbrother. "I'll massage your aches away. I'll enjoy it." His voice was low. Intimate. And it sent a shudder of desire speeding to her lower belly.

Charlotte concentrated on the steadily growing dot before them. If she concentrated on Sethmet, she knew she'd give away her growing infatuation with the man. William wouldn't approve. Charlotte frowned at the thought. For some reason, he seemed intent on pushing her toward his friend, Justin. The man was polite, his company genial, but Charlotte wasn't interested in him.

William glanced over his shoulder and gestured imperiously at Sethmet.

"Duty calls," Sethmet said with dry humor. He guided his camel to the head of the train and waited for William to warn him off Charlotte.

"Tell me about the ruins. Have they been explored?" William's eyes narrowed. "Excavated?"

"Patria Oasis is isolated," Sethmet said. "We don't have many visitors."

"So we will be the first?" William's voice grew sharp.

Sethmet shrugged. The man could interpret that in any way he wished. Several of the villagers who worked in the English camp as cooks and porters had approached Sethmet complaining of being interrogated about the ruins and history of the oasis. Sethmet's gut instinct told him the man had a hidden purpose.

"You said there are other sites. Tell me about them."

Sethmet stiffened inside although he took care that his expression didn't change. "There are others," he acknowledged.

"I want to visit them all."

Sethmet inclined his head. "As you wish." He could show the Englishman enough sites to keep him busy for months, perhaps years. However, the pharaoh's tomb would remain undisturbed. His family was proud of the shape shifter powers bestowed on them by the pharaoh. They would not part with them lightly for failure to protect meant unleashing the curse. A shiver walked Sethmet's spine as he thought of the evil curse. Years ago, when his grandfather wore the cloak of protector, two men--traitors-- had the life sucked out of them by the evil that aided them in keeping the pharaoh safe. Witnesses still spoke of the day in hushed whispers.

"My sister wishes to paint instead of exploring with the rest of us."

"I will arrange for a servant to help her," Sethmet said.

The Englishman's face had turned red in the sun, and sweat dripped down his face. He slapped at a buzzing insect, his slap of irritation startling his camel into a raucous protest. "How much longer?"

Sethmet smothered his amusement at the man's obvious discomfort. It would get worse by the end of the day, especially since there was no treasure here. "Ten minutes."

William had requested two separate parties and guides so they could cover the large site. This suited Sethmet perfectly. He arranged for two of his most trusted workers to guide a group each through the temple ruins and the outlying buildings. Hopefully, they would keep William busy for several hours leaving Sethmet alone with Charlotte. Each group would assume Sethmet was with the other one, or at least that was the plan.

"Your stepbrother seems determined to see every site," Sethmet murmured as the group of men drifted after the guides.

Charlotte shrugged and picked up the satchel containing her drawing materials. "William spends a lot of time in Egypt."

Sethmet directed Charlotte toward an avenue of sphinxes that led to a crumbling temple. The majestic beasts seemed to watch them as they strolled past and stepped in the cool shade of the temple.

"Exploring?" The man's reputation as a tomb robber preceded him, but Sethmet wanted to know if Charlotte was involved. It would make a difference.

A frown puckered her smooth brow and she hesitated. "I don't really know." An uncertain laugh escaped her, drawing Sethmet's attention to her pink lips. "Strange as it is, I've never really asked. I know he brings back a lot of souvenirs whenever he returns to London."

And sells them at a great profit, Sethmet thought. Just as the pharaoh had feared. The robbers pilfered the tombs dragging the dead back from the afterlife, setting their spirits on an aimless journey in the world between. During life, the pharaoh had shared an affinity with the caracal, and the respect remained even though he now lived at rest in the afterworld.

"Would you like to set up here?" Sethmet asked as they stepped into a shady courtyard on the other side of the temple. Cobras and figures of gods were depicted in the friezes in such intense blue, green, red, yellow and brown colors that they dazzled the eye.

"This is perfect," Charlotte murmured, glancing around with a trace of awe. "I only hope my skills will do the scene justice."

Sethmet nodded and helped her to set up her easel and chair. He brushed a kiss across her cheek then straightened. "I'll bring you some water and food, but first I must check that all is well."

"Thank you." Charlotte smiled.

As Sethmet strode away, he wished they were alone. He couldn't risk making love to her, but he would snatch a few kisses, and gently pump her for information.

\* \* \* \*

Charlotte crept from her tent, thankful it was set apart from the others, and there was less likelihood of her being caught and questioned. From the corner of her eye, she caught a flash of movement. Her heart jumped halfway up her throat before she realized she hadn't been discovered.

The cat.

"Hello, kitty," she whispered, stepping toward it without fear.

The cat was as big as she remembered, certainly big enough to gulp her down for a snack. "Good, kitty."

The caracal turned up its lip in a snarl the second time she spoke. Charlotte stilled, suddenly diffident. The beast *was* wild. Perhaps approaching it wasn't the wisest idea. They stared at each other for a long drawn out moment. Intelligence glowed in the cat's eyes but not menace despite the show of sharp, white teeth. Charlotte exhaled slowly, letting her tense limbs relax, and glanced away from the mesmerizing cat to see if anyone was awake to notice her departure.

Not a soul stirred in the camp. Good. No curious, prying questions to answer. The cat swished its tail then stalked off. With one last glance over her shoulder to check the silent camp, Charlotte followed since the cat seemed to travel in the direction she wanted. Up ahead, the cat broke into a loping run. Awed, Charlotte watched the leashed power of the beast. What would it feel like--running free like that with not a care in the world? No expectations or restrictions. Charlotte sighed as the cat disappeared from sight. She wondered where it lived and hoped she'd see it again before she traveled back to England.

Aware time was passing, she jerked from her reverie and hurried to the edge of the oasis where they had arranged to meet.

"Sethmet?"

A shadow parted from a date palm. "Charlotte."

Sethmet strode over to Charlotte, hugged her tight then swung her in a circle so her legs flew outward as they spun around. Finally, he let her stand on her own feet but maintained his grip of her hand. "I am glad you came. I thought you might change your mind."

"No," Charlotte whispered, brushing a lock of hair from his face. "I want this. I want you." She should have felt like a fallen woman. Definitely wicked, but instead excitement pulsed through her body. She hungered for his possession and couldn't wait to share further intimacies.

"Come," Sethmet murmured.

Tugging lightly on her hand, he led her down a narrow, overgrown path she hadn't noticed. Charlotte's skirts brushed against the sprawling plants that ran rampant. In a nearby tree, a night bird called, then Charlotte heard the flap of wings as it flew off over the water.

"Where are we going?"

"My family owns a small cottage here. I didn't want any

interruptions this time." His voice throbbed with promises that sent awareness flooding to her core. "Here it is." Sethmet opened the wooden door of the stone cottage. He reached inside and produced a lamp. Seconds later, he ushered her inside and shut the door, locking the rest of the world out.

Charlotte looked around, interested in learning more about Sethmet and his family. The cottage consisted of two rooms, the simple wooden furniture fairly impersonal and not telling her much. Sethmet clasped her hand and led her into the second--a bedroom. He let her hand go and lit another lamp. A subtle glow filled the room as he placed the lamp in a wall alcove, and their shadows appeared on the far wall.

Sethmet turned to her, his golden eyes intent. "Let me be your maid tonight."

Wordlessly, Charlotte nodded despite her qualms. George had never seen her naked just as she'd never seen him unclothed. Sethmet dealt with her buttons and the laces on her stays, sliding fabric aside and exposing her breasts to his gaze.

"Beautiful," he said, brushing the back of his hand across one creamy curve. His fingers brushed across her nipple then tugged. Charlotte closed her eyes and clamped her bottom lip between her teeth to hold back her cry of pleasure. "Let your emotions show, Charlotte. Don't hide from me. Open your eyes."

Charlotte managed to lift her eyelids even though they felt as though they were weighted. She caught Sethmet's golden gaze and held it, savoring the innate approval she saw.

"Do that again," she whispered.

"This?" Lazy humor sounded in his voice as he tweaked her nipple. Once. Twice. And then a third time.

"Yes," Charlotte said, fighting the need to close her eyes again. A streak of pleasure shot from her breast to moist feminine folds. More. This man had worked magic with her body before. Call her greedy, but she wanted it again. She wanted more.

Sethmet tugged her skirts down. The stiff black fabric pooled at her feet. Gathering her up in his arms, he lifted her and walked over to the bed leaving her black skirts of mourning sitting in the middle of the floor. He set her down on the edge of the mattress and removed her boots, tossing them aside in a careless manner. A gleam lit his eyes as he stared at her, his gaze traveling the length of her body and back to her face. Charlotte shivered at the heat she saw in him, the strength and leashed power. This man could have any woman but he wanted her.

He sat beside her, the feather mattress depressing with his weight, and rolling her against a muscled masculine thigh. Sethmet unfastened her ribbon garters and peeled woolen stockings down her legs. The act of undressing turned into the most erotic experience Charlotte had ever participated in. Sethmet drew her drawers down, pressing a soft kiss to each inch of skin he uncovered.

"You're perfect," he murmured, leaning back to look his fill. "I knew you would be."

She should have felt awkward, but instead an unexpected wantonness took possession of her body. Her skin tingled for want of his hands, his mouth. Between her legs, in her private, feminine places, moisture surged. An ache, deep-seated and tormenting, sprang to life. Charlotte stirred restlessly wanting to demand he touch her with greater intimacy. But she didn't, years of rules and ladylike manners coming to the fore.

Sethmet cupped her face with his hands and kissed her deeply, sliding his tongue into her mouth, thrusting and withdrawing. The ache intensified. Charlotte splayed her legs, fidgety and impatient yet unable to ask for more. Cool air met warmth, and if anything, the ache in her womb deepened, making her want to beg for him to ease the hunger that tormented and teased.

Rules be damned. She'd already asked once and remained alive to tell the tale. "Please, Sethmet. I want ... Touch me."

"I thought you'd never ask," he murmured, leaning over her. Charlotte heard the masculine satisfaction but instead of shame, need soared higher. Stronger. "For you, Charlotte, anything."

Sethmet blazed a trail of kisses from the corner of her mouth and down her neck. Unhurried. Taking his sweet time. Charlotte murmured a soft protest. Too slow, her mind screamed, especially when fire scorched her body, spreading rapidly until she was a mass of smoldering flames.

Deliberate and leisurely, he kissed his way across her collarbone and across the curve of one breast. Charlotte swallowed, waiting, anticipating the heat of his mouth suckling her breast. Instead, he kissed the area surrounding her nipple.

"Too slow," Charlotte muttered, and she grabbed his head forcibly and placed his mouth exactly where she needed it.

A chuckle sounded, the warm burst of air sending a shudder the length of her body. Charlotte panted as a tight coil of desire gripped her. Then Sethmet drew on her breast, and licked sweet, agonizing circles across her tight nipple. One of his hands trailed across her belly and lower to the triangle of hair between her thighs. Charlotte bucked at the dual sensation--the suckling of his mouth at her breast and the slow, teasing exploration of her moist cleft. The coil of passion wound tighter, stealing her breath, stealing her soul.

Slowly, Sethmet eased away. Charlotte made a sound of protest then saw Sethmet had paused to strip away his clothing. His shirt dropped away, exposing his chest. He sat up to tug off his boots and stockings then opened the flap of his trousers. Seconds later, he stood before her, naked and aroused.

Charlotte gulped. She knew the mechanics of sex well but the width of him, the length. Her gaze rose from his cock, up his waist and chest to meet his amused gaze.

"Like what you see?"

Charlotte's voice failed so she nodded. Her tongue slid between her lips, moistening the dryness away. The man looked firm with not an inch of excess flesh anywhere on his body. Her trembling hand reached out to stroke the length of his shaft. The first sensation was one of warmth. Then awe rose as Charlotte wondered at the inherent strength in him. Her hand curled around the breadth of him and squeezed. Sethmet's sharp hiss of breath steadied her nerves and brought a grin. A deep shudder shook his body when she applied pressure and stroked his cock again. Pre-come collected at the sensitive tip, and Charlotte brushed her thumb across the small drop, smoothing it away. Sethmet made a hungry sound at the back of his throat.

"No more," he said in a hoarse voice.

Before Charlotte could protest, she lay flat on her back with Sethmet looming over her. A feral grin displayed white teeth before his mouth crashed down on hers. He surrounded her, and Charlotte reveled in the weight of him, the sensation of hard muscles against her softer curves. His erection pressed against her inner thigh. Charlotte shifted to align their bodies, and his cock slid deep into her womb. Sethmet murmured, stroking his tongue against hers in a quick punch of heat. Charlotte arched against him, meeting each powerful thrust of his body. Her heart thundered as overwhelming sensations built to sweet agony. She shuddered then exploded in a fury of ecstasy that licked through her veins for long, satisfying moments.

A harsh cry rumbled from Sethmet. His hips pumped. Hard. Fast. Then, he stilled, a moan squeezing past his lips. His eyes were closed, his head thrown back and deep in her womb,

Charlotte felt the spurt of his seed. A satisfied smile crept across her lips. She, Charlotte Webster, had made him moan.

"You look smug," he murmured, his golden eyes intense and mesmerizing as he stared down at her.

A soft gasp escaped Charlotte. She stared back, her hand creeping up to caress one lean cheek then paused to finger his lips. In that moment, he reminded her of a wild beast. He reminded her of the kitty.

## Chapter Four

For the third morning in a row, Sethmet escorted Charlotte back to her tent just as the sun started to peep over the horizon. He held her close for a moment then brushed a kiss over her smiling lips.

"I'll see you later, sweetheart."

Charlotte smiled as he strode away, holding memories of last night close. The experience of making love with Sethmet would remain with her always. It was one she'd drag out during the endless round of society balls and soirees--one that would remind her of a few weeks of perfect freedom.

After spending time freshening up and changing into clean clothes, Charlotte peeked through the door of her tent. Daylight had arrived and servants scurried about the camp carrying out their duties. A flash of movement caught her attention. Charlotte started forward then halted to watch the heated discussion between William and his friend, Justin. Justin wore a scowl. He seemed to digest whatever William said then stated his opinion forcibly using his finger to drill holes in the air for emphasis. Curious, Charlotte crept past her tent and sidled close enough that she could hear.

"But the fact remains, we haven't found anything," Justin snapped in a hard, cold voice. "We had a deal, and I expect you to stick to it."

Charlotte wrapped her arms around her body to counter the chill Justin's tone sent rippling across her skin. This didn't sound like a fight between friends.

"I will. You have my word, but I didn't expect to have so much bad luck," William countered. "It's never happened on any other expedition."

Of the two, he seemed calmer, but Charlotte didn't intend to test his temper by being caught eavesdropping.

"A curse. Bah!" Justin swept his hand through the air. "Nothing but superstitious dribble."

"You have to admit the way Martin was injured was damned spooky. He swears a cat clawed him. Damned if the marks all over his body don't look like claw marks yet there were no prints on the ground where we found him."

Curious indeed, Charlotte thought, wondering uneasily if the caracal had something to do with the strange attack. No, she decided. Not her cat. Her kitty wouldn't harm her. William and Justin showed signs of moving so she decided she'd better make her presence known. She crept back to her tent then swished the canvas back loudly as though she'd just exited.

"Good morning," she said in a bright voice. Charlotte glided over to the two men. "Where are we exploring today? I swear my sketchbook is almost full, but there are so many interesting things to record."

"Good morning, Charlotte." Justin took possession of her hand and bent over it. At the last minute, he turned her hand over and pressed an intimate kiss on her wrist just above the pair of short gloves she wore. Under normal circumstances, if she'd met him in a London ballroom, his attention would have flattered her. With his cool English looks, blond hair, blue eyes and independent means, the man was a matrimonial prize. Yet, he left her cold. Instead, a man with golden skin, tawny eyes and dark hair made her blood sing. And strange pointy ears, she thought with a grin, that he hid under his long hair. Sethmet had acted embarrassed when she discovered them, but she thought the imperfection cute.

"Good morning, Justin."

"Charlotte." He retained her hand for longer than proper, his bold eyes sweeping over her in a manner that made her distinctly uncomfortable.

As she tugged her hand away, Charlotte caught the satisfaction on her stepbrother's face and wondered at it. Despite his encouragement, she felt she'd managed to keep Justin's attentions at a distance.

A gong rang out, the dull sound vibrating through the campsite.

"It seems our meal is ready. This heat is parching. I am ready for a dish of tea," Charlotte said.

The three wandered over to the shaded area set aside for

dining. Justin pulled out a chair for her. Charlotte subsided into the upright seat and smiled at Justin, thanking him for his assistance.

Sethmet strolled into the camp not long after, and Charlotte couldn't help staring at his lithe, masculine grace.

"Charlotte," William said sharply, noticing the direction of her eyes.

Charlotte's attention snapped to her stepbrother, and her cheeks heated at being caught ogling Sethmet. If she weren't careful, she'd give her interest in him away.

"Have you made the arrangements I requested?" William demanded as soon as Sethmet reached them.

Charlotte tensed inwardly, indignant on Sethmet's behalf. William spoke to Sethmet as though he were a servant with not an intelligent thought of his own. She knew otherwise. Sethmet was cultured and witty. A secret smile lifted her mood. And he was her lover.

Sethmet dipped his head. "Yes, all is arranged as you desired."

"I trust there will be no mishaps today."

Sethmet shrugged carelessly, his dark hair falling over his face to hide his expression. "I have no control over the curse."

Justin snorted in the background. "Superstitious rubbish."

"There's no such thing as a curse." William took a final sip from his dish of tea then placed it down on the table. "Let this be an end to the discussion. Charlotte, if you're finished I'd like to have a word with you before we leave."

Charlotte opened her mouth to protest and glanced down at her dish of tea. She'd only had time to take one sip. Surely there was time for her to drink more?

"*Charlotte.*"

Sighing inwardly, Charlotte stood. She knew that tone and it didn't bode well. William walked to the edge of the camp then waited for her to catch up.

"I want you to be a little more courteous with Justin. He's important to this expedition."

Charlotte gaped for an instant then snapped her mouth shut while she wondered how to respond. Finally, she said, "Exactly how courteous?"

"Don't take that tone with me. All I'm asking is that you spend time with Justin. It's important that he's kept happy since he's funded the expedition to search for the pharaoh's tomb...." William trailed off and commenced pacing--short lines back and forth in front of Charlotte. He paused and threw up his hands. "All the holdups are making things difficult in our search. If I didn't know better, I'd start believing in curses."

"Your search?" Charlotte stared at her stepbrother. It sounded as though he searched for a long lost tomb. He'd lied about sightseeing. "Let me get this straight. Lord Banning, Justin, has financed our trip to Egypt."

"Yes, so I need you to play nice with him." William's hand curled into her upper arm with bruising intensity. "It's not much to ask."

Charlotte didn't recognize this driven man. It was as if another being inhabited William's body. She glanced over at the assembled servants and the protesting camels being loaded up with supplies for the day's expedition. Sethmet directed the whole procedure with ease and authority. "We'd better go. We're keeping everyone waiting."

William grabbed her arm again. "Don't forget what I said, Charlotte, otherwise you'll be sorry." He laughed and there was no humor in the sound. "Hell, we'll both be sorry."

\* \* \* \*

Charlotte rode the same camel she'd ridden in the past. Despite the blond camel's constant griping, Charlotte was becoming fond of the beast. It didn't have the most pleasant teeth or breath, but her camel had character and was a definite flirt, fluttering long eyelashes at the other beasts.

Charlotte clambered on board, with the ease of practice, swaying back and forward as it fell into step with the rest of the train.

Up in front, William spoke with Sethmet. Justin caught her eye and halted his camel until Charlotte reached along side.

"Have I told you about Banning House?" he asked in a jovial tone, his blue eyes full of heat.

Distinctly uncomfortable with his clear intent, she realized that Justin had paid marked attention to her all along. But she'd been so preoccupied with Sethmet she hadn't paid much attention to anything else.

"Ah, yes. That would be nice," she said faintly. Not that she had much choice. With her stepbrother's words ringing in her ears, she forced a smile. Too bright, she thought with horror when Justin beamed back. William hadn't told her everything this morning--she was sure of it. Knowledge was power so George used to say when he'd arrived home after long meals at his club. Charlotte decided to ask William a few questions next time they were alone.

"Of course, my mother takes care of all the household details for me. She's always saying that it's time for me to settle down in England and raise a family."

All the more reason to avoid Justin even though he had a title. Of course, her one regret was that her marriage had remained childless even though George had visited her bed regularly. Charlotte stroked her gloved hand across the camel's coarse coat maintaining a placid smile all the while. Desire for a child was not a good enough reason to bind herself to Lord Banning, not since George had left her comfortably situated financially.

In the small silence that followed, Charlotte risked a quick glance at Justin. His eyes were fixed on her breasts. She froze and a small croak escaped before she could call it back. Justin raised his gaze to hers without apology. If anything, the heat in his eyes grew.

"You must know how I feel about you, Charlotte."

Charlotte cleared her throat, desperate to dislodge the escalating panic inside. She did not wish to lose her freedom again so soon. "I am still in mourning, my lord. Justin," she added hastily.

"Are you painting today, Charlotte?"

Never had an interruption been so welcome. Charlotte beamed at Sethmet. "Yes, I had thought watercolors."

"Do you not have instructions to issue? Other things to do?" Justin snapped. "We were having a private discussion."

"We have arrived," Sethmet said.

"Where? I see nothing but rocks," Justin snarled.

Charlotte scanned the horizon, seeing nothing but hills of terracotta rocks and the brilliant blue sky. Already the heat of the day made the cotton fabric of her lightest dress itch. They dismounted from their camels. Sethmet first and then he aided both Charlotte and Justin.

"These are the tombs of a pharaoh," Sethmet said, his expression serious. "They are well camouflaged to deter tomb robbers."

Charlotte witnessed something that looked like greed flash across Justin's face, but the expression vanished so rapidly, she wasn't sure.

"We'd better find something today," Justin snapped as he accepted a drink from a servant.

"We're all tired of chasing our tails," William said in an icy voice from behind them. "Let's hope today will be more successful."

Fury whipped through Sethmet. Inside, the cat snarled for freedom. Anger must have shown in his eyes because the Englishman took a step back.

Of course, they'd find nothing here. And they'd leave Patria Oasis with nothing more than the possessions they'd arrived with. That was his job as guardian for the pharaoh.

\* \* \* \*

"I believe you're taking us in circles," William snarled at Sethmet as they toured yet another site.

Sethmet hid his amusement by concentrating on the crumbling pillars of the old temple. Of course he was, but now was not the time to confess. "I gave you a list of sites in the area. You decided which ones you wanted to look at."

"I don't know why we bothered with a guide," Justin added. Red dust covered his white shirt and black trousers while sweat covered his face.

Sethmet thought he'd caught too much sun despite the top hat the man insisted on wearing. With his bright red cheeks and glittering eyes he appeared crazed. William, on the other hand looked like a desperate man. Sethmet thought the cat would do a little eavesdropping tonight before he met up with Charlotte. As always, his loins tightened at the thought of joining with Charlotte. The English woman was becoming important to him. Sethmet didn't know if he'd be able to let her leave Patria.

William stomped away from Sethmet, picked up a stone and tossed it at the end column. It smashed against the frieze of Egyptian Gods that decorated the columns then bounced off to hit a servant. William ignored the servant's pain and picked up another stone. "Nothing! There's fuckin' nothing here but empty ruins."

"Take care where you're aiming." Sethmet clenched his fists as he glared at William.

Charlotte stepped between them. "It's getting late, and we're all tired. I'm ready to go back to camp." She sent her stepbrother a measured glance then strode off to where her camel waited.

Amusement replaced Sethmet's fury while the two Englishmen started to mutter between themselves. Finally, they stomped over to their camels.

Sethmet followed more slowly, his mind on Charlotte. Every

time he'd tried to speak to her during the last two days either William or Justin had interrupted. Sethmet intended to meet up with her tonight--one way or the other.

\* \* \* \*

Charlotte retired to her tent earlier than normal to escape Justin's pointed attentions. No matter how politely she rebuffed him, he kept forcing his company on her. She stripped off most of her clothing and lay down on her pallet. Night approached rapidly, but it was still too early to meet up with Sethmet. Charlotte sighed and closed her eyes, thinking of the caracal. She hadn't seen it lately but sometimes, in the morning, there were paw prints near her tent. Instinctively, she scuffed them out so no one else would see, but it thrilled her to know the cat watched over her.

"My good luck charm," she whispered.

Charlotte picked up a pillow and hugged it to her chest. She wished it were Sethmet she held in her arms. An intolerable ache that only he could quench burned strongly within Charlotte. She stirred restlessly, rubbing her thighs together and clenching her womb tightly. The sweet pain only intensified. She'd have to wait for Sethmet. She closed her eyes and instead of picturing woolly sheep like her nanny had told her, she imagined graceful caracals. Charlotte started counting....

The night air chilled Charlotte, but her thick coat kept the worst of the frigid air at bay. Sand tickled beneath her paws. A soft cough alerted her to the presence of another. She turned, flicking her ears and scenting the breeze for signs of danger. Then she relaxed as a larger cat padded up to her and affectionately nuzzled her neck. Pleasure rippled through her body. The lynx nudged her sharply, leaped forward then halted to look back expectantly. Her ears twitched, and she bounded after the larger male. The wind whistled through her fur, the scents of the oasis registered before she gave into the sheer pleasure of running free.

"Charlotte." The loud whisper intruded on her joyous scamper along the sand. "Charlotte."

A hand traced down her cheek. Charlotte's eyes flew open. A dark shadow loomed over her. She opened her mouth to scream but a hand across her lips contained the sound.

"Shush. It's me."

"Sethmet?"

"Were you expecting someone else?"

"Of course not. But what if someone sees you? I thought we

were meeting at the cottage."

"Fret not, sweetheart. Everyone is asleep." Sethmet lifted her face for his kiss. One taste of his seductive mouth and every thought of protest faded. "Besides," he said slyly, "the idea of discovery--of being discovered brings a thrill all of its own."

"You don't need to worry about your reputation." Charlotte tried to sound stern but failed dismally. The wretched man was right. The risk of being discovered with a man in her tent had her all hot and bothered.

"We can go to the cottage if you wish, but why waste time?"

In the inky blackness of the tent, Charlotte couldn't see a thing. She wished it were light enough to see his face, just to see his expression and if his mouth and eyes matched the humor of his voice. He wasn't a man that smiled a lot, but when he did, it was compelling.

"You still have your stays on." Nimble fingers skimmed down her side to cup her bottom and pull her flush with his body--his erection. "And your drawers."

"You have more clothes on than me," Charlotte pointed out, even though she couldn't see to confirm.

Sethmet stood and moved away from her. Instantly, Charlotte wanted to recall her words and draw him closer.

The rustle of clothing sounded. Charlotte bit her lip, her heart jumping with acute expectation. Her hands went to the laces on her stays.

"No, let me," he murmured. "I like to undress you."

Charlotte's heart beat even faster. In the last few weeks she'd become addicted to waking up with a warm, naked body curled around her smaller frame. And when they weren't sleeping-- well, she'd become obsessed with making love with Sethmet as well. The thought made her pause. Returning to London and slotting into the old routines would present difficulties. Part of her rebelled at the idea of forcing herself into the old mold she used to inhabit. Yet, there was no alternative. Charlotte knew that too.

"What's wrong?"

"I was thinking about going home," Charlotte confessed.

"You want to go home?"

Charlotte hugged Sethmet fiercely then pulled away to lay her cheek against his naked chest. "Of course I don't! I love the freedom I have here. I like being independent and answering to no one." Charlotte paused, wrinkling her brow. That wasn't quite true. George had left William as executor of his estate. Whenever she wanted money, she had to obtain it from her stepbrother. And then there was the fact he wanted her to cultivate Justin's friendship. In truth, the freedom and independence she had at the moment was just an illusion. "In fact, I like it so much in Egypt I dreamed I was a caracal running across the sand."

## Chapter Five

"Didn't you sleep well last night? You look like a mouse dragged in by the housekeeper's cat." William's intense eyes seemed to pierce right through her. Charlotte fought to keep her composure. He couldn't know about her and Sethmet. And she wasn't surprised that she looked tired given that they'd slept little during the night.

"I'm fine," Charlotte said. No, he seemed preoccupied. It was something else troubling him. She glanced over her shoulder to see if anyone was within hearing range. A servant stoked the fire while another prepared bread rounds to cook on the hot embers. Justin sat on a chair outside his tent while his valet shaved him. In the distance, a camel called. No doubt, the camels were on their way from the oasis ready for the day's expedition.

"Justin has asked me for your hand in marriage, and I've accepted." William's blunt words hung in the air between them. They stared at each other. "Did you hear me?"

"I am not marrying Justin." The idea of the man touching her intimately sent a shiver of distaste surging through her body. Charlotte folded her arms across her chest in a protective manner. "I refuse."

William pulled a face and placed a hand on her shoulder. "At least think about it. Help me out of a jam."

"William, I don't want to marry again." Charlotte met and held her stepbrother's gaze, trying to make him understand. "Not straight away. I went from the schoolroom to marriage with no time in between. I want to enjoy my independence, and with the inheritance George left me, I have that luxury."

William glanced away, and Charlotte's heart skipped a beat. Was that guilt she'd seen? "What haven't you told me?"

"There's no money left."

Something in his tone raised alarm. "What ... what are you talking about?" One look at his stark face made her breath catch. "What have you done?"

William whirled to nail her with a glare. "You will marry Justin as soon as we return to England. The arrangements have been made, and I expect you to act civilly to him. He's a friend and soon, he'll be a member of the family." And before Charlotte had a chance to refute his orders, William stalked off.

"William, wait!" Servants looked up from their tasks to stare, but Charlotte didn't care. She chased after her stepbrother and grabbed him by the forearm. "Stop. You can't order me to marry Justin then walk off without explanations."

"You want explanations. I'll give you explanations. I have debts--debts that need paying."

Gaming debts according to the gossip in London. Charlotte eyed William uneasily. She'd thought he'd stopped gambling. Evidently not. "Use my money to pay them off. You're welcome to it. My wants are simple. I don't need much."

William's laugh raised the hairs at the back of her neck. Not amused and with a shade of bitterness, it sent her stomach swooping with fear.

"What have you done?" she whispered.

"Your money has gone. Every penny."

"The house in London. The land?" Growing horror brought a stammer to her voice. It couldn't be as bad as it sounded. It couldn't.

"Mortgaged to the hilt," William confirmed. Not a trace of remorse showed on his pale face. His eyes were unrepentant. "If only we could find the treasure."

"You could have told me."

"You couldn't have done anything," he pointed out cruelly. "George gave me authority over you and your assets. I have used them as I saw fit."

Charlotte's legs trembled so much she knew she had to sit before she fell. Somehow, she found herself over in the area of the campsite they used to dine. The canvas shade flapped in the gentle breeze. Charlotte stepped under the shade and fell onto a wooden chair. Without money she was powerless, dependent on her stepbrother's largesse. Charlotte shot a resentful glare at William. He'd manipulated and used her to further his own means. Even though he'd confirmed he searched for treasure, she hadn't believed he was an unscrupulous tomb robber who removed every valuable from the dead, leaving nothing to comfort them in the afterworld. The scientific papers he'd spoken of were probably fiction too. Either that or he stole them.

Tears formed at the back of her eyes and a lump of regret and intense sorrow threatened to close up her throat. Independence for Charlotte Webster was nothing but a dream now. She'd have to marry--it was either that or starve.

William stormed over to join her. He sat opposite her and gestured for a servant to pour coffee for both of them. When the servant had left he quirked a brow at her in silent mockery. If William expected her to follow blindly wherever he led then he was in for a shock.

A sudden thought occurred, and she turned her narrowed eyes on him. "If I refuse to marry Justin what happens?"

"Ah, my dear." William reached across the table to grip her chin with a cruel pinch of fingers. "But you will marry Justin. I've given my word, and a man's word is sacrosanct."

Charlotte jerked from his touch, the burn of temper fuelling her determination. Somehow she had to resist her stepbrother's efforts to tie her to Lord Banning. "The camels have arrived for today's expedition." When in doubt change the subject. Besides, she needed time to think, time to plan.

"This discussion is not over," William warned.

"I'm a widow capable of making my own decisions." Charlotte didn't wait for his reply but rose and made a dignified exit.

Sethmet appeared from behind the supply tent. "What's wrong?"

Embarrassing tears flooded her eyes. She wiped them away angrily and wondered why nothing was ever easy. "Nothing," she murmured. "I'm looking forward to today's sightseeing. I'm almost ready. I just need to collect my hat and drawing materials." Charlotte turned away before Sethmet could comment on her distress. Her attempts to hide her emotions in the English way had failed dismally. Tears started to fall in earnest. Charlotte quickened her pace. The irony of the situation didn't escape her especially since she'd been congratulating herself on her independence. In one strike, every scrap of freedom she'd possessed had disappeared.

"Charlotte, what is it?" Sethmet curled his hand around her upper arm and dug in his heels so she had to stop her retreat. Gently, he turned her to face him, his face a picture of concern. "Let me help you."

Charlotte shook her head. "I ... I've had some bad news," she murmured finally. Although she treasured the time she spent with Sethmet, she'd known it had to end. Charlotte had to stand alone--there was no one else to rely on. "There's nothing anyone can do to help."

"You there!"

The fury in William's voice made Charlotte jump.

"Our equipment tent has been broken into. Line up the servants. I want to question them."

Sethmet inclined his head then stalked off to arrange an immediate meeting. He resisted the urge to comfort Charlotte. Something had happened. He'd seen her talking with her stepbrother and suspected William had done something to upset her. It didn't surprise him. The man was a selfish bastard. Greedy too. Sethmet knew William and Justin had been leaving camp late at night to check out sights he hadn't taken them to yet.

Sethmet's mouth lifted in a sneer. He wagered the two men wouldn't like the surprise he had in store for them. The minute the English men had started searching on their own they'd crossed the line. Sethmet wasn't about to let his family die at the hands of the pharaoh's curse.

The servants stopped their chores and milled about the center of the campsite in an uneasy silence. Sethmet stood in full sunlight, his eyes watchful while William and Justin consulted in a private huddle.

Charlotte hurried off to her tent. She disappeared inside, but her soft sobs were clearly audible to him. Sethmet had to force himself to hold ground, not to go to her and offer comfort. It was difficult when he felt as though his heart was being ripped out.

"Who sorted the equipment and put it away last night?" William strode up and down the line of servants, glaring at each of them until they shuffled uneasily. "Answer me. Who put away the equipment?"

Several of the men eyed each other uneasily before one stepped forward. He muttered in a low voice.

"Speak up, man," Justin snapped.

Sethmet stepped forward, ready to take the brunt of the men's anger. "He doesn't speak English. Let me question him."

The quiet sobs continued to distract Sethmet, making it difficult to do his job and concentrate on protecting the pharaoh. Sethmet could smell her flowery scent on the breeze. His hands clenched and unclenched at his sides. Despite the need to comfort, he didn't have the right. Their worlds were oceans apart. He had to remember that.

"Question him," Justin demanded, breaking into Sethmet's unhappy thoughts.

William thrust his face close to the man who'd stepped forward. His cheeks and neck had turned bright red with anger and a nervous tic throbbed in his jaw. "Ask him what he did with the barrel of gun powder."

Sethmet met William's anger with a hard stare. "What would a party of tourists want with barrels of gun powder?" Tomb robbers, he thought in disgust, his suspicions confirmed yet again. "If you're looking for treasure, you're at the wrong oasis. There is no treasure here."

"I have information that says otherwise," William spat, "and I don't intend to leave without finding it."

"Despite the cursed bad luck you seem to be having? The death of a man last week. The disappearance of equipment. It's true that others have sought treasure at Patria, but they have left broken men. I don't know why men insist on coming here. There is no treasure, only death to those who search."

"Ask the man what happened to the gun powder," William insisted, not backing down despite being caught out in a lie. Sethmet fired off the question. The man shifted uneasily, but Sethmet felt it was because William was so incensed. He nodded when the man finished then ran his gaze across the rest of the men assembled for William's interrogation.

A loud scream rent the air. The servants burst into excited jabber. Sethmet heard the word, curse mentioned more than once. Another scream galvanized Sethmet to action.

Charlotte.

He sprinted to Charlotte's tent. Just as he arrived, Charlotte lifted the tent flap and stepped outside.

"Charlotte, you're all right," Sethmet said with relief. He had to forcibly remind himself not to embrace her in public. Not touching her was difficult but seeing the dried tear tracks on her face was even harder.

"Who screamed?" Charlotte said. Unhappiness hovered in her blue eyes. "Is someone hurt?"

Sethmet glanced away and hoped he hadn't given his concern for Charlotte away with his mad sprint to her tent. He suspected her stepbrother would make things difficult if he knew of their relationship. "I don't know. I thought it was you."

A third scream, long and high with panic, directed them to a petrified woman servant.

"What is it?" Sethmet said. His sharp tone seemed to pierce the woman's panic. With a trembling finger, she pointed. Sethmet saw the pottery flagon she'd dropped in her terror. Wet sand surrounded the vessel while a short distance away two scorpions scuttled across a pair of sandaled feet. The soles of the feet pointed upward as if the man were buried head first in the sand, his feet the only visible part of his body.

Charlotte came to stand at his side. "Do you know who it is?"

Sethmet shook his head. "Dig him out," he directed several of the milling servants.

"All this is a distraction," William snarled. "I will find out who stole my equipment, and when I do that man will suffer."

Sethmet squatted beside the buried man. He caught a whiff of gunpowder. Standing, he strode around the man. The scent grew stronger. "There's your gunpowder," Sethmet said pointing to the thin black trail that led from the dead man into the desert.

William cursed and whirled about. "You there! Go and get a spade. We can still use the powder if we collect it up again.

A gust of wind appeared from nowhere, whistling and whipping up galabiyyas around the servant's legs, sending sand and gunpowder swirling through the air.

The wind disappeared as quickly as it appeared. And the silence that remained was so complete and unexpected, it raised hairs at the back of Sethmet's neck. The pharaoh. Even from the tomb, his spirit aided Sethmet and his family in their task.

The servants glanced at each other in uneasy silence.

"The curse," one of the more daring whispered.

"This is ridiculous," Justin drawled. "I say we go on with the day's excursion."

"We must do something for this poor man first," Charlotte protested.

"He's nothing to do with us. Come, Charlotte." William crooked his arm and waited with clear impatience.

Sethmet caught Charlotte's hesitation and liked her for the sensitivity she showed for a man she didn't know.

"No go," one of the servants cried. He broke from the group and ran off without looking back.

"Come back here," William ordered. He turned to Sethmet. "Do something. You're in charge of labor. Get them ready for departure."

The fury in William's voice made the servants edge away. The wind whistled across the open sands and a final blast sent the sand flying through the air.

The curse.

Eyes rolled in fear, showing the whites, and as one, the servants turned and raced for the oasis.

"Wait, damn you!" William hollered.

Justin shrugged. "Let them go," he said as he carefully inspected his fingernails. "We don't need them. There are other ways."

"We can visit this new site without the servants," William said.

"It is a long journey which will require two nights away from your camp." Sethmet tried to gauge how hard to dissuade them. The two Englishmen were determined to visit the site they'd heard about, but he didn't want to refuse in case they went without him. The site was uncomfortably close to the pharaoh's tomb. Sethmet wanted to go along so he was on hand to act should the men discover the tomb. Yes, there were traps laid for the unwary explorer but they weren't foolproof.

"Do you think the journey is wise?" Charlotte asked. "Without servants it will certainly be difficult."

"You don't have to go," Justin pointed out.

William glared at his friend. "She can hardly stay here alone without a chaperon."

Sethmet watched the two men as they silently communicated. William continued to glare until suddenly the scowl transformed into a grin. He didn't like that smirk. It boded ill for Charlotte. That settled things. He couldn't leave her on her own with the two men.

"If you are willing to wait until tomorrow I will arrange supplies and servants for the expedition to Zuweila Oasis."

The men glanced at each other and seemed to come to a decision.

"Tomorrow will be suitable. Charlotte, come," William said.

Charlotte stiffened. Her beautiful mouth firmed, and she cast a beseeching look at Sethmet.

Sethmet's lungs constricted. He wished he knew what was going on. Although he'd patrolled the camp as much as he was able, he hadn't discovered evidence of a traitor until the pharaoh had pointed the men out. Now it was up to him to discover if the traitors worked alone or there were more in the camp. He must concentrate on protecting the pharaoh not his lust for Charlotte. Even so, Sethmet gave her an encouraging nod, trying to tell Charlotte with his eyes that he would watch over her and keep harm away. Icy cold slid over his face then as another thought occurred. If Charlotte had deceived him and she was in league with her stepbrother then there might be nothing he could do to save her from the pharaoh's wrath. The notion was like a swift kick in the gut, and just as painful.

## Chapter Six

Night fell rapidly, and Sethmet paced, waiting for the camp to settle. Impatience got the better of him and he dragged off his clothes. After thrusting them under a tree at the edge of the oasis, he let the change take him. Tendons and sinew twisted, bones lengthened and his jaw transformed. The pain of the change balanced on the fine edge of pleasure. Sethmet shuddered, the rush of enhanced senses a rich sensual experience that he never tired of. The cool night breeze ruffled his fur as he padded across the sand to the English camp. Without conscious thought, Sethmet prowled straight to Charlotte's tent. Her soft breathing both reassured Sethmet and called to him. The desire to go to her, shift into human form and sink his cock deep into her warmth nipped at his self-control, dividing his loyalties. Sethmet's chest rumbled in a low growl of conflict. His tail swished in agitation before his loyalty to the pharaoh and his family over ruled his heart, and he turned to patrol the camp. His gut told him more danger lurked. Learning the identity of the dead servant had yielded few clues since the man had been a loner from another oasis. Men often left the caravans to take a break at Patria Oasis. That was the problem--at any given time, there were many strangers present. Sethmet knew most were honest men but some, who had no loyalty to his family, had hidden motives and it was these men who presented the challenge. Perhaps he should let gossip do his job for him--let the servants' superstitions and natural fear spread alarm. That would work, and yet, Charlotte would leave when her stepbrother left. He'd lose her. Sethmet paused to scent the air.

Lilacs.

Charlotte.

Sethmet found himself outside his lover's tent, his heart jumping and every sense attuned to each move or sigh she made. He snarled low and deep and determinedly padded over to William's tent. A lamp burned inside sending shadows playing across the canvas. Two silhouettes were outlined and the tinkle of glasses told Sethmet that William and his companion were drinking. His ears twitched as he raised his head to the breeze. The peaty fumes told him they drank whiskey.

Sethmet stalked closer, sitting quietly as he settled in to listen.

"I tell you the man is stalling us."

Sethmet's lip curled in disdain. Of course, he was bloody stalling them. With luck, the boiling temperatures of mid-season would drive them homeward. But then again, perhaps not. William was looking increasingly desperate, his temper uncertain and boiling over at the slightest infringement.

"I have the map," William countered. "It's not perfect but there are not many more sites to check. Once we find the site with the two hills and the small temple of the cat, then we know where to commence the dig."

"I don't know why you didn't ask the guide straight out. We're paying him enough."

"I did." William's tone was sharp as if his temper balanced on a pinnacle. "The man told me there were many temples dedicated to the cat around here. Damn me if he wasn't correct. All the sites we've visited so far have had some of the features on the map but not all."

A glass clinked against a bottle, and Sethmet heard the whiskey sloshing into a glass.

"Ask the man for more details. Offer him more money," Justin said.

"I have. He's frightened. This damned curse and the death of his friend has put the fear of God into him."

"What about the guide?"

"The damned man is too full of himself, if you ask me. He's a bloody servant and he acts as though he's a lord. I asked him early on."

"What did he say?"

"He said that while the money I offered was an attractive incentive, he couldn't accept. The bloody man had the effrontery to say he'd lived in Patria all his life and knew of no treasure. It simply didn't exist so I would be foolish to pay him."

Justin barked out a laugh. "Upstart."

Interesting, Sethmet thought. But it didn't help him in weeding out the traitor.

"Have you talked to Charlotte? Will she accept my offer?"

The lustful note made Sethmet stiffen. Had that been the cause of her upset earlier today? His ears signaled his disquiet, his rush of jealousy. Sethmet stood and prowled a circuit around the tent in an effort to soothe his rising agitation.

"She has some silly notion of enjoying her independence," William drawled. "But don't worry, she'll come around."

"Did you highlight the monetary incentives?"

"Oh, yes. Believe me, I pointed out every single benefit to Charlotte."

William sounded determined to marry Charlotte off to his friend. The idea of Charlotte being married to and sleeping in the same bed as the Englishman ratcheted his jealousy up another notch.

To hell with it. He'd learned most of what he needed to know. It was as if a giant clock ticked away the time before Charlotte left and she was lost to him. Sethmet padded to her tent and after a quick glance to check for prying eyes, he shifted to human form. Then, he untied the laced door and crawled inside the tent, desperate to exert his claim on Charlotte.

\* \* \* \*

Firm masculine lips caressed hers. Charlotte's eyes snapped open, her heart galloping, not in terror but in expectation. "Sethmet," she murmured arching against his solid, muscular body. Her hands squeezed masculine buttocks. Naked, masculine buttocks. A laugh bubbled from her lips. "Where are your clothes?"

"I was in a hurry. I wanted to speed things up."

Charlotte's heart pumped out two rapid beats before she caught her breath. Already, moisture gathered between her legs in readiness for his possession. Charlotte pushed against his chest, struggling to free her arms from her voluminous cotton nightgown. Skin. She wanted to rub against him like a cat. Charlotte ached. She fought to free herself from the constricting cloth and managed to trap a lock of hair. A pained cry escaped.

"Hush," Sethmet soothed in his smoky, accented English that never failed to heighten her arousal.

Minutes later, she was free and running her hands down his flanks. "Now," she urged. "Hurry."

Sethmet turned, flipping over on his back and lifting her at the same time so she straddled him. "Ride me," he murmured. "I want to see your breasts and watch your face while you come."

Charlotte thrilled to his sensual words. She laughed breathlessly, while her hand cupped his testes and then his cock, feeling the shape and the strength of him.

"It's dark. You can't see me when it's this dark," she whispered, positioning his erection at the entrance to her womb. She sank down, savoring the tight fit, the stretching, the promise of the joining.

"I can see you. I have very good eyesight." And to prove it, he said, "You have a small brown mole on your right breast."

She sank to the hilt and paused to torture both of them. A ripple swept through her, urging her to hasten the pace.

Sethmet gripped her hips with both hands. "Ride me, Charlotte. I need you."

Charlotte lifted then sank back down. To be needed--that was special. No one had ever needed her before. She quickened her pace, rising and falling until they both gasped. Ripples of pleasure streaked through her body. Below her, Sethmet stiffened. Deep in her womb, his seed gushed. Charlotte slumped forward, and Sethmet closed his arms around her, holding tight.

She closed her eyes trying to hold onto the pleasure and the closeness. Instead, shadows intruded. She would have to return to England and marry--probably Justin. No wonder, her dreams were of cats running free in the desert. Charlotte craved a life she would never have, and it had spilled over into her dreams.

\* \* \* \*

When Sethmet arrived at camp to head the overnight expedition to Zuweila Oasis he found the place in an uproar. A group of servants formed a tight knit group near the cooking fire. Steam rose from a pot suspended over the glowing embers, but that was all that had occurred in the way of breakfast preparations. William screamed orders, punctuating them with waving arms and insults but everyone ignored him. Instead, the servants cast frightened looks over their shoulders and muttered between themselves.

Sethmet bit down on his tongue to suppress his grin. He had a fair idea what the fuss was about.

"About time you arrived," Justin snarled. "Tell the natives to get to work."

Sethmet bowed, his lips quivering as he battled the need to laugh out loud. "Certainly, my lord."

Sethmet strode forward and the servants parted, fanning out in a semi-circle around him. "Why have you stopped preparing for the journey to the oasis?"

The men fidgeted and stared at their sandaled feet.

It was clear none of them were willing to speak first so Sethmet scanned the faces and picked. "Bahar?"

Footsteps, the swish of stiff fabric and the scent of lilacs told Sethmet that Charlotte approached. Despite his worries about taking the Englishmen so near the pharaoh's tomb, Sethmet was looking forward to spending more time with Charlotte.

"What's going on?" Charlotte's soft voice sent a frisson of awareness through Sethmet.

He cleared his throat. "That's what I'm trying to find out. Bahar?"

"Ghost cat," the man whispered, glancing over his shoulder as if he expected the mythical beast to pounce on him.

"A cat?" Charlotte stepped close enough that Sethmet could feel the heat from her body. "What did it look like?"

Bahar paled. "Bad omen, missy. Not see cat. Foot prints all around camp." A shiver swept through his thin frame. "Bad, bad omen."

The muttering started again.

"What's the man talking about?" Justin demanded.

"He's right about footprints," William muttered. "They're all around my tent--as big as my hand. They look like cat prints to me."

"There are big cats around here," Sethmet said, smiling at Charlotte. "And of course, the cat is a sacred animal in Egypt. There are many temples dedicated to the cat."

"I don't care about bloody legends," William snapped. "I want to get moving."

The man's sweaty face and red cheeks showed clear strain. It wouldn't take much more to push him over the edge. Sethmet offered a placating smile. "And you will," he promised. "Just leave it to me."

It took all of Sethmet's persuasion to get the workers to carry out their normal duties let alone prepare for the expedition.

"The ghost cat seeks prey," one muttered, his arms flapping so much he reminded Sethmet of a stork trying to fly. The wind aided the vision in his mind's eye as the man's cotton galabiyya snapped in the persistent breeze. Sethmet lifted his head. A storm was coming--he smelled it in the wind. The pharaoh was agitated and showing it with the powers he had at his command.

Never fear, my pharaoh, Sethmet pledged silently. I will keep you safe--no matter what.

It was a dangerous game he played since a cornered man was a desperate foe. William appeared increasingly edgy. Justin, on the other hand, remained the arrogant Englishman ordering the workers around, sending them on countless trips to his tent for items he simply couldn't do without.

Finally, they were ready. The workers still squawked like agitated birds.

"The ghost cat will come. We will die in our sleep," one intoned.

Sethmet resorted to guile. He gestured them together to listen. "It is broad daylight," he said. "If the cat follows we will see for we travel across the flat where there are no dunes."

They digested the information.

"This is true."

"The master is right. We will be safer if we leave the oasis."

Several of them nodded agreement.

"Good," Sethmet said. "Then I will start loading the camels." A smile hovered on his lips as he turned away. He wondered what they'd think if they knew the ghost cat traveled with the camel train and would stalk the campsite tonight.

* * * *

Charlotte thought the servants seemed happier as they set up camp for the night. The man stirring a stew over the fire hummed while another squatted by the fire and tapped on a goatskin drum. All was not well, however with William and Justin who spoke in low undertones.

"Is there a problem?" she asked, finally having enough of being ignored. It wasn't as if she could talk to Sethmet even though she preferred his company. The power her stepbrother had over her frightened Charlotte. He'd already gambled away her money. Charlotte suspected there might be worse in store since they kept glancing at her. "What is wrong?" she repeated. "Do I have a smut on my nose?"

"Of course not, my dear." Justin stepped over to her and claimed possession of her hand. He pressed a lingering kiss to her wrist. "We were merely discussing business. Nothing to worry your pretty head about."

If she'd worried earlier she might have prevented William spending her inheritance. Charlotte reclaimed her hand and resisted the urge to wipe it on her gown. "It's getting chilly," she said. Outside the U of white rock formations protecting the campsite, the wind whistled, sending fine white sand swirling into the air. Charlotte shivered. The white desert was a lonely, ghostly place. "I think I'll get my shawl."

A shout rang out to announce dinner was ready.

Charlotte exhaled with relief when the meal finished and she could escape to her tent. William and Justin continued to speak quietly between themselves. Charlotte wasn't sure she wanted to know what they were discussing, but she still picked up several words. Treasure and marriage among them. She stood, deciding she'd had enough. "Good night."

William and Justin broke off their conversation. Justin stood and Charlotte moved quickly so the table sat between them.

"Good night, my dear."

Charlotte nodded and hurried off. The man made her feel distinctly uncomfortable because of the way he'd starting eyeing her as though she were a tasty slice of roast beef. Charlotte hurried away before Justin decided to escort her to her tent.

She peered through the gloom, trying to see if Sethmet was waiting for her. To her acute disappointment, he was busy instructing the servants. She heard his low, husky tones and sighing, stepped inside her tent flap. Probably for the best, she thought. The aches in her body from the camel ride seemed bone deep. It was either that or the tropical climate was disagreeing with her, and she had caught the ague or some other tropical disease. Charlotte frowned in annoyance, knowing she didn't have time to get sick. It would leave her vulnerable and that was a situation she disliked heartily.

Charlotte undressed slowly, the persistent aching in her bones making her wince when she raised her arms. She felt her forehead in the way her governess used to when Charlotte was pretending she was sick. A soft chuckle escaped at the memory. Fishing and exploring the woods with the neighboring children had seemed much more fun than practicing her French and needlework. Nothing wrong with her temperature, she decided. Perhaps she would feel better in the morning. Charlotte drew her nightgown over her head. A shaft of pain shot the length of her body, and a moan squeezed past her lips.

Charlotte lay down on the pallet, but the noises from the

campsite seemed louder than usual. She could hear the low murmur of William and Justin talking together, probably in another huddle. Dishes clacked together loudly and the persistent bang bang of the drum reverberated inside her head. A man spoke in their native tongue, the voice familiar and reassuring. Sethmet, she thought, her heart aching in time with the throb that shook her body. Suddenly, her breasts and nipples felt tender and swollen, the weight of her nightgown too much for her to bear. She shifted fitfully, trying to relieve the ache but it intensified, transforming into excitement. Charlotte twisted and turned until her nightgown worked up baring her legs to the air. Charlotte's heart pounded, her mouth dry and her body on fire. Where was Sethmet when she needed him? She moved yet again and an arrow of heat shot to her core. Unbidden, her hand glided across her belly then lower to tangle in her pubic hair. She swallowed, desire overwhelming her. Tempting. Her hand crept lower, sliding across slick feminine folds. A jolt of pure, heady sensation arced through her body. The gentle rotation of a finger drew a moan from her tight throat. Molten fire licked through her veins, yet she felt empty and alone.

*She wanted Sethmet.*

Her finger stroked, massaged, building the sensation, until her pulse raced and urgent hunger jerked her hips.

*Sethmet, where are you?*

Suddenly, unsteady footsteps outside her tent stilled her hand. Charlotte bolted upright on the pallet. The footsteps halted outside her tent and a light shone, casting shadows against the canvas. Her stomach clenched tight. Sethmet? Harsh breathing and a whiff of tobacco and snuff answered her silent question. Not Sethmet. He never brought a lamp. A flicker of apprehension swept through Charlotte when the ties that kept the flap closed were tugged open. The flap lifted and even in the darkness, Charlotte could identify the man.

## Chapter Seven

"What are you doing in here? Wait!" Charlotte held up a hand in front of her body. "Don't come any closer. Leave now, and we'll forget this ever happened."

Justin held his lamp up so he could see Charlotte more clearly.

"But my dear, that's no way to greet your future husband." He stalked closer. Setting the lamp aside, he grabbed her, planting a punishing kiss on her lips.

Alarm yielded swiftly to anger. Charlotte softened her body, melting against his chest. "Oh, Justin," she cooed, batting her lashes at him.

The man puffed up like a proud peacock. "I knew you'd see sense," he drawled. "I need an heir straight away. No sense wasting time."

"Oh, Justin." Charlotte sighed and simpered up at him. *Pompous toad.*

Justin let her go and stepped back, his gaze traveling the length of her body. "You are very beautiful, my dear. Of course, I know you were married for some time. It's possible you may not be able to bear children. I must have an heir."

Charlotte's anger almost choked her. She took a slow, deep breath, her eyes narrowing. "So, you would like to spend time with me before we return to England."

Justin advanced on her, a hot look in his blue eyes. "I'm glad we understand each other, my dear."

Charlotte forced a wide smile. *Come a little closer, Lord Banning.* She slid her hands down her hips, holding the fabric of her nightgown against her body so her shape showed through.

"I'm so glad you're being sensible about this." Justin reached for her, and Charlotte raised her head. She heard the faint sound of footsteps outside the tent, but then the moment she'd hoped for happened. His eyes slid shut and she struck, jerking her knee upward into his groin with all the force she could muster. He dropped to the ground like a felled tree giving a pained groan that came from deep in his chest. Charlotte stared down at him with disgust and resisted the urge to kick him while he was down. If her bones hadn't ached so badly she just might have.

A growl sounded just outside the tent.

"Kitty?" Pleasure suffused Charlotte. She rushed toward the flap and lifted it to see the snarling face of the lynx, its ears twitching in agitation. The tense set left her shoulders because instinctively, she knew she was safe from Lord Banning now. The caracal turned and loped off then stopped to glance back as if he waited for something--something that he wanted her to do.

Charlotte glanced over her shoulder then without another thought limped from the tent determined to find somewhere else to sleep tonight. Kitty would help her find somewhere safe. She hurried to catch up to the cat, every muscle throbbing, each of her bones sore and tender.

The cat paused as if to make sure she followed. It picked up its speed, breaking into a trot, leaving the camp behind. Charlotte tried to follow. She stumbled, a wave of nausea sweeping through her belly. Her heart thundered. She had to go with the cat. She had to follow. For some reason, it seemed imperative that she kept the caracal in sight. Charlotte struggled to her feet but pain speared through her. A whimper sounded, soft and forlorn in the darkness. The agony suffused her body from the top of her head to her bare feet. She scrunched her toes into the sand, and her hands clenched as she rode out the pain. Unexpectedly, the sensation changed. A wave of pure, heart-rending pleasure poured over her in waves. She balanced on a knife-edge, sometimes pleasure and sometimes pain. Her skin glowed hot and sensitive as though it might pop and it felt as though her bones were being stretched on a rack. Her cotton nightgown was an unbearable weight on her sensitive skin. With shaky hands, she drew it off and let the breeze cool her heated body. Another sudden wave of pain sent Charlotte to her knees. The sand beneath her hands and feet sent a whimsical notion through her confused head. Sounds bombarded her: a man snoring, the crackle of the campfire, the sleepy yawn of the man who tended the camels and the soft snarl of the cat. The urge to run was a siren song--it lured her much like the cat drew her awe.

A soft growl attracted her attention. The caracal stood in front of her with its ears twitching and tail swishing. He padded closer and rubbed his head against her shoulder. His rough tongue licked across her cheek before he padded away then turned back to wait.

Charlotte desperately wanted to follow. She crawled, tensing, expecting pain, but it didn't come. Confused, she glanced down to see she'd changed into a cat much like Kitty.

A dream, she thought hazily.

Charlotte moved smoothly after Kitty and then broke into a run, barreling into his muscled shoulder. He let out a surprised grunt, gave her an affectionate nudge then swatted her with his paw.

Growling, she raced off, stopping abruptly to see if he followed. He did. Kitty loped easily at her side, keeping pace as she ran and ran and ran. The freedom was like a heady tonic. The wind ruffled her fur as she ran while her sharp eyes picked up small creatures that scuttled away at their approach. Gradually, her pace slowed, her sides rising and falling with exhaustion. Kitty kept pace the whole time and slowed when she did. He licked her muzzle, and her face, rubbing against her until she quivered. His eyes glowed as he gently shunted her in another direction.

Different sounds--human noises--made her hesitate even though she couldn't see the camp yet because of a rocky outcrop. The scent reached her at the same time: men snoring, their sweaty bodies tossing and turning as they slept. Stealthy footsteps wandered through the camp. Without warning, Kitty slammed into her shoulder, forcing her to stop.

Startled, she froze. Kitty prowled in front of her. A mist shimmered around the cat and before her stunned eyes, he transformed. Seconds later, Sethmet stood before her, proudly naked.

"Change, Charlotte," he murmured, his voice low and seductive. "Concentrate. Picture legs and arms in your mind, and the change will happen."

Charlotte fixed on his words and concentrated as Sethmet instructed. Pain tinged with pleasure rippled across her skin. She shuddered inwardly as her body transformed back to human form. Sethmet caught her close when she stumbled. Chest pressed to breast, and Sethmet stroked her back, murmuring in a low, soothing tone.

"I'm sure you have questions," he murmured.

Charlotte lifted her head to study him closely. "You're Kitty. That wasn't a dream."

Sethmet scowled. "I am *not* a kitty. Come. I'll grab my clothes, and we'll talk in your tent."

"What about my nightgown? And what if Justin is still in my tent?"

"I'll kill him," Sethmet snarled. "You are mine."

Charlotte opened her mouth to hotly dispute his ownership then snapped it closed again. Perhaps there was something in his claim. And he was right--she had questions. *Lots of them.*

She had changed into a cat. A caracal. She'd run free just as she'd dreamed during the last few weeks.

"I might exact my revenge anyway," he muttered, his eyes glowing hotly as his gaze wandered across her bare breasts. "He touched you." Raw, savage anger burned in him, and she had no doubt Justin was in extreme danger.

Charlotte placed a placating hand on Sethmet's breastbone. "I dealt with him myself. He won't forget it in a hurry. What just happened? I turned into a cat just like Kitty."

Sethmet glared. "Don't call me that."

Charlotte ran her hand across his shoulder then down his biceps. She stood on tiptoes and pressed a kiss to his lips. Instantly, Charlotte forgot every one of her questions. Sethmet's arms came around her and he took over the kiss, ravaging her mouth. Tongues dueled, mouths mated, and his cock swelled against her stomach.

"My mate," Sethmet said, cupping her bottom and lifting Charlotte so her legs parted and curled around his waist. His hands stroked in a long and luxurious stroke down her back while he nuzzled at the smooth skin of her throat. Sethmet led Charlotte into a world where sensation ruled, and he was everything to her.

His hand probed slick feminine folds, strumming her swollen clit, driving her higher. Deeper. One finger slipped inside and thrust slowly. Charlotte trembled, as he feasted on her mouth and pumped his finger in and out. A violent spasm of pleasure streaked the length of her body, making her gasp.

"Harder," she moaned.

"Not with my finger," he said, slipping his finger from her tight channel. "I want to feel you clutching at my cock." Holding her firmly, he placed his erection at her entrance and slid home, stretching her, filling her. He gripped her hips with both hands, his strength evident from the ease in which he lifted her so effortlessly. The spicy tang of arousal surrounded them. Flesh slapped against flesh. Frissons of excitement pounded Charlotte, and her whole body shuddered on the cusp of orgasm.

"Touch your breasts," he ordered. "Pretend it's my hand caressing you. Tug your nipples."

Charlotte hesitated then did as he instructed, gliding her hands across her breasts then plucking at her nipples. Each tug sent a corresponding twinge surging to her clit. Sethmet thrust harder. Quicker. The simmering pleasure gathered momentum growing bigger, pushing her higher until it spilled over. Hard pulsing waves swept through her womb, gripping Sethmet's cock. Sethmet groaned, thrust again. Once. Twice. Then he stilled, clutching her tightly to his chest.

He dipped his head, pressing his forehead against hers. "You're my mate, Charlotte."

The possessive tone made her smile. "Maybe." When she received some answers.

A growl vibrated deep in his chest. "Time to talk." Sethmet separated their bodies and let her slide down his body to stand on her own feet. He clasped her hand and started for camp. "My family comes from a long line of shape shifters. We are guardians. We protect the pharaoh's tomb from people like your stepbrother."

"But that doesn't explain what happened to me tonight. Will it happen again?"

"Would you like it to?" he countered, his expression telling her nothing.

Charlotte thought of the restrictions she faced in her everyday life with the ton. The freedom she'd experienced since being in Patria Oasis had made her realize what a pointless and aimless an existence she led in London. And meeting Sethmet had opened her eyes in regards to the men she met in the ballrooms and private parties. They were like plain copies or imitations of the real thing.

"I ... yes." Charlotte nodded her head. "Yes, I'd like to run free again."

"With the secret of the cat comes responsibility." Sethmet met her gaze and held it, his dark eyes serious and a trifle grim. "There are disadvantages."

"What disadvantages?"

Sethmet studied Charlotte closely. His heart still pounded from their lovemaking. He had climaxed yet he wanted to repeat the experience again. But most of all he wanted to know what Charlotte intended to do. He loved her--she was his mate, but he didn't wish to hold her like a caged bird, not if she didn't wish to remain in the oasis. "Do you wish to return to your home in England?" Great. Smooth. Very polished. But he waited anxiously for her reply, admitting the truth to himself even though he didn't say it. He'd rather cut out his heart than let Charlotte leave.

When she shivered, he said, "My clothes are under the rock to your right. Put my shirt on."

Charlotte stooped to tug the clothes from underneath the rock. She handed the trousers to Sethmet and watched while he stepped into them.

Sethmet couldn't restrain his grin. His brows rose. "My turn to watch now."

A gun blasted through the silence of the night.

Sethmet started to run. "Stay there," he shouted over his shoulder. Seconds after his order, he heard footsteps behind him.

"I am not staying put," she muttered.

"Someone's shooting in the camp. You must keep safe."

"What about you?" Charlotte demanded.

Sethmet rounded the base of the white outcrop at a sprint. The blood moon peeped from behind black clouds casting a ghostly crimson glow over the tents. Servants milled around in terror, jabbering at the top of their voices.

"What's going on?" Sethmet demanded.

"A gun!" One of the servants pointed at the cook.

"He shoot," another said.

The wind roared and whistled through the campsite. Canvas snapped and galabiyyas flapped wildly. Then, the wind stilled. An uncanny silence left the men staring at each other uneasily.

"The ghost cat," someone whispered.

"I heard gun fire. What the devil is going on?" William's bed cap sat askew on his head as he glared around the terrified servants.

"That's what I'm trying to find out," Sethmet said. He watched Charlotte dart behind William's tent and head for her tent.

Justin limped up to them. "What's the melee about?"

Sethmet's eyes narrowed on the pale and drawn Englishman. If he had his way the man wouldn't have walked from his tent.

"The ghost cat. He is controlling the wind," a servant said.

"But not the guns," William snapped, holding up his lamp and shining it around the circle of faces. "Who fired the gun?"

"What is going on? Why is everyone awake?" Charlotte said.

Sethmet turned in her direction, willing her to step next to him so he could keep her safe. She smiled faintly, as though she could read his mind, and sashayed up to him, stopping beside him. Sethmet exhaled slowly, feeling easier now she was here. And clothed again.

"I thought I heard a gun," Charlotte added.

William spun away. "I'm going back to bed."

Two shots rang out in quick succession. A servant dropped to the ground, and a high-pitched scream echoed through the campsite.

"Ghost cat!"

The servants scattered in all directions, fleeing as though they ran for their lives. The injured servant crawled behind a tent.

The wind picked up again, the mournful wail sounding eerily like a man crying.

"Come back here, dammit!" William roared.

"The shots are coming from over there," Justin said.

"It's the cook," Charlotte whispered in his ear. "Can you see him? He's still got the gun."

"I see him," Sethmet murmured, wrapping his arm around Charlotte's waist and discreetly placing her behind him. A bullet would have to go through him to get to Charlotte.

The servants came swarming back into camp like frightened children.

"The ghost cat surrounds the camp," a servant said.

Another servant shuddered, rolling his eyes wildly. "The cat commands the wind. There is nowhere to run."

Another shot rang out. William clutched his chest, and red bloomed on his white nightshirt. Blood dripped down his hand and arm and he dropped to the sand.

"William!" Charlotte raced to his side and sank to the ground to check his chest.

The cook staggered closer, dropping his gun and waving his hands wildly. His hair stuck up giving him a crazed look. "Forgive me," he cried.

As he spoke the wind sent a mournful wail echoing through the campsite. The camels bellowed and snorted from the other side of the outcrop. Several of the servants cried out in terror, backing away and calling to the Gods to protect them. A wave of sand rose up from the ground, racing toward the cook.

"Traitor!" The word boomed through the campsite, loud and eerie, echoing for long moments afterward.

Sethmet watched, the hairs on his arms and legs prickling even though he suspected the pharaoh was the source of the voice. As he watched, the sand engulfed the man. His frightened shrieks battled with the wail of the wind. Then, the cook's body disintegrated, starting from his feet and rising upward until only his terrified face remained. Gradually, his face faded away, his pained screech reverberating for long moments afterward.

"What ... what was that?" Justin's frightened voice broke the horrified silence.

"Ghost cat," one of the servants moaned. "The curse."

Justin's head snapped from side to side as if he looked for a tangible source. "It won't come back?"

"I don't know," Sethmet said, but even as he said the words, the cry of the wind intensified. The sand rose up, swirling up like a funnel and racing toward Justin.

"No! No," he shrieked, backing up then turning to flee. "I had nothing to do with him. I am innocent."

The sand wave raced after him, catching him and engulfing him. His petrified screams faded as his body dissolved in front of their eyes. The sand wave dropped, dispersing on the desert and the wind disappeared leaving an uneasy silence behind.

"Sethmet?" Charlotte's frightened voice drew him.

"It's all right, sweetheart. How's William?"

A tear rolled down her pale cheek. Even though William had treated her badly, he was all the family she had left. "He's dead."


## Chapter Eight

Charlotte was thankful for Sethmet's calming presence. He spoke to the terrified servants and gave them instructions before leading Charlotte to her tent.

"Come," he murmured, his arm propelling her forward into the tent. "You need some sleep before we return to Patria in the morning."

Sudden panic nipped at Charlotte, and she clutched at Sethmet. "Don't go. Don't leave me."

"I will never leave you," he promised, and Charlotte took comfort, sensing the truth of his words.

Charlotte lay down on her pallet and shifted to allow Sethmet to join her. She went into his arms and cuddled against his chest. "What happened? I was there, but I still don't understand."

Sethmet hesitated, and Charlotte saw it clearly. "The truth, if you please."

"The pharaoh felt threatened. His tomb is nearby."

Charlotte worried her bottom lip between her teeth. "But I thought you and your family were guardians."

"That is true. We are, but the pharaoh sometimes acts on his own and takes vengeance." Sethmet pressed a kiss to her bare throat.

"But we are safe?" Charlotte hated the uncertainty in her voice, but then it wasn't everyday a woman witnessed two men disintegrating before her eyes or changed into a caracal.

"We are safe. I promise you." Sethmet's arms clasped her tightly then he raised her chin with his fingertips and kissed her slowly. Deeply. Almost as though he were sealing his promise. Her lips moved under his, and she opened her mouth so she could taste him. Instead of being seduced, he gentled the kiss then pulled away to look at her.

"I have no family left in England. And no money," Charlotte blurted. "William spent all my money. I have nothing."

Sethmet tucked a lock of hair behind her ear and smiled at her, tenderness in his eyes. "You have me, Charlotte. I love you. Stay with me in Patria. Be my mate."

"You love me?" Wonder bloomed along with hope. Could it be her destiny to stay in Egypt with Sethmet?

"I love you, Charlotte. I don't want you to go back to England."

Charlotte found herself smiling, her decision made in a heartbeat. "I love you too. I would like to stay here with you. I feel more at home here than I ever did in London."

"Wait." Sethmet placed his fingers across her mouth. "Let me tell you a little more of the guardianship before you make your decision for there will be no going back."

"This sounds serious," Charlotte said gravely.

"It is. As guardians of the pharaoh's tomb we are given the power to shift into cat form, but that comes with a price. If any member of our family should ever turn traitor or fail to keep the tomb safe, we lose our ability to shift."

"Everyone in your family?" Charlotte asked.

"Everyone, no matter what his or her age. And worse, the traitor will die and our family will suffer from a curse." Sethmet sought her gaze and held it. "We will die."

Charlotte shivered, remembering the expression on Justin's face before he had faded from sight. Terrified and as if he were in extreme agony. She never wanted to die that way. She inhaled deeply and asked the final question that had been bothering her. "I don't understand how I was able to shift like you. I am not family."

Sethmet smiled then, his teeth dazzling white even in the dark tent. Her eyesight and hearing had improved since she'd gained the ability to shift. But she still didn't understand although it appeared Sethmet did.

"You carry my child. Our child, Charlotte."

Charlotte gasped. She pulled away from Sethmet, a trembling

hand creeping to spread over her abdomen. "A baby?" Wonder, excitement and uncertainty swept through her.

"Are you pleased?" Sethmet murmured.

A tremulous smile sprang up on her lips spreading to pure joy. "A baby. I thought ... I thought I was barren." Tears of happiness fell unchecked down her cheeks, and she wiped them away impatiently. "A baby. Oh, Sethmet. A baby!"

"So, you'll stay here with me even though there is the danger of dying with the curse?"

Charlotte smiled and stroked her hand down Sethmet's cheek. "We will make sure we serve the pharaoh well. The curse will not trouble us."

"Charlotte." Sethmet pressed a tender kiss to her forehead then lowered his head to move his mouth over hers, devouring her softness.

She leaned into him, her lover, her mate, a sense of rightness and well being flooding through her. Her smile was wide and held confidence. "I love you, Sethmet. And I would be honored to join your family."

Freedom--yet a home and family too. Her smile turned misty.

A life with Sethmet was her dream come true.

# ANIMAL INSTINCT

By

## Michelle M. Pillow

### Chapter One

Eve Matthews stumbled drunkenly into her office trailer at the Jameson Wild Life Rescue and Preserve. The trailer was dim, but she spent more time in it than in her own apartment and didn't need light to find her way around. Everything was neatly organized and put away. Her desk sat in the corner, dominating much of the small front area. An old brown couch was next to it. The poor piece of furniture had seen better days, but she couldn't see spending the Preserve's money on a new one when they had so many rescued animals to take care of.

Plopping down on the couch, Eve kicked her feet up on the broken coffee table and sighed. She rarely drank, but a night spent with her overbearing socialite parents was enough to warrant the rare occasion.

"Evelyn dear, why didn't you bring a date?" her mother had scolded the second she walked in the front door of the mansion home.

"No, hi, how are ya?" Eve growled under her breath, feeling a small measure of drunken comfort in talking to herself. "How's the job? Save any lives today? We missed you, Eve, glad to have you home."

Nope, what she got was, why don't you have a man?

If it wasn't bad enough, the entire party had heard her mother's comment and it was all anyone wanted to talk about the entire evening. Are you dating? When are you going to settle down? What ever happened to that nice doctor you were seeing? What was his name? Henry Statton? Yes, what ever happened to Dr. Statton? You were so perfect for each other.

Eve frowned. A reflection of moonlight caught her eye as it landed on the small scrap of paper hanging on her wall. Evelyn Matthews, Veterinarian. You'd think that would have been enough to make her family proud.

Suddenly, a dark figure leapt from the floor to settle next to her. Eve jumped in surprise to see the black panther. A small giggle left her lips as the large animal set his head in her lap. She stroked him behind the ears, drawing comfort from the animal's friendship.

"What do you think, Midnight?" she asked the big cat. She called him Midnight because of his beautiful dark coat of fur. It was so black it was almost blue. "Do you think I should have told them about Henry? I could just see it. Mom. Dad. I know you like Dr Statton, but after I found him in a dress, his cock shoved down his male receptionist's throat, I just couldn't bring myself to marry him."

The panther nudged her hand and lifted his face close to hers. She chuckled, feeling the animal's warm breath on her neck. Eve loved all animals, always had since she was a girl. She found them easier to talk to. They listened, didn't judge her, and she didn't have to worry about them telling her deepest secrets. Animals didn't betray their friends. Not like humans did.

She usually made the rescued animals sleep either in the lab or out in the large prairie they had set aside for the cats. But Midnight was different. He had come to her a mangled, broken mess. It had been the worst case of neglect and abuse she had ever seen. He'd been found in an old barn. No one knew where he'd come from. The best they could guess is that he'd escaped his owner and crawled to the barn for safety. That's when she'd been called in. The stupid police officer at the scene had wanted to put him down. Eve wouldn't let him--not when he had a chance to live.

For long months it was touch and go and she'd almost lost him on several occasions. He needed constant supervision those first weeks and so he had slept in her office while she nursed him back to health. Sometimes, thinking about all the cat had survived, she was astounded that he'd lived at all.

Ruffling his fur, she grumbled, "Oh, I am really going to miss our little talks together, you know it. But it's not fair to keep you locked up in this office all day and night. You deserve to live out in the open with the other cats."

Eve closed her eyes and leaned her head back on the couch. A little moan left her lips and a small tremor worked its way through her body. She absently kicked off her shoes and pulled her socks off with her toes.

"Why *don't* I have a man, Midnight?" Her head pulled up so she could look into his entrancing golden eyes. "My mom's right. I am kind of pathetic. Why couldn't men be more like you? Fierce and wild, strong, silent, knowing when to give comfort and when to take it. Protective."

A sound of misery and discomfort rumbled the back of her throat.

"And do you know how long it's been since I've had sex? Not that the sex I've had has been anything to brag about, but at least it was something. Sometimes, I think I'm so aroused I'm going to explode from the pressure. Not that you understand any of this, I'm sure."

The panther's ears twitched as if it truly listened. Eve frowned at him in thought, stroking her hands over his face. Sometimes, when she looked at him, it almost seemed like he did understand her. Midnight's eyes closed as he enjoyed her attentions.

"Uh, I think I'm going crazy. I'm going to end up alone--the old cat lady children run away from in fear. It has been way too long, that's for sure. But the only men who want to date me are stuffy, boring doctor types and I'm too much of a coward to go after what I really want. I am not sure I even know what I really want. If there ever was a truly sexually repressed human, that would be me. But, you don't have that problem do you, boy? I bet not. I bet panthers never have to think about it. They just act on instinct, pure animal instinct."

Eve pushed up from the couch, walking to the small bedroom in the back of the trailer. The room was set off from the larger front office with a small bathroom next to it. The queen sized bed was covered with a mountain of pillows and blankets. A small dresser was along the wall, next to a full-length mirror. She began undressing, not caring that Midnight followed her and watched.

Throwing her silk shirt on a chair, she then jerked her long legs out of her slacks. Stumbling before the mirror, she looked at herself in the dim light. She was pretty or, according to her mother, she would be if she put on more makeup and did her hair in something other than a sloppy bun. Her body was toned from spending hours on the prairie caring for over three hundred animals. Her skin was tan and her blonde hair streaked from hours in the sun.

Tugging at her hair, she loosened the blonde waves down over her back. "I lied Midnight, I know what I want. I want just one night with no commitments, like a stranger I don't have to talk to. I want him to be a wild, untamed lover. I want ... I want him to be bold."

Eve began running her hands over her body, feeling the weight of her breasts through the tight hold of her white silk bra. Her nipples hardened with instant longing. It really had been too long. She was frustrated beyond belief and masturbating had long since lost its appeal.

Eve sighed and fell back on her bed wearing only her white silk panties and bra. A dreamy sigh came to her lips, as she closed her eyes. "Mmm, that's exactly what I want. I want a big strong man who can pick me up, crush me against a wall, and fuck my brains out. I want someone who doesn't care what others think of him--a true rebel. I want someone sexy and wild and confident, with a motorcycle and tight black leather pants that mold to his deliciously firm ass. Someone who'll just look at me and make me melt into a puddle. Mmm, that's what I really want. But I'm a coward, Midnight. I'm too scared to go and find him. Besides, guys like that aren't attracted to safe, boring veterinarians who live in trailers, talking to animals as if they were people."

Eve started to laugh, a sad sound that held no merriment.

"It's just as well," she murmured, too tired to move. "I wouldn't know what to do with a man like that anyway. I'd probably tense up and start crying out of fear."

Midnight jumped on the bed and lay close to her side, not touching her skin. She sighed, long and loud, and absently patted his back before falling into a deep sleep.

## Chapter Two

Viktor looked over the gorgeous woman who lay unmoving on the bed next to him. He could see her perfectly in the dim light of the bedroom. Only a soft blue glow came in from the window. She was ravishing, so much so that he couldn't take his eyes off of her. Just his luck, he'd find the first woman he truly desired and cared for in his eternity of living only to be stuck in his shifted form, unable to do anything about it.

She unintentionally tortured him day and night with her presence. She talked to him about herself, telling him secrets, whispering her fantasies. It was pure torment. She undressed before him, letting his cat eyes see her body without hesitation or thought. During his time spent under her care, he'd been afforded numerous views of her form--in the shower, the bed, dressing and undressing. A few times, when she didn't know he looked, he'd watched her pleasure herself--wiggling her hips against her exploring fingers, stirring up her feminine scent until it clouded his mind, jerking and panting as she brought herself with a silent cry of release. If he were shifted to human, he'd groan in anguish at the memories of watching her climax by her own hand. Since he was panther, he merely growled low in discontent.

Feeling a tingling in his limbs, Viktor urged his body to transform. It had been a long time and it hurt like hell. He endured the pain exploding in his body, as he shifted to human once more. Black fur began to be replaced by tanned flesh. His muscles lengthened and stretched, arching and curling until they molded into a hard, masculine frame. His lips parted in a silent, agonizing scream. Soon it was over and he was again a man.

Viktor took a deep breath, trembling weakly as he readjusted to the energy it took to be in the larger form. He knew he wouldn't be able to stay a man--not yet anyway. But, once he was completely healed, the human form would again be his dominant shape. He'd have changed back sooner, but the wounds he'd suffered would have killed him.

Lying naked on the bed, he looked at Eve with his dark, human eyes. He knew she was drunk, could smell the liquor in her veins mingling with her woman's scent--a scent that it had finally driven him to the point of risking exposure to her, a scent so sweet he'd risked shifting before his body was ready.

Running a masculine hand down his ribcage, he suppressed a

groan. His eyes flickered over Eve, landing on the soft rise and fall of her round breasts. His long, tapered fingers wrapped around his thick cock. Shifters weren't known for suppressing their sexual appetites and it had definitely been too long since he'd indulged his. The heavy length of his shaft lurched and throbbed beneath his hand as he stroked it.

Moving with liquid grace, he turned onto all fours and crawled to be closer to the woman on the bed. His breath came in hard gulps as he looked at her. He couldn't resist. He'd been forced to gaze at her creamy breasts and athletically smooth thighs for too long. He wanted a closer look. He wanted to touch her, taste her. He wanted to fuck her.

Viktor licked his lips and sat back on his heels. Sexy lace panties hugged her narrow hips, the straps falling over where her hipbones protruded slightly from her skin. He knew when he pulled them down that he'd find a narrow patch of dark blonde hair guarding her opening.

Her thighs parted slightly as she stirred next to him on the bed. He couldn't resist lowering his face between them to breathe in her exotic feminine smell. Without thought, his lips parted and his long tongue reached forward to taste her through the silken barrier.

Eve lurched against him at the contact, wiggling and moaning in her sleep. A soft pant came from her lips and her legs fell open to him, as she inadvertently begged him for more. Viktor grinned and could not deny her plea.

"Mmmm," he moaned in the back of his throat, bathing her panties with his tongue until they were soaked and clinging to her hot, moist pussy. His breath panted against her. He could taste the sweet cream of her body trying to saturate through the silk.

He pulled back and she whimpered lightly. Her hand found hold on her own breast and began massaging. Her legs stirred, as she mumbled, "No, don't stop. Please, don't stop."

Hearing her soft, sleepy voice, he couldn't help but obey it. His fingers ran up her warm thighs to grab her panties from her hips. He worked them down, off her body. Seeing the soft glistening of her drenched pussy, he adjusted her around on the bed and spread her legs wide to him.

As his mouth latched onto her clit, drinking furiously, his fingers rode up her flat stomach to help her massage her breasts. Their fingers intertwined on the soft globes. With a rip, he tore open the bra, freeing the mounds to his searching fingers. He rubbed the nipples, pinching and squeezing them into hard buds. His teeth nipped lightly, making her squirm against him. He moaned and dipped his long tongue into her slick channel for a deeper taste.

\* \* \* \*

Eve felt the heat of potent arousal burning in the apex of her thighs. Her drunken mind tried to pull out of its haze as she cried out in pleasure. Whatever touched her, she didn't want it stop. A warm tongue lapped her body, stroking the length of her slit until she couldn't tell if the wetness was from her body or her dream lover's caressing mouth.

"Ah, yes," she cried, breathless and needy. She kept her legs open wide, giving him room to explore as she rocked her hips up to his mouth in encouragement. A long tongue dipped into her, stroking deeper and faster than should have been humanly possible. Her body quaked, sinfully aware of every touch.

Fingers gripped her breasts, holding her stomach down with their connecting arms. She felt the man's strength and it excited her to know he could overpower her--was overpowering her.

Her hips bucked against her dream lover, thrusting wildly into his expert mouth as she tried to find release against his deepening kiss. Her leg hooked over his shoulder, pulling at him to smother his face in her needy pussy. Teeth latched onto her clit, gently raking the sensitive nub.

Eve screamed as a tremor hit her in an urgent, intoxicating wave. Cream released itself from her body in a sign of pleasure to flood his mouth. The man moaned in approval and she felt him drinking her essence into him.

"Oh!" she begged. "Don't stop ... please ... oh ... yes ... there. *Nooo!*"

Suddenly, the mouth was gone. She felt the bed shift, as if he would leave her. He couldn't leave her, not yet, not like this, not needy and so close. Her feverish brain tried to hold onto the dream.

"Please fuck me," she whispered softly. "I need it so badly. Don't go."

A low chuckle answered her. The deeply masculine voice sent chills over her shivering flesh. "I'm not going anywhere."

The bed shifted again. Eve felt him next to her and lifted her arms to touch him. Her mind became more aware. She realized she couldn't see him. But the blindness of the dark room only enhanced her other senses. Her nerves jumped, reaching for him. She could smell his scent--so strong and all invigorating man. She could hear his breathing, deep and even. Her mouth watered, wanting to taste him.

"Who are you?" she asked.

There was a small silence, before the seductive voice answered, "A fantasy. Would you like me to continue?"

"Yes," Eve moaned in acceptance. What did it matter if she was in some drunk-induced wet dream? It felt real and she wanted more of it.

Her fingers discovered the ridges of a muscular stomach. She pulled herself up to face him. Her hands hesitated as they felt the pulsating heat radiating off his cock.

"Don't stop," he ordered harshly.

Eve's fingers lowered and she gasped. If she doubted she dreamt before, she now knew she had to be. The large shaft she discovered was thicker and longer than she'd have thought humanly possible. Her fingers glided over the smooth mushroom tip in her excitement, and she was thrilled just by the thought of what it would feel like inside her. She'd been with some big men before, but nothing of this girth.

Veins protruded from the hard shaft. After what seemed like miles to her hazy brain, she reached the base. Eagerly she stroked, squeezing hard as she made her way back up to the top. Small animal sounds came from her throat.

It was a dream, so what did it matter what she did?

Eve leaned over, touching her lips to her hand as she guided the tip to her mouth. Her tongue flicked over him, tasting the sweet flavor of his cock. He shivered as she licked playfully at him, boldly stroking him with her hands.

"This is my dream, right?" she asked. "I can have whatever I want?"

A growl answered her.

"Then I want you to ride me hard. I can't take this playing around. It's been awhile since--"

Strong hands pushed her back on the mattress, cutting off her plea. Eve moaned. Soon his body was above hers and she parted her thighs to give him access to her slick opening.

The dream man grabbed her wrists and pinned them above her head in a savage motion. She whimpered. His large cock found her ready slit, only to probe boldly into the narrow opening. She felt a momentary wave of panic at his size, but soon relaxed, determined to enjoy what the dream had to offer.

Eve felt her body stretch to fit him and thought she'd faint from the pleasure-pain of it. He glided forward, sliding in her juices, filling up her womb to the brink of her tolerance and beyond. Her hands were still pinned above her head and all she could do was wiggle her hips as her channel adjusted to his heavy shaft.

"Ah, you're so tight," he growled. She could hear the approval in his hoarse words. "So wet and hot. Your pussy feels so good on my cock. It makes me want to pound into you until your hot little cunt is the shape of my hard shaft."

Eve couldn't answer as he withdrew. She'd always wanted a man confident enough to talk dirty to her, but had never had it. In fact, aside from Midnight, she'd never confessed the longing to anyone. Her heart raced in her chest, thrilled by his naughty words and his sinfully wicked body moving in hers.

"I'm going to fuck you until you come so hard you can't breathe." He quickened his pace, instinctively knowing what she needed and giving it to her.

Eve needed sex, release. She needed to be liberated of the tension that built inside her, pulling her body into a tight cord. With confident strokes he thrust, grinding his hips along hers in a primal rhythm that had her twitching beneath him. She called out in continuous pleasure, knowing no one would hear her.

Sweat beaded on her flesh as he drove her towards the rapturous height of her passions. Her channel began to quiver, clenching violently around him. She cried out in ecstasy as an explosion sparked in her hips, traveling like a tidal wave over her whole body, rippling against her flesh, drowning out her voice.

His hips only pushed harder, faster, deeper, slamming his shaft to the hilt, fitting so deep his balls seated themselves in the cleft of her ass. Eve jerked but he didn't stop, pushing her until his body exploded with hers. He grunted his release, spurting hot waves of seed into her womb. Her body drank him up, milking him of every last drop of his essence.

Too fast, he pulled himself from her. She blinked, trying to see in the dark as she searched for him. She was too weak to move more than a few inches. Her breath came ragged and she suddenly felt cold without his heat.

Eve lay still for a long moment, listening to the silent bedroom. When she could finally stand, she pushed off the bed and stumbled across the floor. Hitting the light switch, she turned to look around. The room was empty, aside from Midnight on the bed. The cat yawned, looking at her with his knowing eyes for a brief moment before falling asleep.

"You'll never believe the dream I just had," she whispered, grabbing her dizzy head. She wondered how a dream could leave her so sated and yet so incredibly sore. She headed into the bathroom, stumbling into the doorframe as she passed. Weakly shutting the door behind her, she whispered, "I think I need a shower."

\* \* \* \*

*Soon,* thought Viktor, stretching out on the bed as he heard the shower turn on.

Soon he would be well enough to show her who he really was. His body was just barely sated by their lovemaking. The one brief taste only made him want her again. And again he would have her. Once he was well enough to hold his human form, he would seduce her right. He'd make every single one of her torturous fantasies come true, for now her fantasies were his.

## Chapter Three

Eve watched Midnight sprint out into the prairie, running in long strides over the grassy plain. The cat looked completely recovered. He didn't even limp from his ordeal. She smiled, happy to see him running free. However, even as she was happy for him, she was sad too. She was going to miss his company. Suddenly, her little office trailer seemed small and lonely.

"Dr. Matthews, phone call!"

Eve frowned, turning to one of the many Jameson Preserve volunteers. She could never remember their names so didn't even pretend to try. They were mostly college students helping out for a class credit. All of them had a noble sense of excitement being there, but Eve got tired of having to retrain them each semester. She sighed. It was all part of the job.

"Yeah, thanks," Eve mumbled. She turned back to watch Midnight only to discover he was gone. A phone was thrust at her and she took it. Turning her back on the volunteer, she began to walk away from him. "Dr. Matthews."

"Evelyn, darling!"

"Oh, hi, mom," Eve said. The phone dropped slightly from her ear.

"Evelyn, darling, so glad to have gotten through to you! I've been trying every day for two weeks, ever since you ran out on the party," Cynthia Matthews said.

*Darned volunteers!* Eve flinched. She had a standing order that only business calls were supposed to get to her. Everyone else had messages taken.

She blushed, remembering the vivid dream she'd had that night of the party. She didn't realize she'd drunk so much champagne before being driven back to the office. At first she worried that it was real, but as none of the college boys working for them looked knowingly at her, she relaxed. The sex had been just a wild, albeit wonderfully erotic, dream. Or how her thighs were sore, as if she'd had a rough night of sex? Well, that could easily be explained away. She must have stumbled into something while feeling her way around the dark office.

"Evelyn? Evelyn, are you there? Are you listening to me, dear?"

"Uh, no mom, sorry, must be a bad connection. I am out in the field right now. Have you been trying to call?" Eve asked. She flinched, feeling bad for lying. "You know how it is with volunteers. They don't always get me my messages."

Eve braced herself, knowing what was to come. She wasn't disappointed.

"Evelyn, dear, that's why I keep telling you to get a real job." Cynthia sighed, a truly wistful sound that drove her daughter to distraction. "Or even better would be to get a husband with a real job! Oh, which reminds me, the reason I called. After you left Dr.--"

"Mom?" Eve yelled into the phone. A mischievous smile curled onto her lips. "Mom, are you there? I can't hear you!"

"Evelyn? Evelyn?" her mother called, clear as day.

"Oh, I hate these phones. Mom, if you can hear me, I'll call you tonight!" Eve yelled, trying not to laugh.

"No, Evelyn, no, you can't tonight. We've got the Mercy Hospital Banquet. That's why I'm calling. I want you to go with us!"

Eve grimaced. "Mom? I can't hear you. Huh, guess it's dead."

Pulling the phone back, she hung up on her mother. She'd seen the Mercy Hospital Banquet in the paper and knew her mother thought it an excellent place to meet eligible doctors. Really, if she wanted to be some man's piece of eye candy, she'd have become a cover model.

Eve again looked over the beautiful landscape of the north field. A wide-open area stretched into the distance, covering nearly fifty acres of land. A forest nestled in the valley of some hills. She knew a creek flowed through the long line of trees. This was just one of the many fenced in areas the Jameson Preserve owned--all thanks to her.

The phone started ringing, getting her attention. She knew it was her mother. Taking a deep breath, she said, "You know, I've worked hard. I deserve a little break and it's not like I'm going to meet anyone hanging out here."

Lifting the phone, she said into it, "Mom, I'll go. Send the car at seven."

Cynthia Matthews gasped in stunned excitement. "Oh, I'm so glad. Wear the red dress I bought you! I'll send over some shoes and jewelry to go with it. In fact, let me just come to get you right now. You can go to the spa with me and later we can go to the house and change. I just know Edwardo will get you in. He owes me a big favor...."

Eve sighed, letting her mother ramble on for a few more minutes. She shaded her eyes, looking for Midnight against the horizon. She couldn't see him. Tonight might very well turn out to be a boring disaster, but anything was better than spending it alone, missing a cat. Breaking into her mother's long-winded excitement, she agreed to be ready in an hour for the spa. Then, hanging up, she began to make the long walk back to her empty trailer.

\* \* \* \*

"Why did I ever agree to this?"

Eve swore under her breath, looking for an escape route from the crush of people. The Mercy Hospital Banquet was held each year in a small castle some eccentric rich man had built in the 1890's. The long marble front hall was beautiful, decorated with floral vines and white banners emblazoned with the burgundy dove of the hospital's logo. As far as the eye could see, there was nothing but doctors and the plastic dolls they called wives.

Whatever made her think she would find one decent person to talk to at a function like this? She'd have been better off at the office playing solitaire.

Artfully placing her champagne glass down as a tray passed, Eve lifted the skirt of her long red dress and maneuvered her way through the crowd. Seeing her mother in the crowd, she ducked in the opposite direction. Cynthia's laughter trilled perfectly over the long hall in the completely fake way Eve hated.

Eve made her way out a side door, rushed down a long empty hall, and turned through a long corridor before anyone could come looking for her--not that she thought they would. Soon she was outside, standing alone on a high balcony.

The rough stone rail beneath her fingers was thick and cold as she gripped it. A deep breath forced its way into her lungs, as she looked up at the starry night. It was truly lovely out and for a moment she lost herself in the vague memories of a dream, a dream of dark eyes and a silken voice. His words were hazy, but the feeling they gave her still lingered. She was hopelessly haunted by it.

Below her were the gardens, lit by the yellow glow of artificial torches. Paths wove around the manicured lawn in perfect symmetry. It was beautiful, but she much preferred the wild, untamed look of the prairie at the Preserve.

"A beautiful lady all alone tonight, how can this be?"

Eve gasped, spinning around. The voice was low, edged with an accent she couldn't make out. A rush of feeling overcame her, making her excited and fearful at the same time. Her round eyes darted to a shadowed corner. She saw a brief flicker of movement.

"I'm sorry, I ... I didn't know someone was out here." Eve tried to skirt past, but the man stepped forward into the blue moonlight. She froze, unable to move.

Dark eyes met hers, sending a chill over her flesh in instant awareness. Her body quaked, growing so weak she was afraid she'd fall to the hard balcony floor. She blamed her obsession with the dream man for her reaction to the stranger.

The man wasn't exactly smiling at her, but he wasn't frowning either. His firm lips curled ever so slightly, as if he knew her. He stared boldly, as if he had her already memorized. Whoever this man was, he was gorgeous in a dark and dangerous sort of way. He didn't look like a typical doctor and yet here he was at a benefit, wearing a tux. Suddenly, Eve's knees buckled and she stumbled forward.

A strong hand shot out to steady her, curling boldly on her arm. Shock waves of heat washed over her from his hold. Her mouth fell open and she couldn't even manage to whisper her thanks. A long moment passed and they didn't move. His hand stayed on her bare flesh, not moving, just holding.

Eve, realizing she held her breath, panted and forced her eyes away from his dark ones. Already the penetrating gaze was emblazoned in her mind. Her heart raced, pounding uncontrollably in her chest. She couldn't breathe, couldn't think. She wanted to run away in fright, but she couldn't move.

"Are you well?" he asked her, his lips pulling up as his jaw lowered.

*Russian*, Eve thought, too insensible to move. *He's Russian.*

"Doctor?" he asked, concerned.

"You … you think I'm a doctor?" Eve asked, still staring in amazement. His words washed over her. He thought she was a doctor, not some piece of eye candy dating a doctor?

"Aren't you?" His smile widened.

"I … I drank too much champagne I think … I did," she mumbled, swallowing. Then, trying to blink herself back to awareness, she hastened, "I have to go."

Eve tried to rush past, but his hand tightened on her arm to stop her. A weak sound whispered past her lips.

"No, you don't," he said. "You must stay."

"Here?" Eve asked. She felt like a fool, but she couldn't think. There was something familiar about this man, as if she knew him intimately--which was impossible. She shivered, her body straining to be closer even as her mind begged her to move further away.

\* \* \* \*

Viktor looked down at Eve, taking in the fine structure of her face. It was all he could do not to kiss her full lips. Already he had tasted her body and he wanted it again. It was agonizing torture to stand so close to her, and yet be unable to do anything about the burning need in his body.

He'd never seen her as striking as she had been caressed by blue moonlight. Silk clung to her curves in a way that would surely drive him mad if he didn't feel it for himself. The open back of her dress fell low to her hips, baring her spine. He wanted to kiss the long length of it, tender and slow. He wanted to touch her until she squirmed and called out his name, begging him to end their torment.

She wore makeup, something she rarely did. Her hair was swept up off her shoulders with delicate blonde wisps blowing in the breeze. Her lips trembled and, to his carnal delight, she licked them. Her uneasiness made him smile. It was quite endearing to watch. He'd seen her on the job. She was normally cool and collected. He liked that his nearness unnerved her.

"You want me to stay here?" Eve asked weakly, again licking her lips.

"Yes." Viktor nearly groaned, wanting to suck her tongue between his teeth. He took a step closer, pulling her forward at the same time. His hands became caressing, moving up and over her arms.

"With you?"

"Yes," Viktor said. "With me."

\* \* \* \*

Eve didn't know what to do. She couldn't think as the strong masculine smell of his body came over her. She shivered beneath his warm hands, liking the way they felt against her skin. It was insanity. He was a stranger and all she could think about was how much she wanted him to kiss her.

His eyes dipped down to her lips as he drew forward, seeming to understand what she wanted from him. She stiffened, pulling instantly away. "I have to go."

Eve ran through the door and left the banquet as gracefully as she could without drawing notice. Her heart raced in her chest, lodging in her throat until she could barely breathe. Her parents' car took her back to the Preserve. She didn't want to go back to her lonely apartment, she wanted to go home.

## Chapter Four

Eve looked out over the moonlit prairie for Midnight. She knew it would be nearly impossible to see the black panther in the dark, but she tried to find him anyway. She still wore the red silk gown, having walked out to the prairie pathways instead of going to her office. Her hair had fallen loose as she rode in the limo to the Preserve and now hung about her shoulders and back.

She was on a wood plank bridge with rope sides. Before her the wild grasses grew, rolling like ocean waves in the blue moonlight. The bridge led to a path in the woods. She knew the area well, but it wasn't wise for even the seasoned staff members to go in there at night. No one had ever been hurt at the Preserve, but she didn't want to risk it.

Eve looked down at the creek flowing gently beneath the bridge from the woods. A nervous smile came to her lips, as she thought of the handsome Russian. Her heartbeat sped in her chest. He was a stranger and yet she'd felt connected to him.

She really needed to stop drinking. It was making her loopy. All she could think about was her wild dream, only this time, Mr. Dark and Dangerous was the unknown face above hers and his was the silken accent that gave her chills. On a basic, primal level, she had wanted him to kiss her, to keep kissing her until they were both hot and feverish with need. Then, she'd wanted him to make love to her right there on the balcony. Only, she'd chickened out and had run away like a coward.

Hearing a noise, Eve jumped slightly. She turned and smiled to see Midnight. She had hoped he'd find her. Leaning down, she held her hand out to the cat. His powerful body moved, perfectly healed, as he stalked forward to her. His golden gaze watched her with his silent intensity.

"Hey, how was your first day out in the wild?" she asked in a soft whisper. Automatically, her fingers ran over him to make sure he was unharmed. Satisfied that he'd not gotten into any scrapes with the other cats, she let him go. He looked at her and she shivered. Without knowing why she confessed it, she said, "I met someone tonight."

Midnight watched her.

"He ... he was gorgeous," Eve said. She again reached to stroke the cat's fur. A secret smile came to her lips. "He tried to kiss me and I ran away from him. I didn't even learn his name."

Midnight didn't move. Eve's smile faded.

"I did just what I always thought I would in a situation like that. I ran away like a coward. I should have ... oh, Midnight! I should have just done what I wanted. But, I started to worry. Was he married? Did he know my parents? Would he think I was a whore? Who was he? Why was he interested in kissing me? Why would he be interested in me at all? Before I knew it, I had talked myself out of any adventure by analyzing it to death. And now I'll never see him again."

Suddenly, Midnight stiffened and sprinted off into the nearby woods. Eve started to follow after him and then hesitated. She couldn't break her own rule. The cats weren't used to humans being in their forest at night. Even though she'd nursed them all back to health, they were still wild animals and she respected that.

She craned her neck, looking for Midnight for several long minutes, hoping he would come back. He didn't. He was gone.

Sighing, she turned to go back to her office. Suddenly, Eve froze. The handsome stranger was there. She couldn't see his face and yet she knew who it was.

"What are you doing here?" she asked, nervous.

"I came to find you," he answered in his low, sultry tone, sending chills over her entire being.

"Me?" Eve asked. It was like a dream come true and that scared her. "Why?"

"You ran away before I could introduce myself." The handsome man came towards her, stalking with liquid grace to reach her. He no longer wore the tux, but a pair of tight blue jeans that molded to his hips and strong thighs. A black T-shirt hugged his well-built stomach, hugging delectably large biceps and a thick chest, bending with each flex of his perfect muscles. His body moved with effortless charm. "I am Viktor."

"Just Viktor?" Eve asked with a nervous laugh. She couldn't move. The bridge beneath her feet shifted slightly with his weight. Dark hair spilled over his shoulders in brilliant waves of blue-black. His dark eyes penetrated, like a wild beast. She shivered, her body heating at the look. She grew damp between her thighs. It was the same instant attraction she'd felt on the balcony and it again took her by surprise.

"Yes, just Viktor."

Eve shivered. His voice was silk, gliding through the air to caress her. "Evelyn Matthews. I'm in charge of the Jameson Preserve."

Did her voice just become husky? What was happening to her?

"I know," Viktor said. His gaze dipped down to her lips and she knew that he wanted to kiss her.

"You know?" Eve asked, growing suspicious. "Are you a patron? Is that why you're here?"

"No, but I wish to be." Viktor lifted his fingers to touch her face. "And I am here for you. I know all about you, Eve. I know of your kind heart, your love for these animals and for this place."

Eve's throat worked nervously. The way he looked at her-- deep and probing--as if he knew every intimate thought in her head unnerved her. She fought to hold still. The potent ache he caused stirred deep in her belly and she wanted to pull him closer.

"And I know what you want." Lashes dipped low over his eyes as his gaze raked over her silk dress. "I know what you need, what I need."

Eve's mouth opened, but she couldn't speak. Her breasts ached, the tips reaching for him. People just didn't speak so plainly, so boldly, so directly. They never just laid it out there, good or bad, without some kind of hidden agenda. But, looking at him, she knew that there was no other motivation than what he said. He wanted her--simple as that. And he meant to have her.

Viktor didn't give her time to protest. He moved forward, cupping her face in his hands as he pressed his firm lips to hers in a gentle kiss. A weak moan of surprise escaped her, but she didn't pull back. Her blue gaze widened, meeting his. By his confident stare, she'd expected him to be untamed in his passions. His eyes searched hers before closing.

Eve heard another moan and realized it was his. His lips began to move, parting to suck her bottom lip into his mouth. He drank gently from her mouth, as if savoring her taste. She gasped and his tongue slipped past her teeth to explore her depths. Weakly, her hands lifted to rest on his strong arms. His fingers slid back into her hair to pull her closer.

Viktor groaned louder and she could feel it rumbling all the way to her toes, trailing liquid desire with it. As his kiss deepened, his mouth became more insistent. Slanting along hers, his tongue massaged her depths and his teeth raked her lips to nibble gently. His hands slid down over her body. Eve's knees gave out and she fell hard into his chest. He caught her before she fell.

She pulled her mouth back, her eyes wide and dazed with astonishment as she looked up at him. The silk gown was a weak barrier to the heat of his body. The unforgiving steel of his muscles pressed into her, molding hard against her trembling frame until there was no mistake of his desire. She felt the throbbing heat of his arousal, fighting to be free of the denim.

"This is insane," she whispered, breathless. Unable to help it, her stomach wiggled against the denim-lined protrusion of his shaft. Her nipples tingled, sending shock waves down her spine to her soaking pussy. "I don't know you."

"Close your eyes," he instructed.

Eve obeyed. How could she not? Her entire being shook, whispering his name through her limbs. *Viktor, Viktor, Viktor*....

"Now, Eve, just feel me against you."

She nodded, reaching out with her other senses to detect him. It wasn't hard. His nearness overwhelmed her completely until she could think of nothing else. She felt connected to him, a strange feeling she didn't care to explore. She tried to tell herself it was the champagne, but she knew it was more than that. There was something about him that made her want to throw caution to the wind and act the part of the animal, surviving on pure instinct, fulfilling each animalistic need as it arose. He smelled of power and strength. It was an intoxicatingly raw scent of man and it called to her.

"Feel my mouth." His accent rolled over her and she parted her lips willingly. His direct words captivated her. Viktor brushed his lips to her swollen ones. "Feel how I want to taste you."

Eve panted, feeling the soft kiss shooting throughout her body, arousing her further until she wanted to scream with fervent need. His tongue edged her lips, tracing around the outer edge, just as her body wanted his erection to trace her most intimate opening. With her eyes closed, she could practically imagine what it would feel like to have him there, thrusting hard.

"Feel how my body is hard and ready for you." Viktor groaned, as if he could sense her thoughts. To prove his point, he ground his hips forward, bending his knees to rub his cock into her sensitive stomach. Suddenly, his hands were everywhere-- tangling in her hair, gliding over her arms, gripping her waist, edging the skirt up and over her hips.

"Ah, yes," she panted. Eve's head fell back on her shoulders, gladly meeting the rocking of his hips with her own. Her fingers glided around his waist to squeeze his tight buttocks and pull him closer, urging and controlling his hips in her desperation. She lifted a thigh to rub along his, spreading her body open to him.

"You know me, Eve," he whispered into her ear, his voice hoarse and hot. "Your body knows me."

Eve couldn't explain it, but she knew he was right. She'd never be able to reason it aloud, but every fiber in her being recognized him and wanted him. She couldn't fight the burning need any longer. Her fingers clawed at his clothing, pulling the shirt up and over his shoulders. She sighed in pleasure to discover the dark muscles of his chest. Lightly, she brushed kisses over his chest, flicking her tongue against his nipples until they budded beneath her touch.

Viktor pushed the straps of her dress off her shoulders, unzipping it from behind to free her breasts to him. A light moan escaped him as he discovered she wore no bra with the gown. He devoured her neck, kissing and licking over her throat and ear. His fingers flicked her nipples as his hands massaged her aching breasts.

Eve cried out in pleasure, clinging to him for support. His lips made a hot trail of discovery and exploration to her breasts. Explosions fired beneath her fevered skin as his mouth pulled a hard nub between his teeth, only to bite and kiss and lick in a mystifying rhythm.

"This is crazy," she whimpered. Her hands fumbled to free him of his jeans, eager to discover if he was as big as he felt rubbing against her. She pushed the denim slightly from his hips.

"Do you want to stop?" He pulled back to look at her, his eyes tortured by the very idea.

"Mmmm, no." Eve dipped her fingers to touch him, grabbing his hard shaft in her hands. His eyes closed and she gasped to feel his enormous size, so much bigger than she'd imagined. She grew wetter just thinking about it. "Oh ... my ... Viktor. Wow."

Low, animalistic sounds came from them as she stroked his large cock. Viktor's hand jerked her skirt aside, gliding to find her moist center. He groaned as his fingers cupped the lace-covered slit, soaked with the cream of her body. Pushing the panties aside, he worked around them, moving to stroke her intimately with his hand.

"Ah, you're so fucking wet," he growled in approval. He thrust a finger up inside her and her hot channel convulsed and tightened around him. His lips devoured her neck. "You drive me mad."

"I want you ... now!" she demanded, fierce and sure. She gripped his cock firmly in her hand to emphasize her meaning.

With stalking precision, he backed her towards the end of the bridge, bringing her back to settle along a thick post. She didn't take her hand from him, loving the feel of his strength in her palm as he moved. Her body was on fire for him, drenching her pussy. Never had she felt the insanity of pure lust, never until him.

"Fuck me," she insisted, arching her back into the post. The night breeze caressed her skin, keeping her nipples hard. Then, almost shyly, she begged, "Please, Viktor."

He smiled, a devilishly handsome look to his dark features. His black hair blew over his shoulders as he lifted her up. He held her before him as if she weighed no more than a leaf. Her legs wound around his strong hips, jerking him close.

Insistent, he guided his hips up to hers, rocking his smooth shaft up towards her slit. He let his cockhead rub along her in several strokes, lighting a fire from her clit all the way down past her soaked opening. Her body jerked as he neared the cleft of her ass and his grin deepened. She hit his shoulder weakly, loving the sensations, but hating that he teased her with them.

The waiting became too much for them both and he couldn't hold back. Adjusting her body, he thrust forward, roughly sliding into her core, letting gravity pull her down until she was seated completely on his throbbing shaft. Eve tensed, surprised by how full she was, how deep into her womb he touched. She cried out in pleasure.

Viktor's call matched hers as he began to move. He gripped her hips, controlling her completely as he began to thrust. Her legs flailed weakly behind him and her hands held onto his shoulder and neck for support. He drove himself into her hot passage, only to pull out and do it again, conquering her moist depths. The natural rhythm of his hips sped up. Animalistic grunts of passion came from them, loud and primitive.

Eve felt the tension of her body, centering on her rocking hips. She held onto him, helpless to do anything but ride out the agony of pleasure. With each hard thrust it felt like he pounded deeper until she was sure her body would be ripped in half by his massive size.

Firework explosions erupted between her thighs. Eve screamed as her orgasm racked her body, fiercer than any she'd ever felt. Viktor didn't stop as she trembled, releasing a wave of hot cream like molten lava over his cock. As soon as he felt it, his body exploded, washing her womb with his seed as he came in hard, jerking shudders.

Their trembling continued for what seemed like both an eternity and an instant. Her body too weak to move, Eve dropped her head to his shoulder. Her legs fell like dead weights and he let her body slide from him to the ground. Crushing her to the pole, he began to kiss her gently, moaning softly in the back of his throat as if he never intended to let her go.

## Chapter Five

Eve moaned, weak and completely sated as Viktor pulled back from his kiss. His dark eyes gazed deeply into hers and his mouth opened as if he would confess something. Suddenly, he tensed. His eyes glimmered with gold as he looked at the forest. Eve blinked, dismissing the strange sheen as a play of the moonlight.

Without looking at her, he began to adjust her clothing. His eyes scanned the trees as a worried frown marred his brow.

"It was probably just one of the cats," Eve began weakly. "Don't worry. All the animals that show signs of dangerous tendencies are caged in a different area. I come out here all the time at night and have never had a problem."

Viktor looked at her and frowned, as if he wanted to say something to her, but held back. Or was it that he wanted to scold her for coming to the fenced prairies alone? She started to ask about it, when he pressed his mouth to hers in a swift, searing kiss.

"Go to your office and lock the door," he commanded. Eve trembled in a combination of fear and shock. "I'll explain everything tomorrow."

Eve didn't move. This was her territory and she wasn't scared.

"Eve," he began, only to pull away. "Please, just go. Trust me, please."

"But, you're a stranger." Eve's rational mind was slowly trying to return. Her comment was insane after what she'd just done with him. A wave of panic overcame her as she realized she'd just slept with a strange man without using protection. She started to feel sick and soon after came the confusion.

"Damn it!" Viktor frowned, again looking to the woods. He didn't bother to right his clothing. "I ... I don't have time to explain this. You know me, Eve, just trust that you do. And I know you. Now, please, I beg you, go inside."

Eve looked him over. She couldn't help it. He was half naked and so very beautiful. His dark eyes stared at her with a strange, possessive light.

"What is going on?" she asked, her words soft.

"Eve." He hesitated. Then, as if a dam burst inside him, he rushed, "I love you."

Her face fell in disbelief. She shook her head. She could see that he thought he meant his words, but that was impossible. Suddenly worried she was standing before a psychopath, she backed away.

"Eve...?" he began. He started for her, but then stopped. He struggled for a moment, then turned to run into the forest. Eve stared after him, not knowing what to think. Silence penetrated her numb brain, interrupted by the babbling of the small creek beneath the bridge. It was as if he hadn't been there at all.

Frightened by her reckless actions that night, Eve began to run. She didn't stop until she reached her office. Locking the door behind her, she stared dazedly at it. What in the world did she just do?

\* \* \* \*

Viktor hated to leave Eve the way he did, but he didn't have time to explain. Running into the forest, he shifted into panther, dropping down on all fours without breaking stride. The remainder of his clothing fell from his body as he ran faster. An old enemy was in the forest this night and he couldn't risk being seen with Eve. If Bartel discovered his feelings for the woman, the shifter would use them against him.

It was Bartel who had jumped him from behind, stabbing his human form in the back before beating him near death. He had managed to get away, crawling broken and bruised to an old barn. He was sure death was coming for him. When the farmer found him and then the cops, he was sure they'd finish what Bartel started. He'd seen the fear in the cop's face. He'd seen him draw his gun from the holster to put him down.

But then, an angel from heaven had appeared. He remembered her perfectly, her clothes crumbled from sleep, her angry blue eyes flashing as she stood between him and the cop's bullet. He had been in too much pain to hear her words, but she'd screamed at the cop, calling him a long list of names from incompetent to inbred. Viktor inwardly chuckled each time he thought of it.

She'd approached him without loathing or fear. Her gentle hands had probed him and she'd stayed by his side, talking to him, urging him to drink, to eat, and later to stand. She had a good heart--all the cats at the Preserve said so. And, in those long hours, listening to her as she cared for him, he had fallen in love with her.

Only, he couldn't believe he'd let the words slip. The plan had been to take it slow, to make her fall for him as the man, before he revealed his secret to her. Now, remembering the look of shock and horror on her face, he was worried that he might have ruined his chance at winning her heart.

Running faster, he let the worry slip from his mind as he concentrated on tracking down Bartel. The next time he found the deceitful tiger, he wouldn't be caught so off-guard. When they next fought, it would be to the death--only this time Viktor didn't plan on being the one left for dead.

\* \* \* \*

Eve looked around her apartment, sighing at the plain white walls devoid of photographs. She hardly spent any time in it and at times she wondered why she bothered keeping it at all. It was hardly a home. There was a couch and a coffee table--both gifts from her mother. Several boxes lined the walls, waiting until she got the urge to unpack them. That day hadn't come in the two years she'd rented the place.

Crossing the kitchen barefoot in only her white robe, she grabbed a cup from the cabinet and poured herself some coffee. It was the only thing she had in the cupboards. If she wanted to eat, she'd have to either go to a restaurant or back to her office at the Preserve. Thinking of the office, she shivered. She'd stayed locked up until dawn, before making a run for her car.

"What was I thinking?" she moaned, looking down at her coffee cup. She didn't even want to think of the fact that she might be pregnant by a stranger--or worse, diseased. She knew better than to have casual sex! "*Argh!* What the hell was I thinking!"

The little voice inside her laughed, seeming to mock, *I know what you were thinking!*

A small, unaware smile came to her lips as she remembered Viktor. She dipped her finger into the coffee's surface and made little ripples in it. His dark eyes had penetrated her, capturing her soul. The memory of his voice gave her chills. Oh, but he was handsome! And his body inside hers felt so ... so ... so incredibly good that she ached with wanting him all over again.

Eve couldn't quite place it, but she would almost swear she knew him somehow. She thought of the endless parties she'd been to with her parents and couldn't for the life of her remember him. Surely, she'd remember meeting a man as gorgeous as he was.

She closed her eyes, as a wave of hot longing shot through her. It wasn't fair. One man shouldn't hold so much control over her.

*I love you.*

Eve froze, stopping her hand from reaching beneath the robe to touch between her thighs. Had he actually professed his love for her? No. He couldn't mean it. But, something in his eyes had said he believed the words to be true.

"Ahhh," she moaned aloud into the empty apartment,

slamming her palm on the countertop. "He's a lunatic. I had unsafe, unprotected, unbelievably great, extraordinary sex with a complete lunatic."

Eve banged her head against the cupboard door several times.

"*Mmmm* and what's worse, I want to do it again."

\* \* \* \*

Eve was nervous stepping out of her car in front of her office, but she knew she couldn't avoid going to work. There were a lot of animals that needed her attention and care if they were going to get better. Her morning went fairly smooth and, after three hours working in the Preserve's lab, she left it to make her daily inspection of the grounds.

Looking for Midnight first, she was disappointed not to find him. She went to the main security compound to check the hidden cameras. They covered nearly all the Preserve's grounds. She searched every acre, unable to find him. She asked the guards about him. They told her they hadn't noticed the black panther about, but one mentioned having seen a tiger they hadn't noticed before.

Eve thanked them, though in truth she doubted they could tell a lion from a housecat. There were no new tigers on the grounds-- not for the last year at least. It's what she got for hiring men barely out of their teens to work for her. Half the time, she thought it was the cool uniforms that attracted them to the job more than helping to guard the animals.

Eve sighed in frustration, hoping Midnight was all right. For some reason she couldn't discern, she felt closer to him than the others. Suddenly, she thought of Viktor. He'd run into the forest the night before, the same direction Midnight had earlier. Not understanding what, if anything, was going on, she made her way back to the bridge.

That evening, after hours of searching the forest, Eve had to admit defeat. She checked in with the security guys once again and even questioned all the volunteers. No one had seen the black panther. However, a few of the volunteers did confirm the report of a new tiger on the grounds. Eve frowned, realizing that it was quite possible some idiot had dropped off a cat on Preserve property and left it for them to take care of.

Her stomach in knots with worry, she left instructions to cancel all morning activities while they went out in the jeeps to look for the new tiger. If there was a new cat on the loose, it was quite possible he'd attack the others--possibly even Midnight. Pushing into her office, completely spent and ready to take a shower, Eve shut the door behind her.

"You're out late," Viktor's voice came from behind her. "I was beginning to worry."

Eve jumped at the sound, even as her body responded. Her thighs began to throb with need, as moisture pooled between them. She whirled around, her face tense as she looked for him in the dim light. Going to a light switch, she flipped it on.

When she found him, Viktor was in the process of standing from her couch. He smiled at her, almost shyly as he held out a bouquet of wildflowers. Eve eyed the flowers suspiciously and then him.

"How did you get in here?" she asked, unsure if the shaking of her limbs was fear or excitement. Her heart pounded violently inside her chest.

"You left it unlocked," he admitted. "I would have waited outside, but I wasn't sure you'd want your co-workers seeing me."

Eve slowly nodded, conceding the point. She paused, taking the time to look him over. He again wore jeans, a dark blue T-shirt, and a comfortable pair of sneakers. She much preferred the relaxed outfit compared to the tux she'd first seen him in. By the time her gaze made its way back up his very firm body, she was blushing.

"You look lovely," Viktor said.

Eve realized his eyes had been giving her the same examination. Looking down, her blush turned to a look of horror. Her jeans were covered in dirt and mud, as was her button down Preserve uniform shirt. She could just imagine what her hair looked like--frizzed out about her head.

"I spent most of the day in the forest looking for a missing cat." Suddenly, she frowned in worry, forgetting her concern over her appearance. "I couldn't find him. I'm worried."

"Which cat?" asked Viktor.

"Midnight." Eve turned slowly making her way towards the little refrigerator by her desk. She was starving. Seeing only an old sandwich and some cans of soda, she opted for the soda. She offered one to Viktor. He shook his head. Then, as she popped the top on her can, she watched him set the flowers down on the coffee table. "He's been missing all day. I saw him last night on the...."

Viktor grinned. Eve instantly forgot what she was talking

about.

"Ah, you should go, I have to take a shower," she said, as if suddenly aware of how close he was to her in the small trailer. Every fiber in her being begged her to jump the distance between them and demand he give her a repeat performance. "I need to get some sleep if I'm going to get up early to start a search."

"All this for the panther?" he asked.

Eve's brow again furrowed in worry. She had no idea why she didn't just throw him out of her office. Instead, she answered, "Yeah, but there were also reports of a new tiger on the grounds. I think someone might have dropped off an animal without telling us. It happens sometimes. There is no telling if the tiger is diseased or hurt, or if it's even tame enough to be out in the open area. Some of them are really mean when we get them. It takes some time to rehabilitate them. I can't risk him getting the other cats sick or attacking them."

"You really do love it here, don't you?" he asked. His tone said he already knew the answer.

"Yeah," Eve admitted. "I do. I'm happy here--for the most part."

"The most part?"

"It can get a little lonely talking to animals all the time. Usually, I don't mind it, but sometimes it would be nice to have them answer back." Eve shrugged. Coloring slightly, she changed the subject, "What are you doing here, anyway?"

"I wanted to see you," he admitted without embarrassment. "And I hoped you'd want to see me."

"Wait a minute," Eve frowned. "I never said Midnight was a panther. How--?"

"I thought about you all night," Viktor interrupted, letting his voice dip seductively.

"I think you should go," Eve said. Her stomach growled, loudly rumbling.

"Come to dinner with me," he said, easily changing the subject. "You have to be starving and I've got a car parked out back."

"No, I don't think--"

"What? You aren't scared of me, are you?" he asked, his eyes glimmering with mischief.

Eve slowly shook her head. No, she was definitely not scared of him. But, she was scared of how she felt about him. Already, her body was wet and ready. Her head was busy sending her images she'd rather not remember of his oh-too-delicious hips thrusting into hers. She ached for the feel of his cock buried deep inside her.

"No, it's just I'm not dressed to go out and I need a shower." Eve gave a meaningful look down at her muddied outfit.

Viktor smiled a truly charming smile. His fingers reached out to touch her face. His accented voice dipped to a husky murmur. "I'd be more than willing to lend a hand."

Eve's cheeks pinkened. "I ... I...."

Viktor cut her words off with a heated kiss, slanting his mouth boldly against hers until her knees weakened. When he pulled back, he whispered, "I'll wait in here for you. If you wish for me to join you, just yell."

With a gentle swat of her backside, he turned her towards the bedroom door. Eve gulped, walking through her office to the back. Shutting the door behind her, she nearly swooned onto the bed. She lay there for a long moment, debating whether or not to open the door and invite him in.

"Is everything all right in there?" Viktor called.

Eve jumped up from the bed. "Yeah, just fine!"

Hurrying to the bathroom, she shut that door too. Then, without further contemplation, she jumped into the shower--alone.


## Chapter Six

Eve was surprised to find that Viktor drove a jeep, much like those she used on the Preserve. She smiled. She had figured him for a flashy sports car type of guy. Most doctors were.

"So, do you work for Mercy?" she asked, lightly. She'd slipped on a casual outfit to match his--blue jeans and a white button down shirt.

Viktor blinked in confusion, glancing over to her. "Mercy?"

"Mercy Hospital," Eve said. "I assumed you were a doctor. You were at their banquet dinner last night."

"I went there to find you," he said easily.

"Careful," Eve teased, not knowing what was coming over her that she could joke with him. But, she couldn't help it. His very nearness put her at ease as if they were old friends. "You're starting to sound like a stalker."

"Mmmm." Viktor grinned. "Well, if I'm a stalker, there is no one else I'd wish to stalk."

"I'm sorry, but something has been bugging me. Have we met before last night? I mean, you seem really familiar--your eyes mostly--but I can't place you."

Viktor chuckled. "Are you saying I am forgettable?"

"Well, no," Eve rushed before she realized he teased her.

Viktor laughed, a deep, rich sound, as he turned into a parking lot. "Glad to hear it."

\* \* \* \*

Viktor was the perfect gentleman during dinner, all except his gaze, which seemed to devour her every move. Eve found she quite enjoyed his company and they had several things in common. He wasn't a doctor, which she kind of liked. He had a quick wit, an easy smile, and eyes that seemed to stare into her soul. He was laid-back, spoke to her with respect, and treated her like a lady. And, to her amazement, he seemed to know more about big cats than she did.

After dinner, he drove her back to the Preserve. Eve wasn't quite ready for the night to end, but she was too nervous to invite him inside, knowing all too well what she'd be asking for. After the night before, it seemed silly that she would be nervous about it, but she was.

"Are you tired?" he asked, pulling open her door for her.

Eve shook her head. "Not really. I don't sleep too well at night."

Viktor gave her a look that seemed to say, *I know*. "Want me to come in? We could play cards."

"Cards?" Eve giggled, though she did play solitaire on many occasions to pass the time and to sort her thoughts out.

"Yeah." Viktor grinned. His eyes dipped over her. "Strip poker?"

"How about just poker?" Eve asked, stepping back.

Viktor sighed, looking properly disappointed, but he nodded in agreement. "Poker it is."

Once inside, Eve got out the deck of cards and sat on the floor across from the couch. Viktor sat on the couch facing her. Every time he looked at her and grinned, Eve felt her heart skip a beat.

"I have to confess, I really don't know how to play poker." Eve giggled, feeling light-headed. Her eyes began to travel over his handsome body as they had all night. Suddenly, she didn't feel like cards.

"Hum," Viktor mused. "Well, I don't know about America, but in Russia it's much better with your clothes off."

"Yeah, right." Eve chuckled. "Isn't this the same country that has a bunch of people jumping naked into icy lakes to swim?"

"Have you ever tried it?" he countered.

"What? Ice swimming? No. I like being warm too much for that." Eve busied herself shuffling the deck.

Viktor lifted his arms and placed them over the edge of the couch. "In Russia, we have many ways for staying warm."

"How long have you been gone?" Eve asked. "From Russia, I mean. You seem like you miss it."

Viktor's eyes dipped down and he looked uncomfortable. "Ah, it has been many years."

"Oh," Eve detected that he was uncomfortable talking about it so changed the subject. "Well, you know, in America, we have ways of keeping warm too."

Viktor glanced up, meeting her eyes. His brow arched on his handsome face.

Eve set the unused deck of cards aside and began crawling around the table on all fours. She couldn't stop herself. She just loved being with him. He was comfortable and for some reason being around him made her confident.

She pushed the light coffee table out of her way and crawled between his knees. Then, running her fingers over his calves, she pressed along the inside of his thighs spreading them open. Her eyes boldly met his, watching for a sign of approval. His smile faded, replaced by passionate intensity.

Dragging her nails lightly, she met with his waistband and pulled the button free. She could feel the hard heat of his arousal through the denim. She'd noticed his large erection most of the evening. She'd have had to have been blind not to. It had been there since she'd first walked into the trailer to find him on her couch.

After spending the evening with him, she found that he was indeed reasonably sane and not the crazy stalker she first feared him to be. Since they were both adults, they could do whatever they wanted and right now she wanted nothing more than to make love to him in every way imaginable--starting with his tempting cock in her mouth.

Eve's mouth watered just thinking about it. Watching his eyes, she unzipped his pants. Then, glancing down his hard body as he adjusted his hips, she smiled to see he wore no underwear.

Her fingers caressed him, rubbing along his thighs, as she leaned over to kiss the smooth mushroom-shaped head. Viktor's breath hitched in his throat and his hands gripped tightly to the back of the couch. Eve licked him several times, flicking her tongue over his flesh as she sampled a taste. Viktor moaned and his hips jerked ever so lightly. Parting her lips, she kissed the head. Viktor's moans turned to pants. Eve chuckled with power, taking him deeper with each passing kiss of her lips.

As she sucked him deep, her hands moved over his taut stomach to his thighs. She pulled the jeans from his hips, before settling her fingers on his thick shaft. His cock was too big to take all the way in her mouth, so she stroked him with her hand, cupping his balls underneath.

Viktor fingers shot forward to stop her. "Enough, a man can only take so much of that and I would not come so quickly."

Eve pulled back at his insistence and grinned up at him, licking her lips.

"My turn," he growled. Before she knew what he was up to, he grabbed her waist and flung her over to lie on the couch. With deft fingers, he freed her of her jeans and red lace panties with one swift pull. "Mmmm, much better."

Viktor trailed kisses down her parted thighs, moving his tongue in lazy circles as he neared her wet slit. Eve watched him in fascination. His dark gaze bore into her. As his mouth latched onto her clit, she cried out in pleasure.

Viktor's long tongue caressed her, licking her in long strokes. His fingers delved into her wet passage, massaging her until her cream covered his fingers. Then, slowly, he edged down the cleft of her ass, parting her cheeks as he rimmed his finger around the tight rosette. Eve bucked, never having been touched there. She panted, her eyes wide as she discovered the pleasure he could give her.

Viktor's expert mouth brought her to the brink of release. He pushed and probed in just the right way until she twitched and panted beneath him. When she pushed at his shoulder, he only sucked her deeper, thrusting his tongue into the moist cavern of her body. With a cry, she came hard against him, spasming her release into his mouth.

Viktor pulled up and gave her a cat-like grin. Crawling above her, he gently leaned over to kiss the racing pulse at her neck. "I will give you a small break to recover, but I am nowhere near finished with you."

"Who said anything about recovering?" Eve grinned. "All I want to know is, do you want to stay here or do you want to move to the bed?"

"Mmmm. Definitely the bed--more room to move around," Viktor murmured between kisses. He pulled up and gave her buttoned shirt a meaningful look. "And this time I want you completely naked."

"I think that can be arranged." Eve giggled, thoroughly enjoying herself.

Viktor growled as he swept her up and threw her over his shoulder. He gave her ass a light smack and she kicked her feet in pleasure. Striding across to the bedroom, he deposited her on the bed. Eve stood on the mattress looking down at him.

"Well?" he demanded, hands on hips. "What are you waiting for? Strip."

Eve purred a low moan, slowly unbuttoning her shirt as she swayed before him on the bed. Viktor grabbed his dark T-shirt, gracefully tore it from his shoulders, and threw it to the floor. By the time he worked out of his jeans and stood naked before her, she'd managed to unbutton the shirt, but nothing else.

"Let me help you with that," he growled, leaping up on the bed.

Eve watched his body. Her eyes were mesmerized by his athletic form and sculpted grace. He was a man who knew how to use his body and did so to perfection.

Pulling the shirt off her shoulders, he tossed it over his head. She stood before him, clad in only her white lace bra. Eve leaned forward, grinding her mouth to his in a searing kiss. Their tongues battled as his fingers tested the weight of her breasts, pushing them over the lacy barrier.

"I'm going to fuck you so good, baby," he groaned into her mouth.

Eve shivered in pleasure at his words. Moisture dripped from her, coating her slit in anticipation. Her hands left his body only long enough to undo the strap behind her back. Her breasts fell free and she let the bra drop to the bed. She grabbed his thick cock and stroked it hard.

"I want you on your hands and knees," he instructed. His accented words were hoarse. "Ah, please Eve. I want to watch myself ride you."

Eve kissed a trail down his body as she sunk to the bed, stopping briefly to suck his cock into her mouth. Then, turning around, she waited for him on her hands and knees, wiggling her hips in his direction.

Viktor groaned and she felt his weight shift on the bed behind her. First his hand found her, massaging her clit in agonizingly slow circles. His fingers slid over the cleft of her ass as his other hand moved forward to probe her wet pussy.

"Ah, yeah, you're so wet for me, aren't you, sweetheart?"

"Yes!" Eve cried pushing back at his fingers, wanting him deep inside.

Viktor played with her awhile longer. "What do you want, sweetheart?"

"I want you to fuck me," Eve demanded. All her inhibitions flew out the window. It was like Viktor knew all her secret fantasies and was intent on giving them to her. She'd never told anyone about them--well, no one but Midnight. "I want your cock inside me now! I want to ride your hard cock until it comes and then I want to ride it again."

"Mmmm, yeah, baby, keep talking," he urged. "Tell me how good I make you feel."

Eve moaned as his cockhead probed her slick opening. She almost couldn't think as he began to press into her. "Ah! You're so big!"

Viktor chuckled.

Eve felt a momentary wave of embarrassment at the generic statement. But, as he pressed deeper, she forgot all about it. "Yes, you feel so good. Your body makes me hot. I'm so wet for you. I want you to take me, Viktor. *Please!*"

Eve thrust her hips back to swallow him inside her. She couldn't speak, as he filled her up completely. Eager, he began to move, thrusting wildly in her silken depths, pounding hard against her core with an almost bruising force. She didn't care. She loved the feel of him, the power of his untamed movements. His hands grabbed her hips, pulling and pushing her body on his, faster, harder, deeper, gliding in the juices of her slick pussy. The tension built between them, echoed in the harsh pants of their breaths.

Pleasure racked Eve with each stroke, pouring into her limbs as she began to tremble with her violent release. Her hand lifted, roughly massaging her clit as she was brought to completion. Viktor yelled a conquering sound as his seed exploded from his body, shooting in a hot stream inside her clenching depths. Her pussy squeezed him hard, milking him of every drop. Her loud cry joined his as wave after endless wave of pleasure coursed over her entire frame.

Viktor fell onto the bed next to her, too sated to move more than his hand over the small of her back as she lay face down in the mattress. Her heart hammered violently in her chest and her limbs were so shaky she was afraid she'd never move again. She moaned lightly, a sound of pure contentment as she angled her face to look at him. He winked at her and shot her a crooked grin.

"We really shouldn't be pressing our luck," she murmured. "We need to start using protection. I know I'm clean, but...."

"You have doubts about me?" he asked, and she could see that she had hurt him. "Do not have doubts. I am clean."

Foolish as it was, she believed him. "Still, there is pregnancy."

Viktor closed his eyes and shifted his face towards the ceiling. "You do not wish for children?"

"Well, I ... I never really thought about it," she whispered, not understanding the seriousness of his tone.

"I have already told you how I feel, Eve," he said, not looking at her. "The rest of our lives is up to you."

The statement was so simple, so honest. Eve shivered. But, instead of fear, she felt an entirely different sensation curling in her limbs, soaking her body once more for him. A smile came to her lips as she looked at his naked form, lying perfectly before her on the bed. His cock was only half aroused, but she bet she'd be able to change that.

\* \* \* \*

Viktor waited for her response, his blood racing so fast in his veins he was sure he'd never recover. The sex between them was great, but she said nothing of her feelings for him. Hell, who was he kidding? The sex between them was phenomenal. In all his years of living, he'd never felt the like. Her body responded to him with little provocation. It had driven him to near madness to smell her sweet, ready fragrance all night during dinner and not be able to pounce across the table.

It amused him some that she had tried to deny her feelings for him. He could tell each time her thoughts drifted to sleeping with him. She'd bite the corner of her lip and look perplexed, all the while staring at his cock protruding through his jeans. Gawd! But that look had kept him hard and aching all evening.

Instead of hearing her answer, he felt her hair brush over his chest. His eyes opened to see what she was up to just as her mouth came down to kiss his shaft. His body jerked, growing to instant life under her lips. He would not have thought it possible, but as she kissed him, he was ready to go again.

Eve sucked him until he was hard and ready. All he could do was lie back and let her. She looked at him through the long length of her lashes, and said, "You promised we'd do it again."

Viktor groaned, helpless against her will as she straddled his hips. She controlled him, owned him completely, and there wasn't a damned thing he could do about it. As she lowered her body on his to ride them to their next climax, he couldn't speak. He was mesmerized by her thrusting body, so raw and passionate, and he could only hope--so completely his.

## Chapter Seven

Eve yawned, refusing to open her eyes to the morning. Her body was loose, yet achy, and filled with a deep, sated contentment. Suddenly, a smile lit her face as she remembered the night before spent intertwined in Viktor's arms. If anything, he was an accomplished lover.

To no small embarrassment, she realized they'd had sex nearly four times the night before--not counting the times she came by his mouth. She'd thought of protection once, but not again. She knew she should be worried, but with as good as she felt, she'd just have to save worrying for later. For the first time in her life, she felt reckless and carefree and she loved it. Smelling coffee, her eyes popped open and she sat up in bed.

"Finally awake?"

Eve blushed, turning to the bedroom door where Viktor stood against the frame. He looked like he'd just been waiting there, watching over her as she slept.

"What time is it?" she asked.

"About ten."

Her face fell. "I'm late. I was supposed to meet the group four hours ago to begin the search for that new tiger. And I still have to find Midnight. I hope they didn't try to go it alone!"

Viktor said nothing as she hopped out of bed. Eve dressed in a hurry, too preoccupied to notice he watched. Then, pulling her hair back, she stopped beside him only long enough to take a drink from his coffee cup.

"Thanks," she said absently, as she headed for the front door.

"Wait." Viktor set his cup down and went after her. His hand shot out to stop her from leaving. His eyes softened to look at her. "I'm going with you."

Eve paused, startled as she gazed up at him. Slowly, she nodded. "I suppose it would be nice to have another expert along if there's trouble. These college kids don't know what they're doing half the time. Only, I can't be responsible for you, so don't get hurt."

Viktor smiled. When she tried to pull away, he jerked her into his embrace and placed a firm kiss on her mouth. Her eyes widened in surprise and she didn't return the affection. When he pulled back, he flashed a devilishly handsome smile, saying softly, "Good morning, Eve."

\* \* \* \*

Eve was angry. The volunteers had taken it upon themselves to split up into groups of two to try and find the new tiger. It would have been so simple for them to go to her office and wake her up, but no--they had to take matters into their own hands. Most of them could be called back by the two-ways, but a couple of the groups didn't have two-ways as the Preserve had run out.

The first lost couple was found making out in one of the fabricated caves of a new section that was under construction. Needless to say, they hadn't seen the new tiger. The last two missing volunteers were still unaccounted for. Eve frowned, gripping her two-way, as she glanced at Viktor.

"Anything?" she said into the handheld.

"Nothing yet," came the answer back.

"They probably left to go hang out at the pizzeria, thinking I'd sign off on their hours," mumbled Eve to Viktor. "I swear I need to hire someone just to keep track of them."

"It seems like you could use a lot of help around here," he answered honestly.

Eve narrowed her eyes to look at him.

Viktor held up his hands in defense. "I didn't say you were doing a bad job, I just said you could use help."

Eve relaxed, reading in his dark eyes that he truly didn't mean anything by it. She nodded. "Perhaps, you're right. But I hate to take away funds from the animals just to make my life a little easier."

"I don't think the animals would mind too terribly." Viktor's hand lifted to brush back a strand of her long hair.

Eve shivered at his nearness, too worried at the moment to wonder at their relationship. Something so familiar again struck her about his gaze. To her amazement, she watched it change, flickering and filling with a subtle gold. She started to open her mouth to speak, but stopped when movement caught her attention. Viktor tensed, spinning around to look at the forest.

"Get out of here, Eve," he commanded.

Eve was too stunned to move. "How…?"

"Eve!" Viktor demanded, reaching behind him to grab her arm. "Midnight?"

\* \* \* \*

Viktor smelled the presence stalking them from the forest. He had been waiting for Bartel to show himself. He hadn't wanted to let Eve come looking with him, but she did know the back paths and he knew she wouldn't have just stayed home without good reason.

He heard a twig break in the forest. Eagerly, he tried to push Eve back along the path. Bartel had come for him, not her. If he could just get her to run....

"Midnight?"

Viktor tensed, hearing the soft sound of her confused voice behind him.

"Oh, Gawd! Tell me it isn't true. Tell me I'm crazy." She didn't move behind him and knew the stubborn woman had no intention of listening to him.

Against his better judgment, Viktor spun around to face her, putting his back to the trees and to danger. He grabbed her arms and shook lightly. "Eve, listen to me. It isn't safe. I need you to go back. I'll be right behind you."

Eve stared insensibly at him, her shoulders jerking at the sound. The two-way fell from her fingers. "Your eyes … you … they changed. But, I don't understand. How…?"

A loud roar sounded from the forest. Before Viktor could turn around, Bartel leapt from the trees. The tiger's claws slashed through his arm. Eve screamed, reaching behind her back for a tranquilizer gun. Viktor threw her behind his back, trying to get her to run.

\* \* \* \*

Eve stumbled to the ground, only to hurry back to her feet. She watched in horror, as Viktor's perfect body began to shift. His tanned skin filled with a familiar black fur. His body contorted, molding and changing its shape. Within seconds, Midnight stood before her, pitted against the aggressive tiger.

She blinked, trying to deny what she'd seen with her own eyes.

It wasn't possible. Men couldn't change into cats. Cats couldn't change into men. Viktor was Midnight? She trembled, tears filling her troubled gaze. The things she had confessed to him, the panther him. She had told him things she had never told anyone before! That's how he'd known what she liked in bed!

Mortified by the realization and terrified by the two wild animals now stalking around each other in a circle, she began to back away. Trembling, she looked around. The gun had fallen to the ground and she tried to edge towards it without drawing attention to herself. Every fiber in her body told her to run, but she refused. She knew she couldn't leave Viktor to fight the angry tiger alone.

Her breath caught as she reached for the gun. The panther and the tiger began attacking each other, batting their long arms, growling and snarling viciously. Eve dove to the ground. The tiger heard her and turned. She saw his large body leaping through the air, ready to strike.

Eve screamed, covering her face with her hands as she waited for the heavy body to fall on her and tear her apart. The blow never came. She heard a thud. Her whole body shaking, she slowly lowered her arms to the ground. Viktor stood over the motionless tiger. He'd torn the throat from its neck. Eve gasped, automatically crawling forward to help the dying animal.

As she moved, she stumbled over Viktor's discarded clothes. She jerked as her hand touched them, almost as if they burnt her. Cautious, she reached to touch the fallen tiger. Her training bid her to help the creature.

"Eve?"

Eve froze. It was Viktor's gentle voice behind her. She couldn't look at him.

"Eve, leave him."

"No, he doesn't understand what he did. He's just an ... an animal," she answered. Her fingers shook as she tore her shirt, trying to stop the bleeding. Even as the blood rushed over her fingers, she knew she was too late. The tiger was dead.

"Bartel knew exactly what he was doing," Viktor said weakly.

Eve still couldn't look at him. She needed time to think. "What's going on here? Who are you?"

"I'm the man whose life you saved," came a gentle whisper.

"I saved a panther," she countered, staring at her hands. The veterinarian inside her mourned the life she couldn't help.

"Eve, I--"

Eve heard a thump as Viktor fell to the ground. Spinning, she turned. He again was shifted into a black panther. He lay motionless behind her, his eyelids drooping weakly. It was then that she saw the large gash in his side.

"Viktor," she whispered in worry. "Hold on."

Without hesitation, she began tending his wound. The cut was deep, but after a few minutes of care, she knew he had a chance-- if she got him back to her lab.

Crawling over to the two-way, she heard him make a weak noise. Her heart leapt into her throat and she could barely breathe as she called for help. As she spoke, she made her way back over to him. His golden eyes stared out at her, trusting and sad. Lightly she touched his face, and whispered, "Don't worry, Viktor. Everything will be just fine."

\* \* \* \*

Eve left Viktor in the lab to heal, instead of bringing him back to her office. His wounds were deep, but with a little time and care, he would recover. He'd lived through worse, he would live through this. The tiger was buried in the prairie by the volunteers. She recorded the incident as a rabid, abandoned animal that was already too far gone when she got there.

She left most of Viktor's care to the staff, only doing what was necessary to assure he lived. His golden eyes followed her every movement, full of questions that he couldn't ask. She realized he had always looked at her like that, as if something was on his mind when she talked.

Eve made sure she was never alone with him, not wanting to give him an opportunity to turn back. Once he was healed, she planned on sending him away. She never wanted to see him again. Well, if she was perfectly honest, she did *want* to see him again, just knew that she was too much of a coward.

As the days passed, she was all too aware of the confessions she had made to him when she thought him to be just a rescued cat. To her amazement, the fact that he shifted bothered her less than the fact that he knew her deepest desires, her darkest secrets. She'd told him things--embarrassing things. She'd changed in front of him, bathed in front of him, and for all she knew she could have touched herself in front of him. Eve was definitely mortified.

Making love to a stranger was one thing. But a stranger she really knew nothing about? Who had been told everything there was to know about her? It didn't seem fair.

However, despite this, she did miss his presence. She missed the feeling of having someone else around in the lonely office. She missed how she felt when he touched her. It was strange to think that she'd only known the man for a few short days, but she felt as if she knew him longer. She felt connected to him in a way she'd never felt connected to anyone or anything. And, whereas she was not attracted to his panther form, she did feel a special friendship with it that transferred itself onto the man.

Eve shook her head. If anyone could read her thoughts, they'd think she was crazy.

Pushing open the lab door, she turned to make sure the student volunteer was behind her. The kid nodded his head, grinning in an absentminded frat boy sort of way. His head bopped to a tune only he could hear as he sang to himself.

Eve hesitated. It had been two weeks since Viktor fought the tiger. She bit her lip, knowing it was time to let him go. His golden eyes turned to her, and she could see darkness swirling in them, begging her to give him a minute alone with her. She lifted her chin and refused to send the boy away.

Her fingers trembled as she examined his wounds. He healed fast and she assumed it had something to do with what he was. After a half hour, she nodded at the volunteer.

"He's ready to be released. Take him out to the South field and let him go," Eve said.

"But ... Dr. Matthews?" the boy said, surprised. "You always release the animals yourself."

"Don't worry about him." Eve glanced at the boy, almost ashamed that she couldn't remember his name. Then, nodding her head in encouragement, she said, "He won't hurt you."

"Well ... ah ... no, I guess not," the boy said. He turned to grab a leader off the wall.

Eve turned to Viktor and, without looking him in the eye, quickly whispered, "I want you to leave and don't ever come back here. I want nothing to do with you."

Viktor made a small movement of protest, standing up on the table with a low rumble in the back of his throat. Eve turned, nearly choking on her tears. She waited long enough to hear the boy attach the leader around the panther's neck. When he had Viktor well in hand, she left the lab without a backwards glance.

\* \* \* \*

Viktor left the Preserve. Eve couldn't believe it. A small part of her had hoped that he'd see through her bravado and come to her, despite her being a coward. He didn't. He just left and Eve was crushed.

A month went by without a word. Slowly, Eve integrated herself back into work, attacking her job with a renewed force, staying up until all hours of the night so she wouldn't have to go back to the office. She gave notice on her apartment lease and paid a mover to go in and clean it out. It wasn't hard since everything was still in boxes.

Her mother came to the office a few times, horrified by the news of her moving completely to the Preserve. She'd even convinced her to go on a few blind dates. Eve did it, if only to keep the woman from nagging. The men were polite, kind, self-absorbed. Every time she thought about letting them have a simple good night kiss, a twinge would begin in her stomach, quickly rolling into a debilitating cramp that would last most of the night. She missed Viktor, both forms of him, and longed for him with every beat of her heart

Eve sighed, glancing sadly around the long cement clearing of the lion's den. The den was populated with only two cats--the female she now tended and a male who paced next to them as if worried about his mate. It was hard to concentrate on work, but she forced herself to get back to the task at hand. Lifting the lioness' paw off the ground, she studied the small cut she found. Acting on a thought she'd been toying with, she glanced around to make sure they were alone before looking at the lioness. Quietly, she whispered, "Are you a ... do you shift ... change form?"

A low chuckling sounded to her side. Eve dropped the lioness' paw and spun to where the lion had been pacing. The lion was gone, but in his place was a naked man crouched on the ground, staring at her. He had incredibly chiseled features, a broad muscular body, and long blonde hair that spilled to his waist.

Eve blinked in surprise, turning to eye the lioness that had backed away from them. Her mouth went dry and she couldn't speak. She'd taken care of the lion for nearly five years now, after he'd been found roaming the countryside without a sign of an owner.

"She doesn't shift," the lion man said.

Eve turned back to him and bit her lip. "King?"

The man chuckled, a deep, rich sound. "I always was fond of the name you gave me. Though, in the human world, I am simply Cade."

"Oh," Eve breathed, unable to think of any other way to respond.

Cade stood and stretched his back. Eve turned her eyes politely away from his naked body and he chuckled again. Hearing him clear his throat to get her attention, she turned back to him. He held out his hand for her to take.

"I'd like to thank you for caring for us as you have. Many of the shifters here stay only because of you."

"There are more of you?" Eve asked.

"Yes, just under half the population I believe. Finn, ah Pouncer to you, actually is trying to buy the Preserve. You saved him from a--"

"A hit and run," Eve finished. "His back was fractured and we didn't think he'd walk again. We always wondered how he got on the highway."

"Shifters have a knack for healing quickly," Cade answered with a nod. "It kind of goes along with the whole immortality thing."

Immortal? Viktor was immortal? Unable to hold back, Eve asked, "Do you know where Viktor went? The black panther?"

"No. I haven't had the pleasure of meeting him," Cade said. "But, if you like, I'll spread the word you're looking for him."

Without giving her time to answer, his body began to grow with fur. Rolling his neck, he folded over onto all fours, once again becoming a lion. King tilted his head and let loose a series of roars. The lioness ran back to stand by his side. When he finished, Eve numbly nodded her head at him and shut the cage door. The lion watched her, seeming to smile.

Eve slowly made the rounds to all the pens, calling out for an introduction. Some shifted right away, some hesitated before revealing themselves, and some didn't change at all. Eve was amazed by just how populated her Preserve really was. Most thanked her for her care, some made suggestions as to what the other cats needed, and others simply nodded and shifted back without words.

Finn, the mountain lion she called Pouncer, greeted her with a warm, affectionate hug. He was glad that he was finally able to reveal himself to her, for he was indeed buying the Preserve. It was his intent to turn it over to her complete care and to hire whatever staffing she needed. She was known as a heroine to the shifter kind and they were all more than willing to donate money and time to her glorious cause. They had a long talk about shifters and humans before she finally left him to his supper.

By the end of the talk, she wore a small smile. Stopping by the security booth, she destroyed the tapes from the day to hide any evidence of the shifters' presence. Then, her smile fading slightly, she went home to her lonely office.

Chapter Eight

"He is your mate," Cade said simply, looking up from her office couch where he sat with Finn. Eve blinked. She hadn't said anything. Cade grinned, wiping a bit of mustard off the side of his mouth with the back of his hand. Both men wore clothes and were completely demolishing the hamburgers she had gotten for them from a local fast food restaurant.

It was late evening and the staff had been sent home. It turned out that they really had no need for security on the Preserve, being as they had a high population of shifters who were more protective and more effective than any security guard she'd ever hired.

"Viktor," Finn clarified with a small mischievous grin she was becoming to know in him. His blue eyes sparkled. "He is your mate. That is why you have that look in your eyes."

"Mate?" Eve tried to dismiss with a wave. "I ... I hardly know him."

Cade and Finn both chuckled, shaking their heads.

"Things are not so complex in the wild," Cade said. "It is why so many of us choose to stay away from the complications of being human. As a cat, if you are hungry you eat. If you are tired, you sleep. If you are threatened, you fight. And, if you love, you mate for all eternity."

"But, we aren't mated," Eve protested weakly. "I mean, I never said I love him."

The two men laughed harder.

"Whether you say it or not doesn't matter, Eve," Finn said. He wiped his hand on a napkin and wadded his trash into a ball. Tossing it at a nearby trashcan, he smiled as he made the basket. "If it's true, it's true."

"How can we mate forever when I will die and he will live on? It doesn't make sense." Eve sighed, looking miserably at her new friends.

"Eve, you're one of us now," said Finn, almost as if he was surprised she hadn't figured it out for herself. "It's how we knew we could reveal ourselves to you. We can sense our own kind."

"But, I'm not ... I can shift?"

The men laughed again and she frowned.

"No, but you're mated to a man who can. Your life is combined with his. Since he is immortal, so too are you," Cade said with a delicate shrug.

"Is that the way it is between Mia and you?" Eve asked, thinking of the lioness. "She will be yours forever?"

Finn really started laughing. Cade turned red. "No, she's ... we don't...."

"Shifters do not mate with cats," Finn allowed, still laughing. "We merely feel a kinship with them."

"Well, I guess I can take the birth control out of your food then. It would save quite a bit of money," Eve said, thoughtful. Finn only laughed harder. She made a face. "I give it to you as well."

Finn's face fell and he looked down as if she had kicked him in his manhood. It was Cade's turn to laugh.

"You said I had a look," Eve said. "What look do I have?"

"The look of your heart dying."

Eve froze, her eyes widening as she whirled around to her bedroom door. Viktor leaned against the frame, a sexy smile hesitant on his lips. He looked as if he'd been standing there for some time. Suddenly, she understood just what Finn and Cade had been laughing so hard about.

"Wh--how?" Eve couldn't move. Her heart beat a violent rhythm in her chest.

"I know because I too carry the same feeling," Viktor said softly.

Eve was vaguely aware of her two friends standing next to her. Finn touched her shoulder and said, "He came while you went to get food. Since we recognized your mark on him, we thought it was all right to let him in."

Eve nodded. She couldn't take her eyes off Viktor. The door to the office opened and closed, leaving them alone.

"How ... where ... why?" she tried to reason. Then, acting on pure instinct, she ran forward and leapt into his arms. She was a woman starved for her man. Her lips parted and she kissed him, driving him back towards the bed.

Viktor made a weak sound as he landed on his back. She pounced on him, straddling his waist between her thighs.

Hungrily, she tore at his shirt, ripping it from his shoulders. Her mouth worked its way from his lips, journeying over his strong shoulders, kissing his solid chest, down to the indention of his navel. Lightly, she licked him. His body tensed, stiffening beautifully beneath her as her fingers worked the button to his jeans.

She worked his cock free from the confines of denim. Her lips parted, eager to continue. She'd missed his taste so much.

"No, Eve, wait," Viktor said, grabbing at her arms to get her attention. She blinked, not wanting to come out of the daze she was in. "We should talk first."

"Mmmm, no, we should definitely do this first." Her tongue flicked out to tease the tip of his shaft. Viktor groaned, helpless against her pleasurable torture. She took him into her mouth, sucking him gently, nipping lightly, caressing him with her tongue and hands until he couldn't stand it. Only when he was pleading for mercy, did she let up.

Crawling off him, she stripped from her clothes, not caring that he watched her every move. She was empowered by his desire for her, by the rigid power pulsating in the veins of his cock. Her slit was soaked with her need, nearly dripping as she tugged the jeans off his hips.

Slinking up his body, Eve dragged her nipples over his calves and thighs, budding them into hard peaks as jolts of desire worked their way into her blood. She stopped to once more lick kisses to his shaft before continuing her journey up to his lips. Their mouths slanted together in a deep, searching kiss.

Without breaking contact, Eve lifted her body over him and thrust down, slamming his heavy length hard into her. Her muscles jerked around his enormous cock, remembering the feel of him, squeezing him tight within her hold.

"Ah, baby, yeah," he groaned, parting from her mouth. His fingers moved over her back and waist, only to grip her hips and jerk her further along his shaft until she was seated tight against his pelvic bone. "Oh, fuck, yeah."

Eve loved watching the pleasure on his dark face. She knew in her heart that Finn was right. Viktor was her mate. She hadn't felt whole without him. She understood that now. The idea of him leaving again tore at her heart. She wanted to speak, but the passionate aim of her body took control and she knew she'd need to find release before she could form a coherent thought.

She pulled up only to have his grip slam her back down. Eve

cried out as every nerve in her being tingled in approval. Pushing up, she used his chest for leverage as she began to pump her hips against him. She rode him like a woman possessed, as she slid his cock in the juices of her body.

Her fingernails gripped his chest, digging into the hard muscles she found there. Her hips rocked fast and hard and so very deep, growing in speed and intensity as the fire ignited between them. Viktor's primal grunts of pleasure joined her wild screams. His hands left her hips, reaching to pinch her nipples and massage her breasts. Eve growled in feminine approval. Her hips worked harder as she rode him. Her own fingers found her clit, circling the sensitive nub with frantic pulls, as she fought to obtain the brilliant surrender of her climax.

"VIKTOR!"

Her scream pierced through her body just as the rampaging tremors of her release exploded in her thighs, running rampant through her form as she stiffened and convulsed around him. Viktor's grunt turned into a full cry as his seed shot into her womb.

Eve dropped down along his chest with a heavy sigh, purring contentedly. "I missed you."

Viktor tensed. His fingers lifted to push the strands of her blonde hair from her face to study her. "Only because of this?"

"No, well, this is great." She grinned, settling her hand on his chest. He was still buried deep inside her and she didn't feel like ever moving. "But, because I love you, too."

A wide smile formed over his lips as he pulled her body up to lie next to him. Draping his leg over her hip, he cradled her to his chest. "I'm sorry I didn't tell you about me sooner. At first I couldn't shift to do it, and then … Truthfully, I didn't want you to be embarrassed about talking to me."

Eve's face colored. Viktor kissed her soundly before she could pull away. He hugged her tighter and groaned as if in torment.

"No, never be embarrassed. You nearly drove me mad. I swear I healed by willpower alone just so I could make love to you," Viktor said. He kissed her temple, her cheek. "Just so I could live out every one of your fantasies with you."

Eve chuckled, suddenly not feeling so self-conscious when she heard his approval. "So that was you, that night before we officially met at the banquet?"

"Ah," Viktor chuckled. Eve loved the sound of his accent as it rolled over her in pleasant waves, making her desire him anew.

She doubted she'd ever get her fill of him. "It was. I tried to stay, but it took all my energy to shift and I couldn't hold it."

"And the tiger?" Eve asked. "He was one of your kind as well?"

"His name was Bartel. He was young, wild. He had no care for any life but his own. I stopped him from raping a woman outside a bar about a year ago and he wanted revenge for it. He stabbed me in the back and left me for dead."

"So there is no more danger?" she concluded.

"No, no more danger," Viktor said. "Unless…"

"Unless what?"

"Unless you try to send me away again." He growled. "I planned on giving you time to adjust, but now that you know the truth, I am never going to let you go. You're stuck with me."

"You won't mind living here at the Preserve?"

"No, in fact Finn has given me permission to build us a house right here in this very spot. I figure we can start construction right after the wedding."

"Wedding?" Eve gasped, her eyes growing round.

Viktor grinned. His hands began to stir against her. Before she knew what was happening, he flipped her over and began nipping at the back of her neck. His hand strayed down to grab a full cheek in his palm. Squeezing her ass, he whispered in her ear. "I see you need some more convincing before you'll agree to be my bride."

Eve whimpered as he fitted his legs between her thighs and spread her wide.

"Do not worry, love." Viktor said, rubbing his cock into her moistening pussy and up the cleft of her lovely ass. "I know every one of your fantasies. And I know just how to make them all come true. By the time I'm done with you, all your doubts will be gone."

The End

# BEST INTENTIONS

By

# Mandy M. Roth

### Chapter One

Lillian pulled up outside the *Thioshpaye* Cabins and waited for the courage to get out of the vehicle. The thought of what she'd come to do still made her slightly nauseous. She wasn't the type of girl who slept around, and she certainly wasn't the type that cheated, but she knew what had to be done. Besides, Jack had been the one to file for a divorce, not her. He'd been the one that had decided he couldn't do it anymore. Sure, he begged her to forgive his error in judgment and take him back, but there was something she needed to attend to first.

Lily glanced over at the bar, *Igmú*, adjacent to the cabins. Renee had told her that she could find plenty of sexy men willing to shack up for a night or two at the bar, no questions asked, and that's exactly what she needed. No muss, no fuss. It didn't appear to be a dive and that surprised her. She'd expected the entire place to be flea bitten and crawling with lowlifes. The place not only looked like it was well kept, it looked like it turned a decent profit as well. The Native American theme seemed a bit much, but other than that, it was perfect. She was a bit disappointed that her grandmother wasn't alive to see the place. She would have loved it. She'd been part Native American and had tried to instill some of the ways of old into Lily.

She pushed the door to the office open and stepped inside, her attention still on the bar next door.

"Can I help you?" A deep voice asked.

Lily looked at the man behind the counter and drew in a deep breath. He was stunning. From what she could see, he looked to be made of pure muscle, and the white t-shirt he wore showed off his sun kissed skin. Sandy blonde locks fell just below his shoulders and whips of sun-bleached white strands ran through it. It was clear to see that he enjoyed the outdoors.

"You all right?" he asked, cocking a light brown eyebrow at her. Stark blue eyes looked out at her from under his thick lashes.

Her pulse sped as she inched towards the counter. "Yes, I'm fine. I need a cabin for the weekend."

"You by yourself?" he asked, standing up, taking her breath away. His six foot one inch body was pure perfection.

*Oh Gawd, he's even more gorgeous than I thought.*

\* \* \* \*

Brayen's heart raced as he watched the tiny brunette walk into the office. He rarely got excited over a woman upon first glance, but she did it for him. Her curves were where they needed to be and she actually had enough meat on her bones to not look fifteen. He hated the way women starved themselves trying to be a size zero. This one was perfect, not too big, and not too small.

Her green eyes locked on him and he wondered if his face was as red as it felt. He'd never been prone to getting embarrassed-- this was a first. The way she stared at him, made him both nervous and excited all at the same time. He hated to interrupt her, but she didn't appear to be making any headway in the introducing herself department.

The scent of her arousal filled his nostrils and he had to close his eyes a moment to prevent her from seeing them shift. She wasn't a lycan, he could tell by her scent, yet here she stood in his establishment. The Shaman had said that normal humans could not see the hotel or bar, they'd see it as abandoned and continue down the highway. He'd paid good money for the old man to work his magic on the place and wasn't happy to find out that this little one found her way past it.

"You want a cabin for the weekend, huh?"

"Yes ... yes, please, if there's one available," she added softly.

Bray nodded his head and eyed her up. "Sure, I've got room, but wouldn't you be more comfortable in the city? It's only another fifteen-twenty minutes from here."

Her head snapped up and something flashed in her green eyes, anger perhaps. She moved her jaw around and Bray could smell her body changing. Yep, she was pissed. He smiled at her feistiness and looked out into the parking lot. "Need any help with your bags?"

"I can manage on my own. Thank you very much." She said sternly. Her strong will only made him want to touch her more.

"Tell ya what. I'll give you a cabin for the weekend for half price if you let me carry your bags to your room."

She balked at him. "Money's not an issue for me. I can pay your fee, and I can carry my own bags … Mr…?"

"Name is Brayen, but Bray will do Miss…?"

"Lily will do for me," she said, still glaring at him.

"Lily it is then." He moved from behind the counter and came to a stop before her. She was so much smaller than he was that she only came to his chest. He wanted to pick her up and see how well she fit against his body, but he didn't. She reeked with desire for him, but his bet was on her being cold as ice if he tried anything. It was a shame too. He hadn't been this attracted to anyone in his life. His 'condition' prevented him from getting close to too many people.

He took a deep breath in and savored the sweet scent of peaches. He wasn't sure if she'd just eaten one or if it was some sort of lotion, but it drove him mad with desire. He stretched his shoulders and started for the door. The need to put some distance between them was great. "Let's get you settled in. It's getting late and tomorrow's the full moon."

He brushed past Lily and she tensed up. The smell of her arousal hit him again, causing him to stagger backwards. She grabbed his arm and it took everything in him not to throw her to the floor and fuck her then and there.

"Are you okay?"

He glanced down at her tiny hand on his arm and let a smile creep over his face. "I'm better now, thanks."

She rolled her eyes and pulled away from him. "Can I just get the key to my cabin now?"

"Oh, in a hurry?"

"As a matter of fact, yes I am. I want to get a bite to eat at the bar. They serve food, right?"

Bray's gut clenched. They'd serve her there if she wasn't careful. "They sure do. Can I buy you dinner?"

Her eyes narrowed on him. "Why?"

"Why not?" He bent down and put his face dangerously close to hers. Her full, rose red lips were so close that it took all his strength not to clamp his mouth down on hers.

\* \* \* \*

Lily stood there, gazing into the handsome stranger's crisp blue eyes and had to fight to concentrate on what he'd said to her. She caught buy dinner and that was it. She tried to look away from him, but she couldn't. All she could do was shake her head slightly.

She hadn't intended to find anyone that she was this attracted to. The most she'd hoped for was to find a man that at least caught her eye, spend the weekend fucking his brains out, and leave--no strings, no phone numbers, no contact again.

The attraction she felt for this man, Bray, was more than she'd hoped for and more than she felt comfortable with.

*Use your head, Lily, you need to be able to walk away from this man and not look back! Jack is who you love, he's the only man you've ever loved.* She scolded herself as she stared at Bray's lips.

He stayed locked in one spot for what seemed like an eternity. The door to the office opened and a strong gust of icy cold wind blew in. Lily cried out and moved forward and the wind seemed to encircle her, thrusting her forward. She ran right into Bray's lips with her own, her mouth parted slightly from the yelp. She went to close her mouth and felt his warm tongue invade her. Her insides flared to life and her inner thighs pulsated with need. She put her hands on his chest and pushed back from him.

"Do you ... do you mind?" She panted.

Bray looked at her a moment and then around the office. Lily looked too. She felt something, someone touching her back, before it pushed her into Bray again. She looked up at him and shook her head. "Something's here ... behind me."

He put his hand out to her and she took a step back, afraid that if his skin touched hers that she'd take him to her bed instead of a man for whom she felt little. He laughed softly. "Don't mind them. They rarely do more than kick up a wind. They must have thought we needed to get a bit closer. If I were you, I'd follow the advice of the spirits. They don't mislead anyone."

Lily glanced out at her car and back at Bray. He closed his eyes slowly and shook his head. "Listen, Lily. You don't have to be afraid of me."

"Who the hell would be afraid of you, Cougar?" A husky voice bellowed from behind her. Lily jumped and spun around to find a tall man standing in the doorway. His dark hair reminded her of Jack a bit and guilt for why she was here swept through her. His dark brown eyes fell on her as he stopped in his tracks. "Well, what do we have here?"

Bray stepped in front of her quickly. "Mason, this is Lily. She's just here for the weekend."

Mason peered around Bray and smiled widely at her. She was still trying to get over how gorgeous Bray was. Adding another hunk to the mix was almost too much. Lily smiled and extended her hand. Bray stiffened and for a minute, she thought he might slap her hand away from Mason. He didn't. "Hi, I'm Lillian. My friends all call me Lily."

Mason took her hand in his and brought it to his lips slowly. "Then I hope I get to call you Lily."

He was a fine specimen of a man and the fact that she felt little when he kissed her hand proved that he should be the one she spent the weekend with.

*No attachments!* she reminded herself.

"You here by yourself?" Mason asked.

Bray growled and Mason just grinned at him. Lily nodded and took her hand back slowly. "Yes, I'm here for the weekend. Needed to get away for a bit."

"Everyone eventually does," Mason said knowingly.

Lily pushed past Bray and stood between the two men. Each was over six foot and dwarfed her. Thoughts of an erotic sandwich filled her head and she had to shake them off. An affair with two men was definitely not something she was up for. "Do you think you could give me a hand with my bags?" she asked Mason.

"It would be my pleasure."

\* \* \* \*

Bray's jaw twitched from the rage in him. How could she stand there and flirt with Mason right in front of him? She wasn't attracted to Mason, at least not in the way she'd been with him. His heightened senses made him very aware of her body's chemical reactions and there was no way she wanted Mason as much as she wanted him.

*I sound like I'm in junior high.*

Lily walked out to her car and Mason turned to look at him. "You all right? You're not thinking anything serious can happen with her, are you? She's so human that I almost choked on it. How the hell did she find this place? My grandfather said that he put a veil on it. She shouldn't have been able to wander in here. I'll put a call in to him in the morning and get him out here to repeat the ritual."

"No," Bray said, putting his hand up. "She felt the spirits of the land rush through. She's human, but some powerful blood runs through her veins, that's how she found us. Leave Running Elk alone, he's not as young as he used to be."

Mason laughed. "The man will outlive us. He's got to be pushing a hundred now."

"With as slow as we age, I'm betting over that." Bray said, peeking over Mason's shoulder at Lily. Mason smiled at him and followed his gaze.

"Cougs, if you like her, just tell me and I'll keep my distance. Wouldn't want to piss the *kitty* off." Mason growled as he wrinkled his nose.

Brayen rolled his eyes and laughed at his old friend. "I think I'm in love."

"You just met her, and she's human."

"I know, and I know. Doesn't change the fact that I'm in love."


Chapter Two

Lily applied a thin layer of lip-gloss and double-checked her outfit as she fluffed her towel-dried hair. She hoped that the tiny black dress didn't scream sleazy, but in truth, she was desperate to find a man to sleep with her tonight, so the hooker get-up was completely in order.

She turned slightly and nodded in approval at the low cut back of the dress. It just missed showing her butt. She slipped her thigh highs and heels on and headed out the door. The cool night air smacked her bare skin and she cursed herself for wearing something so skimpy.

*I'll not only get laid, I'll get pneumonia too.*

The night was darker than she remembered them being in the city and she glanced around nervously. The hairs on the back of her neck stood on end and she knew that someone was watching her. The unmistakable sound a wolf howling followed next and she broke into a run.

\* \* \* \*

Brayen sat in his office, finishing up the end of month books. He hated the work, but it needed to be done. He ran a legitimate business, even if it did cater to the supernatural. No one had investigated how the seemingly abandoned old hotel turned such a profit yet, and Bray guessed they never would.

His thoughts drifted back to Lily. He'd spent the last few hours thinking bout her. It had taken everything in him not to take her, fuck her, and claim her as his mate. It was in his makeup to want to take a mate. It seemed that all weres had the overwhelming drive to find that one person who they could breed with. The idea that his one person could be a tiny, spitfire of a human was almost laughable.

Brayen logged his last entry and stopped when he heard the cry of a wolf. He knew that sound, it was one used before the wolf attacked its prey. He'd been charged with keeping the shifters in the area in line. He was their guardian for lack of a better term and he wasn't about to let a rogue werewolf spoil it for the bunch. If the damn thing did manage to kill anything the police would be crawling all over the area looking for clues and Bray couldn't risk one of them being gifted enough to sense the lycan compound.

He stripped his shirt and shoes off as he ran outside. If it came down to a fight, he didn't want to ruin any more clothes than he had to. The cougar within him caught scent of the wolf and he ran in its direction. It was closer to the cabins than he would have liked to see. Normally, even the craziest of shifters would stay back from the compound grounds. This one was bold or incredibly stupid. He couldn't figure out which.

Mason ran out of his cabin and looked at Bray. "It's not one of mine."

"Rogue?" Brayen didn't want to hear the answer to his own question. If the wolf wasn't part of Mason's pack then they had trouble on their hands.

"That's my guess."

"Shit!"

"Yeah," Mason said, stripping his shirt off as well.

They ran towards the scent. Bray stopped in mid-stride and Mason came close to knocking him over. "Hey, what the hell are we stopping for?"

Bray put his hand up and motioned towards Lily. She stood near the edge of the property staring at a pack of wolves. Bray could feel her fear as if it were his own. "Don't move, baby. Don't move," he said softy. She started to turn her head in their direction, but stopped. "That a girl. Don't move. We're coming up behind you. Once we're there, run."

A large black wolf, no doubt the alpha, growled at Bray and Mason. Bray's body burned for the change. He wanted to shift into a cougar and have at the wolves. He knew he was stronger than they were. It had always been so. Mason's great-grandfather, the local shaman, had told him that he was born to be the guardian and that in that gift came great strength. He told him stories of his mother, Rose, showing up pregnant and alone. The people at the reservation had seen to her needs and when she'd died during childbirth, they'd cared for him as if he were one of their own. And in a way, he was one of them. Different as his cougar DNA was, he still was a shifter all the same. Mason was like his brother. They were both powerful and could take on any other shifter. So far, he hadn't met an opponent that could hold a candle to him--at least not yet.

A white wolf snapped at Lily and she screamed out. The wolves took her fear and ran with it. They lunged forward, leaving Mason and Bray no choice but to shift to defend her.

Bray's body transformed in mid-air as he leapt over Lily. He landed on all fours at her feet and batted out at the alpha wolf, catching its snout and ripping it wide open. Mason, in wolf form, appeared next to Bray. He looked over at his friend, all black and lethal, before setting his attentions back on the rogues.

\* \* \* \*

Lily stood frozen as she watched the events unfold before her. Her mind tried to make sense of the scene, but failed. A large tan cat, possibly a cougar, turned its amber eyes to her and snarled. She fought to get her feet to move.

"Bray?"

She looked around, but couldn't find him anywhere. The was no doubt in her mind that he'd spoken to her right before the white wolf leapt at her, but she couldn't find him.

"Brayen!" She yelled, frantic now that he may have been attacked as well.

*Go into the bar NOW!*

Lily turned around looking for Brayen. He sounded so close.

*Go, Lily!*

The command startled her and brought her back into the moment. Standing in the dark with a huge group of wild animals was insane. Brayen wasn't out there, she must have hallucinated him. She ran towards the bar, and stopped when another wolf appeared before her. It bared its teeth at her as it lunged off the ground. Lily screamed out and attempted to jump out of its path. It dove past her, and slid in the dirt.

\* \* \* \*

Lily's scream caught Brayen's attention and cost him dearly when the alpha rogue sunk its teeth into his neck. He slashed out at it and caught it across the face. It released him quickly and ran off in the other direction. Mason looked over at him and Bray knew that he would go after the wolf so that Bray could go to Lily.

*Thank you, brother.* Bray pushed out with his mind. He'd known how to communicate with the wolves since he was just a boy.

*Go see to your woman,* Mason said, running after the alpha. *If she has been bitten and exchanged blood then she will turn.*

The thought of Lily being turning into a lycan scared the hell out him. Few survived the change and she was already so small.

Lily screamed again and Bray shifted back into human form before jumping between the wolf and her. He caught it in midair and twisted its snout hard. He felt its jaws breaking under the weight of his grasp and he had to fight back a smile.

"Get off my property! I will kill you if you set foot on it again," he said, throwing the whimpering lycan across the yard. He whirled around to check on Lily. Her eyes were wide as she crab walked away from him, shaking her head. He'd taken every precaution to prevent her from seeing him shape shift so he didn't understand what the problem was.

He made another more towards her and she fell onto her backside. "You're bleeding and you're ... naked."

*Shit, I forgot about that.*

Brayen glanced down at himself and back at Lily. "I don't suppose you could overlook the fact that I'm walking around in the buff and trust me to get you to your cabin safely?"

She blinked twice before settling her gaze on his groin area. The minute her green eyes locked on him, his cock acted of its own accord and hardened instantly. Painfully. The need to bury it in her was too great. He stalked over to her and didn't ask if it was all right to pick her up, he just did. Her desire for him filled his nose. She wanted him damn near as much as he wanted her and that did little in the way of helping his throbbing problem.

"Put me down," she whispered. "You're bleeding all over the place."

"I'll buy you a new dress."

She balked. "I don't care about my dress. I'm worried about you hurting yourself more by carrying me. In case you haven't noticed, you're huge and if you should happen to pass out I'll never be able to get you to safety if the wolves come back."

"They won't come back." Brayen slowed his pace and looked down into her sweet face. No one had ever worried about him before. He was the guardian, the keeper of the lycans. He made sure they were safe. No one looked out for him. Need pulsated throughout his veins. He would have her tonight if he didn't put the brakes on.

"Lily, if I carry you into your cabin I'm staying the night with you. Tell me now if you don't want me because once my foot crosses that threshold there will be no turning back. And I think we both know what will take place if I stay with you."

"Carry me in."

His heart stopped. "Are you sure?"

"I think you've lost too much blood and it's affected your hearing. Carry me in already, would you?"

Her sass appealed to him even more than if she'd been submissive. The need to claim her drove him onward even though his neck was raw and she'd been right, he had lost too much blood. The werecougar in him made him able to stand more pain and to sustain injuries that would kill a human. It also made his lifespan close to ten times longer than a human's. He didn't want to think about out living Lily. He couldn't.

He opened the door to her cabin slowly, watching the expression on her face as he went. There was no way that he'd take her without her consent. It didn't matter that he'd die from need, he'd see to his mate's happiness first.

*My mate? Why do I keep calling her that? Humans can't be our mates. It's not possible.*

He set Lily down on the bed and backed away from her slowly, letting his eyelids flutter shut for a moment. The cougar in him was trying to surface and he wouldn't let it out. He wouldn't let it claim her.

"Bray?"

"I need to clean up. I'll be right back."

"You need a doctor." The worry in her face made him want her even more.

He reached out and caressed her cheek gently. "I'll be fine. I promise. I just want to wash the blood off me. You deserve better than this."

Lily looked off towards the wall and he watched closely as her expression changed. "Please don't put me on a pedestal. I don't deserve that."

Something in her tone told him that this was bigger than she was letting on. "Lily? Do you want to talk about it?"

Her gaze came back to him. "No, I don't want to talk. I just want to be with you."

Need rippled through him as he looked down at her. "I'll be right back, baby."


Chapter Three

"Hey, can I help?" Lily's sweet voice asked.

Bray stiffened as Lily opened the shower door. His hungry eyes skimmed over her naked body, soaking up its glory. His cock responded instantly. The need to pull her into the shower with him was great, and he gave into it.

"*Oh,*" she gasped as he lifted her quickly.

"*Oh,*" he echoed with a small grin.

With her in his arms, she was finally high enough to kiss comfortably so he took full advantage of that. Pressing her tiny body against the cool tile, he found her mouth and forced his tongue into it. She met him with a fury, her arms going around his neck, and her breasts pressing against his chest. The feel of her hard nipples against his skin made his cock throb.

"Wrap you legs around me."

Lily listened and as she wrapped them around him, he felt her hot core near the tip of his penis. "You're wet."

She let out a sultry laugh and kissed his jaw line. "We're in the shower."

Bray worked his hand down her side, running his fingers over her breast on the way down to her core. "That's not what I meant," he said, shoving his finger into her, finding her even wetter than he'd first thought. He licked her lip and bit at her tongue gently as it came out to greet his. "So, tight...."

They moaned together. She tipped her head back, thrusting her breasts up into his face and he was left with no choice, he had to enter her or burst. He positioned the head of his cock and thrust in hard and fast. Lily screamed out and clutched onto him. He stopped in mid stride.

"Did I hurt you?"

Her green gaze found his blue one as she dove at his mouth, pulling his bottom lip with her teeth. "More...."

He obliged. Pumping the length of shaft into her repeatedly, savoring every second of having her tight sheath encompassing him. "Do you feel that? You were made for me."

She answered him by planting tiny kisses on his throat. She pulled back quickly and caught his face in her hands, forcing his eyes to hers. "What are you? You're healed."

The thought of lying to her never entered his mind, and that should have scared him. The existence of his people depended on humans not knowing about them. Brayen did use his gifts to coat his voice with a bit of reassurance. It was easy to do, yet he found that he rarely used that talent. "I'd never hurt you, Lily. I'm a shape shifter. Like the legends of old. My animal is the cougar."

Her eyes widened and he waited for her to scream. She didn't. "You were the tan cat that saved me from the wolves." She glanced away a moment. "Oh, *Gawd*, those weren't wolves, were they?"

"No," he answered honestly.

"They would have killed me."

"Among other things."

Lily ran her hands through his hair and traced her way over his shoulders, and down his arms. He began to move within her, slowly, unsure how to take her calmness. He expected hysterics.

"Is your condition genetic?"

Her question caught him off guard. He'd set himself up for her to scream bloody murder and demand that he exit her body immediately. "*Umm*, I guess, but I don't know. I can't have children until I find my mate."

She looked saddened by his news. "How many mates do you get?"

He pumped himself into her slowly, filling her, and feeling her body tighten around him, trying his best to stay focused on their conversation. It was hard to do when her breasts seemed to swell beneath his touch. "I only get one. Do you want me to stop? Are you afraid of me?"

"I'm not afraid of you for the reason you'd think. I'm afraid that I won't be able to walk away from you."

"You don't have to walk away, Lily. You could stay with me."

"*Shh*," she said, pulling his mouth to hers. He quickened his strokes and let out a muffled cry as she bit down gently on his tongue.

He reached down and rubbed his fingers over her swollen clit. She jerked and bit down harder on his tongue, drawing blood, and pulling the beast within him to the surface. A growl emanated from him as his body shook. Lily's tight pussy milked him and brought his own release on suddenly. Brayen almost lost his footing as the water beat down on his back and his seed spurted into her womb. His incisors lengthened and he bent his head down to sink them into her soft skin.

Lily cried out and grabbed hold of his hair as her blood flowed into his mouth. He felt her channel constrict again as the pleasure of his bite brought an orgasm. Before he knew it, he was coming again as well, spilling his seed into her, filling her womb with his power.

He pulled back from her slowly, running his rough tongue over the bite mark. The realization of what he'd just done sunk in. He'd marked her while having sex. He'd mated with her. Brayen pulled back from her quickly and let her legs slide down him.

She stood before him and ran her hands over his stomach, before wrapping her arms around him. Her embrace felt so right, so perfect. She was his other half. The one he'd searched for all his life, yet she was human. He couldn't explain it to himself, let alone to her.

"Come on. Let's get you cleaned up before the shock of what I am sinks in."

Lily tightened her hold on him. "I'm not shocked at all. My grandmother told me about you. She said that men like you existed and that I was born to walk among them. Of course, I took everything she said with a grain of salt. That will teach me," she said, with a laugh. "I mean who believes that they were destined to meet people who can turn into animals?"

"Did she also tell you that you'd end up mated to one the rest of your life?"

Lily's arms dropped away from him. Sorrow filled her voice as she spoke. "We have the weekend, Bray. That's all we'll ever have."

"No, we can have eternity. All you have to do is say the word."

She put her hand on his chest and shook her head. "I can't give you anymore than the weekend."

If she thought for one minute that he'd let her walk out of his life she was not only wrong, but crazy as well. They were married in the eyes of the were community, and that was not something that was taken lightly. She was now the guardian's wife--his mate, and hopefully, if they should happen to be blessed enough, the mother of his children.

He turned the water off and lifted her from the shower. The sweet smell of her sex permeated upwards and he found himself instantly aroused. Her tiny fingers wrapped around him causing him to moan.

"You are insatiable," she whispered.

"When I find something that makes me happy I tend to run with it."

"I see that."

"Say that you'll stay longer than the weekend," Brayen pleaded, needing to hear that she'd consider it. Though he was sure that she had no idea just what she was to him now. In her eyes, he was a one-night stand. In his world, she was his wife. He laid her damp body out on the bed and pushed her legs apart with his knee. He edged the head of his cock near her still soaked pussy and leered down at her.

She bucked beneath him, trying to get him to enter her. "Please...."

"Promise me more than the weekend, Lily."

"I can't."

He let the tip of his penis slip into her. Still tight, she seemed to seize hold of him. It took everything in him not to slam himself down to the hilt. He needed to hear her promise to stay. He wasn't sure why it was so important to him, but it was. "Lily, let me love you more than a few days."

"Bray," she sighed his name out.

Seeing that he had lost this one battle, but refusing to lose the war, he plunged into her, determined to lay claim to her in as many ways as he could. A scream tore from her throat as he sank his teeth into her breast, riding her body with his the entire time. Each thrust, each draw of her blood, put him closer to the edge of sanity.

Lily raked at his back. He felt the blood running down him, as the fiery hot feel of her sharp nails continued to dig into him. She came with a start. "Brayen, oh yes, Brayen … yes … fill me up, give it to me."

How could he resist such a simple request? He thrust into her again, this time holding himself down on her as his cock pumped, shooting forth his come.

## Chapter Four

Brayen took a deep breath in, holding Lily's sweet scent in him. His insides churned. He'd never experienced anything like this before. Waking up with her tiny body wrapped around his after a night of unbelievable lovemaking was almost too much.

For a tiny thing, Lily was insatiable. They'd made love every way possible in the tiny cabin. So many times in fact that he'd thought for sure they'd both be unable to move for days.

He reached down and ran his hand over her lower abdomen. Afraid to say it aloud, he just let his hand rest there, hoping that the gods would see fit to give them a family someday. After the passion they'd shared, Lily couldn't just walk out. She could say that they had only the weekend until she was blue in the face, but leaving him would hurt her as much as it would hurt him. They were connected now--mated.

*Cougar*, Mason's voice pushed into his mind.

He stirred slightly, careful not to wake Lily. *What is it?*

*The rogue wolves were spotted in the area again. I'm going to take a group out to hunt them at dusk. I thought you might want to come too.*

Brayen looked down at Lily and exhaled slowly. *I can't.*

*I understand. Stay with her and I will do my best to assure that she doesn't see any of us shift.*

*She knows what we are.*

Dead silence greeted him. He knew that Mason was attempting to understand why Brayen had told an outsider about them. The laws of their kind were clear. No outsider was to know of them and live. Lily wasn't an outsider anymore. She was his mate now.

*Cougar....*

*I took her as my mate,* Brayen said quickly, not wanting Mason's wheels to spin.

*She's not one of us.*

*I know, but that doesn't change the fact that she's my mate. Look at us. You consider me your brother, yet my mother came here, pregnant and alone, without an ounce of Sioux blood in her. Running Elk took me in. I am as different as she is, yet I am your family.*

He felt the weight of Mason's thoughts. *That's different, Brayen. Grandfather knew instantly that you carried the gene of a cougar in you. The human does not carry a were gene ... not unless you infect her with it. That could be the answer to all our problems.*

*NO!*

*Brayen....*

He cut communication down with Mason instantly. He wouldn't entertain bringing Lily over. The change could kill her.

Brayen gathered Lily in his arms and pressed his lips to her forehead. She was his now and he'd never give her up or let harm come to her. If his people weren't willing to accept her as she was then he'd leave. It was that simple. His wife came before all else.

\* \* \* \*

Lily woke slowly, still sore from the incredible night of lovemaking she'd shared with Brayen. How a man could go that many times in one night was beyond her. They'd done so many things, things she'd never dreamt of doing with Jack, that she blushed again thinking about them.

She smiled sheepishly as she thought about Brayen holding her hair as he commanded her to 'suck him off', and oh, how had she. She taken every last inch of his abnormally large cock into her mouth until it had hit the back of her throat. She could still hear his soft moans of pleasure and feel his abs tighten under the weight of her fingertips as he spit seed down her throat. It was one of the most erotic experiences she'd ever had with a man and it hardened her heart to think about it.

*I have to walk away. I have to go home. I have a life there, waiting for me to put it back together again. I can't leave Bray, I've fallen in love with him.*

She stopped dead in her tracks. *Love?* Where the hell had that come from? What had provoked her decision to stay? She hardly knew the man and the little she did know would have scared anyone else to death.

Lily shook the thoughts from her head and looked around the cabin for Bray. He was nowhere to be found. She sat up, slowly.

The discomfort from being rode hard by Brayen left her a bit worse for the wear.

She crept over to the cabin door, tucking the sheet from the bed around her more, and opened it slowly. Shocked at first by the fact that it was dark out again, she inched her way out of the cabin.

She would have turned around and waited in the cabin for him, but the sound of his voice, raised in anger grabbed her.

"I will not turn her!" Brayen shouted.

"You'll turn her or we'll have no choice but to deal with her, or I will have to...." Mason's voice followed close behind his.

Brayen snarled. "Don't even fucking think about laying a hand on her, Mason, or I will forget that I call you brother."

"Come on, Bray. Be realistic. Turn her or kill her. If you don't, one of the others here will. Do you want them sticking their dicks in your woman for the rest of your life? Claim her fully or they will--if you're lucky. They could always just kill her. Let us pray that it's a swift death because you know how some of them like to play with their food."

"God damnit, Mason! Why does it have to be this way? Why can't I just love her as she is?" Bray asked. He sounded like he might be crying. "She's still refusing to stay with me. She says that we only have the weekend and that she'll go then."

"Did you tell her that she couldn't?"

"I asked her not to."

Mason chuckled. "Tell you what, brother. I'll hold the rest of the pack back until tomorrow night. If you haven't turned her by then, then we'll be left no choice but to protect our secret ... whatever the cost."

"NO! If it comes down to it, I'll deal with her. No one else is to touch her. Am I clear?"

Lily choked back a sob as she hurried back into their cabin, leaving them to finish their conversation. Brayen was going to force her to become what he was or kill her. Her heart sped and she had to fight to keep from screaming.

Something sharp pinched in her lower abdomen and her eyes widened in horror. "No, I can't be." Instinctively she knew that it was true.

The door to the cabin opened and Lily had no more time to think about what she'd just learned. Brayen stood there smiling at her like he had no cares in the world. "How do you feel? Not too sore I hope."

"Fine," she said sternly.

"Is everything okay?"

She couldn't tip him off that she knew what he had to do. She forced a smile onto her face and let the sheet fall away from her body slowly. There was no way that she'd stay through tomorrow and put him in the position of having to decide how to best handle her, but there was also no way she could leave without feeling his body in hers one more time. Like it or not, she was addicted to him. In love with him, and deathly afraid of him.

Lily put her hand out, summoning him to her. His golden hair caught pieces of the moonlight streaming in from the window. He looked like a god standing there, and she knew that he too held the power of life and death in his hands.

He let a wicked grin spill over his face. "*Mmmm*, I believe your sex drive may rival my own." He covered the distance between them and pulled her into his arms. "I love my smell all over you. Don't get me wrong, I love the way you smell, but," he drew in a deep breath, "I like knowing that you're mine. Always and forever."

She choked back the tears that threatened to fall. Oh, how she wished that what he said were true. Somewhere along the line, she lost the will to return to the life she once knew and wanted only to be loved by him for the rest of her days, but if the rest of his 'pack' had anything to do with it, tomorrow would be her last day. Panic welled up inside her and she clutched on to Brayen's strong arms to stay grounded.

"Lily? What's wrong?"

She fought to regain her composure and leaned up to meet his lips. "Fuck me."

Brayen stiffened at her words. His nostrils flared slightly and she almost screamed when his eyes flickered from blue to amber. When he spoke, his voice sounded labored and deeper than normal. "Woman, you shouldn't talk to me like that. The beast is hard enough to control around you."

He turned her around quickly and she yelped. Material ripped behind her and it only took a moment to figure out that it was Brayen's clothing. He pushed the sheet away from her body as he forced her to her hands and knees. His fingers seemed to caress her entire body. Heat built up inside her and she screamed out as he tweaked her nipples.

"Such ripe berries … they taste as sweet, you know."

Lily only moaned in response to him as Bray slid his hands down her body and found her swollen clit, plucking it, sending white-hot stabs of pleasure through her lower regions. Gasping for breath, she clawed at the floor, trying desperately to find her center. She failed, as an orgasm ripped through her, leaving her out of breath and falling forward.

Wrapping his arms around her waist, Brayen leaned in to her, his rigid cock pressed against her soaked entrance. "I'm not done with you, my love."

*Love?*

"I can't take ... anymore," she panted.

He growled near her ear, and rubbed the head of his penis in and out of her pussy. "That's it, baby." He slid the length of himself into her quickly. Unable to hold her exhausted body up, she fell onto her elbows. Brayen stroked her back tenderly. "I'll do the work, my love. Just stay there and enjoy it. You do like it?"

"Yes," she whispered. "I love it. *I love you.*"

Her confession came just as Brayen slid a finger into her anus. She cried out and tried to crawl away from him. His other arm encircled her, pulling her back to him, forcing his cock deeper into her womb, and his finger further into her anus. She was so full. Too full. "Brayen...."

Angling her hips upward, Brayen pumped harder into her, hitting her g-spot. The orgasm blindsided her, leaving her contracting on both his cock and finger. "So fucking tight ... Lily ... so fucking perfect."

He slammed his body down hard in to hers, jerking as he came deep within her. "I love you too, Lily, with all my heart."

She froze. He'd heard her confession. She'd assumed that he hadn't, but now as he held her to his body, still spilling semen in her, she knew that he too shared her feelings.

The tears that she'd tried so desperately to hold back flowed freely. She did her best to steel herself to the reality of what she was about to do. She would wait until he fell asleep and then she would leave without so much as a goodbye. There was little choice for her. There was more than just her own safety to think about now.

## Chapter Five

Brayen touched Renee's shoulder and gave her a halfhearted smile. "Thanks for inviting me. This is nice."

"*Whoof*, nice he says." Renee jabbed him in the rib cage and narrowed her eyes. "Nice is you finally getting out and seeing people. You stay locked away with...."

Bray's jaw tightened. "Say it ... animals."

Renee shook her head and glanced nervously at the kitchen door. "I'd never call you or others like you animals and you know that. My father was one and I loved him with all my heart. I grew up wishing that I'd gotten the gene that causes it."

He froze as he heard Renee confess to wanting to be a shapeshifter. He wouldn't wish it upon anyone. Having normal friends was rare. Renee was one of the only humans he interacted with and that's only because he'd known her father. The only other human he'd ever gotten close to had walked in and out of his life in a matter of two days, but had left a gaping hole in his heart that would never heal.

"Bray, you all right?" Renee asked, eyeing him suspiciously.

He nodded and grabbed the plate from her hands. "Here, I'll take that out to Will, those burgers smell done enough. Anymore and we'll be chewing on charcoal."

Renee laughed as he headed towards the back door. He opened the French door and stopped when he caught scent of *her*. He looked around frantically and spotted her standing there. She was still as beautiful as the night she walked in needing a room for the weekend.

Lily was dressed in a pale yellow sundress that hung to her ankles. Her dark brown hair seemed a little longer than the last time he'd seen her, but other than that she hadn't changed in almost six years.

Something brushed past Bray's hand and he drew in a sharp breath as a tiny shock passed through his skin. He glanced down to find a little girl standing next to him. She looked up at him and smiled wide. A tiny dimple formed on the right side of her face and her blue eyes locked on his. "She's like an angel, isn't she?" she asked, softly.

"Who?"

The little girl pointed out towards Lily and reached up to take his hand. He stood still, reluctant to touch the tiny being next to him. She seemed so small that he feared he'd crush her with just one touch. She pressed her hand into his and looked out towards

Lily. "I tell her that she looks like an angel all the time, but she doesn't believe me. I can tell you think she looks like one too."

Bray let out a chuckle. "Oh, you can? You seem awfully young to know so much."

She balked. "I'm five, and I'm very smart for my age."

"Ah, I see." Bray said, stiffening as he saw a man approaching Lily. The man looked as though he'd fallen out of the pages of GQ or at the very least was a Kennedy. Bray's muscles flexed as the man's hand ran up Lily's back like it belonged there. She settled back into his arms and it was clear to see how very happy she was. The man wrapped his body around her and swayed back and forth with her.

Blinding rage overcame Bray and he clutched hold of the doorframe to keep from growling and drawing attention to himself. A tiny cry sounded next to him and he looked down to see the tiny brown-haired girl staring at him with wide eyes. He looked at his hand and realized that he was clutching her small hand. With his lycan strength he could crush it without thought. Bray dropped to his knees next to her and inspected her for injury.

"I'm sorry, sweetie, did I hurt you?"

Her lip puckered out. "Just a little. How did you do that?"

"Do what?"

She moved up closer to him. "How did you make the same noise that I make? The sound like a mean kitty?"

Bray hadn't realized that he had made any noise. He smiled at the little girl and touched her hand gently. How he hadn't crushed all the bones in her hand was a mystery. "What's your name?"

"Rebecca-Rose, but everyone calls me Becca. What's yours?"

"Rose? That was my mother's name. You must be a very special little girl to have a name like that," Bray said, giving her a wide smile.

Becca reached up and touched his cheek softly. Her tiny finger went to his dimple and her eyes widened. "You've got the same hole when you smile. My momma says that she can see all the way through my head when I smile big."

Bray let out a throaty laugh and patted her head gently. "I think your momma sounds like she's a good mommy."

"Oh, no, she's the bestest mommy ever!"

"Rebecca-Rose, what are you doing bothering this nice man?"

Bray's nostrils flared as he looked up to see the Kennedy

standing over them. The man gave Becca a sideways glance and then started to laugh. "I leave you alone for five minutes and you're harassing Renee and Will's guests." He looked at Bray and put his hand out. "Hi, I'm Jack Preston, and I see you've already met my daughter Becca."

Bray stood slowly and took the man's hands in his. He could smell Lily on him. They'd been intimate recently and the thought of that sickened him. Becca touched his arm lightly, keeping him from shifting and ripping Jack Preston's head clean off.

Jack looked down at his daughter and reached for her. She leapt into his arms, but kept her eyes on Bray. "Daddy, he can make the kitty noise like me."

Jack glanced nervously at Bray, but forced a smile to his lips. "Oh, he can, can he? Does he get into as much mischief as you too?"

Becca looked at him and shrugged her shoulders. "I don't know, Daddy, maybe. He's strong too."

"I'm sure he is, peanut," he said, setting her down gently. "Mommy's looking for you. She wants you to sit down and eat something. I told her not to bother, but you know your mom."

Becca nodded. "I told him that momma looks like an angel. I think he believed me."

Bray's gut clenched tight, and he scanned the yard for signs of Lily. She was a mother now, and a wife? That couldn't be. She was his wife, and supposed to be the mother of his children someday. He watched as Becca scattered away, leaving him standing face to face with Jack.

"She's a cute kid. You and your wife must be *very* proud." Bray almost choked on the words as he said them.

Jack nodded and walked over to the cooler. He grabbed a bottle of water. "You want a beer or anything?"

"No, I'm fine," Bray said, watching him carefully. "Only water for you?"

"Yeah, I'm on call at the hospital. They've got someone in the ER now, but if things get backed up I'll need to head in."

Of course, Lily would be married to a doctor. A nasty thought popped into his head. "So, if you don't mind me asking, how long have you been married?"

Jack reached out and touched Bray's shoulder. He wanted to bite the man, but stood tall. "Lillian and I have been an item since high school. I loved her from the moment I laid eyes on her and we've never been apart. I married her right out of high school and made it work through college. It was rough, but we made it. My family didn't approve. They even managed to come between us for a while there, before Becca was born. I didn't think we'd make it for a while there, divorce papers were already filed ... oh, look at me ramble on. That was more I information than you wanted."

"You can say that again." An identical replica of Jack said as he approached.

Bray looked at the twins and his nausea only intensified. *Of course, they'd come in pairs.*

Jack smiled at him. "Ah, this is my brother Lewis. Lewis this is...?"

"JACK, your pager's going off!" Lily's voice floated over the crowd.

"Better run, wouldn't want to keep *her* waiting," Lewis said sardonically.

It was clear to Bray that Lewis didn't like Lily. He could smell his hate for her rolling off the man, and he found himself wanting to snap both their necks. Jack looked at Bray and ran his fingers through his short black hair. "Work needs me, sorry that I couldn't introduce you to Lily. She'd love to meet the man who charmed Becca." He smiled and turned to go. "See to it that Lily and Becca get home safe if I'm not back," he said to Lewis.

"No problem, brother," Lewis said, as he watched Jack run off. He made a gagging sound and glanced up at Bray. "Does it sicken you too?"

Bray jumped a bit startled by the question. "Does what sicken me?"

"Seeing the two of them together."

"I take it that you don't care much for your sister-in-law."

Lewis let out an icy laugh and looked Bray dead in the eye. "He could have done so much better than a little squaw half breed piece of trash. Hell, anything would have been better than that."

Brayen saw red, but did his best to stay levelheaded. "From my understanding, Jack's wife has only a tiny bit of Native American blood in her, and she is quite proud of it. I'd love to be a full blooded Lakota"

Lewis didn't ask how he knew that. "Lak ... what?" He waved his hand in the air. "Please, you don't have to pretend for my sake. Nobody wants the red man's blood in them, least of all me. It sickens me that Jack tainted the Preston name with that stain. I told him to let the half breed suck his dick, spread her legs and that was it, not put a ring on her damn finger. Our mother never approved. Right up until she died she begged him to reconsider his choice in a wife."

Bray resisted the urge to smash Lewis' head into the wall and watched as he walked away into the crowd of people. Renee walked up behind him and tapped his shoulder. "Planning on taking that plate out to Will or are you willing to eat your meat cooked for once?"

"Would you mind doing it? I've got ... *umm* ... I've got a bit of a *problem* with keeping my problem at bay." He hoped that Renee would understand that if he took one step out that door after Lewis he would shift into the cougar and rip the man's throat out.

Renee took the plate from him and walked outside. "You are so going to have to fill me in on what's going on with you when I get back. Try not to eat any of my guests."

"Renee, have you seen Lily's keys? Someone's parked behind me and the hospital needs me," Jack said, appearing behind Bray.

Renee looked back and pointed towards the countertop. "She always tosses them in the basket with mine. I swear, the woman should have been my sister, she's here enough. I'll give her a ride home later, she can't drive your stick shift."

"Thanks, doll!" Jack said, snatching the keys up. "Watch her, she's a wild one."

"Daddy, Daddy...." Becca cried out, running past Bray to Jack. "Don't go today Daddy, please."

Jack's eyebrows came together. "Peanut, you've never asked me not to go in to work before. What's wrong? You know that sick people need Daddy's help, right?"

Large tears welled up in little Becca's eyes and Bray felt his own heart break with the fall of each one. "I know, Daddy, but don't go today, please. I have a bad feeling, Daddy. The kind that pulls at my tummy and makes the kitty noise come again."

Jack kissed her forehead and wiped her tears away. "I'll be back soon, and we can have a tea party. I'll even wear one of those silly hats, okay?" He set her down and looked up at Bray. "Sorry to ask you to do this, but could see to it that she doesn't run out behind me? Lily will be in here in just a minute."

Bray nodded and moved closer to Becca. He watched Jack run out the door and had to pick Becca up to keep her from following him. "Put me down, put me down!"

"Your *father* asked me to keep you here until your mommy comes in." Bray tried to sound gentle, but he'd never been around small children and wasn't sure how to handle this type of situation.

Becca twisted in his arms and snarled at him. Bray's heart leapt to his throat. He knew that sound. He'd made it enough himself. He took a deep breath in and held it. Becca's scent was familiar, she smelled of Lily and, he took another breath. He staggered backwards a bit, but managed to hold her steady. Becca smelled of cougar, like him. She twisted in his arms and looked at him, her blue eyes shifted to amber before she snarled again.

He let out a throaty growl as a warning to her not to try anything and she stopped moving in his arms. Her wide eyes fell on him and tears filled them. "He won't be back."

Bray looked towards the front of Renee's large home. "Sure he will, sweetie. He just had...."

She shook her head. "No, Daddy won't ever be back, and Mommy's heart will break." She put her head on his shoulder and he smoothed her long hair down. "You'll help make it better, won't you? I know you will make it better."

Brayen wasn't sure what to say to her. He couldn't come out and tell her that he thought he was her father, no, Jack had filled those shoes all her life. It was clear that she loved the man, and he her, but Bray had to know. He turned with her in his arms and found Lily standing behind him, her mouth open.

"Brayen?" She said his name softly. She looked at Becca in his arms. Her face paled, and she grabbed hold of the countertop to steady herself. That was all the confirmation he needed. She'd left him almost six years ago in the middle of the night, pregnant with his child and never told him about her. He hugged Becca to his chest and shook his head at Lily.

"How could you not tell me?"

"Bray," she said, moving closer to him and lowering her voice. "I was, am, a married woman. I, we ... Jack and I couldn't have ... I...."

The realization of what she was saying sunk in. He'd been nothing more than a sperm donor. She was his mate, his world, *his* wife. He'd thought that what they had was special, now he knew that it meant nothing to her. Bray fought back the tears that tried to surface and did his best not to let Lily see the hurt in his eyes.

Someone pounded on the front door and it burst open. "LILLIAN, LEWIS!"

Lewis burst through the back door and Lily followed close behind him as he ran to the front room. "Chief Sisel?"

A tall man stood there, covered in blood. His eyes were wild as he looked at Lily. "Lillian, there's been an accident, just down the bend, near the river. Jack's...." He dropped his head down.

"NO!" Lewis cried out.

"No," Lily whispered softly, as she took a step back. "No, Adam, no … don't do this … don't … no, Jack's fine. He's at the hospital now, they needed his help … he's fine … he's...."

Chief Sisel made a move towards her and she darted away from him. "Lillian, Jack's gone. Beth and I were on our way up here for the picnic and I watched him lose control of your car and … I tried to save him … I radioed in for help and the squad was there in a matter of minutes. Lillian, they said that he died instantly."

Brayen turned with Becca in his arms and ran towards the backyard. She clung to him sobbing and mumbling about how she knew her daddy wasn't coming back. He spotted Renee and ran to her. "There's been an accident … Jack."

Renee reached for Becca, but she held tight to his neck. "Sweetie, go to Renee, I need to check on your mommy." Renee gave him a puzzled look, but didn't question him.

"I want to stay with you. You can't leave us now, he'll hurt mommy. He doesn't like her … please!" Becca said, between sobs. Bray passed her to Renee and kissed her tiny cheek quickly.

"I won't leave you, sweetie," he said softly, wondering who *he* was.


Chapter Six

Brayen ran to the front yard and found Chief Sisel holding Lily in his arms as she kicked and screamed at him to let her go to Jack. She lashed out again and caught the Chief's cheek. He loosened his grip enough for her to weasel out of his grasp.

"Lillian!" Chief Sisel called out after her.

"Let her go, maybe we'll get lucky and the bitch will die too," Lewis whispered under his breath. The Chief missed the comment, but Bray's ultra-sensitive hearing let him pick up on every bit of it. He shot Lewis a nasty look and raced down the drive after Lily. She'd covered quite a bit of ground in a short period of time and Bray had to grab her around the waist to get her to stop.

She pounded on his chest as he spun her around. "Let go of me!"

"Lily, please stop. Let's go back up to Renee's and...."

"And what?" She demanded. "He's gone, Bray ... Jack is gone. He can't be dead. I didn't mean for it to happen. He should have punished me, not Jack."

Bray held her to him and shook his head. "Who should punish you, and what the hell are you talking about?"

"God, he should have punished me, not Jack. I'm the one who lied. I'm the one who lied."

"Baby, please, I don't understand. I want to help you, but you need to get a hold of yourself. What did you lie about?"

She cried out and slapped him hard across the face. He didn't flinch. He just let her hit him repeatedly. "I lied to Jack, when he found out that Becca wasn't his ... he asked if I loved her father." She took a deep breath in, "and I said no, I looked him in the eyes and I told him that I never loved you, that I only used you. I lied to him ... oh God, I lied to him."

Brayen set her down and grabbed her wrists. He pulled her body to his and let her cry as he held her. "It's okay, baby. It's okay. You weren't being punished. It's okay."

"It's not okay! I lied to him! It was bad enough that he found out that she wasn't his. I couldn't bring myself to hurt him more. I love him, Bray, I do ... *did* ... but not as much as I love you and now he's dead because of me! I need to go to him, right now. I need to see him." She clutched onto his shirt and clawed at his chest. "I thought that we were going to make it. Jack said that he understood, but now he's gone. He can't be gone. They're wrong. He's fine. I'm sure he's fine. Right?"

Bray did his best to hold his emotions in check. On one hand, he had his mate confessing to loving him more than her husband, yet on the other hand, he felt her pain and sorrow. "Come on, baby, let's get you back to the house, Becca needs you to be strong now."

## Chapter Seven

Lily looked out at the for sale sign and pressed her forehead to the window. Renee had told her to keep the house, that it was what Jack would have wanted, but she couldn't bear to live with memory of him all around her. Every room reminded her of him, and she couldn't do it anymore. He'd been gone for six months now and she still couldn't go to his gravesite. Her shame over their last few weeks together was too great.

Becca's eyes had shifted, that was the first sign that something was different with her. Lily tried to make excuses for it, but she knew why. She knew that Brayen's 'dark gift' had been passed to her daughter and that she one day would be able to change into a cougar at will. Jack had finally cornered her with blood tests that his brother Lewis had run on Becca the last time she was in for a check-up. Being married to a twin whose other half was also a doctor had never been easy, but Lewis' deception had almost cost Lily her marriage.

The hurt in Jack's eyes was so great when she walked in and found him holding the paternity papers that she knew instantly what had happened. She just didn't know why Lewis had done it. Sure, he disliked her, he always had, but to come in five years after the fact and pull a stunt like this was too much!

They'd been happy. She'd done what she had to do to have a baby and Jack had understood. He'd forbidden her to seek medical attention because he didn't want his colleagues knowing that they were having trouble conceiving a child. She'd honored that wish and when he'd left for the conference in Chicago for the weekend, she'd seized the moment and gone to the bar she'd heard Renee mention once. Her intent had been to get pregnant, not to fall in love. She'd succeeded in one, but failed miserably in the other.

Her cell phone rang. She looked at the display screen and rolled her eyes when she saw Lewis' name. "Hello?"

"Lily, I need for you to sign a few papers for me. It has to do with Jack's share of the family practice. You'll maintain control of it, of course, but I just need to get the okay for a few things."

The last thing she wanted to deal with right now was more paperwork. "Whatever, Lewis. Becca and I will stop by before we leave town. Are you at the office or home?"

"I've got to make a quick stop tonight, Lily. Why don't you meet me...." The phone lost its reception. Normally she would have been ticked that her phone had once again popped out on her, but the fact that it cut Lewis off was a blessing, so she went with it.

\* \* \* \*

Lily listened close and heard Becca's voice coming from Jack's old office. Lily hadn't been able to set foot in there yet. Lewis had handled packing up all of Jack's belongings for her. She'd had to leave the house when he did. Seeing the exact replica of Jack wandering around the house had been too much for her.

She stopped just outside the office door and listened to Becca talking softly. "Yes, Momma is still sad. I tried to get her to smile today, but she doesn't ever smile anymore. No, I want her to leave. He's bad and he'll hurt her. You know he will."

Lily cracked the door open and found Becca sitting in the center of the empty room. "I know that you love me, Daddy, but I can't get Momma to stop missing you," Becca said to the empty room. Lily's stomach tightened. Now wasn't the time for her daughter to take up talking to thin air and pretending it was her father. She started forward to put a stop to it, but stopped when she felt a rush of cold air blow around her. Something whispered to her, but it was muffled. Lily gasped and ran towards Becca. She snatched her daughter up in her arms and ran from the room.

"Daddy!" Becca screamed, reaching over her shoulder towards the vacant room.

The gusting wind followed Lily down the hall and she thrust the front door open. Strong arms grabbed hold of her and she screamed out.

"LILY!" Brayen shouted.

"Bray?" She threw herself against him, smashing Becca between the two of them. "Something was in the room with Becca … I heard it … it was cold, like ice," she panted.

Bray touched Becca's head and she looked up at him. "Momma was scared of Daddy. It's just Daddy coming back to tell her to be careful and to trust you. He told me to find the man who makes the kitty noise too, that he would always love me and Mommy."

"Rebecca-Rose, you will not talk about your father like he's still here."

"But he is, Momma."

"Yes, he is." Bray said, looking directly at her. She hadn't intended to be insensitive, and yes, biologically speaking her father was here, but that wasn't what she'd meant.

A cold blast of wind blew past them and on it came the whisper of Lillian's name. She screamed out and Bray pulled them both out of the house. He hustled them towards his jeep and didn't stop shoving them until they were safely inside.

Lily buckled Becca into the backseat and waited for Bray to climb in. "You felt it too."

"Yeah, and I heard it as well," he said, starting the jeep.

## Chapter Nine

Bray carried Becca into his house and took her up to the loft. He kissed her gently as he tucked her under the covers and brushed the hair from her face. He'd ached to see her tiny face again and had made the decision to just show up on her doorstep. Lily hadn't returned one of his calls and had asked him to stay away. He'd honored that until he was no longer able to bear not seeing them.

Renee had understood and given him a call to tell him that if he wanted to catch Lily and Becca he needed to act fast, they were moving away. The thought of never seeing Lily or his daughter again sickened him, and he was happy he'd decided to go to them, but he couldn't stop himself. He needed them, and they needed him no matter what Lily thought.

Becca purred softly in her sleep and Bray smiled. She was his, it didn't matter that she called another man daddy--she was totally his. It was as plain as the dimple on her face, and her ever-changing eyes--she was his.

Every night since the moment he'd learned she existed, he'd looked up at the night sky and wondered what his little girl was doing. He'd even stood on the sidelines at Jack's funeral, hidden away--just to be sure she was okay. Now, she was here, in his home, where she belonged, where they both belonged.

He turned to find Lily and stopped when Becca cried out softly in her sleep. She opened her eyes and looked directly at him. "Daddy?"

"It's just me, Bray," he whispered.

She nodded her head. "I know, but Daddy told me that you're my daddy now and that you're special like me. He said that you'll love me like he did. Will you love me like he did?"

"Yes, Rebecca-Rose, I love...." She was asleep again before he got the words out of his mouth. He still wasn't sure how to be a parent, but he knew that he'd never let anything happen to her and that he'd ached to hold her to his chest and to hear her sweet voice again. If that was part of being parent then he'd do just fine.

It saddened him that Becca still felt the need to talk like Jack was still around, but after the incident at the house, Bray wondered if he really was. He glanced around the loft and shook his head in approval. The moment he'd returned home after learning of Becca, he'd redone the upstairs area just for her. Sanding the wood for her new bed, and building the dresser from scratch had been all he had to occupy himself with while he gave Lily her required time to grieve.

The three-story dollhouse that he'd made her caught his eye and he hoped that when she woke it would catch hers too. He kissed her lightly on the head and turned to climb down the stairs. He took a deep breath in and knew that Lily was on the porch. Come hell or high water, that woman was going to talk to him.

Bray thrust the screen door open and headed out to her. She stood there with her arms wrapped tightly around her body, holding her cell phone in one hand.

"Who did you call?" He asked.

"Lewis, I was supposed to meet with him and sign some papers tonight and I didn't want him worried about us."

Fat chance of that, Brayen thought to himself.

Lily shivered slightly. He knew she was cold, the night breeze had picked up. He wrapped his arms around her petite frame and pulled her back into his body. She stiffened.

"Damn it, Lilly. Stop! I love you."

Her head fell back against his body as she touched his arms lightly. "I wonder everyday if I wouldn't have got in my car and drove to the *Igmú*, would Jack still be alive?"

"You wouldn't have Becca. *We* wouldn't have Becca," he said, avoiding the desire to defend their love for one another.

"No, we wouldn't. Would we?" She dropped her head down and let out a deep breath. "What in the world does *Igmú* mean?"

Brayen smiled in spite himself. "It means cat in the Lakota native tongue."

"I should have known, *Cougs*."

\* \* \* \*

Lily turned in Brayen's arms and let him hold her tight to him. She'd dreamed of a moment like this for over six years, but hated the price she'd paid for it. Still, being in Bray's arms felt right and seeing him carrying Becca to bed made her guilty for keeping them apart for so long.

"Bray, I screwed up everything. Every choice I made was a bad one. I didn't mean to hurt you, Jack, Becca, anyone...." His lips crashed down on hers, barely giving her time to breathe let alone think. His tongue dove in and found hers ready and willing. She clawed at his back and he pressed his mouth down on her even harder. His hands roamed up her back and stopped when he reached her neck. He jerked her head back from him.

Bray's eyes burned amber and a gasp escaped her throat. She pressed her fingers to her swollen lips and tried to back away from him. He held tight to her neck. "No," he said, his voice raspy and deeper than normal. "You won't run anymore. This is what I am, who I am, and this is what OUR daughter is. You'll accept it now, Lillian. You've no other choice."

"Bray...?" Terror gripped her. She couldn't watch him shift again. It had been what had driven her away all those years ago and what had kept her away every night that her body ached for his touch. No it wasn't, she overheard Mason saying they were going to kill her.

He took a deep breath in and smiled, showing that his teeth were now elongated. Lily yelped and pushed on his chest. "Brayen, no ... don't do this. Please don't do this."

"I've wanted you for six years, Lily. Six damn years!" He jerked her face towards his and snarled at her. "You carried my child in there." He cupped her sex harder than was comfortable and backed her up against the railing. "I didn't get to share that with you. I didn't get to be there with you, to watch your belly grow with the life I helped create. I didn't get to hold her in my arms and tell her how much I loved her, and I didn't get to be there the first time she experienced this...." He let go of her neck and allowed claws and fur to sprout forth from his hand. Lily screamed out, but he held tight to her. "I should have been there to help her get through it."

"I'm sorry, Bray ... please...." She jerked back when his claws came near her face. Hot tears burned her cheeks as she watched the mix of hate and pain on Bray's face. "What do you want me to say? I'm sorry!"

He shook his head. "No, tell me how you could disappear after you claimed to love me? Tell me the truth, Lillian."

"I'm sorry," she panted.

Bray's clawed finger touched her cheek and he applied enough pressure to let her know that he could hurt her, if he wanted to. "THE TRUTH!"

"I heard you talking to Mason," she blurted out. Bray jerked his hand away. "I heard him tell you that humans couldn't know about lycans and that I needed to be 'dealt with', turned … killed." She looked into his amber eyes and watched as blue pushed its way through. "I also heard you agree to 'handle the situation yourself'. I ran from you, terrified by what I'd seen, by what you are, and what you were willing to do to me to protect it. I knew I was pregnant before I left. I had a gut feeling and I wasn't about to let you or Mason harm our child. I knew the baby would be special. I knew she'd have your gifts, and I didn't care, Bray. I loved you so much that I'd do anything to hang on to a piece of you, and that meant running before you or Mason could stop me!"

Brayen's eyebrows came together, leaving a crease on his forehead. "*Ohmygod*, Lily, you only heard part of the conversation. I told Mason that I planned to marry you, and announce you as my mate to protect you in the lycan community. He agreed to support my decision." He reached for her and she took another step back, hitting the railing hard. "I've loved you from the moment I laid eyes on you. I'd never harm you or our child. I'd die to protect you both."

Lily shook her head in disbelief. "I thought … I thought…." Her legs gave out from under her as the realization that she'd walked out on the love of her life sunk in.

Bray's arms wrapped around her and he lifted her in the air. "I'm sorry that you heard that. I didn't know."

"I love you, Brayen. I always have."

## Chapter 10

Bray carried Lily inside and walked her directly to his bedroom. Hearing her say that she loved him had chased away the hurt. She'd thought that he would kill her to protect his secret. He would have run as well if he were in her position.

She'd done what she'd thought was right for their unborn child and he couldn't blame her for that. He wouldn't. He had a healthy daughter and Lily back. He'd want for nothing again.

"I need you tonight, Lily."

"I've needed you since the night I met you."

He dropped his head down and clutched her to him tight. "I'm so sorry."

"No, don't apologize. I made *more* than my fair share of mistakes. Let's just be happy that we found each other again. I don't want to think about how much time we missed out on with each other--with Becca-Rose."

"Have I told you that I love her name?" He stopped for a moment and planted a kiss on the bridge of her nose. "Have I told you that I love her, and that I love you?"

"I knew that you'd love her. I knew in my heart that you would, but I was so scared of what the rest of the lycans would force you to do … I could risk my happiness. I couldn't risk her though, Bray. I couldn't let anything happen to our baby."

Her words ripped at him, pulling at his gut, forcing unshed tears to his eyes. "Shh, baby. Don't do this. Don't take the blame on yourself."

"But Brayen, you didn't get to be with me when I had her. You didn't get to hear her first word. See her take her first steps."

Kissing her again, lightly, he moved his hand up and under her shirt, needing to have skin to skin contact with her. "So tell me, what was her first word?"

Lily let out a half sob, half laugh. "Kitty."

Brayen's laughter spilled forth from him as he cupped his mate's breast.

*My mate.* The words sounded even sweeter in his mind as he replayed them.

He moved over her slowly. "Can I have more than the weekend?"

Lily looked up at him, her eyes wide. "You can have me for a lifetime, if you want me."

"Oh, I want you Lily. I want you more than life itself."

He dropped his mouth down onto hers, losing himself in the taste of her mouth. Peaches. He loved the way she tasted. He pulled at her clothes, letting a claw extend from his hand as he went. There would be no barriers between them now.

Bray moved down Lily's body, needing to taste her, see her, touch her again. It had been so long--too long. His cock throbbed with the need to be buried in her, but first he needed to taste her. Take her scent in.

Licking his way down her, she moaned when he parted her legs, exposing her quim to him. "Lilly," he said, sinking his face into her folds. He lapped up the cream that oozed from her tight channel before putting his mouth over her swollen clit. Sucking gently, he inserted two fingers into her, feeling his cock harden to the point of pain as she tightened around him.

She clawed at his head, pulling his hair as she ground her hips into his face. He let out a throaty laugh as he continued to roll her clit around in his mouth. He knew the instant that she came. Her fingers dug deep into his hair and her pussy clenched down on his fingers. Brayen was nowhere near done with his assault on her and continued to lick her and pump his fingers into her until she was left with no choice but to try to crab walk away from him.

Grabbing hold of her hips, and kneading his fingers into her ass, he pulled her back to him. "No you don't. I intend on making sure you never leave me again," Brayen said, nibbling playfully at her core.

"Oh, really? Want to tell me your plan?"

He kissed her inner thigh before moving up her body and positioning the head of his cock at her entrance. "*Mmmhmm*, it involves me sticking my dick into you, making you beg for more, before I deposit my seed into you."

Her eyes widened and she shook her head slightly. "Bray, you can't come in me. I'm not on any sort of birth control."

A feral grin crossed over his face. "I know."

"But...."

"But what, Lily? I have my family back now and I intend to watch it grow. You and Becca are my life. According to lycan law, you have been my wife from the moment I marked you and intend on honoring that vow to you. And...."

Putting her fingers over his lips, she smiled up at him with tears in her eyes. "All I've ever wanted was to hear you say those words to me. Now, shut up and fuck me."

A shaky laugh fell from his lips. "I believe that very phrase got you in trouble once before. Did it not?"

She smiled. "I was hoping you'd punish me."

"Oh, I will, baby. All in good time, but right now I just want to make love to you. Will that do?"

"Only if you promise to fill me with enough of your seed to

give me another wonderful child."

"Baby, I'll soak you in it. And we will be blessed with another, I'm sure of it. I want to see your belly swell with the life I put in it."

"You say that now, when you want some."

He sank his cock deep within her, silencing her. She clutched onto his arms as he continued his onslaught, not wanting to ever be without the feeling of Lily beneath him again. He pressed into her again, and fought to keep claws from springing forth from his fingertips. The excitement and thrill of being in her again was almost too much.

"Yes, Brayen ... oh *Gawd* ... I'm coming, Bray. I'm coming."

"That's it, baby." His balls jerked up as he ejaculated in her for what felt like an eternity.

## Chapter 11

Lily kissed Brayen's forehead lightly before tiptoeing out of the room. She checked on Becca before slipping her shoes on and putting on one of Bray's thick shirts. Opening the front door slowly, she stepped out into the night.

When she'd woken to the feel of what she was sure was her ovary accepting Bray's seed, it took everything in her to keep from waking him. She wanted to share the news with him and would as soon as she was able to confirm it. Becca would love being a big sister. She'd always wanted someone else like her and now she not only had her father, but also a baby brother or sister.

The sound of a twig cracking brought Lily out of her trance. She looked out and over the large wooded lot. The cabin rentals were down the hill a bit, along with the bar. The thought of a stray drunk shifter scared the hell out of her. Turning to head back into the cabin, she froze when she heard the sound of her name.

"Jack?" She called out, unsure if she'd really heard him, or if it was just the wind.

*Lillian.*

"Jack?" She ran down the porch and towards the sound of the voice. She'd meet her fate head on. If he'd come back to punish her then so be it. He'd been a wonderful man and she would always love him.

*Run!* The sound of Jack's voice telling her to run sent her into a panic, but instead of heeding his warning, she froze.

There was a clicking sound behind her as a cold, hard object pushed against the back of her head. "If you scream, I will shoot you and whoever else comes running out of that door."

"Lewis?"

He rammed the end of the gun into her head. "Shut your fucking mouth, squaw. Now, move!" He said, pushing her towards the woods.

She bit back the scream that was on the tip of her tongue, afraid that Bray and Becca would hear her and run out to their deaths. Her feet stopped working right, and she fell two times before Lewis finally grabbed hold of her arm and began to drag her down the side of the mountain. When they were a good distance from the cabin he pushed her down to the ground.

Lewis looked down at her, his eyes wild and locked on her. "It was supposed to be you, you know?"

Lily shook her head slightly, not wanting to upset him, but unsure what it was that he was talking about.

He pointed his gun down at her. "In the car, you stupid bitch, the day that Jack died. It was supposed to be you and that mongrel abomination of an offspring, NOT my brother." His voice was wild, and high.

The realization of what he'd just confessed to sunk in and Lily had to swallow down the vomit that rose in her throat. "No, Lewis. No."

He hit her hard across the face with the back of his hand. "I had the car tampered with so that you would die and take that freak with you. Jack deserved better than you ... you stain. How could you spread your legs for a monster, give birth to one, and force my brother to raise it as his own? You sicken me."

"Becca's not a monster," she said, shutting up when she saw the hate flicker through his eyes. It mattered not what he said, she knew in her heart that her daughter was pure.

"I did the blood work, bitch. I know that she's not human and when I told Jack he confessed all her little secrets to me. The ability to sprout fangs, claws. The eyes changing and that growl." He let out a methodical laugh. "He wanted me to track down others like her and seek their help so that he could teach her how to control her 'gifts'. How the hell the man could call them gifts was beyond me. You poisoned him against me.

Against our mother. And you used him. I'm sorry that he died, but at least your meal ticket went when he did."

"I loved Jack."

"NEVER speak his name! Never." He struck her again, this time with a closed fist. Lily's vision blurred and she fought to stay conscious. A metallic taste filled her mouth. Lewis said something to her, but her ears were ringing too loudly for her to make it all out. When she did not answer right away, he struck her again.

"Answer me, bitch! What did you do to him? Did you use your Indian magic to put some kind of spell on him or did you use this?" he asked, dropping down and cupping her sex quickly.

She jerked away from him, only to have him reach down and claw at her pajama bottoms. They tore away easily for him and she screamed out as he thrust a finger into her. "That's it, isn't it? You used this to lure him away from us. Tell me, if I fuck you too, will I be as hooked? Will I be willing to give up my career, my money, my pride?"

Lily kicked out at him only to have her shot deflected as if she were no more than an insect. "Do that again and I'll start shooting you in places that won't kill you. I want you alive while I take my turn with you. You've let every other man in the world in there, why not me too?"

He unfastened his pants and let the length of himself spring free. She drew in a sharp breath and tried to crawl away from him. He pinned her down quickly, positioning himself above her as he went.

\* \* \* \*

Something pushed on Brayen's shoulder. It roused him from his deep sleep with a start. He let out a snarl and jerked upright, only to find Becca-Rose's blue eyes wide and terrified.

"Daddy?"

The sound of her sweet voice calling him daddy melted his heart. He looked down, suddenly very happy that Lily had insisted that he put some pajama bottoms on. He'd been used to sleeping in the buff. He reached out to Becca and lifted her up onto the end of the bed, glancing over to see if he'd wakened Lily with his antics. She was gone.

"Lily?" He called out softly, terrified that she may have fled again. The only comfort he had was that Becca was still here, and he knew that Lily would never leave her.

Becca jerked her head around wildly. "Hurry, Daddy. He's got her."

"Did you have a bad dream, sweetie?"

She shook her head no and blonde curls fell into her face. Bray brushed them back and smiled at her. "Let's get you back into bed and I'll send mommy up to tuck you in, okay?"

Her eyes flashed to amber and she clawed out fast at his bare chest. Her cut was shallow, but still stung all the same. "REBECCA!"

"My *other* daddy told me to wake up and get you. He said that momma was in trouble and that she and the new baby would get hurt real bad if I didn't wake you up. So get up already!"

Becca's words sunk in and Brayen remembered his first meeting with Lily, when the spirits of the land had rushed in the door and pushed them together. She'd been able to feel them, so it stood to reason that Becca might very well be able to communicate with them as well. If that was the case then Jack had reached out from the spirit realm to help Lily.

Brayen jumped to his feet, taking Becca with him. "Did he say anything else?"

"Uhhhuh, that Uncle Lewis is sick and that he was the one who made Daddy go away from us."

*Uncle Lewis?* Bray's stomach dropped when he realized that Lewis had been the one behind Jack's accident. He also remembered how Jack's car had been blocked in so he'd borrowed Lily's.

*Oh God! Lewis wanted Becca and Lily dead.*

*Brother?* The sound of Mason's voice pumped through his head. He was attuned to Brayen's feelings and no doubt sensed his fear.

*Lily's in trouble. She can't be too far from here.*
*I'll get everyone out. We'll find her.*

Bray looked at his daughter and set her on the bed gently. "I need for you to be a big girl and stay right here. I have to go find your mommy. I will send someone to be with you. If you smell Uncle Lewis coming, run and hide. I will find you, I promise."

"I want to come too!"

"Becca, sweetie, I don't have time to argue with you. He'll hurt mommy if I don't get to him."

"And the baby?"

Lily was pregnant again. He'd think more on that once he knew she was safe. "Yes, sweetie, and the baby."

"I'll stay here."

"Good girl. I love you." He kissed her cheek and ran for the door.

*Mason, have two of our people come to my cabin immediately. My daughter needs their protection.*

*Daughter? Cougs, you've got some explaining to do.*

*All in good time, brother. I need my wife back first.*

*Consider it done,* Mason said.

Brayen hit the front screen door with such a force that he tore it clean off its hinges. It didn't matter. All that mattered to him was his family. He'd do anything to protect them.

He drew in a sharp breath and tried to find Lily's scent. The wind seemed to close in around him, pulling him towards the left-hand side of the property. The air had a male feel to it and he knew right away that Jack was there, guiding him to Lily.

"I'll find her and bring home safe. I promise." He whispered to the wind as he ran through the forest.

He heard Lily's cries before he saw her. His heart went to his throat and it felt as though time stood still when he saw her pinned to the ground, her legs spread wide, and Lewis above her. Lily struck out at Lewis, preventing him from completely entering her.

The beast within Brayen took control, shifting him quickly into the cougar. Primal instincts took over and lunged at Lewis' body. Scoring a direct hit, he rolled with the man a small way. He bit down fast, aiming for Lewis' throat, but coming short and clamping down on his shoulder.

Something pressed against his chest and he heard the cocking of the gun before he felt the bullet tear through him. Giving little thought to the wound, assuming it would heal instantly, Brayen held tight to Lewis' shoulder. When an overwhelming pain rippled through his body, he felt himself shifting back into human form. He struck out hard and fast, afraid that if he didn't, he'd die before Mason had a chance to get here and save Lily.

\* \* \* \*

Lily scrambled to her feat as she watched Bray, in his tan cougar form, roll with Lewis. They struggled and she heard the gun go off. Brayen's body jerked back violently. He lashed out at Lewis as he shifted back into himself. The gun flew out Lewis' hands.

Lewis laughed. "That's right," he said, clutching his bleeding neck. "I used silver bullets. Know, as you lie there dying that I WILL be putting one through that child as well. No part of your bloodline will leave here tonight."

Brayen tried to get to his feet, but collapsed on the ground with a thud. Lily stopped thinking and dove for the gun. Lewis lunged at her, but he was too late. She rolled onto her back and fired it.

Lewis' eyes widened, and she had to push the fact that he looked so much like Jack out of her head as he tumbled down onto her. Their size difference left her pinned beneath him as he let out his breath. Something knocked Lewis' body off hers and she screamed when she saw the head of dark hair, and large brown eyes looking down at her.

"It's safe now, Lily. It's me, Mason."

"Mason?" She let him help her up, unconcerned with how exposed she was to him. Her only thought was Brayen. He hadn't moved since he fell. She crawled over to him, sobbing. "Bray ... no."

Lily turned his body and pulled his head on to her lap. "Bray ... no, don't leave me. Please don't leave me ... don't leave Becca-Rose."

Mason touched her shoulder gently. "I need to take him to Running Elk. My people will escort you back to the cabin. They're with your daughter now."

"I can't leave Bray."

Mason scooped Brayen up in his arms. "He is my brother, Lily. I will give my life to save his, if that's what it takes. He needs the help of our Shaman. Please...."

Grabbing her mouth to keep from screaming, she nodded.

## Epilogue

"No fair, you're cheating again, Uncle Mason," Becca-Rose said, with her tiny hands on her hips.

Mason looked shocked by her accusation. "Why you ... I never cheat. I am the world's greatest checker player, ever. Bow to me little one."

"Oh, please. It's getting deep in here, Uncle Mason."

Lily's mouth dropped open. "Rebecca-Rose! Who did you learn that from?"

Becca giggled and Mason turned red. "Lillian, I may have sort of slipped up and...."

"Mason," Lily scolded, doing her best to hide her laughter.

"Uncle Mason, wanna have another tea party?"

Mason groaned, glancing up at Lily for help. She shook her head and laughed. "Oh, no way I'm getting you out of that one, buddy. You said that kids were a breeze and that you didn't see what the big deal was."

"That's before I got a good dose of your daughter," Mason said, winking at her.

Strong arms slid around Lily's waist. "What's wrong with my little girl?" Brayen asked, running his hands over her swollen belly. "I love you," he whispered in her ear.

"I can hear that," Mason said sardonically.

"Like I care," Brayen shot back. He slid his hand lower and Lily felt the baby kick as if he knew that his daddy was touching him. "Oh, he's a feisty one."

"Can I just say that your children have the odds stacked against them?" Mason said, tousling Becca's curls.

"And why is that?" Lily asked, not sure she wanted to hear his answer.

"It's simple, they are part kitty and stubborn as hell. They come by it honestly though."

"I can't wait for you to have some of your own, brother."

"For that I need a woman."

"What do you need a woman for, Uncle Mason?" Becca asked softly.

Mason opened his mouth to answer her and Brayen ran over to cover their daughter's ears. "Oh, no you don't!"

THE END

Printed in the United States
34302LVS00003B/61-390